(THE ENDLESS WHITE SEA)
GEISTESCHREIEN FOREST

TRANSTREMERIA

TEMURITE NOMADS

THE GREAT SHIELD RANGE

CISTREMERIA

SAMARITE NOMADS

SOLNII

SALT SEA

TRIBES

VYAHTKEN PLAINS

COLTAI

ALAUS

SAPPHIRE COAST

RHOREGIA

BALTAI

Nor.

Balt

NORAI

Rhor

Vargas

VARANGIA

Ammercy

GREEN DELTA

MARBLE SEA

DOLOR SEA

THE CONTINENT

ALLONIA

CAPE OF THE KNIFE

THE SWORD OF MERCY AND WRATH

NC KOUSSIS

NCK PUBLISHING

Cover art: Nino Is

Cover design: Deranged Doctor Design

Map & Interior illustrations: Sara Ferrari

Editor: Sarah Chorn

Proofreader: Lee Seater

See more at www.nikitaskoussis.com and sign up to the newsletter to get the novella, *The Sword of Salt and Smoke* free!

BY THE AUTHOR

FOREWORD

This book has graphic depictions of the darker side of disability, abuse, mental illness, violence, and sex. I have not done this to beat you over the head with shock like a blunt weapon, but to provide a dialogue into the horrible things that people are capable of and to not shy away from showing the darker side of life. I do this to highlight the brighter side of life: perseverance in the face of inhumanity; dogged persistence of heroism; bravery when all one feels is fear. I say dialogue, after all, and I hope that if you feel something from this story, good or bad, you let me know. I'd love to hear from you, and my email or DMs are always open.

Please see my website at https://nikitaskoussis.com for a full list of content warnings.

Nikitas C. Koussis
March 2023

For Shannon

Contents

VOLUME ONE

Demon. Wukodlak. Turnskin. Shapeshifter. *Versipellis* in High Istryan. These terms describe the same creature—man or woman—afflicted with Sigur's curse. The curse was the punishment for all the descendants of the traitors who sided with the Great Fiend, the Harbinger, the Devil.

The demon is terrifying and unsettling in its monstrous magnificence. They are shapeshifters who take the form of a giant man-wolf on two legs, with wicked teeth, thick manes, and sharp claws. Those afflicted possess the strength and stamina of ten men, the ability to leap vast distances and run at great speed, and the ability to return from the dead.

Sigur's worshippers, especially those of His priesthood, are pact-bound to hunt down the creatures. The Order of the Golden Sword are Sigur's hunters par excellence, given authority by their counterparts within the church, as the Will of Sigur. The Order eschew all forms of temptation, be that body or mind, and leave behind mortal concerns such as war or politics. They do this for the immortal soul of mankind. The cursed beings are evil incarnate, and it is the duty of all good men to hunt them until there are none left.

— *Modern History of the Istryan Empire*, vol. II.

The relationship of the Sigurian Church and the Order of the Golden Sword is contentious, and one that the Church disavows and relies upon in equal measure. The Order acts with impunity, scouring through various lands, recognizing not any human authority, claiming that they are the embodiment of the will of Sigur himself. They respect not the natural laws of due process, or of fair hearing, exterminating towns wholesale if they believe it will root out 'heresy'. The greatest and most present example in recorded history are the mass pogroms that took place over a five-year period from 784-789 Aetate Discordiae. The whole continent was brought to its knees with infighting, suspicion, and lawlessness. Brother turned on brother, neighbor on neighbor, all in the pursuit of 'purity'.

In preparing for their work, the Order employs obscure and magickal weapons, traps, and poisons. The identity and existence of this arsenal are closely guarded secrets. Given that they often kidnap and indenture talented thinkers (alchemists, smiths, engineers, and others), it is no surprise that they have developed some advantages over other forces of the time.

— *Truth, or A Regard for the Fanatics of Sigur, Anonymous*

1

TRISTAIN

Fervum, 1044

The curse tears through family lines. An infection, not passed through teeth, but through pups. The son inherits the curse from the father.

— Lord Notarius Gian Adalla

D OUBT MEANS DEATH. WHEN the fighting's thickest and you're grasping a sword by your fingertips, there's no room for it. When all you're doing is stab-stabbing, hands numb, face numb, eyes streaming with sweat. When you can't tell friend from foe. Tristain wanted to think he'd learned that lesson but life kept reminding him that he hadn't.

Leon's powerful kick sent him stumbling. The knight's sword crunched into the mail along his side. He gasped as pain shot through his ribcage. Tristain raised his shield, expecting a blow. But nothing came, and he relaxed.

"Know your range, squire," Leon's voice carried from across the yard. "If you're close enough to hit them and you haven't, they'll be sure to hit you."

Enough talking, Tristain thought, grinding his teeth. *Just hit me already.*

Leon held his sword and shield by his side. Tristain charged. His opponent's sword swept upwards and Tristain blocked. Flipping his sword for the reply, Tristain missed. Leon had already moved back. They circled each other.

"Where are the weak points, lad?" Leon's voice was muffled by his face-plate. He liked to test Tristain's memory in the spar.

"Armpit, groin, neck, back of the knee, and ankle," he yelled, punctu-ating each word with a step forward. Leon maintained his distance. Still, they continued to circle each other. "Why are you holding back?"

"You're not ready, Squire."

Not ready, my arse.

Moving in fast, Tristain brought his sword low. The knight's feet looked unsteady. He'd finally caught Leon off-guard. Tristain reversed, bringing the sword back up. Changing his footing, he ran the flat of his blade along his opponent's curved helm. He pivoted, hooking the sword behind Leon's head. He pushed, sending Leon over his outstretched leg. The crashing sound reverberated through Tristain's helmet.

Leon's red beard seemed to explode from his face as he threw open his visor. He howled with laughter.

"I yield! I yield!"

Planting the tip of his blunt training sword in the dirt, Tristain helped Leon to his feet. "I thought you had me, Sir."

"Cheeky fucking *sal'brath*." Leon swore in Hillard, the language of the people from the South Hills. It meant fish-breath; how everyone from the mountains thought of people not from the mountains. "Where's my flask?"

A servant boy had it on hand. Leon unbuckled his helmet, tossed it aside. Throwing back his neck, his muscles flexed as brown liquid ran down his chin. The Hillman was shorter than Tristain, but twice as wide and all muscle. Tristain could sometimes beat him in a swordfight, but in pure strength, Leon had the best of him.

"You're learning," Leon said, wiping his face.

Tristain smiled at that. Still, he wished the knight would take him more seriously. He wouldn't get better if Leon took it easy on him. For a man given the moniker Leon the Strong, he could be irritatingly cautious.

Inside their canvas tent, Tristain racked his armor and washed his face in a small basin, then changed into finery. As the son of a count, a lot was expected of him. His chest filled out his forest-green doublet, snug from two years of Leon's training, while russet-red hose hugged his muscular legs.

He wiped his hair. Dirt got everywhere—in his underwear, in his ale, on his clothes. The army had burned the fields months ago, and the land was still barren, little more than a dustbowl.

He eyed the small writing desk, its papers in a scattered pile—his half-written letter to Selene sticking out like a rude gesture. *What can I say to her? That I haven't found a way yet?*

"I'm going for a walk," Leon's voice came from behind. Tristain turned. Shaved head and flowing red beard, Leon wore the clothes of a lowborn knight—loose-collared linen shirt and black trousers. "You coming?"

Tristain nodded. The letter could wait.

"So," Leon said as they passed a barracks. Ahead, a woman whistled a tune as she hung out soldiers' linens, while a pair on patrol walked past, spears in hand.

Tristain waited for Leon to say something. A minute of stony silence, and they reached a small hill where they saw the besieged city spread out before of them. Rennes' walls stood stark and silent as the sun set behind them. Below was a flat area set with outward-facing spikes, facing towards the city. Beyond the spikes, deep and hungry, laid trenches that would cover the assault. Tristain wasn't sure why they waited so long. Three long months had passed since they arrived, and still no word about the timing of the assault. *Mayhap they expect the city to starve before then,* he thought. *And they'll surrender without a fight.*

The sky turned hues of pinks and oranges. Another night in a foreign land, and Tristain was no closer to his goal of finding employment as a household guard than when the day started.

"Sir." Sharp wind whipped unshorn black hair across Tristain's face. "Is there a reason you think I'm not ready?"

Leon stiffened. He took a sip of his flask. "You're what, Tristain... sixteen?"

Tristain clicked his tongue. "Eighteen, sir." *He should know that... I've been his squire for near on two years.*

"Ah, I forget sometimes. And tell me, what do you want? Money, fame? If you're looking for either, just look at me: ten dozen pieces of silver to my name, and a busted back. They call me the Strong, but sometimes I can't reach my arse to wipe."

Tristain stopped himself from saying something smart. Around them, the sounds of dinner picked up, crashing pots, cooks barking orders to servants, soldiers joking around campfires.

Leon gave him a look of resignation, before taking another swig. "You think I'm spineless, lad, too afraid that I'll hurt you? Don't give me that look. I know what the men say, when they talk over their fires, when they think my back's turned. They say I've lost my touch. And yet... they will die, and yet more after them, before this war is over."

Tristain sighed, folding his arms. Below them, a campwife, the women who followed the army and cooked, cleaned, and served the soldiers, chased a servant boy out of her kitchen.

"If you won't push me, Sir, how am I going to prove myself?" He tried to keep the anger out of his voice.

"I didn't say that, lad. The squad's on patrol duty tomorrow. You'll be in the van, riding with me."

A smile drew across Tristain's face. Riding in the vanguard, Tristain would look important to anyone that saw. He might look important enough to sponsor or hire as a personal house guard. If he was a house guard, his master would offer his mother and adoptive sister somewhere to stay as a matter of course, if he could get them away from his father.

Once, he dreamed of being the lord of a mighty estate, like his father, fighting in tourneys for his own glory and in wars for the empire. How high he'd ride into battle, how nobly he'd spirit a lance into the empire's enemies...

Leon belched as he drained the contents of his flask. "Let's get back." He started down the hill, then stumbled. Tristain grabbed him and kept him from falling.

Leon wiped his face, chuckling. "Ah, you're a good lad. It's what I always told Erken: you treat your elders with the respect they deserve." A dark look flashed across his face.

As they walked back to the tent with the white eagle banner, Tristain thought of Leon's son. Erken was his name, a lad of eighteen, and much like other boys his age, wanted nothing more than to make their fathers proud. Tristain knew little of what that was like, but people often talked about legacy and glory, and he understood the sentiment. His father had talked about it enough for a lifetime.

Erken had died in a battle in the Giant's Footfalls, thirty miles to the north. The army's last major battle before the siege, they had fought hard to gain a hill defended by archers from the Kingdom of Badonnia, the empire's age-old foe, and whose lands they had occupied. The empire had lost over a quarter of their forces—a thousand men in total to gain the hill, and the Badonnians were forced to retreat, fleeing behind Rennes' walls. Leon's son had been one of the dead.

Tristain placed Leon in his bed and quaking snores filled the room. His flask rolled onto the floor.

Tristain sighed. For as long as he had known him, Leon never abstained from drink, enjoying an ale or strongwine with dinner as folk do, but these days, it seemed he never spent a moment without it. Though Tristain smiled as he thought about what the knight had said to him. Riding in the van tomorrow. He was happy to have the chance to prove himself.

As he turned to get dinner from the kitchens, he heard shouting and cursing. He stuck his head out the door.

"You've heard?" a soldier in his breeches yelled, running in the parade ground's direction.

"Minstrels!" the other said, close behind.

Tristain followed. The parade ground was at the center of the camp. Turned into a veritable city by the many folk that tailed an army, it touted tents and pavilions of bright colors, rugs, armor, supplies, anything and everything. For the right price, of course.

It was far from the stark hill dotted with catapults, far from the noise of the drilling grounds, far from the row of latrine pits. The scent of char-grilled meat and smoky spits drifted into his nose. The sweet sound of a harp played quickly filled the air, accompanied by a quicker lute and faster drumming. From what he'd heard, a troupe of minstrels had arrived, causing a great stir.

He had a good view of the musicians as he entered the grounds, but what really drew his eye was the general. The general, Duchess Ilse Adolar, stern of eyes and jaw, carried the face of someone accustomed to hard decisions and the weight of the world on her shoulders.

Tristain pushed down the knot in his gut as he made his way over to the general. The minstrels started their next song, a quick quintain.

"...we'll have to smooth things over with the Order, I'd say," he overheard someone say as he approached.

"No," a man in fine mottled silks and velvets replied. "I'd say this is precisely what they need. They're getting a little too comfortable. They should serve the empire, not work for the highest bidder. Ah, someone approaches."

Tristain bowed. "Your Grace, my lords. I am Tristain Florian Oncierran, son of Sebastian, and heir to Invereid."

"Well met." The duchess tipped her head. "I believe you are Sir Vorland's squire, are you not?"

"Yes, Your Grace."

"Ay-ay," the herald said, a man with a peacock feather sticking from his peaked hat. "And for the next song, we have Glamis of the Tower, a sad tale to be sure, but a treat for the ears."

They sang of Glamis, a man who sought power and strength above all other men. Defeated by a better fighter, he turned to the Great Devil out of spite, and became something more than a man—a terrifying wolf, killing his daughter and his wife. Delivered as an elegy, but Tristain could only pity the wife and daughter.

"Very prestigious, to learn under Leon the Strong," the man in silks said as the harps and slow drums started. He was short, plump, with slick blond hair and a beak-like nose. "How goes it? Has his strength rubbed off on you?"

"I believe we haven't met, my lord," Tristain said.

"No, I don't believe we have. Count Andreas Pagehald of Verania. Vredevoort leads my troops, but I pay them. Though I'm here because who better to monitor my holdings?"

Tristain's eyes lit up. The regiment from Verania was the largest and would've cost thousands to pay. Surely, he would have more than enough to pay for a single household guard. But whether he would want to take the risk of upsetting his father... There was also Vredevoort: the vicious man had led the disastrous battle in the Giant's Footfalls, where thousands had died over a year ago. As well as Erken, Leon's son. Though Tristain would work for Pagehald directly, not Vredevoort, so it might not have been all that bad.

Cheers filled the air as the song finished. People rose from their seats, tossing silver pieces, while young boys gathered the coin. Tristain thought it was a decent rendition, though the strings were out of time with the singer.

"Now, we have our own real-life Glamis here," the herald said, pointing to an obscenely hairy soldier. "You're more hair than man, my friend." The hairy one waved his arms defensively. "Oh, I don't envy your mother if you were born like that! Throw him in the river, they must have said, the midwife's cursed him!"

"Count Pagehald—" Tristain went to speak, turning back.

"Yes, I remember now," the man said, leaning on his back leg. "Your father gave me a thrashing in the August Griffin Tourney ten years ago, I believe. He always had a temper, that one. What news of him?"

"I do not have any, my lord. He was in good health when I left two years ago. It is little wonder, so far from civilization."

"Indeed. I receive writs and reports to sign but once a moon. I sometimes ask if the sun does not set backwards here. And yet, our esteemed Grand Duke wishes to claim these lands? For what purpose?"

"You forget yourself, Andreas," the general admonished.

"Apologies, Your Grace. Excuse us. I wish to speak with Tristain privately, if you'll permit."

The Duchess bent her head slightly as if her neck, stiff from carrying a stone jaw, could only bend so far. Tristain and the count bowed in return and took to a nearby table. The count dismissed those seated with a wave.

"Tell it true, young man." Pagehald ran a hand under his smooth double chin. Though he wore a long tunic with flowing sleeves and a loose belt, it did very little to hide the plump. The days of the count's tourneys were long behind him. "What are your plan after this godsforsaken war?"

"To serve, my lord. My greatest desire is to serve an honorable household."

"Ah, color me intrigued. I would've placed heavy bets on you having dreams of fame and glory. After all, few men of your age want to set down roots in one place."

"I have responsibilities, my lord." *Let him think I have a mistress and children to support if it will keep him from prodding further.*

The man nodded. "Hm... I understand all too well, and I'm not un-sympathetic to your position. You should visit after we wrap up this nasty business in Badonnia. My estate makes the finest wine north of the Bight."

"Thank you, my lord," Tristain said, trying and failing to keep a straight face. He felt like dancing on the tables, kicking over flagons of ale in time to the music. He pushed down his excitement for now. It was only a small step, and he would have to make it through the war first.

"And don't forget, my friends, to tip your campwives," the herald said to the crowd. "Or give 'em the tip!"

After the count bid him farewell, Tristain sauntered off to bed, the sounds of the revelry fading, but his good mood remained strong. Guilt spiked through his chest like a dagger; he was using the count. He seemed like a decent man, and yet Tristain had very little interest in being his guard. He simply wanted the position and everything that came with that. A place for his family to live, where his mother and Selene would finally be safe.

But a familiar pain in his left hand, where his father had shattered his pinkie with a mallet, followed the guilt. Rage persisted over the years, though he barely remembered the specifics. Not because his memory failed him, but because there were too many occasions to count. A mallet here, a chain there. He'd become inured to the abuse by the end, and he wasn't sure if that was worse. It was only when the firstborn Bann died three years ago that Tristain became the heir and golden child. Then, his father's rage turned on Selene, the family's ward, and their mother. He couldn't forget that, even if he tried.

Selene was more than the daughter of a noble family—she was Tristain's love. He would do anything to protect her, and he failed her by leaving. The courts offered no recourse for the abuse because legally, Father had all right to beat his ward if she disobeyed. Even if she didn'tAnd like many families, they cared little for daughters—first sons were kings of their home. Everything else was dispensable. Squeezed by circumstance, Tristain had only left her to find a position that would allow them all to get away.

He welcomed the pain in his left hand. It was a reminder of what he would do, what he was capable of, to get her free.

After he perfected the letter to Selene, he climbed onto the straw bed at the foot of his knight's armor, steel glinting dully in the light of a tallow candle where scarce an inch remained. For the first time in months, he slept soundly.

2

SELENE

FERVUM, 1042 – TWO YEARS EARLIER

Fire, as a vestige of Sigur's light, is preternaturally effective against the creature.

— GRAND INQUISITOR ULRICH VETTERAND

SELENE'S MOTHER WAITED FOR her in the parlor, a smile on her lips. She always held that smile for Selene, like the world only mattered when her daughter entered the room. Often because that's the only time it did. That was the truth, and Selene never shied away from painful truths.

"How did you fare?" she asked.

Selene placed her new dress at the head of the lounge and pulled out her true prize hidden in the length of the frilly sleeve: a waster. A dagger made of solid oak.

"The tailor's son made it for me." She kept her voice low.

Mother sighed, her hand to her chest. "Oh, Selene." The tone was one of admonishment, but Selene noticed her smile never disappeared.

"Where's Father?"

"Upstairs reading. He won't want to be disturbed."

They looked at the wide stairs, visible from where they sat. Tension thickened the air. Pressed in from the gilded walls, panels of oak, scalloped columns of stone. All cracked and fading. The rotten sides of a rotten home.

Selene cut the tension. "Have you heard from Tristain?"

Mother shook her head. "No. I would've thought you knew more than me. He writes those letters to you, not his mother or father. You'd think he was your brother by blood."

He nearly was, at least how she thought of it. But then, they'd also shared secrets, and kissed, and more. These were secrets to be kept out of necessity, along with the contents of their letters.

She longed for when Tristain would tell her stories of brave knights. Those like Leon Strong of Vorland, from the wild South Hills, who slew twenty men with a broken sword.

Father thought it adorable at first, when his son and his adopted daughter chased each other around the courtyard with sticks and buckets for helmets. Then he'd grown tired of it, and the older Selene became, the more she was expected to do her duty: sew, knit, clean, care. Learn the roles of a noblewoman, to be married. Wrapped and presented like a prize pig. Perhaps he intended her to marry Bann, the firstborn, but he'd died not a year ago.

Tristain had gone off to join Leon the Strong, in Archduke Albrecht's war in Badonnia. A dream, some would say. A nightmare for her.

All the bad thoughts gave her a headache. She leaned her head around the corner, measuring the silence, counting her breaths. How long before Father descended those stairs?

She sat on the lounge, facing her adoptive mother.

"Sing a song, Mother," she said. She placed her hands in her lap.

Mother tucked a stray lock of Selene's raven-dark hair behind her ear. "All right, dear."

"Oh, gentle breeze,
I feel you on my cheek,
You pass by me so gently,

And I miss you so sweetly."

Bright goosepimples raised her neck. Selene felt her love pour out for her adoptive mother, like the goddess Eme's amphora into an endless cup.

"Oh, gentle lover,
I feel you on my cheek,
I pass by you so gently,
And I let you go, so sweetly—"

"Where's that bitch!" Father's voice roared across the parlor. Mother turned white; her song choked in her mouth like bile.

"I'm not going to hurt you," he said, marching into the room. The sound of his feet marked Selene's death.

He burst upon them with the fervor of a wild animal, doublet open, his face purple.

"I told you to fix this button," he said, showing her a brass, acorn-shaped button, hanging loose. "You gallivant around town like a common whore, and I suffer for it."

Selene stood slowly. It was like talking into the mouth of a bear. "You gave me permission to go to Invereid."

"Not to spend an entire day there."

"It's not my fault you tore the button." She regretted the words as soon as they left her mouth.

"Sebastian, please," Mother said as she put herself in his path. "She'll do what you asked."

"Get out of my way." Father's voice froze with its coldness, like a rime falling on an already icy land. He took his belt off and wrapped it around his hand. "I need to teach her a lesson."

"Enough. She's just a child."

"She's sixteen. I'd fought for the emperor twice by the time I was her age."

As you keep reminding us, she thought but she kept those words to herself. She didn't feel like being beaten within a hair's breadth of death.

"Go, Sebastian." Mother cooed and put her hands on his shoulder.

He shoved her off and turned against her, facing his side, like a swordsman. A swordsman indeed, one well past his glories.

"I ought to teach you a lesson as well. My only remaining son is off in Badonnia and doubts plague me yet again whether he is even my son. No son of mine would've lost that tournament."

The leather of his belt stretched over his fist, making a horrible noise. He pulled it tighter.

Mother pushed her hand back, finding Selene's arm.

"Hide," she whispered.

Selene nodded. Hiding like a coward. Would Tristain have hid?

Yes. No one faced Father's wrath and survived. She almost thought his firstborn, Bann, hadn't died in Ostelar but had rather run afoul of Father's moods one day.

She ran into the hallway to the left side of the parlor, opposite where Father had come from and the stairs. He cried out after her.

"Get back here!"

"Sebastian, no! Here, I'm here."

Their voices faded as she entered his office. She opened the wardrobe at the back of the room and stepped in, closed the door behind her.

You never know just how loud your breath is until you're hiding from a monster. Desperately, Selene wanted to quiet herself, and smothered at her mouth and lips. Deeper and smaller she shrunk, pushing into the darkest part of the wardrobe. Voices muffled through the wood, full of hate and anger. Selene's chest constricted painfully at the noise. They'd followed her into his office.

"Of course, he's yours," Mother said. They seemed to pace back and forth, their voices getting louder and quieter.

"You weren't pregnant when I left, wench," Father roared, voice thick with irritation. "I was gone for the better part of a year, and I come home to find you've had a son!"

Tears forced their way out of Selene's eyes as their voices went quiet again.

Ginevra, Sigur, Eme, save me now! Praying to the gods, she wanted an end to it, for one of them to storm from the room, as their arguments usually went. But for all her praying, Selene was trapped.

Mother's voice came around again. "...bringing this up every moon. Why don't you believe me?"

His vile threat sounded across the room. "I should've killed him in the crib."

"You know what? I'm glad he's nothing like you. Why would I ever want him to be like *you?* I *wish* he wasn't yours."

Selene heard nothing more. The weight of the silence pressed down on her more than the suffocating blackness around her. She pressed her ear against the door, hoping to hear something, anything.

A piercing scream sent Selene reeling back against the wood. Wet, horrible noises followed, the sound of something fleshy hitting the boards. She threw her arm out, shoving herself from the wardrobe.

A great, hairy beast loomed over Mother's limp body. Father. Selene's breath fled her though she wanted to scream, *No!* Strained eyes flicked over the monster, the bright blood soaking into the floor, the tide of it greater than she thought possible to come from one person. Shivers ran through her legs and arms and hands and neck, and she bowed her knees, brought her elbows in tight. At last, her voice found her, and she howled at the woman's twisted, unmoving face, poppy-red blood settling on her dress of silk.

The misshapen man-wolf that was her father turned its icy gaze on Selene, fixing her to the floor. Lowered to the floorboards, he stalked towards her, nasty and hideous. Bared, curved teeth brought to a savage point. Bright, silvered eyes of blue, repulsive pools of acid. Deep, cruel snarls filled her ears. Selene flinched as the creature reached out slowly for her.

She ran. Sharp pain tore across her back, but she kept running. Out of the room, down the hall. She heard the tumbling of heavy feet behind her. Gasping for breath, she felt the creature behind her, mere inches away from horrible agony.

Bursting through the front door, she screamed for help. Something rough and strong closed around her calf. She fell hard. Her temple and ear wracked with sharp pain as they slapped against the ground. In a daze, she thought she heard people shouting. She rolled over with a groan. Claws dug into her left arm. Agonizing, blinding pain ripped through her very core. She drove her head into the ground, trying to escape, trying to focus on anything but the searing throes of anguish she felt. Convulsing, she felt like even boiling water or a hot poker could not hurt this much. The edges of her vision frayed, darkening with hot excruciation. Then her world went dark.

T RYING TO CLEAR THE edges of her swimming vision, she blinked. She wrenched her head up. A silent, pained scream escaped her. She shook like a leaf in a storm. The big blacksmith Tomas lay on the ground, dead, while Father's half-burned monstrous form sprawled next to him. Only then did she notice the smell of burning flesh and singed hair. The beast wasn't moving—for now—but she had to pull herself away. Who knew if it would come back to life? She tried to pull herself away but felt a weight on her shoulder. And below that, nothing. With a clatter of iron, the still-hot half-made blade fell off her left arm as she pulled with her other arm and pushed with her feet.

Shouts and curses came from behind her, in front, all around. She felt a twisting hole dig deeper into her stomach, numbing her, hollowing her out. She blinked, in a blur already to the stables, her heart beating faster and faster. Her mind screamed to get on her horse. She tried to use her arms to pull herself up, but it wasn't working. The air was impossibly warm and stifling.

Taking a small step, she flung herself headfirst onto her horse's unsaddled flanks, and her left arm flailed behind loose and limp. Wild eyes and even wilder screams from the yard. *Oh Gods... I have to run! What if... what if there's more of them?* She strained, hooking one leg over and using her thighs to pull herself upright. The horse took off, knowing what its master wanted, and she closed her right fist around the creature's mane, fingers white, holding on for dear life.

The landscape passed in a blur. The horse followed a path only it knew for a time, only it kept track of. Heat rose in her chest as her vision blurred. The air grew stifling again. The world spun, and she was on her back. Pain hit her in waves. She lost feeling in her fingers and her toes. Above her, an old man in a black robe leaned over, concern on his face. He knelt, long grey hairs falling over his face. *Old... old man of Sigur...* She was delirious. *As the Gods left this world, so too do I...*

She woke several times in a daze, feeling herself being carried, the sound of hooves and wooden wheels grinding dirt. She heard voices talking over her as she lay. Agonizing pain bit into her spine, shooting through her bones. Blissfully, darkness visited her again.

A S THE ORANGE SUN streamed through a window above, Selene blinked her eyes open. Her vision swam. She moved her eyes with purpose, as though she had to get used to seeing again. A man in a grey robe with a blood-spattered leather apron looked back at her. The room had walls of stone and was chilly, despite the sunlight. She went to sit up, but only one arm did the job and so she fell on her left side. She gasped.

No... Gods be good... She reached over with her other arm and felt only a bandaged stump. Eyes widened in denial. She screamed, again and again, wishing it weren't true. Writhing in panic, loss, mournful sorrow. Two hands grip her tight. The man in grey restrained her. He called for help.

Inconsolable, her tears and screams came unbidden. It took two grown men to hold her fast to the bed. She kept screaming until her voice went hoarse and choked. Someone forced a white liquid into her mouth. Exhaustion settled over her, and sleep came quickly.

S ELENE HAD FALLEN FROM her horse, she was told. Her left arm had barely been attached and had to be amputated. The robed man with the long hair was not an old priest, but a warrior of Sigur, a Golden Sword named Sorenius. He had taken her to a nearby church to be treated, where the doctor was also the priest, Radimir. She blushed as Sorenius came to her in her sickly state. One arm and no good for it. He was beautiful, and she was sure she looked horrible. She certainly felt it.

He had an air of authority, standing straight-backed, with a firm chin and muscular neck. His grey eyes were the only thing dull about him, if that could even be said. Streaks of silver marred his lustrous dark hair, tied down the back, with the sides of his head shaved. It was an odd style, evocative of a woman's rather than a man's. Still, it did him much favor to attract attention to his sharp, rising cheekbones, a mix of fresh and old scars on them. He wore black; a boiled leather jerkin and black trousers paired with black boots.

"Good to see you're awake," he said. "I was afraid the priest was too generous with the poppy milk."

Selene's throat was hoarse when she spoke. All the screaming, she supposed. "Perhaps he should've been... I might've slept forever."

He sat at the end of her bed. "You know why I saved you? You would've died, the corruption ran so deep."

"Corruption?"

"The wound was infected, that was plain. The priest had to take it up to the shoulder to cut away all the corrupted flesh. That happens when demons attack: corruption takes hold, if you're lucky enough to survive. The strangest thing, though, your wound was cauterized. I think that was what saved you from bleeding out, allowed you to make it as far as you did on horseback, delirious as you were. My question stands, though. Do you know why I took you to this place?"

"No."

"I saw your strength in your white knuckles as you clung to the horse's mane when you fell. The determination in your grazed elbows and skinned knees. The courage in your actions. There is no question that hard steel lies your heart."

She snorted. He couldn't be serious. She laughed at his stoic look. Clearly, he didn't think it was a joke. "You're not serious! You may as well have left me. What good am I?"

"Everyone has something to offer the world. There is value in all life. It is as Sigur says, 'Each man to their own place'."

Selene took issue. "What about murderers? Thieves?"

"These are but wayward souls, driven to sin by the evil that lies at the root of the world. We can save them with just punishment."

She sniffed. *Trite answer. But what about...* "Wukodlaks? What value is there in horrible monsters?"

His face darkened. "There is value in their lives."

"How?"

"You wish to bait me? Make me speak something that is not true?" His cold eyes fixed on her. She held his gaze; she would not cower. He sighed, his face relaxing. "Each one dead brings us closer to the return of the Gods.

It was the Great Devil's sin that drove the rift between our world and the Gods. Undoing that will heal the rift."

Selene nodded. She didn't know if his words were to be believed, but he certainly seemed to believe them. There was something comforting about them, the certainty with which he spoke. If life was riddled with doubts and fears, this Sorenius had learned how to overcome them.

"Now," he said, standing. "Time for supper, I think."

A MONTH PASSED, AN agonizing, wrenching month. The priest Radimir removed the stitches, a procedure nearly as painful as getting an arm cut off, and in that time, she had to learn how to walk again, how to move again, as though it was her legs that had been removed, not one of her arms. The church was quiet, the thick stone walls smothering the outside, leaving her in an isolation that was only deepened by her state. She was hardly a prisoner, but where was she to go? Mother was dead, Father was still out there. Better she stay in the sanctuary that the church offered, and hope that Sigur's curse on the werewolves keep her safe.

The inquisitor, Sorenius, was her one shining light in the darkness. The man's visitations were a glowing sun in an otherwise bleak, gray place. But today, he'd gone out, recruiting as he did. Selene was left on her own, bent low, sweeping the floor with a short-handled broom. It was hard with one arm, exhausting to use the same hand to sweep, keep her hair from falling into her face *and* open the door to sweep the dust outside. Gods forbid, the wind would blow it back inside. But she was recovering, getting around on her feet now, so she was at least glad for that. Until she tried grabbing things with her missing arm. Her mind imagined the movement, but her body just did nothing. Untethered. That was how she felt, and it broke her the first night, and for several nights after. But grief and pain eases in time, just as the sun rises in the morn and sets in the eve.

Managing with one arm had felt impossible, but each day that took her further from the loss gave her another day to get used to it. She learned how to dress herself with one arm—easier than you think, seeing as there are only two holes to get through instead of three—and how to brush her hair. Harder to bloody do anything, and slower. But not impossible.

She looked upon the various golden figures purposefully placed around the church. Mounted opposite the main doors was a cruciform sword, plated with gold, pointing to the sky. Prongs of brass wreathed its base, symbolizing light piercing darkness. In a small alcove to the side was the icon of a woman engulfed in flame—a messenger of the Gods burned at the stake by non-believers. On a plinth by the altar was a golden lantern that would remain unlit until Sigur's return to the world.

The church of Sigur was a haven for believers, all of His word. A safe place for kings, peasants, merchants, vagabonds, outlaws all—as long as they believed. Each one of them served Him in their own way, as Sorenius said.

Folk arrived from the local village for midday prayers. She hid. No one should see her like this. She recognized the headman and his family, as well as the smith, the butcher, the baker, and even the shepherd with his stinking sheepskin garments. Her disappearance and the attack at the house would set tongues wagging. It was only a matter of time before people found out.

The priest led them in Gebet, in prayer. His sermons echoed off the stone walls, the vaulted ceiling, in High Istryan, the language of their forebears.

"Sigur harden our hearts against the unwilling, the coward, the selfish, those who pursue power and self-interest above all. I say in the name of the martyrs and the Conqueror, the blood, and the spirit. Father be with us."

As he finished, the congregation sang. The sweet, somber tones lifted Selene's mood. They sang of the strength of Diana, of Orphea, of Martea. Hallowed women that gave their lives for Sigur.

After an hour or so—Selene lost track of time—they finished. She hummed along to the tune. *Mm-m. Mmm. Mm-m. Mm. Mm-m. Orphea found her strength that day...* The congregation filed out the door as the priest caught her eye. He came over to her hiding place and smiled, telling her that Sorenius would soon return. She smiled and nodded, but wondered why he thought it was her business.

She went to her room, unsure what to do now she'd finished her chores. The chores were her condition: not that the priest had asked for payment in swept floors, but they were her own condition, a repayment for all he'd done for her. It was hard work, though, and she was glad it was now over with.

She sat on the bed. Her room was small. There was no gilding on the walls, not like her bedroom at home. No eye-waveringly complex patterns in plaster. No private privies—she shared hers with the priest and Sorenius. Only a bed big enough for one and a sturdy, functional dresser in the corner, behind the door.

A glint of something there caught her eye. She groaned as she got to her feet, feeling more exhausted than she had before she sat. She pulled back the door. It was a dull silver plate, fallen off the counter. Clicking her tongue, she imagined how long it had been sitting there, without a soul to see it. Beauty like that should never be hidden. She lifted the plate and caught herself in the reflection.

Nothing but a stump for a shoulder. She screwed up her face. Maybe before, she could believe it had been a terrible dream, but now that she saw it for herself... she tried to hold back her tears but they only came harder. *Why didn't I have the courage? I should've... I should've fought back. Grabbed the letter knife he kept on his desk instead of hiding like a coward. Maybe Mama would still be alive.*

Her ears pricked as she overheard a conversation through the door. She wiped her eyes. "The girl is young and spirited. She seems to be recovering well," Radimir's voice came muffled through the thick wood.

"Good," Sorenius replied. "Her guardian father is dead. I examined the corpse myself. The blacksmith killed him with a blade he was beating into shape, fortunate that it was still hot, igniting the demon's fur. Unfortunate though that before the demon died, it cut the blacksmith's belly open. And Sigur be true, when the blade fell on her arm, it must've done what you said, sealing the wound."

"Hm. What will you do with her, Inquisitor?"

Inquisitor? She knew the stories. The name spoke to their purpose. They sought out evil. And the man who had raised her... she bit her lip. Had he really died back there, in the yard? It must've been true. Maybe... maybe she could go home. *No. There's nothing for me back there. Only her stiff body left in that horrible, angry place. Tristain is in Badonnia. Perhaps I could go there. But would I make it? And... I'd have to tell him that his father was a monster, and he had slain his mother...*

A long pause drew out before Sorenius replied, "Test her. She may prove herself in time."

T HE NEXT DAY, SORENIUS came to her as she milked the goats in the little paddock behind the church. He held a broom in his hand. Wind whistled through the valley, rustling the maples nearby. The goats were used to being milked. It took a bit to get the hang of it, hampered as she was. Eventually, though, she found an extra hand was superfluous. Maybe to stop them fussing, but once they settled, they let her take as much milk from them as she needed.

"Don't tell him I told you," Sorenius greeted, waving the end of the broom around. "But Father Radimir feels guilty about letting you do things around here."

She kept milking. The farmers' wives told her how to do it—Greta, she thought her name was. *Gods, that was years ago.* She smiled as she remembered. *Mother took me to see them—she would never let me forget we depend on their work for our livelihood.*

"It is as I told him. I want to earn my place here."

He crossed his arms. "And your place in the world?"

She stopped, giving him a confused look. "You speak very cryptically sometimes."

A smile flashed across his lips. Her cheeks flushed. "Hazard of my profession. What I mean to say is, what do you want from life?"

"I still don't understand."

"I mean what I say. What do you *want*?"

She didn't answer right away. She wasn't sure. Marriage, family, children; all things were destined for her. Her father and mother made that clear, but now? *Sorenius is right... What do I want?*

"I suppose I don't know," she said.

He seemed pleased with the answer, nodding. "Come with me."

"But the goats—"

"They'll live."

They went to the foot of a maple tree where leaves were yellowing at the ends. Autumn was coming soon, it seemed. He handed her the broom.

"What's this for?"

"I want you to strike me," he replied, stone-faced as ever.

"Strike you?" *Attack a goddamn inquisitor! What's he thinking?*

"Do it."

Selene hesitated, holding the balance awkwardly with one hand. She thought of her and Tristain's games of chase and pretending to be knights and bit her lip. Never again would she have that, and her heart broke for the loss of it.

She sniffed back tears and braced the broom against her side. He waited for her. She lunged forward with the end. Sorenius flashed a devilish grin. He stepped aside, catching the end of the broom with his hand. He yanked, pulling her off-balance. A trip and a fall later, she was face down in the dirt.

She groaned, rolling onto her back. The shock had dashed all thoughts of Tristain from her mind. "Was that fun for you?"

Sorenius helped her to her feet. "Come now, it's just a bit of dirt."

She brushed the dust off her robe. She even smiled. "So, how was my test?"

Sorenius tilted his head slightly. "Oh, you were listening?" He smiled. "Yes, well. You could be faster, but bracing the broom was clever. Adapt your weapon to your strengths and weaknesses."

"Did me a whole lot of good."

He handed the broom back to her. "Again."

They sparred for a while.

"Again! Faster! Move your feet! Not like that! You'll trip like that. Shift your weight! Pivot on light feet!"

She ended up on the ground time and time again. It was exhausting, and sweaty, and dirty. Her face was caked in filth by the time they finished. She wondered how many different ways he could flip her onto her back, then dropped that line of thinking before it went too far.

Selene panted, leaning on the broom for support. Everything hurt. It was probably the most physically grueling thing she'd done for years. A top ten for her whole life.

She groaned in frustration. "There's no way. You're too quick and I'm too useless."

"Yes," he replied, smugness dripping from his words. She could punch him in the face. If she could bloody touch him. "You keep saying that, but you keep getting back up."

"Piss off."

"Sigur says, 'The strong must defend the weak and the innocent.' You are the furthest thing from weak—"

"And the furthest thing from innocent?"

He smiled wryly. "Let me finish. You're *strong*, in spirit, in heart, where it really counts. How old are you?"

"Sixteen. Truly?" she asked, laughing. Sorenius didn't laugh. "Then why can't I do what matters? What use am I with... *this*?"

"You ask yourself. Ask yourself what you truly want."

What I truly want? A betrothal to a knight... a life of having children... a life sequestered away in some bleak place in some backcountry... like Mother...

She pictured Father's horrible canines closing around her head, tearing it free from her shoulders. She thought of Mother—the woman who'd raised her—and Tomas the blacksmith and wondered how many mothers and blacksmiths and other folk the demons snuffed out every day. Her knuckles went white as she clenched her fist around the broom handle. *What chance do I have? They're monsters, butchers, capable of horrible things. And what am I? Stupid. Nothing. I know nothing of killing.*

No. This man could show her.

"I want to kill demons," she said with finality. "Tell me how."

3

THE DEMON

FERVUM, 1044

I refer to the chrysalis event, known as the quickening, where a demon's full potential is revealed.

— LORD NOTARIUS GIAN ADALLA

THE NEXT MORNING, TRISTAIN rode alongside Leon, high in his saddle, bright-eyed and smiling. He carried the white eagle banner over all of them—Leon's banner. The knight Leon led his fifty spearmen, taking the dusty road that sent them past the latrine pits, past the catapults, past the outer palisades, their spikes decorated with the grisly heads of deserters. Out they went, past the last lookout tower, and towards the forest to the south. The forest was named thus on a map, if a few stark trees on their lonesome could be called that. A hot, dry breeze blew over them, making the journey clammy and uncomfortable. Still, nothing could ruin Tristain's good mood. His horse flicked its tail, shooing flies. Running his hand along the beast's braided mane and down along its side, he felt the smooth leather of the saddle at his thighs.

"What are you so chuffed about?" the corporal Caen said, speeding his feet to walk alongside the horse. Tristain counted the corporal among his friends in this place, though he was still lowborn. From the flat farmlands of the Spear, Caen was lean and strong, with the callused hands of a farmer who worked a plough from childhood. His skin was sun-wrinkled, and though he was eighteen, the same as Tristain, he looked much older.

Tristain chuckled. "Nothing, Corporal. Can't a man be merry?"

"In this place? In this heat?"

Tristain shrugged.

"And what's the plan with that?" Caen said, glancing at the pole with the white eagle banner. "Gonna' find it's home in someone's gut?"

Tristain narrowed his brows. "Has there ever been a moment when you've been serious?"

"Nope, and I ain't gonna start today."

When the sun drew to its zenith, they stopped by a stream, far from the siege camp now. Tristain, naked apart from his breeches, dipped in the shallows with the rest of the men. His gear was in a pile on the bank. He dunked his face, washing like the others. The lieutenant Gida stood guard on the shore, her eyes narrowed over the hazy horizon.

A mirage of the South Hills shimmered in the distance above the Footfalls. Tristain knew it was false because it looked only a few miles away when it was really over fifty. *Fifty miles to the Hills, to the Leviathan Pass. Fifty miles from home.* Four day's march from his homeland of Osbergia, the largest province of the empire. Taking his horse and running would be a stupid idea; he'd be caught within hours. Even if he got away, the keep at the pass was the Empire's and they would ask questions, delaying him long enough that any pursuers would likely catch him. That didn't stop the thought from occurring to him. *To see Mama and Selene again...*

Tristain sat beside a nettle bush. He sighed, wiping greasy hair out of his face. Leon's foot tapped Tristain's leg as he sat.

"Squire," he said, alternating sips of ale with bites of bread. Strung around his neck, over his polished but scratched breastplate, was a small wooden chalice, a token of Ginevra, the Goddess of Mercy and Motherhood. Tristain let it hang. He would've asked anyone else about it, but even after two years, the knight still hadn't opened to him. The most he'd gotten out of him about his son was an angry tirade about Vredevoort the Grim, the one who'd led to Erken's death. He remembered asking Caen about it.

"That one earned his name for a reason," the corporal had said. "Vorland fought to have Erken reassigned, but Vredevoort told him ain't no way. In the Footfalls, Grim sent his men to secure the hilltop, throwing wave after wave at the Badonnians. Hundreds died, Erken with them. I think he blames himself."

"Why would he blame himself for that?" Tristain had asked.

"Why would any father?"

Leon sent two spearmen on patrol, eyes peeled for any enemy approaching on the road or over the dusty plains. Though they didn't expect any Badonnians out here, their army having secured the corridor between the pass and the siege camp, it didn't hurt to be careful, especially in enemy lands.

Caen whistled, drawing his attention. "I saw you've finally finished that letter."

Tristain laughed. "You rifled through my things? Have you no sense of privacy or respect?"

"Privacy? You never stopped talking about it. I had to see for myself. What happened?"

"I spoke to the Count of Verania. He offered me a position in his household guard. That's what I was writing about."

Leon chimed in with a tone of approval. "Household guard? Respectable. You ought to do well."

"Wait, Pagehald?" Caen interrupted. "The Count of Verania?"

"Yes."

Caen looked like he was trying his hardest not to crack with laughter. "You've been 'ad, squire."

Tristain frowned. "Corporal?"

"Verania has more debt than a brothel has whores, and he spends plenty on them, or I ain't a bastard from the Spear. You'll be fightin' off debtors and cutthroats for the rest of your life, short as that'll be."

"Bastard," Tristain said without meaning to.

"I know nothing of this," Leon said from his cup. "But then we don't run in the same circles." Leon slapped his leg. "Ah, Tristain, I'm sorry. But I'm sure he won't be the last lord with an offer. If I were a lord gilded..."

From the perimeter, a private came running, running like the wind, his boots ringing hard on the sunbaked ground. "Sir... Badonnians!" he yelled between breaths.

They rose to their feet, spears clattering and swords rasping. Bread and ale spilled on the ground, and the men arranged themselves into a formation. The private reached them, his knees buckling and his breath sharp and loud. Tristain looked around. Nothing but a sultry breeze came charging at them, and the only sound was rustling trees rather than the whistle of arrows.

"Speak, Sasha," Leon said firmly. "Where are they?"

"I saw hoofprints, sir. Hoofprints by the gully where it's still muddy. Got to be six or seven at least, stopped to give their horses some water." The men relaxed, breaking formation, some of them moaning about a cowardly private and their ruined lunch. The private Sasha, a skinny lad of sixteen, turned beet red.

"Six or seven? They're probably traders or village folk. Have you lost your nerve, lad? We march on."

E VENING FOUND THEM TRUDGING along the east road back to the camp when they came across an alehouse. Tristain's belly rumbled. The air was still and the alehouse quiet, but he could smell roasting meat and fresh bread. *We should keep moving, get back to camp...* but his mouth watered. He imagined ale that didn't taste like piss and bread that wasn't made of turnips.

"Awh, I can smell the chicken roasting from here," Caen said. Murmurs of agreement rippled through the men.

"We should march on," the lieutenant replied. "Find a well-hidden spot to camp."

"Ah, come on, Lieutenant. One ale won't hurt."

"We could meet you later, Lieutenant," Tristain added. "It would be less conspicuous travelling in smaller groups if the enemy is indeed out there." The men crooned in agreement. *And I could use a bath, too, if they have one.* His eyes lit up at the prospect. *I haven't had a proper bath in months.* The baths at the camp were always too cold, or filthy, or more often both.

The lieutenant turned to the knight. "Sir, I really think—"

"Ah, Gida, it's fine. Take half the men and return to the camp. Besides, I don't think all of us'll fit inside. We'll be there before you know it."

The lieutenant sighed and took half the men, who grumbled as they left, complaining that they should enjoy a drink, too. Twenty-five unlucky souls trudged down the road and over the twilit horizon.

Tristain tapped his fingers on the reins as he hitched the stallion. Gida had a point. Perhaps it would be best to keep moving. Or maybe the Badonnians would find them, and Tristain could prove himself in battle. *A sure-fire way to be knighted.*

After a loud tussle for the first bath and settling himself in the warm tub, Tristain thought of Pagehald's deception. The lavender scented water rippled around his chin, wisps of steam curling up from the surface, soothing his muscles. His mind was hard at work. *Had the count really deceived me? Maybe Caen's lying... maybe he doesn't know the truth and they're just idle rumors. Lowborns do love a good tale. But if I say no to the count... the seed has been planted. I'll have to save face somehow, let Pagehald down without causing offence. And I'd be no better off than yesterday.*

He pulled himself out of the bath, hungry and thirsty.

Flicking wet hair out of his face, Tristain took a seat with Caen, Leon, and a fat-faced ox-looking private named Herrad and called for an ale. He needed one.

The innkeeper had, smartly, not turned the men away. Twenty-five blades with the potential to become pointed at his throat was a forceful argument. He wasn't happy about it, though, slamming their tankards and food onto the table. The scowl on his pockmarked face seemed a permanent fixture.

Someone carried a set of dice on them, so they enjoyed a few games and a few ales. Loud chatter filled the room. *You'd almost forget there was a war.*

"The corporal was just telling me about the Spear," the knight said.

"Yeah. Guard Captain Hostein. He was celebrating, 'cause he'd just captured a mighty outlaw, a savage who raided near on ten villages, raped women, killed babies. You know, real scum. So, the captain was a celebrated man. He was a good-looking one, too. Everyone was thrilled to see him. The alehouse kept the booze flowing. The count came down. The baron, the sheriff, they all came down to shake his hand. In fact, Hostein was so popular that towards the end of the night, a few of the village wenches took him upstairs. These girls weren't known for their... timid nature, if you know what I mean. But it was deathly silent downstairs. An hour later, they came back down, untouched as their mothers would have 'em. 'What's happened?' the barkeep asked. They laughed and said, 'He's a looker, but he's about as much use as milk shoes.' And from then on, they knew him as Hostein Milk Dick."

They burst out laughing.

Caspar, Herrad's brother, the man's equal in hairiness and ox-ness turned to face them from the table over. "What's this? Herr, you told them the story about the wench from Taneria?"

"Yeah, right," Caen cut in. "It's what they all say, right? A bit a' wine and Tanerian women are less fickle than an aging whore."

"Don't they also say that men from Triburg have worms for cocks?" Maria said from the next table over, sending laughter through the room.

"Herrad might, but I ain't," Caspar replied.

"You've spent some time comparin'?" Andrea added.

"I don't need to take this from some wench." Caspar pushed himself free of the table, sending ale and chicken carcasses scattering. Both Andrea and Maria drew their weapons, rising to their feet. Lombas the Small laughed, his horselaugh shaking the room. The chubby tavern wench on his enormous lap laughed as well.

"Knock it off, lackwits," the knight bellowed, silencing the room. "Enough fuckin' chatter. It's time to get serious. Who here says they can take me? Squire!"

Tristain laughed and waved his arms.

Caen jabbed him with his elbow. "Come on!"

"Alright, alright... you might regret it, Sir," Tristain replied, to cheers among the men.

They threw back ales. One strongale, two, three. Caen patted him on the back. Tristain felt bile rise in his throat. He wasn't sure if he should be grateful for the support. Four, five, six. Feeling the liquid slide back up, he snapped his mouth closed. He thought it might come out his nose and his ears. The room spun. Leon was unfazed, putting away his seventh.

It was no use. The liquid came flowing out of his nose. Choking, he opened his mouth, coating the floor in foamy beer and stomach acid. The men cheered, slapping him on the back.

"That's no fair," Tristain cried, throat strained. "You haven't got a bottom in that belly!"

The men laughed.

"Alright, alright," Caen yelled. "Who's next?"

Herrad challenged Caen and the big lad from Triburg won handily, then Maria launched into a story.

"So, back home, right," she said, laughing. "The boys used to throw rocks at us, me an' Andrea. It was their way of getting attention, I think. Why are you boys so hopeless at just talking to women? Anyway, one day one of the real big boys, you know, two feet taller than anyone else and cock as big a horse's... you know the ones."

They laughed, looking pointedly at Lombas, the giant lad was taller than most by a foot, and he shrugged his mountainous shoulders.

"So, Andrea and I took him out to the forest for a bit of payback. The poor lad probably thought we were gonna' let him prod us. Well, we might've but... anyway, we went for a swim in the creek, tellin' him to take off his clothes and then we would join him. So, he leaped into the water, prick flailing about like a godsdamned eel. Andrea got in with him, all naked-like, while I hid his clothes in the tallest tree I could find. I'm a fair hand at climbing, you see. I came back, told him we were leaving, and Andrea got out and ran. We didn't look back. We ran so hard that we nearly collapsed." She became breathless, laughing until tears ran down her face.

"Then what? Tell us," Caen said, grinning.

"We..." She couldn't stop laughing. Tristain smiled as he took another sip of his ale. "We hid behind the alehouse, n'... he came runnin', right to the center of town, naked as the day he was born, covered in red, angry blisters from his neck down to his toes. Leeches got to him! Even his prick had a few on 'em! He was furious! But he never threw rocks at us again."

They all laughed.

The innkeeper said something in whispered Badonnian to the chubby woman and she hopped off Lombas' knee.

"We're closing, sorry," the man said in a heavy accent, face pinched.

"What kind of alehouse closes?" Caen said.

"It's fine, Corporal. We've overstayed our welcome," Leon replied. "These kind folks fed our bellies and warmed our bodies. We should be on the road."

The door opened and a strong, wet wind blew over Tristain. The weather had turned.

"Argh, it's raining," Maria said. "First rain in a fuckin' month and it's when we're on the march."

"All the more reason to get to camp, wench," Herrad replied. Maria slapped him playfully with the back of her gloved hand.

Tristain unhitched his horse, feeling the effects of the strong ale now. He nearly lost his footing as the beast buffeted him. Rain dripped down his padded jacket. It fell in sheets now. Thunder rumbled in the distance. The sky darkened.

A man screamed. Tristain turned, drawing his sword. He hadn't realized until that moment just how dark it was, and he blinked, trying to resolve the dark in front of him. Lightning illuminated the sky, and it was as bright as day for a moment. The light dazzled, but through the intense dark blue and white, two figures lay on the ground, dead. Eight grey-plate forms stood abreast above them. Red-gold cloaks on their backs. Steel drawn.

Tristain flinched as the sky went dark again. They were the party from the road. Not a hunting party, or traders, or foot soldiers, but heavily armed Badonnian knights.

One of them bellowed, "*Allae!*"

Heavy crashing footsteps sounded over the rain. Bellowing curses and war cries, they were lit by the sky again. Swinging their weapons in wide arcs, men fell around them, crashing into the ground in wet heaps of mail. Tristain swallowed, throwing himself forward into the darkness. Someone beat aside his sword like it was a mere toothpick, and a plated fist smashed into his jaw. Pain wracked his ear and face as he fell.

A bright fork of light rippled around the knight's raised longsword. Tristain could only watch as it came down like a headman's axe. Then someone crashed into the knight. The Badonnian clattered to the ground. Tristain's wits found him. He scrambled, his fingernails churning up muck and blood.

A heap of mail crashed next to Tristain. It was Caen, his face twisted in pain. His temple ran with blood. Around them, the brawl clashed their way like a storm. A knight lost his balance and stomped on Tristain's ankle. Tristain felt something snap. He tried not to scream, feeling his jaw stiffen from the punch he'd taken. Pushing past the pain, he crawled away from the battle, dragging Caen with him, sword in the other hand. He strained, elbowing his way across the unforgiving mud.

At last, they were free, and Tristain set the corporal aside. He tested his jaw, feeling the stiff muscles and sore teeth. Felt like he might've even lost a few.

Tristain pulled himself to his feet, feeling a sharp tingle through his ankle. He breathed, trying to calm himself. It worked, and his eyes were adjusting to the blackness, making him feel slightly better about the screams and death around him. *Maybe there's a chance... if I can fight back.* He looked down at Caen. *You won't die here.*

He remembered Leon's lessons. The stances. He moved into a back guard, sword edge aligning with his stronger rear leg, his weak leg forward. A red-gold cloak charged at Tristain. Lightning rippled behind his foe. He scanned for weak points. Leon's words echoed in his mind. *Armpit, eyes, groin, back of the knee.*

The air ruptured as Tristain slashed. The blow was deflected, as he expected. Tristain evaded the counter, trading blows. He feinted an attack from above, turning his blade in the air. The knight blocked high, then found Tristain's blade in his armpit. The man howled, dropping to the ground. Bits of food leaked from his opponent's faceplate. He wasn't getting up anytime soon.

More of Tristain's squad fell around him. The Badonnians caught them by surprise, and they were drunk. *Much longer and we'll be finished.* He watched as Leon wrenched a knight's helmet off, snapping the buckle. He roared, burying his dagger into the base of his foe's skull.

It made Tristain sick. Death and horror unfolded in front of him. Half of his fellows were dead, glass-eyed on the ground. Straining, his lungs yearned for fresh air. Despite the rain, the air felt cloying and sticky. No longer able to stomach what was happening, he dry-heaved.

A horseman came charging out of the darkness and knocked Tristain on his ass. The rider whooped as he wheeled the horse around, waving his sword wildly. He yelled something in Badonnian, grinning at Tristain as he got to his feet. *Shit.* Three knights were drawn by the sound. They laughed as they closed in.

"Where do you run," one yelled as he stepped forward and began a flurry of blows. Tristain deflected them. On the last blow, Tristain feinted a cut low. The man blocked, and as he did, Tristain flicked up. The point of the sword went through his attacker's neck. Tristain moved back into guard, pushing his fear and nausea aside.

Two more pounced, forcing him backwards. He countered, disarming one. As he recovered, the other's sword bit into his arm. Tristain howled, retreating. His back sidled up against a tree. The two closed in, and there was no escape. One moved in with a spear, batting aside Tristain's weakened sword arm. He plunged the point in, pinning his shoulder to the tree. Tristain cried in pain, dropping his blade.

An officer stepped forward. The captain, from what Tristain could judge by the deference offered by his comrades, if they had such a thing as deference in Badonnia. He grinned as he approached.

"You," he said, speaking with a heavy accent, "are a lord's son, from your skill."

Tristain spat at him.

He chuckled. "But you die like the rest."

"Sigur fucking curse you," he swore back. "You won't get away with this."

"Your army will perish. All you wester *pudans* will die for nothing and nobody. You will lie in the dirt. Forgotten by all but wolves. Not even your mothers and wives will miss you because we will take them for ourselves."

"I'll kill you, bastard. You watch."

Laughter broke out.

"How can you kill me... if I kill you first?" He stabbed Tristain in the gut. Ice gripped his stomach and pain shot through his body, doubling him over. Only the spear kept him upright. He grasped weakly at the blade, thinking somehow that removing it would stop the pain.

The captain looked at him incredulously. "Why don't you die?"

Tristain groaned as the captain pulled the sword out. Blood bloomed under his jacket. Fear bubbled in his stomach. His breath became sharper. Two others moved in to do the dirty work. Stabbing, cutting, hacking. His vision became hazy, narrowed.

He looked down, seeing himself from above. Looked at the men taking turns to butcher his body. The sound of wet metal rang out, but it meant nothing to him, lost as he was in an ocean of calm.

Then something took hold, wrenching him back into his body. Searing heat swelled from his feet, up through his legs, then his chest, and out through his head, as if he was standing on a pyre. Shooting pain went up his spine. Time slowed, drawing out the excruciating agony. His vision went white with pain.

His teeth were the first to change. They tore through his gums, growing until they were finger-long. His jaw went slack, then broke, the pain causing him to drool. The space around his eyes, nose, and jaw pushed outwards, forming a broad snout. Through the pain, he saw his killers stare, stepping back in horror. Inside, he tried to think, tried to pray. *Gods! Please end this!*

No mercy would come. He was captive for every excruciating moment. Thick black fur sprouted from every pore, like thousands of porcupine needles. His padded shirt ripped at its seams and his mail twisted as his chest ballooned. The spear tip was pushed out as the skin wove itself together. His head pounded as he looked up. It was like having his skull torn open. Claws as sharp as a wildcat's forced themselves from his fingernail beds.

His eyes adjusted, the pain subsiding at last. He could see in the dark as if it was daytime. The smell of the captain's breakfast of ale and beef sausage drifted into his nose. The change took five seconds, yet it seemed like an eternity. He roared. The very air seemed to shudder.

"*Garou!*" The Badonnians scrambled away, yelling and shrieking in fear. Instinct took over. He saw his prey and grew hungry. A scream filled the air as he leaped for the captain.

4

PRAYER

SANGUINUM, 1042

Train the Sword in all martial ways, for that is their purpose.
To be a weapon.

— GRAND INQUISITOR ULRICH VETTERAND

WHEN THE SHADOWS OF afternoon were long and dark and the clouds swelled with the threat of rain, the Gray Citadel erupted in front of Selene, grasped by the southernmost end of a jut of stone and sand, surrounded on three sides by the sea. The stronghold was the centuries-old home of the Order of the Golden Sword in Osbergia, encircled from the north by the capital, Ostelar. At the cliff's base, the water had worn its way into the rock, forming a sheltered cove visible from their approach to the city from the east.

Ostelar and the Citadel were two months from Invereid, and Selene had spent most of that time quietly. The road was tough, but bearable. Sorenius had been enjoyable company—silent and sullen as he always was. They'd trained as they traveled. Her missing arm had given her no trouble, and no infection had come back. The priest Radimir did his work well though her mind still troubled.

In fact, it had given her so little trouble, she often forgot she'd lost it, leading to comical results. One time, Sorenius offered her a hand to get on his horse. She reached out her left hand to take his, only to remember she didn't have a left arm. Another time, she soared over the saddle, thinking to catch herself with her left hand as she did on the estate. She soared right over and tumbled face-first into horse dung.

Other times, the realization came with intense pain. Sometimes, it was as though a nasty god stabbed her left hand, drove spikes under her fingernails. Luck had it she only felt that extreme pain rarely.

Sorenius hitched their horse at the citadel stables, and they made the ascent to the top of the hill. It was hard going. The ground sloped upwards, with outbuildings from the bottom to the inner gates at the top, where the Citadel itself sat. The trapezoidal Citadel keep in bleak, grey stone dominated the landscape. Manned with hundreds of guards, the curtain walls were well-maintained, with bolt-loops and murder holes staring ominously like eyes back at her.

As they walked up the hill, she noted two types of people: black-leather-clads with severe looks and blades at their belts; and demure robe-types going about their duties. The fighters trained in the open square at the bottom of the hill. Sorenius told her of them: arbiters, who fought unusually, their fighting style fit for taking down large beasts than fighting men. One came crashing down near them, having leapt from a high place. She heard the instructors barking orders, "Left! Up! Hold! Dive! Leap! Half-turn! Pirouette!" It was all very confusing, but Sorenius said that was the point. Arbiters worked in pairs or trios—after quick and unpredictable moves distracted the beast, the real threat would dive in from a suitable height, latching onto the creature's back, plunging a blade into the relatively thin-skinned neck. They practiced by using each other as springboards, launching onto targets of her height and once more.

"Their fur is a kind of armor," he said. "Steel can hardly get through, and only properly through the neck. But coat your blade or arrow in poison? Even a slight prick will kill them."

Concocting venoms and poisons were what the grey-robed notaries did. The stench of strong chemicals fashioned by alchemists and apothecaries filled the air, spells and prayers chanted over them to double their effectiveness. A basket *hissed* at her as she passed, and she flinched.

"They milk the adders inside for their deadly venom," Sorenius told.

Once at the top of the hill, she turned. It took her breath away. Though the sky was grey, she could see the entire city. Split by the Alba and Tibor rivers, the city straddled the narrow strip of land down the middle, while in the center, the immense Osterline Hill conquered her eye, a full mile in diameter, the grand duke's ancient White Palace on top. The Inner Ring surrounded the hill, cradling the Noble and Merchant districts, and the Upper Market. Beyond that was the Outer Ring, containing Lower Market and the Slums, which bled west into the port, and the harbor beyond that, to the bay. Beyond the walls and the rivers on either side, were shantytowns known as the Outskirts. After that, the flat wetlands of the Alba and Tiber River valleys for miles around, and the small trading town of Dver north of that.

She felt the inquisitor's hand gently pull her beyond the curtain wall and into the bailey.

"Come with me," a woman said once inside, donned in a bone-white cloak and a stern face.

Sorenius bade her farewell. "You must do this alone," he said. "The rector will tell you where you need to go."

Selene followed her through the giant iron doors into the ground floor of the citadel. Striding along the tiled hallway, Selene's eye drew upwards to the vast, arched ceiling and complex patterns in mosaic and gold snaking across the lime-washed dome, telling the history of the world and Sigur's eternal struggle against the Great Devil. She realized the citadel's exterior belied its true purpose. Truthfully, it was a cathedral. The altar ahead of her held a large golden statue in a forceful pose, Sigur himself, the God of

Light, Death, Strength, and Justice. Priests, both men and women, carted around books, prayed at the altar or icons of martyrs, or simply chatted.

Further inside, dense smoke from incense sticks enveloped Selene, and she hurried along before she lost the woman in the haze. The low light inside didn't help matters, but Selene found her way eventually.

The woman turned before reaching a stairwell. "You'll need this," she said, handing her a set of black robes procured from a nearby stand. "There will be a room for convalescence and quiet to your left when you reach the bottom of the steps. Take your clothes off and leave them there. Change into these robes and proceed down the hall when you are ready."

Selene nodded and descended the steps. The stone spiral was narrow, so she had to watch her step. Now underground, the only light came from candelabras mounted to the wall. They dripped with years of melted wax, mounds of pale stalactites from silver cradles. The candles flickered in the darkness, casting orange light on the stone walls.

Ahead of her, rows of closed doors extended on either side. She looked to her left and found the door in question and pushed it open. A young woman in the same dark robes Selene held kneeled by an icon on the wall, her palms flat on her knees. The icon portrayed Sigur brandishing a golden sword banishing the darkness, similar enough to the rest of them. After shutting the door softly, Selene placed her robes on the floor, undressing. It was a little strange, having someone in the room as she stripped, but the girl seemed to pay very little mind, not turning from the icon for a single moment. *She probably didn't hear me come in.*

Selene swept her black hair behind her ears and unbuckled her vest. She went down to a sackcloth shirt and breeches, a gift from Radimir after having left home without clothing or much of anything. She threw the robes over the top. Taking a deep breath, she steeled herself for what was coming, or rather, what she thought was coming.

"Are you going to ask the Father for His help?" the girl's soft voice came as Selene touched the door pull. Selene turned, cocking her head as the girl stared. She was about the same age as Selene, with cropped red hair that sat just below her ears, framing pointed ruddy eyebrows and a sharp chin. Her eyes seemed odd, like they didn't match. "I am told the training is brutal. I'm praying to Sigur for His help. Pray with me."

"Alright," Selene replied, not knowing where she might start. She barely attended the Gebet, and never knew the prayers by heart. In fact, she was never very religious. She wished Radimir had taught her at least a few, or she'd at least had an ear peeled when he held the services. *What have I found myself in?* she wondered.

She kneeled next to the red-headed girl and closed her eyes. The woman softly spoke, "Mighty Father, your humble servants beseech You. Give us the strength to overcome the trials that wait for the power is Your Name. One day, we shall return what is owed, freeing this world from evil's grasp."

"So, it shall be." Selene recalled how the prayers were supposed to end, at least.

The girl opened her eyes and smiled at Selene. She *did* have mismatched eyes, one half-grey and half-blue, while the other was all blue. A wicked, curved scar ran across her cheek, running from shortly below her mismatched eye across to her ear. Selene tried not to stare.

"I'm Leona. From the Fork."

"Selene," she replied. "Invereid."

"Nice to meet you, Selene from Invereid. You don't know the prayers, do you? 'So, it shall be' is out of date. Now, it is said, 'so, in light'." *Dammit. I knew I should've paid attention when Radimir had Gebet those months ago.*

Selene chuckled, playing with her hair. "No, I... I don't know them."

Leona chuckled too. "That's alright, I'll teach you soon enough." Selene's stomach grumbled loudly. Leona laughed as Selene blushed. "It's alright. I think they'll serve supper soon."

They stood and Selene felt a little better. Maybe the prayers had something to them, after all.

Leona told her where they were going: a training gallery at the end of the entrance hall at the bottom of the stairs, passing the closed doors. Steel rang out and the clanging of shields and the twanging of bowstrings sounded as they approached. The hall opened, and before her stood many people in black robes, recruits like her. They were of all ages, both men and women, though the oldest was probably just shy of middle age. They practiced with knives, swords, crossbows, and shields. Columns dotted the room, one every ten paces, ringed with burning candles in silver cradles, while grates in the ceiling above let sunlight in. She wondered how the geography worked. They must've been below the courtyard above, outside of the keep.

The woman in the white robes shouted for them to gather at the entrance. To Selene's right was a young, scrawny, dark-skinned man, while Leona had her left. The dark-skinned man was probably from Vallonia, a kingdom on the southern tip of the continent, below the Three Republics.

"Before we start," the woman declared, "let us give thanks to the God of Light for our lives, our health, and our strength. Let Him penetrate the darkness and may Godsreturn speed our salvation."

"So, in light," they all replied. Leona glanced at Selene and smiled.

"Good. I am the Rector Palia. For those of you who are new: in the halls of this hallowed ground, I am second only to Sigur himself. I will tell you this only once, so listen well. When you address me, call me Rector, or Teacher. If you address me by chosen name, it will not end well for you. Understand?"

The novices murmured their agreement. The rector stiffened, saying, "Yes, Rector."

"Yes, Rector," they repeated.

"Good. Now, those of you who are new will be assigned an instructor in groups of six. This instructor will assess your abilities and determine how best to train you."

"Yes, Rector."

"Yes, Rector," Selene said, finding herself a bit out of step. Maybe it was the long ride, those long months of sitting in a saddle from dawn till dusk. The dark-skinned man glanced at her. Selene arched an eyebrow. *What's his problem?*

They broke up into groups, and Selene found herself with the dark-skinned Vallonian man; a tall, broad-faced man with a barrel-chest and square limbs; a soldier-type who looked like he could wrestle a bear; another soldier-type that was leaner but still quite strong-looking, and an olive-skinned man with a bushy black beard. She compared the two, and the lanky one was definitely darker. Maybe he was from further south, from across the ocean in Saburria.

"They'll make you shave that off 'fore too long," the broad-faced one said. The olive-skinned one shrugged in response. Selene wondered if the two soldier-types had training—military of some sort. Perhaps they knew how the campaign in Badonnia fared. Tristain was yet gone only a few months, but news was hard to come by.

They stood at the end of the hall, in one of the back corners. Around them sat training targets made of wood and stuffed clothing, made to look like men. They were mounted on tallow-slick slides that Selene tested a little out of curiosity. With each hit, it seemed they would rotate so that the trainee would have to be prepared for a counterattack.

Their setup was common across the gallery: each group was given their own training area with their own targets. Though for safety's sake, Selene supposed, all the archery targets were at one end, placed along the wall.

Their trainer walked up to them. Selene grinned. He met her gaze briefly. *So much for doing it on my own.*

"I am Instructor Sorenius," he said. "I understand that I am to take over from your old instructor. I will dispense with the formalities and get down to it. I do not care what you were before you arrived here. When you descended those steps, you broke all ties with those above, their caprices, and their wickedness. The Order of the Golden Sword is all that you will know. For those of you that are new, we are your family now." She'd heard it from him before, but Selene couldn't think of anything better.

"You, raven-hair." He pointed. Selene stiffened. "Step forward." He fetched a knife and handed it to her, taking a length of chain for himself, winding it around his forearm. "Attack me."

Selene knew this one. She lunged forward with her right arm. The man easily stepped aside, caught her outstretched arm with the chain, and bit. She yelped, not expecting it. He yanked, tearing the knife from her grasp.

She groaned, feeling the muscles ache underneath. Sorenius sighed as he unwound the chain. It was painful, but she swore to herself she would not cry.

"Again," he said, this time handing her a spear, taking a sword for himself. She rubbed her leg. *What's he doing?* "Perhaps you are more comfortable with range?"

She stood out of range of his sword, she hoped. Her spear was long and she cradled the shaft under her arm. The wood was polished, cool to the touch. She swept it from side to side, keeping him at bay. He sprang forward, faster than she could blink. He easily got past her guard. She had no chance. She frantically tried to block, but he swept the spear aside with one hand. Holding the point of his blade to her neck, his eyes flashed with disappointment. The look said, *have you learned nothing?* She wilted, letting the spear fall to the ground. The dark-skinned Saburrian let out a chuckle and the trainer flashed with fury at him.

"Taking it out on the novices, Instructor," the rector said. "I see. On the heels of a successful hunt, too. Mayhap you're still agitated?" *A successful hunt?* She could only recall one night when he'd disappeared, returning in the morning. *Had it been then?*

"Assessing her skills, Rector, in fact." Sorenius spoke matter-of-factly. "Of which she has none."

Selene chewed her lip. She felt tears bud in the corners of her eyes.

"Inquisitor, you are here to train them, not to break them down. If I wanted that done, I would let the torturers have them."

The man looked determined to respond, but simply nodded. "Very well, Rector. You four. Pair off, sword and shield each. I gather you have some training, brown hair?" The thick-limbed one nodded. "Good, take them through drills of blows and blocking. Remember, keep moving. A stationary Sword is a dead Sword. And you two." He pointed to Selene and the other soldier-type. "Start with throwing knives. Go to the targets and tell the keeper there that your instructor has sent you."

The targets were a long row of densely packed haystacks with an abundance of crossbows, short-limbed training bows and long war-bows. There was a crate full of knives as well, which Selene took a handful of, gingerly, making sure not to cut herself. They were all shapes and sizes but had the same general form of small finger-long handles, and razor-sharp two-sided blades. They were for throwing rather than close fighting.

The soldier-type went first, missing wildly, his clumsy fingers fumbling with the small-handled knives. Selene went next, landing hers.

"Nice shot," he said. Selene smiled, feeling slightly better about that dressing-down from before. She put the aloof, arrogant inquisitor from her mind.

She took a second, then lined up another shot. It landed with a soft thump very near to the center.

The soldier-type whistled in admiration. "You're good. I'm Ruprecht, by the way."

"Selene," she replied, tucking a bit of stray hair behind her ear. Ruprecht was kind-faced, with short-cropped brown hair drawn to a widow's peak above his eyebrows.

"Not like that," the inquisitor told as he walked up. Selene wilted. "You think that in the heat of combat, someone is just going to wait for you to hit them with a knife while you line up your throw?" She shook her head. "That's right. Toss them as fast as you can. At least one of them is bound to hit. Aim for here." He pointed to his chest, drawing a box around his torso.

I'd aim for there with a crossbow, she thought angrily.

"Like this." He flicked his wrist, without turning head, three times in quick succession. All three knives landed square in the center. Selene stared, not knowing if she would ever become that skilled.

Sorenius nodded and left. Infuriated by his cold regard, she huffed and turned away. Ruprecht tried again, missing again. Two recruits next to them chuckled, and he grew frustrated. "Maybe I should just do something else," he said. "I'm no good."

Selene sighed, before trying the trick she saw the instructor do. She threw the knife forward, underarm, spinning it counterclockwise. *Thump.* She blinked in surprise. It wasn't dead on, but it was close enough.

Ruprecht laughed. "That prick's got nothing on you!" She turned as the other novices approached.

Leona was grinning. "Supper," she said.

THEY SAT AT LONG tables in the dining hall, in the annex, outside the keep but still inside the curtain wall. It was late afternoon now, and orange sunlight filtered through the lead-light windows. Selene gorged herself on the delicious soup and crusty rolls on offer. The journey to the citadel had been long, and Sorenius was loath to stop unless they had to. They had often ridden all day. There'd been little choice as she rode with him on the front of the saddle. She had laughed when he brought it up, believing passers-by would think they were lovers on a ride. Those concerns had soon vanished as he suggested she could walk instead if she wanted to. His warm manner and his frosty regard switched places often. She could never figure out his moods.

Selene stopped raising her spoon to her mouth. The others watched with mild bemusement.

"You know we have to wait for the rector, right?" Leona whispered. Selene looked up. No one else was eating. She put her spoon down gingerly, wiping her mouth. The rector strode into the room. The woman eyed Selene, then announced the start of pre-supper prayers.

"Join me, please," she said, closing her eyes and tilting her head down. They all did the same. Their voices in unison, they prayed to Sigur for the food in front of them, and for strength in their coming trials.

"So, in light," they finished.

"Now, you can eat," Leona whispered. Selene didn't wait. She dove into the soup again, a pleasant blend of potato and leeks. She bit a piece off the heel of bread. It was all very unladylike, she was sure, but damn it, she hadn't eaten in nearly two days. She was in the middle of a bite when Ruprecht asked her where she came from.

"You heard the inquisitor," Leona said. "We have to forget our past when we come here."

"Oh, come on," he replied. "We have to get to know each other, at least."

Selene coughed, indigestion rising in her chest. "I'm from Invereid."

Ebberich grinned. "Me too. Small bloody world, isn't it? What's your favorite thing about the city? Mine's the river."

Selene nodded. She liked the river, and on the rare occasions she would ever leave the estate, it was to visit Invereid. Not that she could ever see the river up close, out of her sedan—no, there was never enough time between parlor visits and dress fittings. Her guardian father would never allow her to see the city on her terms, and her governess followed this order to the letter. He would never babysit her, of course, it was always the governess. A small part of her was sad that she'd never see her friends again—the mayor's two daughters and the nice tailor's assistant.

"You don't talk much, do you?" said Ruprecht, bringing his spoon up to his mouth and giving it a blow.

"She's probably slow," Salim said. Osbergian was clearly his second language, though he had no trouble with fluency and wordplay.

"Don't be a prick, Salim. It's her first day—she's probably still fresh from the road."

Raul slurped his soup loudly, the brown liquid filtering through his beard. "You'd never hear that from a Vallonian," he said in his strong accent. They turned their heads.

"What's that?" Ebberich replied.

"Nothing," he replied, getting up from the table. He left a half-eaten bowl, walking out of the dining hall.

"Speaking of someone who doesn't say much…"

Supper finished as Solni dipped below the horizon. The twin Gods did their dance at opposite ends of the horizon, and now it was Luni's turn. She came out, her bright form for all to see. It was time for Vespers when novitiates would go to places of quiet reflection and pray. After that, it was bed.

Leona took Selene to a small chapel attached to the annex. The chapel held a few kneeling posts, and there were some black-robed novices there already. The icon hung over the altar was a shimmering form of a sword piercing dark clouds above, held aloft by a woman, Sofiya, the famed martyr and defender of the Godcity against the Great Devil's armies. Her voluminous, golden hair billowed in the wind and her eyes flashed with lustrous fury.

Leona bowed her head as she entered the chapel. Selene did the same, following her lead. She led them in prayers, and they went to bed.

S ELENE TOOK A LONG time to get used to the closeness. The crowds at Invereid were on a scale much larger than the Citadel, but the Citadel proved the more intense of the two. Invereid was quicker, like a fast river, and if you allowed yourself to fall, you'd be pulled under. She could at least find a lifeline in returning to the Oncierran estate, though that presented its own problems. With its endless corridors and chatter filling its halls, the Citadel ebbed and flowed with its own moods and waves, like a languorous ocean.

She found herself thinking of home, and of Mother, and how that lifeline had been cut, pitching her into the black depths. Sometimes she'd think about those moments where Mother would sing, or brush her hair, those moments she held onto with her fingernails. If she let them go, she didn't think she would ever find land ever again.

It was one of those times, Selene whistled to herself as she passed Leona and the others in the cloister, that she thought of Mother and how she might be happy that at least her daughter had found somewhere far from Father. At the very least, out of all the death, that one good thing could come of it.

Leona gave a mismatched grin, to match her eyes, and took Selene's hand in her own, locking their fingers. Selene suspected that she was happy to have made a friend her own age, a girl, out of all the boys that surrounded her.

I wonder if we'll brush each other's hair.

It was strange, to feel comfortable with the unfamiliar. It felt wrong to allow herself a moment of joy, a moment of kinship, after knowing that Mother still laid on the floor of Father's office, a savaged corpse in her mind.

She took Leona's hand, and the girl let out a surprised noise.

"Come here. I want to show you something."

They took a path she'd only discovered a couple of days past, two weeks after the day she'd arrived. Behind the abbey, a garden rested under the shadow of an old oak tree. The air wafted with the smell of lavender and roses. Bees buzzed around the petals of the flowers, and at the foot of the oak, a plaque read:

Praise be to the Martyrs
Their sacrifice knows no end
Of gratitude
Lest we forget.

"This is the preceptor's garden," Leona said. "The head priest."

"Is that so? I only came here because I smelled the lavender. My mother always wore a perfume of lavender. She used to take me down to the garden every day to have me rub some behind my ears."

Leona smiled. "That sounds nice. My mother beat me with a switch when I didn't do my chores."

Selene grimaced in reply. "I'm sorry."

"It's all right. I'm here now. Far away from them."

"As am I." A giant sigh left Selene's throat. It wasn't one of relief, or of loss, but of something like peace, if that could be found. Father and Mother were dead, but in some awful way, their deaths hadn't been in vain.

"Who are the Martyrs?"

Leona grinned as though delighted she'd get an opportunity to explain something about Sigurian worship.

"The Book of Light says that the Martyrs died for our sins—our sins in failing to slay the Great Devil's minions during the Age of Light."

"I see."

Martyrs, great devils, age of light. They all sounded high-flown, something time and legend had turned into myth. *That's probably heresy for a novitiate to say—to think.* She stopped herself before she said something she might regret.

"But how do the other gods come into it? Did they fight with Sigur?"

Leona twisted her mouth. "Hmm. Well, Ginevra did, or so they say. She was Sigur's wife, after all, though the Book of Light is a bit contradictory in this. It's said she offered succor to the minions of the Great Devil. Haven't you read the Book?"

Selene touched the ends of one of the lavender stalks, running her fingers over the pungent petals. "It's been a long time."

That wasn't necessarily a lie, but this girl didn't need to know the truth.

"I hope to learn some, here."

Not necessarily a lie, either.

"You'll have to commit it to memory," Leona said. "Or so the instructors say."

"Got it."

"Well, I can be your tutor for now, hm?" If the girl's grin got any wider, her eyes might disappear.

"Veles sided with the Great Devil, though some volumes of the Book use the names interchangeably. It's a bit confusing, but canon law considers Veles worship heretical. Ginevra and Eme took the side of Sigur since they were both His concubine. Both Solni and Luni remained neutral, since Sigur sealed them in the sky to perform their faithful duties. That's what the Book says."

"I see."

"Anyway, you're getting ahead. I like telling it from the beginning!" Leona brushed Selene's arm and giggled like a girl, which Selene supposed she was.

"Fine, tell it from the beginning."

"Yes, all right. Well, when Sigur formed us directly by spinning yarns of light, He saw the world as a formless, shapeless void, with which to make anything for us. He gave to us Solni, the sun, so that we might have a pale reflection of His light to give us warmth in the void. He gave to us Luni, giving us the first night, so that we know shadow from His light. Then He made the Continent, and all the world, so that we might have a demesne of our own, as He has the world and all the void and all the stars in the sky, and His eternal city behind the sky.

"His brother, the Great Devil, grew jealous and resentful of our love of Him. He created his own creatures, twisted and misshapen, a reflection of his hate."

"Demons. Wukodlaks."

"Monsters," she corrected.

Selene nodded. Mother used to tell her tales about the Continent and Sigur, though the stories seemed as muddy and contradictory as any myth. These people seemed to believe every word that was written in their Book of Light. The stories, spoken by Leona, were robbed of their mystery, as though she shone a penetrating light on them, revealing their facets to Selene.

"In his jealousy, he struck the Lightfather and great gluts of blood fell into the oceans. Those oceans coalesced, forming Ginevra, Eme, and Veles. Together they warred with the Great Devil, until Veles was swayed with promises of power over his father. Meanwhile, the demons warred with mankind as the gods warred in the sky."

Selene recalled that the purpose of the Order was to hunt down Sigur's enemies, leading to the conclusion that Sigur had failed in His war. She wondered if it was heresy to suggest that Sigur could fail at anything, let alone something with stakes as high as that. Though her existence now was testament to the god's failure—if you believed the Book, that was.

Later, the classes confirmed what she'd been told. No one liked to talk about the war that Sigur had lost. She'd risked the question to Rector Palia, once, and all the woman offered was a mighty frown.

"Sigur was tricked. The Great Devil, having swayed Sigur's firstborn, Veles, fell into a trap set by him. He was wounded, and fell back to the Golden City to recover, ending the Age of Light. One day, He will return, and we must be ready."

The words looked as though they'd taken a toll on the rector's face, leaving her exhausted. That was all she said, and she snapped at Selene, barking at her to return to duties.

5

BETRAYAL

FERVUM, 1044

Soldiers have but one duty to the empire: to die.

— DUKE ESTRAD, COUNT PALATINE

LEON HEAVED, PUSHING THE mass of bodies off his frame. Sweaty, hot air filled his lungs and throat. His shoulders strained at the weight—there could've been dozens on top of him for all he knew. The world was dark. A pauldron shifted, sending a gush of water into his face. He spluttered, groaning. At last, he pulled his face free, and threw his visor up, taking a cool, fresh breath for the first time in minutes. The first rays of dawn fell on his face. *At least it's stopped raining.*

He looked around. Carnage unfolded before him. Not anything he wasn't used to. More times than he cared to count, he'd seen a man stretched and quartered by horses; heads on spikes along a palisade; faces contorted into more expressions than a skilled actor. One thing was new, though. Never had he seen so many limbs unattached, so many bodies unrecognizable as human. He pushed it out of his mind.

He unclasped his dented helmet, feeling blood run down his cheek. A Badonnian had smacked him in the head with a hammer, he remembered now. He dragged himself free and checked for injuries. His back ached, his head pounded, and he was pretty sure he had a dislocated wrist. Sigur, he needed a drink. He reached for his flask, but it was gone. He frowned. Plate-covered boots thumping on the muddy ground, he checked each of his company for signs of life. Both Triburg brothers lay in bloody heaps, a spear sticking from one, open stomach on the other. Both had shit themselves. That was something Leon noticed; no matter where you were from, no matter what kind of life you lived, all men smelled the same in death. He found a flask still attached to their belt, and uncorked the cap.

"Ah, just water," he growled, and threw it away.

He moved on, kneeling next to the corporal, Caen. The man had a bloom of dried blood on the side of his face. He checked the blood; dried. Leon brought his ear close to his mouth. Shallow, soft breaths. Leon gave him a hard smack on the chest.

Caen gasped, thrust awake. He clutched at his head. "Aghhh, can't you let me have some fuckin' sleep?"

Leon swore in Hillard, "*Sal'brath.*" Fuck, the corporal was an idiot sometimes. "We have to move."

Caen groaned as Leon helped him to his feet. "I think I got stabbed."

"Relax, it's not deep. Find any survivors."

"Right."

They began checking men for breath. Each one they came to was quiet, chests still. Disappointment grew. Leon felt a vein in his forehead pulse. Heat filled his chest. It happened again. He'd let the lot of them down.

Leon was glad for the scruffy-haired corporal from the Spear. He didn't think he could handle it if he woke up alone. Through them all, though, he never saw one face in particular.

"You seen my squire anywhere?"

"Over here," Caen replied, then he vomited into a bush at his feet. Leon walked over. Lifting aside a branch, the smell hit him first. The smell of blood and death, hanging heavy in the air. Distilled. The sight nearly brought last night's ale onto the ground.

"*Ugh*," the corporal said, wiping his lip. "I can't say I've seen something like that before."

Tristain lay in a circle of bodies... no, bits... around his prone form. The man was immaculate, aside from his clothes. The lad was bare-chested, his mail and shirt discarded in pieces, like the figures around him. Heads, stomachs, intestines... scraps, scattered all around. *I thought I must have hit my head... but, here it is... Sigur's fucking balls.*

Leon walked up to the squire. He tapped him with his foot cautiously. "Think he's dead?"

"*They* sure are," Caen replied, waving his sword around.

Tristain's eyes shot open. Caen swore in surprise. The squire sat bolt upright, gasping, like he was choking for air. He glanced around, unaware of what had happened to him.

"What? What... happened..." He then turned and vomited.

Leon tried to imagine the white bits in the spew weren't what he thought they were. They weren't bones—human bones. Something demonic had visited the squire.

He kneeled. "Are you injured, lad?"

"I don't think so," Tristain said, voice flat. He looked past Leon. Staring. "What..."

"Listen... I don't know what happened here, but we need to move. It won't be long before the Badonnians realize their patrol went missing. Let's go. We'll come back to bury the dead, preferably with an entire regiment."

Leon picked his helmet back up. As he did, he caught a flash of scared innkeep from behind a curtain. *They're not on our side, are they?*

Now, to find the fucking horses so they could get back to the shithole they called a siege camp. Sometimes, he wondered why he even bothered, when all it led to was dead men and soiled pants. Enough dead to last a lifetime—several, even. Guilt tore through him every time, like a sword in the guts. He thought maybe the guilt would stop, one day, but it never did. It would be easier if it did.

More to add to the pile of bodies he'd left in his wake. His son was among them, and they all called out in his dreams, every single one of them.

He went searching through the corpses, rifled through their belts, opened their tunics. The dead didn't complain. He yearned for that familiar burning as it slid down his throat, the coldness a swallow left him with, the warmth as it slithered into his stomach. *Just one drink, any drink*. He'd settle for the fermented marsh water the men made back home.

Leon Strong, reduced to picking through dead bodies, looking for a flask or a skin.

"I wonder sometimes what the women back home would make of things," Caen said. He worked a chunky gold ring off one of the knights' fingers. "There's little under the sun I haven't done as a soldier, things I would never speak of."

"Aye," Leon said. A cold chill settled over him. They left it at that.

Horse hooves echoed over the rattling leaves, breaking the morning silence. Leon lifted his head, put a hand to the sword at his hip. Caen did the same.

Leon snorted as he saw who arrived. The tan-skinned republican, the general's steward, and a few men-at-arms behind. And the lieutenant. *I was wondering when they would show up...*

"Sir Vorland," the steward said as he rode up. Leon lowered his hand. He sat clean and proper, on a fucking pony, his black hair brushed back with slick oil. *Slick, like a fucking snake.*

"I'm sorry, sir," Gida said from beside him.

"Seize him," the steward yelled.

Three men-at-arms wearing the general's colors snatched at him. He jerked his arm out of reach, swung around, and broke a nose with his fist. It did nothing to stop their advance, and they penned him in. He bellowed as they threw him to the ground, writhing in anger, swearing in every language he could think of with such profanity it would make a sailor blush. Mud entered his eyes and mouth as the soldiers shoved him against the ground.

"You've been charged with dereliction of duty, knight," the steward sneered rather than spoke. Nothing seemed to make him happier than Leon's face pressed against the mud. The bastard had always had a problem with Leon, and he was hardly the only one—Leon was a lowborn, knighted, but still the son of a poor farmer.

"For drunkenness leading to the deaths of soldiers. Seize the squire and the corporal as well. I wish to speak with them."

"On whose authority?" the corporal shouted, drawing his blade.

Leon spat mud out of his mouth. "Stow your blade, Corporal," he yelled. *No one else is dying on my account.*

The steward grinned. "The general's authority."

T RISTAIN'S SHACKLES CHAFED HIS wrists and ankles. The cage was stark, only a hard mat of straw to lie upon, and that was shared with three others. Their privy, if you could call it that, was a bucket that backed up against the jailor's quarters. They were afforded no privacy, of course. There was something satisfying about defacing their captor's lodgings. Caen sat across from him, joined by two deserters headed for the noose. Tristain wasn't quite sure where he was headed. Caen said he'd like to go back to the Spear one day, watch his daughter grow up.

Tristain laughed. "You've a daughter?"

"What's so funny about it?" Caen had replied, folding his arms awkwardly with the chains around his wrists. He was serious.

"Nothing, it's just... you're not much older than me."

Caen grunted. "Yeah, well. It's nothing I planned. It was the miller's daughter. A little dance under the miller's nose, we had. Then she was with babe. I left for the war. I was no father. But a while back, I was told she had a daughter. Thought I might go one day. See what I spawned into the world."

"She's like to be a witch," a deserter had said. "Witches and cravens is what come from lone mothers."

"Really? Now we know what your childhood was like."

Tristain chuckled. "What's her name?"

"Vera."

"Interesting name. Any meaning?"

"It's Hillard. Means mercy."

"Mercy..."

Caen hung his face low. His expression wasn't sullen, but thoughtful. *He thinks he'll never see his daughter again. I wonder if I'll ever see Selene again.*

The two deserters stood. "Right, here's to Vera," one of them said, placing his fist on his chest in salute. It was a little ridiculous, if sincere.

The other folded his hands one of the other. "May Ginevra bless her with long life." It was about the only invocation the craven would know. He'd likely never seen the inside of a church. "We're headed to the rope. Gods know we need some fucking mercy, right now."

I T WAS THEIR THIRD night inside the cage, and Solni had long set. The deserters were right. They needed mercy, and they had it, it would be through a noose. A long drop with a knotted rope would be a mercy if there were any left in the world.

The jailor kept watch, torch in hand, yawning. A group of drunk men-at-arms jeered at the prisoners as they passed. Catching their tongues, they went quiet as a group of men in gray cloaks walked past. One of the graycloaks caught Tristain's eye and asked the jailor a question, keeping his eye on Tristain while he spoke. Their voices were too distant, too quiet to hear, but it was clear what they were asking. To speak to the prisoners. *What do a few priests want?* The jailor nodded, and they came over.

"Sigur's blessings upon you, good men," the graycloak who caught Tristain's eye before said. He seemed to be their leader, or at least the one who spoke for them all. "I'm afraid we bring troubling news."

"Aye, and who you supposed t'be?" Caen said, leaning on the bars.

"We are servants of the Holy Order of the Golden Sword. We have uncovered a field of mangled bodies and evidence of devilry and corruption. You two wouldn't know anything about that?"

Tristain was about to open his mouth when Caen shot him a look. A chill moved up Tristain's spine.

"Aye, Swords," Caen replied. "We know not of any devilry or corruption. T'was a fierce battle. But we spoke to the general already. Talk to the duchess. You'll hear right."

The graycloak seemed to think through Caen's words, but simply said, "Very well. We'll speak to the general."

As they walked off, Tristain leaned back against the bars, quiet, consumed by thoughts of that night outside the alehouse. Flashes of faces in pale terror. Blood, flesh... The taste of copper on his tongue, as real as the air he breathed.

Tristain felt Caen shake his arm.

"Hey, squire," he said. "You can't dwell on what happened. It happened. And it won't be the last time."

Tristain wiggled a finger in the mud. "It might be the last time. We don't know what the general wants from us. And what do these priests want?" Caen went silent.

After a short while, he crossed his arms, chuckling to himself. "I don't know if I should thank you or curse you."

"For what?"

"You killed the bastard about to bring an axe down on my head. Still not clear if that was a blessing or a curse."

"Hm. I guess we'll find out."

"Psst," a voice came. Tristain turned. In the darkness, he spotted the scruffy servant boy's face.

"Nikkel," he said, shuffling over.

"Had to see it for myself," the boy said, leaning on the bars. He was Leon's serving boy, Tristain realized. "I thought you were dead."

"No such luck. Any news about Sir Vorland?"

The boy grimaced. "They have him caged in the parade ground. The steward's given the men free reign to pelt him with food. It ain't right. Slimy Republican bastard."

"He eats well, then," Caen cut in.

Nikkel laughed. "I suppose he does."

Tristain took something out of his pocket. It was a letter, addressed to Selene. "Listen. I have a feeling this might be the last chance I have to do this." *If at all.* "Take this to my father's ward, in the Oncierran estate outside Invereid."

"How—"

"Find my horse."

"You're kiddin'. I don't know how to ride that beast."

"He likes apples. Be careful—he bites if he's hungry. Water him when he starts to tire and stick to the roads. He gets a little jittery on unsteady ground. My father'll give you lodging for returning my horse home, and for the letter. He might even have work for you."

"What do you think's going to happen?"

Who knows, but I have to get a letter to her. "Will you do it?"

The boy sighed. "All right. Your father better have work for me, though."

"I'm sure he will. Tenants are always looking for more hands."

"Oncierran," a gruff voice said, approaching.

"Go, Nikkel." The boy ran off, letter tucked into his shirt. Tristain muttered a quick prayer to Ginevra for his safety. *You'd better take good care of my horse.*

"Oncierran lad," the voice came again. Tristain turned. A torch fell upon him. His eyes adjusted as the cage door opened. "The general wants you." It was a guard in the general's colors. They lifted him to his feet, unlocking his shackles.

T RISTAIN SAW THE GENERAL'S anger in her clenched shoulders and the tightness of her jaw. She waved her hand for Galeaz, her steward, to speak. She carried the weight of thousands, and the heavier aspirations of the archduke.

Albrecht, the first son of the emperor, given the title of archduke, ruled the southernmost province, Osbergia. It was the largest with the most fertile land, and shared borders with the merchant republics of the south. Tristain heard the emperor was fond of his first son first. Of course, the sons were less fond of each other. If the general failed, it meant that weight would come crashing down, leaving the other princes of the Lion Throne to take advantage.

Tristain thought of another Prince of the Lion Throne and ground his teeth. But that was the past, and he could never go back to that, no matter how much he wanted. *Selene.* Could he even face her like this? Worse yet, would he even survive this?

"Squire," he said, standing rigid. "You've been called here to recount the events outside the abode known as The Ox's Balls, two nights past, and the circumstances that led to the deaths of twenty-five men-at-arms."

"We travelled up the north road from the southern forest, patrolling, as instructed," the squire replied. "We were making our way—"

"Get to the point, boy, where we lost twenty-five good men for no reason," the general interrupted.

"There... there's very little to say, my lady. They ambushed us outside the Ox."

"Was that all?" the steward said. "Sir Vorland made an unscheduled stop, did he not? And he drank himself into a stupor?"

"I will not lie, my lord. The patrol was tiring. A quick drink was all that was needed, and a warm bath."

"It was more than a few drinks, wasn't it?"

Tristain stiffened. "It... was no more than three." *Seven.*

"And then?"

"We were leaving the Ox, and a storm deadened our hearing until the Badonnians were on us. A group—"

"A group of knights, yes. We spoke to the lieutenant already. She wisely suggested that the convoy keep moving, stay off the roads."

"That she did."

"Is there nothing else?" The general had pursed her lips hard enough they turned white around the edges. *She cannot say it to my face, but she wishes to rid herself of the knight. The question is why?*

Tristain sighed inwardly. *Perhaps... perhaps it would be easier if Leon was out of the way. He knows what I am. Maybe he deserves it. A lowborn knight, and a drunk. His hens are finally coming home to roost.* Heat rose to his cheeks. *Am I truly capable of that? So much for loyalty. Besides, their blood is on my hands as much as it is his.*

"I... I suggested we stay," he said. The general sat up in her chair. "It was foolish of me. The lieutenant was right. We should've avoided the roads." *Maybe things would've been different.* The taste of blood. The screams.

"Your honesty is commendable," Adolar replied. "But not actionable. Your knight should've known better."

"He should hang," Galeaz said.

"And you should watch your tongue, Republican. Sir Vorland is a knight of the realm."

"An incompetent fool and a drunk."

The general sighed. "What is the feeling amongst his men?"

"The lieutenant has voiced her concerns. Some of the men are displeased, but none so far have been insubordinate. They accept Vorland has failed in his duties."

"The other knights?"

"Sigibund and Clearwater are of the opinion that only the emperor can sanction the disenfranchisement. Vredevoort suggested dragging him behind a horse."

"He would." She rubbed her temples. "My mind feels heavy. If you'll excuse us, squire."

"General—"

"You'll be assigned to Vredevoort's regiment for now," the steward said. "Report to Sergeant Dengeld." Tristain bowed. *I'm not dead. Was it really this easy? But... now I have nothing. My knight is disgraced, and his shame will turn to contempt for me. I have no hope of becoming a knight, now.*

Now outside, he chewed his lip in frustration. He felt like punching something. The graycloaks watched him, their eyes on his back.

"What!" he screamed, turning to face them. "Sigur be praised. What do you want?"

They flinched, all but the leader. A sinister grin spread across his face. Tristain felt the hairs on his neck rise. Tristain cleared his throat and left.

He made his way back to his tent, wondering what the next few days would hold for him. No one he knew. A new captain: Vredevoort the Grim. He knew the stories about the harsh, violent man. And these troubling graycloaks, asking altogether too many questions about what happened that night.

Breathing a sigh as he flopped down on his mat, he wondered if the ordeal of the past few days was finally over, or if his ordeals had only just begun. Certainly, something snagged in the back of his mind. He didn't feel in control of himself. His skin felt slippery, as if he could shed it at any moment and become something terrible. The passage in the *Histories* flashed in his mind. *Demon... Devil... Shapeshifter.* Unease settled in and a shiver went down his spine.

6

KNOWLEDGE

SANGUINUM, 1042

*Demons present a confounding problem: what to do if any
man, common or noble, has the strength of ten of his peers and
cannot easily be killed?*

— GRAND INQUISITOR ULRICH VETTERAND

T HE DINING HALL BUZZED with excitement. Novitiates talked excit-
edly, turning their heads to the entrance each time someone walked
in, as they did to Selene. She felt embarrassed, as if she'd done something
to deserve their looks, but they turned away just as quickly.

"What's going on?" Selene asked as she joined the group at the table.
Leona smiled as she sat.

Ruprecht tore at the heel of bread with great effort, like an animal.
"They're-mm... each month-mmh, novitiates who are near their rites have
a skirmish. It's called *Velitore.* That's what everyone's worked up about. By
Sigur, this has to be more stale than usual."

"Yeah," Ebberich said. "It's about the only exciting thing that happens
around here. It's a bit of fun, and everyone gets into it. They fight a
wukodlak. If they live, they get to be confirmed."

"*What?*" Selene's jaw gaped. "They—we have to fight a wukodlak?"

"Uh... yeah? That's what Swords do. Why do you seem surprised?"

"I just..."

"How long have you been here for?" Leona said, rubbing her chin.

"About six weeks," Ruprecht said.

"Three and a bit," Ebberich said. "We haven't been here long."

"Alright, novitiates," the rector said from the entrance. Everyone turned their heads, and the room went deathly silent. "Come with me."

She led them to the entrance hall underground, and further down, through one of the locked doors. The corridor packed with bodies, a snaking line of black robes jostling for position, to be the first through the doors. They went through yet another set of doors and the line fanned out. Selene looked upon a, well... an arena. It was as simple as that. A pit of sand, about thirty strides wide, lay in the center, forty feet below them. A wide, heavy iron door sat at the back of the pit, driven by a set of pulleys and chains that disappeared into loops set in the stone wall. A short railing encircled the pit, itself flanked by cascading tiers of stone benches. A set of stairs proceeded down to a sturdy iron gate, access to the pit. Someone shut the gate.

Orange light from a large brazier hung from the ceiling flooded the stands and the pit below, while daylight from a grate in the ground above shone through. The air smelled slightly of sweat and blood.

Selene took a seat next to the others as the stream of black robes continued. Eventually, everyone was inside and something snapped the grate above shut, creating a red, moody ambiance. A black-haired man in extravagant white and red robes walked to the edge of the pit. The novitiates clapped their hands and cheered. He threw his hands into the air in a welcoming gesture. Cheers and shouts died down, as did the chatter.

"That's Lord Inquisitor Rotersand," Ebberich whispered, seeing the look on Selene's face. "And that's where the fighters'll come out." He pointed to the iron gate at the bottom of the stairs. "And there..." He pointed to the huge iron door. "That's where the beast'll come through."

"Please be seated," the lord inquisitor announced. "I appreciate your enthusiasm, and there is much to be enthusiastic about. But first, let us bow our heads and give our thanks to the Lord Sigur." They prayed, asking for strength in the great trials to come. "We have a special gift for you, today. This won't be our usual *Velitore*. Our inquisitor in the ascendant, Sorenius, delivered not one, but two of our mortal enemies upon our doorstep. Bring them forward!" *Delivered?* Sorenius hunted not one, but *two* wukodlaks when he'd been with her?

Grinding gears and chains signaled the door open. Selene had no time to think. A team of men in grey cloaks filed out, pulling something behind them. Behind the heavy iron door, a wooden platform appeared. Selene gasped, joined by many others. Gasps and screams of terror, laced with excitement.

Two enormous man-wolves—one a dark brown, the other a russet red—were wheeled out. Men in dark robes pulled the platform to the center. Thick steel chains around the werewolves' thick necks bound them to the mobile platform. They had brawny limbs, chests that were slabs of muscle, wolf-like faces, and wild eyes and broad snouts that curled steamy breath. Deadly sharp teeth jutted from their mouths. Their snarling faces turned Selene pale. Menacing intent lurked behind their bright pupils. They would tear apart every person in the room given the chance. Her breath was short and sharp. She felt pains in her chest. Bile burned the back of her throat. *Gods... I'd almost forgotten what a thing it was...* Leona placed her hand on her leg. Selene turned, tearing her eyes away from the demons. *It'll be okay,* said the look Leona gave her. Somehow, she thought it would.

The lord inquisitor cleared his throat, calling for silence. The arena went quiet, until the only sound was the soft growling of the two man-demons.

"But this is not all," he said. "We have a hypocrite for you. A magistrate, who passes judgments of the law, and yet steals from the people, and debauches himself with wenches!" The crowd hissed and booed. The magistrate was dragged out, swearing and shrieking at the sight of the two monstrous creatures in the center. His disheveled outfit would have been nice, once, but now it was ripped and torn. Chains strained and rattled as the creatures smelled the man's fear. They yearned to be freed. And then the chains snapped, sending the guards scrambling. The iron door clattered shut just as they made it inside. The wukodlaks seemed like they didn't quite know what to do, but it wasn't long before their gazes turned to the magistrate. They licked their chops.

The man screamed, trying desperately to scramble up the smooth walls of the pit. Raul jumped up, watching with a grin on his face. And he wasn't alone. Though most of the crowd watched with a mixture of curiosity and horror, there were more than a few who became giddy at the events unfolding in front of them.

The magistrate's face was a cocktail of fear and outrage, twisting into a terrified grimace as he realized his fate. His fingernails scraped, bloodied and broken, against the cut-stone. It was a waste. The walls had been ground smooth. There were no handholds there, or anywhere.

The demons leapt on him, eyes wild with hunger. The tan one wrapped his giant hands around the magistrate's head. The russet one latched onto his legs. They tore at him like dogs. Selene had to turn away. His sharp, wet screams made her blood run cold.

The tan one took to his now beheaded and bloodied torso, digging around. The russet one challenged the other one with a growl, maybe appalled that it didn't get a look in to the carcass. The tan one responded by taking the magistrate's body to the other end of the pit. The russet stood on its hind legs, arching until it was its full height, over seven feet. It charged, claws forward. The tan was skewered. It let out a clipped roar as the russet lifted it into the air. Cheers erupted from the crowd, watching with excitement as the devils tore each other apart. Selene held her hand over her mouth in horror.

A man in white signaled for the fight to end. A ring of Swords with crossbows took up position at the top of the pit, shooting bolts into the creatures. They both fell, hitting the sand with a thump. The fight was over—the magistrate's body lay in a scattered, bloody mush, while the creatures had collapsed in two huge, furry heaps.

Selene's thoughts were a blur, racing as she walked to her evening prayers. She didn't realize until long after that a drop of blood had landed on her cheek.

S ELENE PRACTICED WITH A blunt-loaded, one-hand-operated cross-bow the week after the *Velitore*. It was easy to lose track of time. She was either training, praying, or sleeping, during what little sleep she could find. Nights filled her sleep with nightmares. They weren't of the demons in the arena. She hadn't thought on that since the day it happened. The terrible dreams involved Tristain. He screamed at her to save him as wild dogs tore him apart. Or once, a wolf.

His hand dug into the earth as they dragged him away.

She threw her hands over her mouth, she remembered, stifling a scream. In that dream, she had both arms. It was as if her unconscious mind hadn't caught up to the reality, like when she sometimes grabbed for things, and nothing happened.

Still, the day-to-day kept her busy, kept her sane. She thrived. She felt good, filled with purpose. Even the phantom pain in her arm lessened.

"I figure you're highborn," Ebberich had said to her yesterday during a break in morning training. She laughed it off. *How could he know? No. Relax, Selene. You're probably not the only highborn in the ranks of the Order...* "Yeah. It's your fingers. No calluses."

"What are you talking about, I have calluses," she replied, waving her hand.

"Nuh. Those little nubby things aren't bloody calluses." He held up his palms. They were wrinkled, rough, the lines scored with dirt that looked as though they'd never come out, no matter how much he cleaned them. "These are the hands of a lowborn. Not to mention you've got perfect skin."

"I'll take that as a compliment," she said, laughing.

"Ah, Sigur. We should get back to it."

"No, come on. Any more compliments? Or am I going to have to tease them out of you?" He flushed red. She laughed, taking it as a sign of victory. "Come, let's spar."

Sorenius barked commands as he watched. "Higher! Half-turn! Pirouette! No, not like that! Pivot on your front leg! Fast! You have to be quick! Keep moving! A stationary Sword is a dead Sword! Good! Right, time for training with poisons!"

They finished after another few hours. She was exhausted, but pleased with herself and how things were going. Her lack of ability hadn't held her back, and she was grateful to Sorenius for showing her how to fight on her own terms, with her own strengths. Though he still seemed disaffected with her, for some reason. He avoided her gaze as he left the training hall.

She had to confront him. She saw her opportunity as he leaned on the curtain wall, watching the novitiates run around doing their chores.

She strode up to him. "What in the emperor's sixth concubine was that?" He had a blank look on his face. "You know what the hell I'm talking about. That first day, it was like you forgot you knew me. What, I fulfilled my purpose, filled your quota of recruits, and that was it? Nice to meet you, all the best?"

"I—"

"And you knew you could beat me—there was no need to show it off for your compatriots. I'd lost an arm... where do you get off?"

"*Get off*—"

"And bloody hell, those months where we didn't stop for nothing more than a few short hours... I didn't complain, not once. Not even when I *had* to stop because my arse was raw, my insides felt like they turned inside out, and below my waist was a fucking nightmare. We rode, and rode, and I grew weaker and weaker. I cried myself to sleep most nights. You never *once* asked me how I was. Never *once* asked me why I wanted to stop more often and getting you to stop so we could just sleep was like pulling fucking teeth. What was the goddamn hurry?"

"I had to—"

"I had a bleed on the third night, you know that? I had to steal a poor fucking woman's hat to clean it up. And despite all that, I kept going. You bloody well forgot I was a damn *woman*? I came with *nothing*. You're lucky it wasn't the first time it had happened. I knew what to do, thank Sigur."

Sorenius found it hard to answer that one, flapping his mouth. "Shit," was all he said, eventually. "I'm sorry."

"Alright."

"And are you now—"

"Taken care of."

"Good. Alright... I'm deeply sorry. I truly am. But... if you're asking me to take it easier on you—"

"I'm not. I'm just asking for a bit of understanding, and a drop of fucking kindness for a change."

"Alright, I'll try. I will. I swear to Sigur."

"Good."

They sat along the wall in silence, watching the sky turn orange as the sun set. Sorenius started to laugh. "*The emperor's sixth concubine...*"

Selene laughed too. "I don't know. It's what came to mind. Sorenius, when did you find those demons? Two, no less."

He sighed. "That was why we had to hurry. Don't give me that look. I said I was sorry. It won't happen again. Anyway, it was reported that of one of them was at a charcoal-burner's camp, out by the Spear."

"So, when we headed east on the small road instead of the emperor's road..."

"That's right."

"And when you disappeared that night?"

"Yes. Turns out there were two."

"And you're okay?"

"It was a tough fight; I'll give them that. Lord Inquisitor Rotersand wanted them alive, which made it even harder, of course. It's much easier to just kill them."

"How did you make it out?"

"The trick is not to get hit."

She blew her lips. "Yeah, right? Poisoned bolt?"

He chuckled, confirming that she would never know for sure, but how else could he have done it? They sat in silence for a while longer until it was time for supper.

"**N**OVITIATE," RECTOR PALIA SAID during supper. Selene jerked upright at the greeting, nearly dropping her spoon. "I would ask you to come with me."

"Yes, Rector," Selene replied, followed her through the hall. They walked out of the annex and into the garden, soft grass under her shoes. The sound of cicadas filled the air. Pollen drifted past, kicked up by a gentle breeze. A small flowering birch tree sat in the center, directly in front of a mound of rocks, upon which sat a plaque that memorialized all the previous lord inquisitors.

"I hope Inquisitor Sorenius hasn't been too hard on you," the rector said. "He can be intense."

Selene shook her head. "No, no, not at all."

The rector smiled. "Good. I would like you to come with me tonight. The Lord Inquisitor is having a ceremony, invitation only. I would like you to have a look in. If you want to, of course."

She had never felt more a part of something than now. *Invited to a special ceremony!* "Of course, Rector."

"Excellent. I will meet you when Solni has departed."

S ELENE STOOD IN THE now-dark garden, digging a fingernail into her thumb. It was a nervous tic, one she had from childhood. The garden took on a different hue after dark, and with no moon tonight, everything was black. She had a candle, but that had long gone out in the wind. The warming days stirred up strong winds at night. Squalls howled, coming up the black cape, while unknown things rustled in the privet hedge nearby. On the curtain wall, she saw torch fire flapping around. At least the guards were still there. She took a deep breath, settling nerves. *It's just a simple ceremony. What's the worst that could happen?*

"Novitiate." Selene nearly jumped out of her skin. The voice came from a cloaked figure by the edge of the garden. *How long has she been there?* "Come with me."

She followed the rector. "Any reason you're walking around in the dark?" she asked, hoping to lighten the mood. The rector didn't answer.

They went down the stairs to the underground hallway. The woman reached for a key hanging around her neck. The mechanism clunked as they entered one of the mysterious locked doors she walked past every day. Selene had almost forgotten they were there in the day-to-day. She followed the rector inside.

Rector Palia turned to face her. "Novitiate, I would swear you to secrecy. You are to repeat nothing of what you see here to anyone." Selene nodded, twisting her hair. Her heart fluttered with a mixture of anxiety and excitement. They came to another door.

The door creaked open, revealing a chanting man in fine robes in a circular room with cut stone walls. He wore a gilded mask, chanting over a waist-high table, lifting a burning thurible into the air, filling the room with a slightly sweet, woody smoke. He was chanting in the language of their forebears, High Istryan. Selene recognized a little of it, but the resonance was so strong, and the syllables so drawn out, it sounded nearly nonsensical. A brazier burned next to him, an iron poking rod in the fire. Three others were watching, a woman in white robes—another high-ranking vestal like the rector—and two black clad men, novitiates. Selene didn't recognize their faces. The rector locked the door behind her and led Selene further into the circular room.

She gawped. A tan-colored demon lay flat on the table, its abdomen cut open. The skin was peeled back, revealing a ribcage and organs inside. The cuts weren't sharp, rather... melted, somehow. It smelled like a strange mixture of rotting meat and alchemy. Selene tasted bile at her back teeth. She swallowed hard, trying to keep it down, sensing the gravity of the situation she found herself in. *Because normally I would puke,* she thought.

The chanting ended and grave silence took its place, like the weight of anticipation pressed the voice from their lungs. He placed the thurible on a metal stand gently, taking care not to disturb the quiet. He turned, facing his observers, and brought one hand to the mask, lifting it off slowly.

Behind, the Lord Inquisitor's deep green eyes bored into Selene's soul. His face was gaunt, and his shoulders narrow. Selene found him hard to look at directly.

"Welcome," he said, every syllable smooth and broad. "I am glad you are here. Glory be unto Sigur."

Selene joined the room in a bow. "Glory be unto Him."

"You novitiates may consider yourselves very particular and exceptional after this night. You are privy to a ceremony that only a select few take part in. Here, to better understand the enemy we fight, we dissect, examine, and coldly separate our emotions from objective reality. That objective reality is that we are weak, and they are strong. But it is not hopeless. They are not unstoppable."

He reached for a knife, waving it back and forth as he spoke. "Before us, we see the demon as he truly is. If you kill one, he reveals his true form. That form is mighty and fearsome at first glance but becomes nothing more than the reflection of their damned souls upon a second look. Demon skin. A material that resembles animal skin, with fur, pores, layers of dermis and epidermis that would all seem familiar. Except—" He jammed the knife into the beast's forearm. *Bang.* Selene jumped.

The knife barely entered the skin. It toppled over, clattering on the floor.

"Nearly impenetrable. The back of the neck, under the mane," he lifted the thick brown hairs of the beast's neck, "is the thinnest part, but even then, a strong thrust only enters a scant inch. Enough to sever the spinal column, so we are lucky in that instance. "However"—a vial of green liquid appeared his hand—"Acid does the trick."

He poured it on the beast's wrist. The nasty mixture reacted immediately, bubbling, popping, sinking slowly into the flesh. It gave off foul, black vapors. A novitiate brought a hand to her mouth, retching. Selene watched with fascination.

"As does fire." Searing flesh and igniting fur, the scarred man swept the brand across the beast's arm, filling the air with an awful smell. Selene covered her nose and mouth, groaning. He tamped down the fire with a wet cloth, putting it out.

"Now, the devil is not so mighty or fearsome as he appears. Of course, the interior is just as fragile as ours."

He picked up another knife with a thin, tapered blade, and placed his hands inside the chest cavity. The long seconds he was inside drew out. Selene expected the demon to wake any moment. But it didn't. He jerked his hand three times. The liver pulled free. He placed the organ, three times larger than it should have been, onto a set of scales.

"Novitiate," he said to Selene, wiping his hands on a rag. "Weigh this for me."

Selene stepped forward. Next to the scales lay a collection of assorted weights, iron masses ranging from several pounds to a few ounces. Stacking them, the scales balanced at eleven pounds.

"How is this possible?" Selene said, the sheer size of it leering at her. It was bigger than her head. Up close, the pathetic creature before her, like this, splayed out—while disgusting—meant nothing more to her than a rotting corpse. She reached out, running her hand along the creature's furry foot, goosepimples shooting up her arms, imagining it might wake up at any moment. But it didn't, and nothing happened. It was dead.

"Nothing to be afraid of," she said.

A novitiate puked on the floor. They turned, the smell turning the rest of them green. Another one lost their stomach. Selene wasn't affected, thankfully.

"Right. This process requires the strongest stomachs, I suppose. Rectors, please escort the novitiates from the room. I must dispose of the body."

SELENE LAY ON THE floor of the sleeping hall, with the rest of the novitiates tossing and turning. Her dreams haunted her. She had dreamt of her adoptive brother Tristain. His body laid broken on the battlefield. His voice echoed, taunting her, calling her a coward, telling her she should've saved his mother.

She sighed, getting up. There was no sense laying on her bed-mat hoping that sleep might free her from her thoughts when sleep brought the nightmares. She wandered the annex. The dining hall directly below the sleeping quarters was empty so late at night, of course, while her candle flickered, casting long shadows across the stone. The darkness outside the window was stark, ominous.

She stifled a yawn as she walked into the hall. Light came from the small chapel ahead, the martyr Brigida's. Leona was there, her short red hair twirling as she turned her head. Selene smiled as she walked in, and the girl smiled back. Selene kneeled next to her on cushions on the stone floor. Leona muttered a short prayer, and whispered, "Why are you up so late?"

"I couldn't sleep." Selene's voice was hushed. "Too much on my mind. And you?"

"Same. We should pray. Perhaps we can ask the Lightfather to still your racing thoughts." Leona took Selene's hand and placed it in her own. "Father of All. Still my friend's mind and bring her the strength she needs."

"So, in light." Selene released her hand, but Leona held onto it.

"I feel I can trust you," she whispered.

Selene blinked. "I barely know you, Leona."

"I know, but... it feels as though we have a bond. I never had a family of my own and I think you feel the same way."

Selene nodded. "I had family, but... we were never close. They left me to the Count of Invereid's care when I was very young. I had no one, except for my ward's son, Tristain." Warmth spread inside her chest as she remembered their games in the grounds, chasing each other with dandelions, trying not to get the flowers on their clothes.

Leona pointed to her mismatched eye. "See this? It made me stand out from birth. One night, my brothers tried to cut it out with a hot knife, believing it would make me better. I'll never forget that smell, as long as I live."

"I'm sorry."

Selene felt Leona's hand tighten. "That's alright," the red-headed girl replied with a smile. "That's why I'm here, for a second chance, to make something of myself."

Selene smiled and Leona grinned back. That was enough, and together they prayed to the God of Strength and Justice.

T HE NEXT DAY, SPARROWS circled around Sorenius's head as he explained the proper use of traps to ensnare, harm, and kill a demon. They were just outside Ostelar, in the narrow estuary between the Tibor and Alba rivers. The air was cold and damp, and the muddy grass covered with morning dew. Trees around them browned with the coming arrival of bruma.

She hadn't seen or heard from Tristain for months now. Still no news of the war, either.

Sorenius held up a mechanical device; two metal loops attached to a spring-weighted pad. "Your basic snare. Press the arms down one at a time and unhook the catch. Place it where you think the demon might appear and cover it with some heath. Alternatively, place a ring of these around your camp or hiding spot, so you won't be caught by surprise. Just remember where you left them!" The novitiates chuckled. "Another thing, tying a chime to one of the arms can be useful—when it goes off, you'll know you caught the demon. Though his roars should give it away well enough.

"Next is poison oak. Be very careful handling this one. The thorns are extremely sharp." He lifted a supple green branch, a bramble of thorns on the end of it. "And they're covered in a sap that'll kill you in minutes unless you have the antidote. For a demon in human form, it'll do the same. For a demon in their true form, it'll cause intense pain and disorientation.

Using a sapling allows you to use its suppleness—tie them to a tree, or just off a path, where the demon is likely to pass, and pull the thorny end back, binding it to the tripwire using a slipknot." He demonstrated by putting one end of the branch under his foot and pulling back hard. "Pressure on the tripwire causes the slipknot to undo, releasing the tension in the branch, causing it to"—the branch flicked back to position with a snap—"come back to position. Next, we have a simple trigger catch on a crossbow, pre-loaded with a bolt with your favorite toxin. Make sure to aim this one a little in front of the tripwire—demons move fast enough that they could be meters away from the shot before it goes off."

"What happened to a simple blade in the gullet?" Ruprecht asked. "If I knew it was going to be this complicated..."

Sorenius scratched his face. "Well, you try it. Try to put your simple blade in my gullet."

"No—"

"Come, try it."

Ruprecht stepped forward gingerly, drawing his beltknife. He lunged. Sorenius caught the knife and threw it aside, kicked Ruprecht's legs out from under him. Ruprecht groaned.

"Get up."

Ruprecht got to his feet.

"How do you expect to get a blade into a beast that moves faster than you, is ten times stronger, and has armor for skin, when you can't even get the best of me?"

The others laughed.

"I wouldn't be laughing." Sorenius cut them off. "Humans are pathetic by comparison. If you're close enough to stab them, you're already dead. Right, we'll go on to scents and camouflage, and why you might want to cover yourself in mud and animal dung. Fresh meat is your best friend, and a bit of straw and spare clothes can also be useful..."

7

SACRILEGE

AETESTA, 1043

Bring no quarter unto the creature and the heretic.

— KONRAD STEPPENWOLF, LORD INQUISITOR OF
ANNALTIA

MONTHS PASSED IN THE blink of an eye. Selene threw herself into her training and he lessons so she didn't have to think of home and of Tristain. Even the nightmares eased their cruel reign on her sleep.

As much as she could call the people she knew in Invereid her friends—the tailor, the tailor's wife, their son, the guards that escorted her to and from the town—they had never been as close as Leona, Ruprecht, Ebberich. Even Salim, the Saburrian who'd insulted her the first day, was coming around. Proximity had made them close, shared struggle had opened themselves to each other. Selene barely thought of herself as incompetent anymore, and it was due largely that her friends never made her feel inadequate.

The supper table had been their confessional, their expression of companionship, a rock to return to when they found themselves troubled.

"Did you have anyone back home?" Leona had once asked, a few weeks ago, at the Warming. The festival of Solni, unobserved but tolerated by the Sigurians, but Ebberich and Ruprecht had brought suncakes. Selene asked how and they just nodded knowingly, saying they had a source in the kitchens.

They munched on the moreish, slightly burnt sweets made of almonds dripping with honey, and talked of their old lives. Even knowing they weren't meant to. But no one could overhear them in the clamor of the eating hall during supper.

"Not me," Ruprecht said. "Soldierin' left little time for that, though there were a few kind-looking girls in the regiment. Not that they ever had any interest in me."

"No one's ever been interested in me, on account of my eye," Leona said, fingering her eyelid. Rubbing it as though it might pop out and she'd be glad for the occurrence. "You, Selene?"

"You're gorgeous," Ebberich said. "I'm sure you had more than a few suitors. Were you married?"

Selene's cheeks flamed. She put another suncake in her mouth so she didn't have to answer.

"Ebberich thinks you're gorgeous, aye?" Ruprecht said. "I bet he'd like to know if you had anyone back home, if you catch my meaning."

Ebberich socked Ruprecht in the arm and Ruprecht cried out in mock-pain and indignance.

"It's not that. I mean... well, you know what I mean."

"You did call her gorgeous," Salim said, talking with a mouth full of half-chewed cake.

"I bet Ebberich had a few lovers back home," Ruprecht said, making kissing noises at him. They laughed. Salim exploded with bits of half-chewed almonds from his mouth, which made them laugh all the harder and drew a few short looks from the rector.

So it was no surprise that today Selene heard Ebberich's unmistakably loud voice from the dining hall.

"We must celebrate!" he yelled.

Selene smiled as she walked in. The hall was a bustling, noisy place before supper, and today was no exception.

"What's happened," she asked.

"Both Salim and Ruprecht are being confirmed, can you believe it?" he replied. "I never thought these two idiots would be before me." They all laughed.

"Give them a break, Ebberich," Salim said. "They don't know what it's like to be a blockhead like you, so much slower than the rest of us."

Selene laughed and Salim caught her eye. He smiled. She remembered when he came around. It was a good day—she had disarmed him, somehow, and kicked him in the genitals. Accidentally, of course, in a way that it half-wasn't. He fumed, ready to grab a weapon and do her in, but then he collapsed, laughing as he clutched his groin in pain. After that, he'd warmed a little, and it had only been getting better since.

Raul was a different matter. She dreaded seeing the Vallonian's face. Ever since the demons in the arena, he'd had a look in his eye that made her uncomfortable. Thankfully for her, he had been unwell the last few days, and been confined to the infirmary.

"Our times will each come," Leona said. "What name will you choose, do you think? I would choose... Rufia, after Sigur's confidant, or maybe Linaria, so it's not too different."

"Oh, Linaria's good," Ruprecht replied. "Pin cushioned with arrows for not renouncing her faith, yeah, that's good. Myself, I would pick maybe... Georgius."

Leona quivered. "Ooh, the great slayer of demons! Fearsome warrior, you are." Salim blew his lips in a fart. Ruprecht socked him in the arm and laughed.

"What about you, Salim," Selene asked.

"Oh, me? Haven't really thought about it." He shrugged. "Yourself?"

Selene scratched the back of her head. "I'm not too sure either. I don't really know too much about the martyrs."

"Well," Leona began. "There's Aella, Sigur's wife. She killed herself instead of letting herself be captured by the Great Devil. Then there's Sofiya, the mighty warrior who held Sigur's golden city for thirty days and thirty nights with just a handful of men. Or Domitice, who was renowned the world over for her skill with a bow, until she was raped and butchered by the Devil and his minions."

Selene chuckled. "They all sound a bit grim. Isn't there a martyr who died peacefully in her bed?"

They all laughed.

"That would preclude the 'martyr' bit, Selene," Ebberich said.

"No." Leona raised a finger. "There was one. Diana."

Ruprecht raised an eyebrow. "Diana? She's a martyr?"

"What did she do?" Selene asked.

"She foretold the coming of the Age of Disarray," Leona said. "When men would be free from the yoke of the Gods and would rise and spread over the earth. She died peacefully in her bed. And yes, some scriptures say she's a martyr since she was pursued to the ends of the Continent for her prophecy."

Ebberich touched Selene's forearm. "Well, there you go. We'll be saying hello to Warden Diana in no time."

Selene nodded, smiling. Inside though, she wondered if she would be alright with changing her name. Her mother gave her the name Selene, after all. It was the only thing she had left of her old life.

S ELENE CRADLED THE BACK of her head in her hand. The five of them slept on the uncomfortable wood of the sleeping hall, like all the other novitiates. She felt dog-tired but couldn't—or wouldn't—go back to sleep. Sleep was a luxury these days, between early-morning prayers and recurring nightmares, but still, she was awake. She thought back to her guardian mother. She had no memories of her real mother, after all. Her perfume—lavender, the scent of the Goddess of Fertility, Eme. She found the plant in the preceptor's garden, and memories came flooding back. The sweet sound of her singing voice, the word games they played, the times spent in the estate's garden, picking flowers. Her guardian father scolded her for getting dirt on her shoes, she remembered. If she had been married, would her guardian mother have come with her? What happened to her guardian mother was awful, but not the fault of anyone but her horrible husband. The images of that day flashed into her mind again. The bloody face of her guardian mother's dead body, life snuffed by her demon husband.

Selene heard shuffling next to her. It was Ebberich, facing her. "What's on your mind?" he whispered. The others snored around them, dead to the world. The training was grueling, and the wake-up early, so they slept soundly.

Selene looked at the beams above. The ceiling creaked in the cold wind outside. "My mother."

Ebberich smiled and nodded. "I'm the same, sometimes. I remember the touch of her hand, stroking my hair as I drift off to sleep. Then I wake and forget it again."

She rolled over to face him, propping up on an elbow. "She was a singer."

"Oh, like a minstrel?"

"No, nothing like that. She sang me and my ward's sons to sleep. Her voice was indescribable, like it belonged to a time before men."

"Sounds lovely. Mine was a clothier. Nothing special, just made linens with a loom."

"But she meant a lot to you."

Ebberich smiled. "Yeah."

Selene leaned back, feeling sleep attack her. She stifled a yawn. "Do you know much about Salim?"

"I don't know. Why?"

"I don't think he likes me very much."

"He's a surly bastard. Don't let it get to you. He probably wouldn't want me telling you this, but he was a slave, not that long ago. He thinks he has something to prove. He doesn't, of course, but he's too stubborn to realize that. I mean, he's being confirmed ahead of all of us except Ruprecht, for Sigur's sake."

"A slave?"

"Yeah... he's from Saburria, far across the ocean."

"Saburria? I thought he might be from Vallonia."

"Me too, at first. But then he told me he was taken as a boy, sailed across the ocean, was sold to some noble in Ostelar."

"How did he end up here?"

"His master was a demon, from what I can gather. He won't tell me exactly, but I figure that's what happened. Swords raided his master's house, killed the master, and rounded up all his servants. Salim ended up being recruited out of that."

Selene nodded. *A slave...* She yawned again. They said goodnight. Sleep came almost as soon as she closed her eyes.

"A GAIN," INSTRUCTOR SORENIUS TOLD Selene.

She lunged for his chest with her dagger. He snatched for her arm. Avoiding his grasp, she did a quick half-pirouette, bringing the blade around. He caught her wrist, but only just. The point was an inch from his eye. The others let out astonished laughs, but her victory was short-lived. He kicked her knee, sending her to the floor. It came rushing up and she braced, landing with a soft grunt. The impact on cold stone hurt her body.

But she was getting used to pain. Pain reminded her she was still alive, after everything.

"Better." Sorenius helped Selene to her feet. "But you leave your back open. It would serve you better to do a full turn. You can still thrust into the eye from that position, just adjust your wrist angle." He showed her what to do and she nodded.

"Alright, next, Novitiate Ebberich. You've been getting better with the axe. I want to see how you fare. Pair up with Novitiate Selene. You two, spar as well." Salim was getting ready for his confirmation and *Velitore* they'd been told, and Raul was reassigned to a group one short of a pair.

"Yes, Inquisitor," they replied.

Selene took up a stance, shifting her weight so she became light on her feet. Ebberich followed suit, wielding a bearded axe in one hand and a shield in another. She eyed the sharpened steel. The novitiates trained with edged weapons, of course, and injuries were commonplace. Luckily, neither her nor any of her friends had been injured beyond a few cuts and bruises, unlike some others.

Ebberich came for her, slowly at first. He swung in an arc, testing his range. She stepped out of the way. He swung again, this time faster. She pirouetted, getting around his guard. She pressed her dagger against his neck. He laughed in surprise, and they reset.

Ebberich adjusted his grip. "Alright... I won't hold back."

"Good."

His eyes glinted in the candlelight. He lunged, sweeping fast. She jumped back, then rebounded while he brought his axe around. He put his shield up, catching her body on it. He stumbled. She quickly brought her dagger under his chin. He laughed again, a goofy sound that made Selene's chest flutter. *He's... charming.*

"You're too good with that blade," he said. "Six months and you're already better than the rest of us."

Selene scratched the back of her head, stifling a yawn. "Come on, Ebberich. Be serious, I'm not that good. Nothing compared to Sorenius." Ebberich laughed, offering her his axe. She looked at him as if he was mad. "What's this?"

"Consider it a handicap." She put her dagger away and took the axe. The heft and bulk were all wrong—she much preferred the swiftness of a dagger or a sword. Still, she took a stance as Ebberich reached for another axe. Ebberich came for her again, but without a shield arm, she had to dodge. He turned his axe mid-strike. The axe came within a hair's breadth as she leapt back. Ebberich blinked, apologizing profusely. She laughed.

"Well, it's not surprising that I've got you with the axe," he said.

She smiled, stretching her neck and shoulders. "Come on, again."

Ebberich smirked. He swept forward. She expected it this time and performed her own little trick. She feinted, coaxing his shield forward. As it did, she flipped her axe down and hooked it under. She yanked, opening him up. She kicked savagely with her left foot, right into his solar plexus. His eyes bulged and he dropped to the floor with a wheeze.

The others gave bewildered looks. "Where in Sigur's name did you learn that?" Ruprecht said, laughing.

Sorenius scowled. "Watch your tongue, Novitiate."

"Sorry, Inquisitor."

They went back to training, another two grueling hours before a break for lunch. The arbiter caught her outside the dining hall.

"Novitiate," he said. "I would like to talk with you about something."

Selene smiled. "What is it?"

"Not here."

They went behind the annex, next to the curtain wall.

"Novitiate," he said. "Your training is progressing well, much faster than I would have expected. Rector Palia tells me you are learning the prayers, and I have seen that you are active at all the Gebet. Tell me, does your past still weigh on you?"

Selene smiled, thinking it over. Still, the dreams of Tristain haunted her sleep, his broken body a threat, yelling horrible things until she woke streaming with sweat. Then there were the dreams where she wandered through the gardens with Mother, where claws came up from the ground and tore them both to pieces. "Yes."

The inquisitor nodded. "And you wish to speed through training? I would tell you that there is no such thing, Novitiate. You are confirmed when you are ready, no sooner."

Selene looked down, chuckling softly. "Please don't mistake me, Sorenius. I am grateful for the Order, and the opportunity to prove myself. I am trying to right a wrong done to me. If it wasn't for the Order, for you, I might have died months ago."

"Hm. I realize vengeance is important to you... but I wonder if you place your personal concerns above the Order, and the good of all people, themselves. You say you are trying to right a wrong—what of all the wrongs in the world that you could right, as a Golden Sword? Do you feel any concern for the people done wrong?"

Selene felt her breath catch. "If I have transgressed in some way, Inquisitor, I apologize."

"Do not worry, Novitiate. It was just a simple question. Meet me in the annex's garden after Vespers. There is something important we must do. Now, let's go, we have more training before supper."

Selene nodded, and they left for the training hall again.

THE MOON WAS BRIGHT that night. Luni hung high, her full face towards Selene. Solni had long completed his journey. It was a warm night, too, and Selene ruffled her robe, aerating her sweaty body. It was nearly the solstice, and the celebration of Solni's Day. More people than usual wandered the grounds in the warm night air, chatting, singing, chanting. Ebberich and Leona rounded the corner.

Selene blinked. "What are you two doing here?"

"The arbiter asked us to be here," Leona replied. "And you?" Selene nodded.

"Bit strange, no?" Ruprecht's voice came from behind. Selene's heart was in her throat. She recalled that night with the Lord Inquisitor, reminded of it in more ways than one.

"Novitiates, good," Sorenius said, arriving not long after Ruprecht. "Come with me."

They followed him into the keep, down the steps. He unlocked one of the doors. This one was new, neither leading to the arena nor to the circular room with the table.

He led them down a long corridor. There were many closed doors on either side, loud voices coming from behind some of them. None of them dared ask what they were, or where he was taking them.

"Here," he said, stopping to unlock a door. The bolt clicked. Unoiled hinges squeaked. Selene's jaw dropped. A dark-skinned man, naked down to his linens, sat in a chair. Salim. His hands and legs were bound, tied to the frame of the chair. The inquisitor closed the door behind them. Off to the side was Rector Palia, her stern face eyeing up the young pack.

"What is this?" Ebberich shouted.

"This," the rector spat. "Is a punishment."

Selene raised her eyebrows. "For what?"

"Novitiate Salim has been shirking his duties. It has also been raised that he does not hold the Lightfather in his heart. However, this is an opportunity. I would have had you four punished for failing to report the novitiate's behavior, but the inquisitor promised me you would prove yourselves."

"Prove ourselves?"

"Yes. Extracting information is an important part of your duty and service as a Golden Sword. Extract from the novitiate the reasons for his transgressions, and you will be rewarded." Selene stepped forward. Salim trembled.

"Selene, you can't be serious," Ebberich yelled. "That's Salim, our friend!"

"Novitiate, calm yourself or you will be removed."

Selene stepped closer to the slave from Saburria, pursing her lips. She would not fail by avoiding the hard things.

"Why, Salim?" she asked. He didn't answer, turning away from her. "Why?" The other novitiates watched, frozen. She turned to the rector. The woman was unreadable. She turned back to Salim. "The Order has given you everything, just as it has us. Why turn your back on them?"

"You have no idea, do you," he yelled. "I had nothing. I will always have nothing. It doesn't scare me to go back." They fell silent. The inquisitor took a dagger from his belt. Selene's eyes narrowed. Salim wriggled in the chair, groaning, as the blade glinted in the candlelight.

Sorenius held it out for her. "You must learn, Selene. I have faith in you."

She sighed, taking the dagger.

Leona placed a hand on her back. "Do it. Sigur tests our faith, but we must be strong."

Ebberich pleaded with her. "Please, Selene! Don't do it!"

"Get him out," Rector Palia said. "Now!" Ruprecht and Leona jerked, taking Ebberich by the arms and pulling him from the room.

"No, you can't!"

"Inquisitor. Make sure that novitiate knows the consequences for disobedience." He nodded, leaving the room. The door squeaked shut. Selene was alone with the rector and Salim. She felt alone, and that was strange. Not long after she'd come to the Order, the constant day-to-day, the dog-tired feeling she was left with at the end of each day kept her mind off what had happened to her. Mostly. She was too busy to feel alone. But not now.

Tristain. The name flashed in her mind. It hurt her to think of it.

She palmed the handle of the weapon. It was smooth, made of ivory, and fit her palm nicely. The blade was well-weighted and nimble. "Why did you do it, Salim?"

"I don't have to answer you, you northern bitch." She narrowed her eyes. She flicked her wrist, drawing blood from his cheek. He recoiled. "Fuck you! Pox and shit on you! Goddamn one-arm freak!"

That was it. She'd heard enough. Hatred boiled inside of her. Salim became the target of all the wrongs that had ever been done to her. It felt good to stoke the fire. She darted the dagger across again, cutting his shoulder. Another cut, and another, and another, quick slashes in succession. She lost count. The man howled in pain, begging her to stop. He blubbered like a child. It only made her angrier. Then the adrenaline wore off.

"Enough! Please!" he screamed.

Selene stopped. She blinked, seeing the destruction she wrought. She pressed her fist to her mouth, suppressing a scream. The man's torso was covered in small cuts, dripping with dark blood in the low light. She swallowed hard, blinking back tears.

"I'll tell you," he said, trembling. "Okay, I'll tell you, just stop... I can't do it anymore. I can't pretend I'm a loyal servant or whatever horseshit they try to shove down our throats, not anymore. Look at us! This is what they do to us! Our enemies are monsters, but they're turning us into monsters to fight them. That doesn't make us better. It makes us worse!" His eyes burned with anger.

"Lies," Rector Palia snapped. "We took you in, we took you *all* in. You were rejected, cast aside by your families, by society. By all those with hate in their hearts. We expected nothing in return but your devotion, and your loyalty. Finish this, Selene."

Salim clenched his jaw, closing his eyes.

"We cannot brook traitors here, not in the heart of our halls... *kill him,* Novitiate!"

Selene's eyes stung with sadness. She swallowed.

Salim blinked open his eyes, looking mournful.

"If you don't do it, you'll join him in hell!"

"Please, Selene," he begged. "At least make it quick." Her hands trembled. Her breath came hot and fast. Then a memory. Her mother singing as she did in the parlor room, so long ago. Selene never tried cultivating any talent for it, her father would never allow such fripperies. But her mother was renowned for her voice.

Oh, gentle breeze,
I feel you on my cheek,
You pass by me so gently,
And I miss you so sweetly.
Oh, gentle lover,
I feel you on my cheek,
I pass by you so gently,
And I let you go, so sweetly.

A tear ran down her cheek, and she rammed the blade home.

8

GOOD MEN

FERVUM, 1044

Never underestimate the cruelty of the fanatic.

— GUILLAUME, PRIEST OF GINEVRA

G OOD MEN LANGUISHED IN cages and died while monsters roamed the campgrounds.

Tristain seethed and watched Vredevoort prance about in his feathered helm, visor up screaming about Sigur, as though he were the most virtuous man in all the Continent.

"Glory unto Sigur," he yelled, clapping his gauntleted hands. "Glory, glory! Light, light!"

The surrounding men clapped in unison. "Glory, glory! Light, light!" Some believed it, but Tristain could see the truth of most of their lazy hands and their half-hearted shouts.

"This is the third time today," someone said.

"Does he owe the priests a tithe or something?"

"More like he's got sins need repenting. Probably that stain on his soul from the Footfalls."

Erken. Leon was still locked up by Duchess Adolar's quarters, though it had been a few days since Tristain had occasion to go there. What would happen to him? They'd send a letter to the emperor, but only the emperor could disenfranchise him and seize his land. As of now, he was still a knight.

"Oi, princely lad," Sergeant Dengeld yelled. "Keep shovelin'!"

Tristain straightened. He took the shovel and struck the ground again. Latrine duty. That's what his life had come to.

Today was Sigur's Day, though you wouldn't know it, from the lack of streamers, lack of handmade little wooden swords hanging from eaves. There wasn't even any cinnamon and raisin strudel that you could dig your hands into, trying to find the coin in the juicy middle.

How could he think of celebrating when Selene was no closer to safety? In fact, she was even further away. Tristain couldn't save her when he was a monster, too. *This world is dead and monsters roam its carcass.*

Bones and blood, as bright as the Grim's tunic, came to his mind. That night outside the Ox's Balls. Flash of lightning and snapping, grating, crunching of bone.

Tristain turned to the pit. He shoved the spade into the ground, again, again, again. Sweat dripped off his nose. His throat made a low growl. Muscles flexed, aching but welcome.

"All right, slow down," one of the diggers said. "You're makin' us look bad."

"Oncierran!" The sergeant inflicted his grating voice on Tristain. He had a moustache, about the only hair on his pockmarked head, that drooped over his lips and had bits of bread in it. His breath stunk worse than the latrines already dug and used.

"Sigur bastards want to see you. I ain't one for disappointing those blabbers and earnin' a holy bollocking, so get to it!"

"Sigur bastards?" He dropped his shovel and eyed the exits. Someone shoved him from behind.

"Get on or get out of the way," the man said. One of the poor fellows who had joined him in latrine duty.

Tristain had barely got to know anyone. He couldn't afford to. They'd all be dead, soon enough, buried face-down in the latrine pits, most like.

He reached up and Dengeld pulled him out of the pit and then wiped his hands. You never could be sure what was dirt and what was something else.

"Go on, lad." He leaned in, gave Tristain a powerful smack in the nose with his breath like a goat's. "Just tell them what they want to hear. I'm sure you've done nothing wrong. They just want to make their reports and feel important."

Tristain eyed him. Past his head, three men grappled with last night's dinner, heaving. Next to them, flies clung to a table of shiny, greasy, stinking meat. The campwife tried her best to shoo them but they returned, tenacious little fuckers. Dengeld might've been a steady, respectable sort, and a good sergeant, but even a master tailor given moth-ridden fabric to work with couldn't make much more than a headache. Too good for Vredevoort, really.

"I'll try my best, sergeant."

Dengeld pointed to a tent just off the mustering field, where spearmen drilled. Only nobles, knights, and their squires fought with longsword. Training for any lowborn usually meant a lot of standing around looking busy and stabbing air.

The gray tent crammed in between the abattoir yard and an animal pen, thrown in like a fox in a hen house. *Does that make me the hen that went inside during the massacre?*

Whatever Caen had said to them hadn't worked, and they'd only gotten more interested in Tristain. He'd noticed their whispers, their sidelong glances. Maybe that slick Republican had said something to them. Galeaz had seen the killing field outside the alehouse, after all. Republicans were notorious for taking from one side with one hand and taking from the other side with the other hand. Problem was, you never knew which hand you had.

Even children knew the tales. The Order of the Golden Sword hunted creatures like him. Monsters. Demons. Killers. He didn't feel like one, though. Sure, he'd kill if it ever came to it. He had, to save his compatriots. As much as that had worked. But rampaging through towns, slaughtering children, eating their livers and choiciest bits... that wasn't him. It didn't feel like it, at least. Either way, the graycloaks were looking for him.

If he tried to run now, with the sergeant and the general breathing down his neck, and that republican bastard lingering around, he'd twitch from a rope inside a week. Besides, he wasn't sure he could rightly forgive himself if he abandoned Leon.

The graycloak at the door to the tent jumped when he saw Tristain approach. He looked young, about Tristain's age, and had downy hair about his chin. Nothing that could ever be called a beard. He stepped out of the way and opened the flap, leaving Tristain to duck his head inside.

Dengeld had taken his sword, of course, but Tristain still had his beltknife if it came to that.

The air smelled sickly sweet, heavy with smoke, coming from a censer that sat at the foot of a tall man in a white cloak. Milk-white, not a mar or a mote of dirt on him. It practically shined. He thumbed through a large book bound with thin metal links. Two men in gray standing beside the one in white looked daggers at Tristain as he entered.

"Tristain Florian Oncierran, son of Sebastian Bann and Eda Marie, brother to Bann Sebastian, now deceased. Squire to Leon Vorland." The man peered over his page. "You're a bit old to still be a squire, aren't you?"

"I'm eighteen, and I'm going to earn my deed of arms." Tristain tripped over his tongue as though this prick had put his foot in front. "*Who* are you?" *What am I, an owl?*

"The more important question is 'how long am I to be detained?' The answer to which is 'if you give us what we need, not long.'"

Tristain looked over the three men. He could probably take the one on the left, he looked scrawny, like height was the only reason he looked down on anyone. The one on the right had muscles under his robes. He would prove to be a bit of a fight. They didn't carry any obvious weapons at their belts, but you never knew. He couldn't trust these bastards. Trust didn't come easy to a man looking at the end of a rope if he said the wrong thing.

Tristain opted to keep telling them what they wanted to hear. "And what do you need?"

"We need a name, that is all. We have our eye on you, of course, but there are other options, here."

"Galeaz. You can never trust a republican. Alanian, or Tanerian, wherever the hell he comes from."

"The general's steward? What makes you believe that?"

"Because he's a slimy bastard, that's why."

Dainty and elegant fingers flicked over the smooth parchment. Tristain spotted words and some runes he didn't understand—the shape of an *F* turned on its side, along with a circle with a line through it. An *i.e.*, which meant nothing to him, along with some gold lettering affixed to the top of the book.

"He's in our minds, but signs point elsewhere. Have you heard from your father, recently?"

"My father? No. I haven't heard from him in over two years."

The man's eyes twinkled. He'd have to be on his guard.

Brows knitted together across his forehead. "Why? Is he dead?"

"Interesting that the mind goes to death."

He shook his head. "I don't think my father could ever die." *A malevolent force like that lives on in the world, keeps punishing even when it's wrong and twisted.*

A long silence stretched out like the doldrums after a victory earned through many dead.

"Well, I told you who I suspected," Tristain said. "It's that republican. You should free Leon."

"The knight? We have no qualms with him."

The Order fellow shut his book with one hand and held it down by his side.

"Do you know what the *Notarii* do?" he asked, with all the bluster of a man more than ready to answer his own questions. Father had been one of those. Tristain ground his teeth.

"We find truths and contain knowledge. There are some truths that are too dangerous to be known by the common man. But I'll share with you one that I've learned in my time: there is no secret that can be kept from the Order for long."

The hairs on Tristain's neck stood on end and blood rushed from his limbs, sending them cold. He shook the feeling away. If they were to kill him here and now, at least them be done with it.

"May I go?"

The man in the white robes let the moment stretch out but ultimately nodded. "Yes, you may. Linger a while though, I may have more questions for you. If you survive the siege, that is. I hear you're in Vredevoort's battalion? Sigur be with you."

His fellows sniggered.

Tristain turned and walked from the tent, blowing his lips. He locked his fingers behind his head and strode from the tent. He dawdled, wondering if Dengeld would see him step out, or anyone from the latrine crews would look over here, curiosity getting the better of them.

Vredevoort's wailing split the air like he wished to purify each of their sins with every insane syllable, as though he could rend the sky and usher in the return of the Sigur himself.

"Sigur, Sigur! Neighbors, friends, do you follow the dark? No! That path leads you to damnation! Drag your neighbor into the light! THE LIGHT COMETH!"

No one looked at him. They were all too busy watching a man reach climax screaming about the god. But then, Tristain remembered the Order. *Is he trying to win favor with them?*

Whatever the reason, Tristain didn't care to stick around to find out. He tossed off his green tabard—Vredevoort's colors—and went down the dirt avenue, like he belonged. That one he'd learned from his brother: act like you belong, and people won't question you. He went to the parade ground and bought a skin of ale from the quartermaster, then walked over to Leon's cage.

A couple of soldiers jeered at him, pelting him with rotten vegetables. Leon sat in the corner, arms folded over his knees, covered in muck. When he didn't react to them, they gave up their sport, mentioning it to Tristain as they passed him.

"You've got the right idea," one said. "Tease him with ale." He looked back. "I bet he's thirsty."

"That's it," Tristain said. "Not sure what he did, but if he's in the cage, he deserves it."

"Aye." The men laughed and went on their way.

Leon peered over his knees at Tristain as he approached.

"Aye, Squire. Though you're not my squire anymore, are you?" His lips cracked with blood and voice rasped when he talked. He stood up, groaning as though his limbs had forgotten what it was like to stretch out and they protested the action.

Tristain extended the skin between the bars.

Leon stumbled forward. "Thank you, thank you, I knew you were my squire for a reason, thank Ginevra—"

He gushed with gratitude like water to a man dying from thirst. Dying from thirst for ale. It was pathetic.

Tristain snatched the skin away before Leon could reach it. The knight growled and pushed his arms through the bars, but the gap was too narrow, and he could only fit them up to his forearms.

"You slick fucking *sal'brath*, what game are you playing at?"

"Did you tell them?"

"Tell them what?" Leon tried again, flailing his right hand around, pushing further into the bars with his left. He'd get stuck if he went much further.

"Did you tell the graycloaks about me?"

Tristain felt bad torturing the man with temptations of ale. Leon's eyes streamed with sweat or tears, and giant dark bags clung to his eye sockets, while barely any of his whites remained. Just red.

"*Sal'brath*, tell them what? They haven't said a word to me. Give me the fucking ale already. Ginevra curse you, boy."

Tristain heard the truth in his words, like a man swearing to his grave. He thought darkly that Leon was near his end, and as soon as he was disenfranchised, men wouldn't see the need to keep a delinquent ex-knight alive for long.

"You'll be dead before long," he said, pushing the skin through the bars.

Leon grabbed the skin and wrenched off the cap with a popping sound, and threw it back, suds and amber liquid pouring, overflowing, muscles working, dripping down his sackcloth shirt and onto the ground. Tristain just shook his head.

"That's all I came here for. Goodbye, Leon."

He turned and walked. The last two years and more had come to nothing. Tristain's squiring left him no better, no closer to knighthood. In fact, it left him even further away, took Selene and Mother further away from safety. Shame slapped his cheeks red, and he looked down, unable to let the world look upon eyes budding with tears.

"Tristain."

Leon's voice. Tristain gave him a glance. It was about all he could stand to spare him.

"I would never tell them, even if they asked."

Tristain forced a smile and nodded.

He went back to Vredevoort's section before they wondered where he went. He gathered himself, wiping his eyes.

He heard shouting, saw dust kicked up from behind a building. Someone arguing as they always were, fighting over something. Ever since the minstrels left, some hope had left the camp, too. Tensions ran high, and it was a small wonder no one had been killed. *The general had better attack soon, and win.*

"Get him! Catch that bastard!"

A young man blurred past, knocking into Tristain. In the tumble, Tristain landed flat on his arse and could only watch as two other men burst past, these ones older, pockmarked. A third man, mustached, followed, planted a boot right between Tristain's legs. Hearing the yelling, soldiers crowded around.

Tristain got to his feet. The mustached one carried a bundle of rope.

The other men snatched up the one that had run, bundled him by his legs and his arms, and shuffled him forward. Not a man. A boy, no older than sixteen. He screamed. Tristain flattened himself against the wall. Somehow, he thought, they'd come for him. Screaming about Sigur, nothing good.

Something set the animals off in the nearby pens. They harked and honked, bleating and barking. Emaciated cows, bone-thin pigs, over-wooled sheep. They could sense the tension in the air, feel it as thick as the soup they were destined for.

The mustached man doubled the rope around the boy's neck, tied a knot, threw the other end around the nearby finial of a barracks, a decorative roof piece but no less sturdy.

The boy got an arm free and lashed out, slapping the rope-man across the shoulder, the arm. He screamed himself hoarse, "*I'm not a demon!*"

Tristain's guts churned. He'd seen men die, but this was something else. That was war. You killed a man in war, and he was trying to kill you back. He held a sword, or a spear at the least. Something fair if that could be said.

This was murder, plain and simple. Tristain wondered where the marshals were, where the guards were, where the general was. She permitted this.

Vredevoort swaggered into the lane, stepping wide, thumbs tucked into his belt. A company followed behind him, watching with sneering grins on their faces. They were the group that was joined with Vredevoort in the orgiastic delight of calling Sigur's name. The war god, the god of strength.

But there was no strength here. Strength meant protecting the weak.

Enjoyment. That's what this was for.

"Don't suffer the demon to live, now," Vredevoort said.

They heaved the boy into the air. His eyes bulged and his limbs flailed. He cried for his mother. They lifted him higher. His legs came off the ground and smacked the mustached man in the jaw.

He recoiled and stood again.

"Hold him down," he said.

The other two hugged the kid's legs and put their weight into it. The boy's breeches darkened, his urine building, breaking its banks until it gushed down his leg. His face turned bright purple, veins popped, like the darkest fruit.

Tristain couldn't move, couldn't think. He shouldn't look, but he couldn't look away. If they caught him looking away, they'd likely put him up with the boy.

The boy's limbs jumped several times before they stilled. The men left him there, standing back to whistle and admire their handiwork. Shorn-hair wiped his mouth.

"Worked up a sweat, there," he said. "Maybe we can feed him to the pigs. That'll shut 'em up."

"Bout what a demon deserves," one said.

"Praise the Lightfather," Vredevoort said, lifting his hands to the sky. "But you, I didn't see you at our congregation."

Tristain glanced once, thinking perhaps he'd mistaken the words for him. Twice when he saw Vredevoort looking right at him.

"Is this one a demon, too?" The men chattered. "He's not wearing the colors, but I've seen him digging the pits."

Fear needled Tristain's hands. He forced himself to stand straight, face them, and reached for the knife at his belt. He wasn't some boy barely grasped deep voice and first chest hairs. They wouldn't kill him without a fight—and now they were out of rope.

"Easy, Sihfting, Vereld." Dengeld fell in from the side, putting his hands forward in a conciliatory manner. "Ed. There's no need for that." He turned back. "Sir, I sent him to the quartermaster. He's to get a skin of ale for each of the men. Pagehald's orders."

They cheered at that, clapping each other on the backs as though they'd done a load of hard work. Sigur came first, but not before ale.

"Make it quick, Dengeld," Vredevoort ordered.

The three men walked off, and the dead boy twitched, the only sign that he'd ever been alive. That was it—just a skinsack holding a bit of meat, hung from a makeshift gibbet. The sum of that boy's few years.

"Don't give me that look." Dengeld's voice brought Tristain back. "I just saved your fucking life. A bit of gratitude wouldn't go astray."

"Where am I going to get the coin to get a thousand skins? Better yet, how am I going to carry them all?"

"Don't you worry about the coin. Pagehald's just had an influx from somewhere. I'm not privy, but he'll pay. Just tell them that. As for how you're going to carry them all?"

He clapped Tristain's shoulders. "You'd best start before it gets dark."

9

CONFIRMATION

AETESTA, 1043

Demons have but one weakness: they were men, first.

— ELIAS ROTERSAND, LORD INQUISITOR OF OSBERGIA

S ELENE SAT IN THE contemplation room below the church, the first room she'd ever come to in the Citadel, thinking about her guardian mother. The room was one of the few places a person could go for privacy. Many outright forgot about it, praying in the many nicer places—the gardens, or the chapels in the annex. She didn't know if she could face everyone after what she'd done. But that was life. Her life. What was life if not a shattering? No sense in mollycoddling herself about it.

A knock came at the door. It opened, the hinges creaking slowly. The red-headed girl with the mismatched eye stuck her head around the corner. "Selene," Leona said gingerly. "How are you doing?"

"I'm... I'm okay," she said, biting her lip slightly. *I'm not... not really.* Images of Salim crying stayed with her like a stain from looking at a bright light for too long.

Leona walked inside, closing the door behind her. "We want you to know we don't hate you for what you did. Salim was a friend, but so are you."

"He's dead, Leona."

The girl went silent. Then she sighed. "I'm sorry."

"Don't be sorry."

"No, I was the one who told them about him."

Selene gasped, flaring her nostrils. "You *what?*"

"I didn't know it would come to this! I thought they might just whip him, or make him say a thousand prayers, or something like that. Not *kill* him."

"I can't believe you would do that!"

"It's not like he didn't have it coming, though... I mean, I know it sounds harsh, but if the Lightfather truly wasn't in his heart, surely, he deserved *some* punishment."

Selene exhaled. She felt queasy.

"No... no..." she muttered, holding her head in her hands. Leona placed a hand on her shoulder.

Selene flinched. "Get away from me."

"No, I'm here for you."

"No, Leona. I... I can't do this, not anymore." Salim was her friend. What business was it of Leona's that he might not have held Sigur in his heart? Gods knew she didn't, not all the time.

"What do you mean?"

"It's that dead part of your eye, like a dead part of your soul."

Leona blinked, tears dripping down her cheek. She breathed hard, her lips trembling. "You can't mean that..."

She wilted, shrinking as Selene got to her feet. "I do."

"Not you, too..."

A well of anger sprang forth. Her voice grew loud. "I hope Sigur *never* forgives you for what you've done. I hope you go to the deepest depths of hell and dwell there *forever.*"

Leona went pale. "No... no..."

"Yes. I hope you wander alone until the day the Gods return, and *never* find salvation, *never* find peace, and then Sigur himself strikes you down."

Leona squeaked, running from the room.

Selene strode to the door, her breath quick and her jaw clenched. She sighed, swearing under her breath as she watched the horrible girl run off crying.

S ELENE WAITED IN THE hall underground for Inquisitor Sorenius to arrive. It was daytime, just after waking. It was the time for her rites, her confirmation, and the inquisitor was her sponsor. Three others were there, waiting for their own sponsors. She had a rope net over her shoulder. Her idea: the net would restrain the creature, so they'd have an easier time killing it. She smiled as she caught the eye of one of her fellow *Velitore* fighters, a woman with blonde hair. They each had their own weapons—two with big crossbows, another with a spear.

She wasn't sure of the woman's name. She hadn't had many friends in this place, hardly knew anyone. It seemed strange, that she felt at home, but barely knew a face among them. *Ah...* Ebberich, Ruprecht. They were her only friends left in this entire place. Leona, once, but not anymore. She hadn't seen hair nor hide of the girl since their argument. They ate together, prayed together, slept beside each other. They talked over meals, passing the time with stories of their pasts, despite Sorenius telling them to renounce them.

Ebberich was the son of a corn farmer and a clothier and had been training to join the army before he threw in the with Order, thinking it was better to kill wukodlaks than men. He found his way to the citadel after an arbiter came through town and hunted a local manwolf.

Ruprecht was the fifth son of the Baron of Triburg, with no hope of inheriting land or titles. He was a guardsman in Triburg until the town was attacked by a demon and he was nearly killed along with two dozen of his fellow guardsmen. They'd been saved by a passing Sword and it was then he decided to join them and fight back.

Leona was the youngest of five, with four brothers. Cursed and disowned for her eye, she was neglected and abused. She turned to Sigur in moments of despair, and joined the Order as soon as she could make the journey. Selene thought perhaps she had been too harsh on her—knowing how similar their childhoods were made her sympathetic—but she still hated her for what she did to Salim.

And Salim, the slave from Saburria, who would never see his homeland again.

She whimpered, bringing a hand to her mouth. A twisted face. Stiff pain in her hand—steel glancing off bone. Glassy, brown eyes. A soft exhale. Selene swallowed, forcing tears back.

"Novitiate," Inquisitor Sorenius said, bringing her back. "Are you prepared?" Selene nodded.

The door opened. They were led out as the Lord Inquisitor announced their presence. The crowd looked on, some with nasty expressions, some eager, and yet others with fear. They were led downstairs where a notary unlocked the iron gate. She glanced behind. A small hole was made in the wall behind the notary, covered with an iron grate. The hole led somewhere dark and cramped—only the first two feet were lit by the brazier. It wasn't locked, but it did seem out of place.

The Lord Inquisitor seemed to speak in a different language, even though he didn't. Selene had her focus on the vast door ahead of her, walking onto the sand. The gate locked behind them. Four novitiates. It was expected that at least one would die. She would make sure it wasn't her.

The huge door rattled to life, chains pulling it open. It was black inside, the prison beyond had been shrouded in darkness. A demon would be let out of its cell, free to wander the halls until it smelled the blood and fear in the arena. Smelling that enticing cocktail, it would come running.

The crowd went silent. Selene's heart pounded in her ears. She went over her weapons again. *Two acid flasks. One dagger tipped with poison oak sap. A hand crossbow and ten bolts, all tipped with adder venom. The net—*

A vicious roar interrupted her thoughts. Selene smelled something acrid. She looked down. The man next to her had piss running down his leg onto the sand. She threw her head forward again. *No distractions. Focus.*

The roar came again, louder. Heavy footfalls. Grunting. A gray werewolf burst into the light. It ran straight at them, bent low for the charge. Selene dived to the side, sending sand into the air. The one with the spear moved in. His weapon was bat aside, and he followed, tumbling onto the ground. Crossbows twanged. The beast dodged.

She threw the net to the ground and unhooked her crossbow. The beast was too far away for the net to be useful, anyway. She lined up her shot and pulled the trigger. The mechanism snapped open, and the bolt whistled through the air. The beast moved unnaturally fast and spun away. It turned its cruel eyes on her. Down on all fours, it leapt at her. Too fast. It knocked the wind out of her. She coughed, hitting the sand. Looming over her, it stared, angry.

It yelped, recoiling in pain. A spear planted in its neck. Blood gushed onto Selene's robe.

She scrambled to safety. The others circled. She remembered the net.

With a victorious screech, she looped it over its enormous head and shoulders. The beast growled in frustration and tried to snap at her. She jumped back and with a shaking hand, tried to reload her crossbow, placing the stock against her belly. The demon hooked an arm into the ropes and pressed down. *Snap-pop.* The ropes unraveled, tearing open. *Snap!* Selene stumbled back.

Her hand rattled. She fumbled the bolt. *Come on!*

The beast broke free. Lashing out, it caught the spearman's arm. Bones crunched. The novitiate screamed in pain. The creature yanked the spear free. With its other hand, he ripped the novitiate's throat out. He died as he hit the ground.

Selene backed up even further. The beast cast the net aside, going after one of the others. It landed nearby.

A net is useless against something so strong! But all I need is one moment, one distraction!

She could use the others as bait. *Better some of us die than all of us.* The woman circled closer to Selene, keeping her distance, trying to reload her crossbow.

The woman grunted in surprise as Selene brought her legs out from under her. Wrapping the ropes of the severed net around, making her entangled. She cursed at Selene, eyes wide with fear.

Selene quickly loaded her crossbow with a fresh bolt. The beast danced around the sand, catching the other one on his own. The man let out a clipped yelp as a clawed fist punched into his chest, spraying blood across the sand.

The beast turned. Its quarry was waiting. *How kind of them, he must be thinking.* If the beast thought at all.

Selene backed up slowly, knowing that quick movement would only attract its attention. *Dumb, predator animals.* It snorted. Sand kicked up behind it as it bound forward. It came after the entangled one, as Selene expected. It leaped, pouncing on its terrified prey.

Selene threw the acid flask. It smashed against the beast's face. The monster howled, reeling. Droplets sprayed all over the novitiate beneath. She screamed as her chest and face started to melt. The pain must've been unimaginable.

The beast recoiled, stumbling, grabbing at its smoking face. Half of it was destroyed. Selene unhooked her crossbow. Her hand was steady. The string twanged and hit its mark. Straight into the beast's gullet. The poison made short work of it. It stumbled, grasping at its throat, before making a choked, gurgling noise and collapsing on top of its prey. The woman's screams were silenced.

The crowd roared as the Lord Inquisitor took up his podium again, calling for quiet. His voice was a blur. Selene groaned as she pushed the beast aside, exhausted, hoping the woman was still alive. She wasn't. The beast had crushed her when it fell.

Selene sat on the sand. Sorenius came to congratulate her, helping her to her feet. She was led up the stairs as the bodies in the arena were taken to the hole. Its purpose became clear now. It was a corpse chute, and probably emptied out into the sea at the foot of the cliff.

"Sponsor," Lord Inquisitor Rotersand spoke in the dark room just off the training hall, the one used for the dissection. Selene was still stunned, disoriented. She couldn't stop thinking about the woman's screams. *It was you or her, Selene. Stop thinking. This is your moment.*

"Do you lay your blessing upon this novitiate," the Lord Inquisitor said, "knowing that she commits her life, body, and eternal soul to the Lightfather himself?"

"I do," he replied.

Selene stepped forward.

The high inquisitor brought his arms high into the air. "Speak the words, Novitiate Hunter."

"I pledge my heart and soul, my body and being," she spoke, willing her mind to be quiet. The death of that woman was avoidable—*but this is the service that Sigur requires of me.* "My mind and spirit, my life, and my eternal soul and service, to the great Sigur, the Lightfather, the Father of All. I pledge to seek out evil and vanquish it. I pledge to bring justice to injustices. I pledge to forgo all pleasures of the flesh, all vices of wine and ale and all others, so that I may better serve Him. I pledge to commit my all to the destruction of the Great Devil, and his agents in this world, and the next."

"Step forth, Diana, Warden of Justice, and drink the blood of your enemies." Selene took her new name of Martyr Diana and was made a Sword of the Order.

Rotersand held out a goblet filled with a thick, dark liquid. The blood of the demon she'd killed. She took the goblet in both hands and drank deeply. It tasted of copper and was still warm. She coughed as she withdrew it from her lips.

"Know that from this day forth, you will always have a home in any church of Sigur. Seek shelter in His walls should you ever need it, and He will protect you from harm. And know that when you die, you will join Him in Hell, to fight in glorious battle."

Diana bowed her head. The Lord Inquisitor went on, giving the other novitiates a slightly different ceremony. Each one approached the altar in the center, saying similar words to her, but with variations as they were all notaries, and did not fight in the *Velitore*. She was the only one who survived the trial.

As the ceremony ended, Sorenius approached her. "Deepest congratulations, Warden Diana," he said, bowing his head slightly.

"I would almost say you're happy," she replied.

"Of course. Why wouldn't I be?"

"It happens all the time, doesn't it?"

"Yes, but that doesn't mean I'm not happy to see it. And besides, were you told?"

"Of what?"

"I'm to be your mentor, to travel with you as a pair. As mentor and apprentice."

Diana chuckled. "Good. I hope you know a few tunes to sing so I don't get bored."

"Careful, Diana, I am still your superior." They shared a laugh. "Come, I'll take you to the armory. This'll be the most exciting part."

A dazzling array of weaponry and armor sat before her. Ranging from small one-handed crossbows hung on the wall, all the way to giant metal arbalests, veritable siege engines, weighing many hundreds of pounds. Dozens of racked blades, from the smallest knife to the largest two-hander. On a small shelf sat a collection of vials, all labelled—poisons, acids, and poultices in equal amounts. In the corner were a selection of pressure traps and snares.

Diana chose a nimble dagger, a foot in length. Its ball-shaped pommel was embossed with a design of Sigur's sword. She then took up a nice hand-crossbow, made with an ebony oak-cored stock, and metal arms. It was much more pleasing to the eye than the chipped and damaged training bows, though her last one had served its purpose well, and she would miss it. She thanked the old girl as she placed it aside. She tucked a dozen spare bolts into her belt pouch, along with a couple of acid flasks to replenish her supply.

A rack of black armor caught her eye. Leather jerkin, trousers, and thick leather tassets over the thighs. The left arm was sewn over, reinforced with a curved pauldron of steel, stamped with seen from above. She grinned.

The inquisitor nodded. "Made, just for you."

She raced off, changing behind a screen. Sorenius turned his back, giving her some modesty. Though she might not have minded had he wanted a peek. *Pleasures of the flesh are forbidden... doesn't mean I can't imagine things...* His neck curved and graceful, but strong with muscle. His jaw, slender but handsome. Those leather trousers that hugged his body. *I'm only imagining...*

She stepped out, fine, tooled-leather boots echoing on the stone. "How do I look?"

"Take a look for yourself." He pointed to a mirror in the back corner.

It was the first time she had seen her own face in months. It was nearly blemish-free, and her nose had matured slightly, becoming higher in the bridge and slightly longer. Black made her skin shine; her long, thick raven hair sitting past her shoulders, wavy and tousled. She was strong, her legs long and her stomach taut. Her dark green eyes, like a pine forest, stared back at her. She smiled wistfully. She never thought she could be prouder of herself at that moment.

"Stunning," she muttered, turning to see her whole outfit. It was form-fitting, but fearsome. Artificers lined the jacket and trousers with interlocking metal plates, but the armor was still breathable and light.

Sorenius caught her eye in the mirror, then turned away, pretending to look at something else. Diana chuckled inside. "We leave tomorrow," he said, fingering the handle of a greatsword idly. "For a village in the Hag's Arm. Now that you're my apprentice, call me Soren."

She turned, surprised. "Oh." *I should see the others before I go.* "Can I say goodbye—"

A scream came from the annex. She frowned, drawing her dagger. Sorenius drew his own weapon.

They rushed over, joining a throng of people crowding around the chapel with the icon of Brigida. They moved people aside, pushing to the front. She saw what they were all looking at and froze. Leona dangled from a knotted bedsheet tied around the rafters.

Diana exhaled. She sank to the floor, numb.

VOLUME TWO

The duty of heavy cavalry at the attack is to shock, disconcert, and shake the enemy's morale. To this end, they should prepare themselves with heavy arms, lances, and long axes. The second line and the footmen should always prepare themselves to cut off the enemy infantry their escape. In doing so, the premonitory general will surround and envelop the enemy, if they are so able. If the enemy have their own cavalry, it is the duty of fast-moving skirmishers and light-armored riders to harangue and distract the charge. The general may also employ fortifications or entrenchments to prevent the charge. Entrenchment, however, is to be considered as a last option only. Either the entrenchment is too extensive to be defended properly, or the enemy may just avoid it entirely, finding a place at the rear to strike. One preeminent example comes to mind in 1044. The army of Duchess Else Adolar had invested themselves inside the walls of the city of Rennes, relying on a series of trenches in front of the walls to slow and harass their enemy. As the Duchess was preoccupied in an exchange with the Emperor's Merovian Guard, Prince Reynard of Annaltia noticed that their camp was unprotected, and open to attack. Soon, the Duchess was fighting on two fronts, and was defeated forthwith.

— *Institutum Militaris,* or *Emperor Franz II Osterlin's Instructions for His Generals.*

10

THE BLACKSMITH

VERNUS, 1043

Any rumors that werewolves possess a weakness to particular alloys or elemental metals is unfounded. A gold or a silver-tipped bolt cannot pierce their tough hides and kill them faster, not over good steel. Poisons and fire, however...

— LORD NOTARIUS GIAN ADALLA

WARDEN DIANA HALTED HER horse on a hilltop overlooking the valley of the Hag's Arm. The northern reaches of the Alba River were fordable, nothing more than a few lazy streams coming from the South Hills. Up here, it was nothing like the enormous river mouth that emptied into the Bay of Empires. Pine and fir forests extended in all directions, untouched by logging and farms. Apart from a tin mine in the distance, there was very little sign of civilization. She didn't know Osbergia went out this far. *How does the archduke get his taxes out here?* Soren didn't know either. They traveled together, making their way east.

They had been on the road for weeks now, on horseback. Diana thought she would have to get used to traveling like that. No parlor rooms or goose down quilts ever again. Despite that, she had fallen in love with these lands, with the way the sun fell lazily behind the horizon, and of a morning, the air filled with the scent of wildflowers.

It was late aestiva, and the nights were warm enough that she could sleep under the stars, and they did so often. More than once, she imagined climbing under Soren's blanket. The codes forbade physical relationships, but who would know? He was handsome, well-muscled, and intense. But maybe he was a bit too intense. Too focused on being a good Sword to share himself with her. Even after being with him all this time, she still didn't know where he was from, or his past before he became a Sword. Once, she tried asking him about his past.

"We must remain professional," he had told her. "I don't ask you about your life, and I would expect you to do the same."

Her horse nickered, and she ran her hand over her neck. She was a beautiful mare, dark brown dappled with white. Fourteen hands tall, she was on the smaller side for a horse. Diana admired the beast's eyes—deep pools of coal tar that spoke to her intelligence. The warden had taken to her immediately. She hadn't picked a name yet.

"Soren, how 'bout that," she whispered. The horse blew a refusal. "Or... hm, what about Eda." Diana nodded. The name seemed right. It took a place next to her heart, and she smiled. The horse swayed its head up and down, like an agreement. "Alright, Eda, it is."

"Are you talking to your horse?" the inquisitor asked.

"Yes, what of it?"

He shrugged. "Nothing. Just strange, seeing as the beast couldn't possibly understand."

"Ignore him," she said.

Eda blew her lips.

The road soon changed from forest trail to well-trodden gravel, and forests gave way to fields. The stink of mud and sheep filled Diana's nose. The road was enclosed by wooden fences in various states of repair, perhaps at one point meant to keep livestock in.

Over the next rise, the village appeared. They rode into the little community of Kuhurt. The mud-sheep smell concentrated more here, bringing a tear to the warden's eye. A thick-set, brown-haired man in a loose-necked linen shirt and a blackened leather apron walked up to them, hammer in hand.

"Who in Sigur's name are you?" he said in a Hillman accent. The man was overweight, but his forearms and shoulders bulged with the work of many years pounding away at an anvil. He wore an angry scowl. *Distrustful of strangers in his village.* Based on the looks of some others, he wasn't in the minority.

They dismounted and Soren spoke, "Good man, we are servants of the Most Holy Order of the Golden Sword. We mean you no harm."

"Holy Order?"

"What's that," a man with a milky eye asked. He leaned on a walking stick and had a flock of sheep at his side.

"Order," Sorenius said. "Of the—"

"What?" the sheep herd yelled.

"T—"

"Huh?" He cupped a hand to his ear. "Can't 'ere 'im."

"Aethelen," the blacksmith shouted. "Get after your flock. *Sal'brath.* They're off again!" The man with the walking stick glanced around, swearing as the sheep ran down the road, taking after them.

"I 'ave 'eard of the Order," the smith said. "Though I can't say you're welcome 'ere. We've 'erd stories that you put whole villages to the torch."

"Good man, we are hunting for subversives."

"Subversives? Like robbers 'n such?"

"And others." Soren liked not to reveal their true purpose, as he described, since shapeshifters hid in plain sight. Any one of Kuhurt's folk could be a devil.

"Ah! Why ya' not say so?" He plopped his hammer into the pouch on the front of his apron and grabbed the inquisitor by the shoulders, huge grin on his face. "Us good folk are just wary of strangers, 'at's all. We're all friendly 'ere. Apologies, we're had some trouble of late, with some robbers 'anging around in the woods." He let go of Soren. The inquisitor was left mildly annoyed, frowning.

"Robbers?" Diana said.

"Aye, young lass. They're out in the forest. Been 'avin' bonfires an' keepin' us up of a night with wild shoutin'. They 'aven't been seen near the village, everyone says, but I'm sure they come 'ere, when we're all asleep, creepin' into our 'omes. That's probably what 'appened to the poor miller's boy."

"Miller's boy?"

"Aye, and no lie, it was a right mess. The poor lad was strung up by his feet down by the river, danglin' from a tree. Looked like 'e'd been nibbled at by a bear or summin'. The miller's still distraught about it. We 'ad to cut the poor lad down. We don't 'ave proof the strangers took 'im, but who else wouldn't done it? We've sent word to the lord but we've not 'eard anythin' back."

Townsfolk began to gather around. One of them was a woman with a long red dress—a kirtle. The dress had a low neckline, and her bust was covered by a loose shift that billowed up from underneath. The woman wore a white wimple on her head to keep the sun off.

The smith greeted her. "This is my wife, Joseline. I'm Baltash."

"Inquisitor Sorenius," he said.

"Pleasure. Warden Diana."

"Pleased to meet you, kind folk," Joseline said. "So, do you drink ale, mead... barley tea?" Her voice was warm, inviting. Diana was reminded of a mother's voice.

"Oh, barley tea, please," she replied. Alcohol was strictly forbidden by the codes. She figured it was because they just didn't like fun. Soren replied with a curt shake of his head.

"Very well, three barley teas."

The smith stopped himself. "Why are yeh's still out here? Come on, let's get out of the sun."

They took the two Swords inside. Their house was small, but homely. Little touches of a hard-working family that took pride in their vocation were here and there. Intricate, looping bronze-work on the front door. A pewter goblet on a mantlepiece over the hearth, their dedication to the goddess Ginevra. Small bronze swords made for children to whack each other with.

Joseline brought out three finely decorated bronze cups and a small jug. Designs in twists of blue and green and yellow were painted on them.

"Oh, these are very nice," Diana said.

Joseline looked at the cups and smiled. "Oh, thank you. My son Toldash painted them."

The inquisitor glanced at her. He thought she was too jovial for the work, but this suited her just fine. *Soren can have his gruff mannerisms and stern looks, but a bit of charm can go a long way.*

The inquisitor queried for more detail about the miller's boy. "Oh, terrible thing, that. He was always so lovely," Joseline said as she poured the amber tea from the jug. Warm wisps of steam rose from the cup.

"You heard them stories that the priests tell, 'a those devils that hide as men?" Baltash said.

"Yes, the wukodlaks," Soren said. Diana took a sip of tea. The taste was nutty, and a bit bitter. She felt the warm liquid slide down her throat easily. It was pleasant after a long ride, if nothing else.

"Yeah, them. I think it's one 'a them that done it. Those strangers are probably all them."

"It's possible."

The husband and wife looked at each other. "So, they're real? I was just guessin'."

"They are certainly very real."

"And you 'unt 'em?"

"We do."

"Maybe you should go ask after them strangers then. Be careful about it though, if they're monsters, you might get hurt."

Two young boys came roaring through the doorway, one chasing the other with a pewter knight in hand.

"Ayeee, stop there, young lads," Joseline called. The boys stopped dead in their tracks. "Come, meet our guests."

"Hello there, little ones," Diana said. The two boys had little button noses, big eyes, and long eyelashes. They were positively the cutest thing she had ever seen.

The boys looked at each other. "Wow, you're really pretty," one of them said.

She grinned. "Thank you."

Baltash introduced the two. "My little boys, Caldash and Toldash. They're learning how to be smiths, like their father, and his father before him. Aren't you, boys?"

They answered at the same time, "Yes, Da."

"Well, they're adorable," Diana said.

The inquisitor snorted.

"Thank you, lady," Caldash said, the younger of the two.

"Thanks, pretty lady," said Toldash.

"How old are you?" Diana said.

"Seven," Toldash replied.

"Five," Caldash replied. Diana chuckled. *They're very cute.*

"Now, run along," Joseline said, pushing them out the door. Soren got up, seemingly having his fill of family time, and waved at Diana to join him.

"Thank you for your hospitality," he said. "But we must continue our search. We'll take our leave."

Diana bowed her head. "Thank you, kind folk. The tea was lovely." They seemed properly surprised that a pretty stranger was so friendly to them.

"You're very welcome, lass," the blacksmith said. The couple waved the Swords off as they left.

"**I** DON'T SEE THE problem, Inquisitor," Diana argued. They rode to the camp in the forest, the one the blacksmith had told them about. "Being friendly goes much further than being rude."

Soren waved his arms. "I'm not rude, I'm—"

"A jackass?"

"No, I'm objective, Warden. Being objective allows me to do my work effectively."

They rode staggered to the place in the forest where the strangers made camp. Late Solni drifted lazily through the trees along the trail.

"Sigur's Lantern," Diana swore. "Objective means you only have to care about yourself."

Soren's forehead creased. He eyed her sharply for the curse. "You'll see, forming attachments as a Golden Sword is a terrible idea. You of all people should know this."

There was a flash in her mind. An unmoving, mismatched eye. "No, I won't let that happen," she said, trying to focus on something else. "I won't be that selfish person who uses others and only cares about themselves."

Soren waved his hand vigorously. "Shh!"

Diana shook at the reins. Eda protested at the sudden movement.

"No, I won't be quiet," she yelled. "You were the one who brought it up!"

The inquisitor scowled at her. "Be quiet! I see something."

He pointed to a figure in the distance, leaning against a tree. She squinted hoping to glean something from the distant shape. "They're dead," Soren said.

"What?"

"Shh! Keep your voice down. I think we're being watched."

Diana gulped. "What should we do?"

"We get off the horses and send them back to the village. No sense in them getting in the way."

"Alright."

Diana gave Eda a hard smack on the rear as Soren did to Sullen, Diana's name for his horse, a grey gelding. She thought the resemblance was fitting, of the name, and its rider. The horses would find their way back to the village or would stop for tasty rushes along the trail. Either way, they were out of the way in case they were attacked. Horses panicked terribly at the sight of devils, and the Order had not managed to breed the fear out of them yet. The idea was that horses were sensitive to the evil exuding from them.

That makes two of us, Eda.

"Quiet. Pretend nothing is wrong and I'll see if I can spot our watcher," Soren whispered.

They walked along the trail towards the body in the distance. Solni dipped below the horizon, long shadows falling across the trail. Diana's hand rested on the dagger's handle, arm coiled and ready. They drew closer and studied the carnage. It was a woman's body, no older than Diana herself. Her torso had been torn wide open. Wine-red blood pattered the ground, feeding the soil. More bodies lie further on as well, much in the same state. Diana's stomach churned. *This could only have been in the last hour or so... the devil's probably still here.*

Bile stung the back of her throat. She swallowed hard, forcing herself to be still and quiet. Luni turned her back on them tonight, and darkness was setting in.

"There!" Soren unhooked his crossbow and ran ahead of her.

She lost him in the darkness. Black shapes blurred past, flitting between the trees. Diana drew her dagger. She whipped around, trying to track the shapes.

Boof! Brown fur filled her vision. She hit the ground with a thud. Groaning, she turned over. A huge brown manwolf with a thick mane towered over her. Its monstrously large teeth bared at her as it snarled. She stared, and it stared at her. She moved to defend herself, but she could sense something behind the eyes. *Is it scared?* The demon stood still.

The expected attack didn't come. It breathed, chest like a man's but three times as large, heaving in and out. Finally, it yelped, a bolt planting in its side, white fletching sticking out. Diana held her dagger out, bracing for the attack. The demon had other ideas. It leapt away, whimpering as it tore through the brush and out of sight.

Thank Sigur. Soren came running. "Are you alright?" he said.

Diana brushed herself off, her breath returning to normal. "Yes." She shuddered. "It just stared at me."

"Maybe it likes playing with its food."

"Come, we'd better catch up with it."

"No need. Its heart will give out soon." She raised her eyebrows, giving him a smack on the shoulder. He'd poisoned the bolt.

"What if you'd hit *me* with it!"

"I wouldn't have. Let's go find it."

They headed off the forest trail, finding snapped branches and snagged fur. Sure enough, they came to a heavy-set man writhing in the dirt. His clothes were tattered, and he was coughing up blood. He moaned, "My children..."

Diana blinked in disbelief. "This devil has children?"

Soren nodded. "It's likely he would have used them against us, had we attacked back in the village."

"What do you mean?"

He kneeled and yanked the bolt out. The monster groaned, writhing in pain. "You don't recognize him? He's the blacksmith."

It took her a second. His rotund frame. Brown hair. Thick arms, uneven from working a hammer in one hand.

"*Sigur, it is!* Gods, he seemed so friendly though!" The man struggled for breath. Diana felt for the man for a second before suppressing that thought. *He's a beast. He ripped apart those poor people back there.*

"Demons would use our own sense of kindness and humanity against us. That's why we must hunt them." The blacksmith fell still and croaked his last. Diana still couldn't believe it. *He really was a monster all along. Maybe it was wrong of me not to become detached.* Life was a series of shatterings, after all. Soren got up and placed the quarrel back into his pouch, wiping it clean of the blacksmith's blood.

"Come. Let's go."

11

THE HERBALIST

VERNUS, 1043

Herbalists persist on that knife's edge of near-heresy. They per-
form vital duties—healing, preparing, caring, abortion, even
quietus. But these duties often leave them like the embalmers:
under suspicion, blame, and on the edges of society.

— GERAINT FALLSTADT, EMPEROR'S HISTORIAN

A MONTH HAD PASSED since her hunt of the demon in the Hag's
Arm. They'd not been back to the citadel since they left for Kuhurt,
while the war in Badonnia was in full swing. Rennes lay under siege, and
news was hard to come by. The day before, they'd encountered one of
the local lord's patrols, men in red and green, bristling with lances and
hammers. They surrounded them, eyeing them warily until they noticed
the inquisitorial badge on Soren's cloak.

"Apologies, lord," the captain had said. "Been too many bandits on the
road, lately. Ever since the knights pissed off with their levies, brigands and
thieves think empty fields and homes sit ripe for takin'."

Diana had to ask. "How goes the war?"

"Poorly, mistress. There was a battle between there and the pass, many
kinsmen died." She knew the place. It was called the Giant's Footfalls, after
the strange rock depressions in the area, shaped like footprints. It was a

barren place and would not offer much cover for an advancing army with too many places for enemies to hide.

"Too many," the man said. "Maric here lost his uncle an' brother. That damn lady Duchess. Ain't right, a woman leading a host. Nothin' a woman good for other than motherin' and whorin'. No offence, mistress."

"Thank you, Captain," Diana replied. "Now, I'll remind you that we are duty bound to the canon law of Sigur, not to the laws of men. Are we to be detained?"

"Ah! Beggin' your pardons, mistress. Alright, men, let's speed out of these holy warriors' way."

They did, and let the Swords continue their travels. She didn't have to remind herself that there were a multitude of reasons she'd joined the Order. That women could excel and face no impedance to doing so was just one of them.

Diana exited the church after the prayers had finished, leaning against a wall. Soren had stayed to talk with the preceptor. She tapped her fingers, passing the time watching a honeysucker flit around the branches of a yellowing birch in the middle of the garden. The preceptory was small, just a church, a stable for their few mules, and a dorm for the priests to sleep and eat, and a high stone wall separating the place from the impure world outside. There was no training hall though; no recruits headed for the crucible. A pair of priests in black robes nodded at her as they walked past. She could pick out the words *beast* and *Badonnia* among other ones, like *corruption in the ranks*. She found herself wondering if the Order had spies in the army—rooting out devils before they rotted it from within. Maybe the devils were why they'd lost their fight in the Footfalls.

Diana walked over to the stables to check on Eda. She was in the stables with Sullen, both taken care of by the half-blind but attentive groomsman. The mules had been moved outside.

"Greetin's, Warden," the man said, his wrinkled jowls wobbling as he spoke. He was stooped, hunched over by a third. He was brushing Eda with a stiff wooden comb, humming as he did so. The mare was enjoying herself, leaning into the brushing. Diana was glad. The horse had been through a lot. She had been near frightened to death on the last hunt.

Soren received a letter from the Lord Inquisitor telling them of a group of village folk just south of the Vinpa river in Annaltia, who'd captured a demon. He was the local tax collector. Diana had laughed, thinking it was a jest, until they arrived, and the beast leaped for Diana on her horse.

She had dodged, leaping off Eda. The beast clipped her as he soared over her head, and they landed together in a tangled pile, rolling off the road into a ditch. The creature growled, snarling as the disgusting creatures did. Its mistake.

Her venom-coated dagger already in hand, she stabbed it three times, lightning quick. The adder venom took its ice-cold grip quickly. The creature writhed in pain, raising its great clawed hand, to no effect. The hand came down with no more force than a soft thump, then collapsed on top of her. It died, then it was nothing but an unclothed man with a sizable paunch and two chins. Soren had a devilish smile on his face as he shoved the fat, naked tax collector off.

"Not how I imagined that going," she had joked.

Soren shook his head. "I know better than to make a comment about something like that."

The village folk should've known better. There was no holding a devil without thick chains, and even then, it wasn't a guarantee if they were sufficiently riled. The only safe demon was a dead demon. The tax collector had escaped, slaughtering his captors in his flight. Even the children hadn't been spared.

Diana ran her hand across Eda's neck, the stain of guilt heavy on her, even if it hadn't been her fault. She could've killed the demon, even so.

The horse snorted in appreciation. She walked back to the yard as the door to the church opened. Soren walked out with the preceptor. The women were a Gods-send. Back in the citadel, any number of helpful philters; for pains, sores or bruises they would provide, no questions asked.

Diana smiled as the two approached. "Mother Cecilia," the inquisitor introduced, "Warden Diana, my apprentice. Mother Cecilia is the preceptor here."

The woman bowed her head. She was in her twilight years, like the groomsman, with a crooked back and her ghost-white hair tucked under her veil; white linen to match her robes. "Pleased to meet you."

Diana bowed her head in return. "Likewise, Preceptor."

"You know the lands we stand on? You know of the ancient kingdom of Evergia?"

"I can't say that I do, not much."

"It was a place of gold, and milk, and honey. No one ever went hungry, and it was said that men lived into old age, just as healthy as they were when they were young. But the Great Devil saw to that—growing jealous of Evergia's wealth and utopian ideals. So, he wiped the place from the Continent."

"I see."

"That's why we fight." The preceptor placed a hand on Diana's right arm. "I see you've had something taken from you, forever, as well."

She looked down. "Yes." *But I fight, so that no one else may suffer the same fate.*

"Someone 'elp, for Sigur's sake," someone yelled from over the wall. Diana glanced at Soren. The three of them strode to the gate, joining a few priests.

"What's so urgent," one of the priests snapped. A group of peasants flooded into the preceptory as the gates were opened.

"Sigur's Blade," the preceptor said, sighing loudly. "We've heard these ones before."

"You're the Order, right?" one of the peasants asked. "We saw the hunters on the road. We're—"

"What is the meaning of this?" Soren said.

"Forgive us, lord, but we've come to plead on behalf a' our eternal souls!"

"They're convinced a demon lives on the outskirts of their village," the preceptor said. "I've had a look, Inquisitor, and I believe it to be nonsense."

"No nonsense where the agents of evil are concerned," Soren answered.

"We'll see into this matter." Diana agreed.

THE WOMAN'S COTTAGE WAS far outside the village. Their investigation had proved to be a tale of two women in one. Some described her with horns, giant teeth, and a vicious glint in her eye, snatching babies and cursing men to impotence. Others described her as a quite normal woman, blessed with the gift of healing. No husband nor children, and in her middle age, but that could also be deceptive, as the monsters were known to hide their true nature.

Nestled beside a brook and a small overgrown orchard, her house was a typical homestead of the region, with a main house and a shed, a hen house, and an herb garden, all fenced off by low stone walls. Wild goats wandered in the orchard, munching on the apples that hung from the unkempt trees bulging with fruit. Hens pecked at the crumbs and seeds discarded by the goats. It really was hard to believe that anyone other than a quite normal peasant woman lived here, if perhaps a bit further out than was usual.

The fowl clattered madly at their approach. Soon enough, a short, sun-darkened woman appeared in the doorway. Her madder-dyed kirtle came down to her ankles, and hair the color of red wine speckled with grey poked out messily from beneath her wimple. Diana dismounted Eda, utilizing one hand and the stirrups at her saddle. The mare pulled ahead, tearing a juicy bulrush next to the stone wall.

Soren climbed down from Sullen. "Good woman," he said. "Sigur lay his blessings on you."

"And you," she said, eyeing the blades at their belts. "Is this about the master? I told you before, the rash will only go away if he treats it every day. The lazy bas—" She stopped herself, tipping her head back slightly. "No, you're Order, aren't you? Been said you were on the road. What're you doing here?"

"Good woman, the ground is cold through our boots. We'd much rather discuss the reason for our visit inside."

She relaxed her face. "I'd prefer you keep your weapons outside, but I've no reason to refuse ye'." They stepped carefully through the woman's garden and headed inside. She passed under the lintel with no trouble. Both Swords had to duck their heads. Inside, the cottage was surprisingly well-lit for its location in a glade. Paned windows and dormers opened the space. The woman headed behind a curtain to the kitchen, sending the fragrant smell of herbs into the main room.

"Expecting guests?" Sorenius asked.

"Nay," she answered. "Just meself. Forgive me if you were looking for a five-course meal."

A woman of the land, Diana thought she might fit right in between the tenants of her old guardians' estate.

"Don't mind us, we're not hungry," Diana said. They'd eaten at the preceptory, though taking food from a suspected she-wolf would've been suicidal. Who knew if she'd poison their food?

Diana looked around. On the woman's shelves were a few curios: a small doll made of wool, clothed like a child; a letter knife; and a necklace made of silver, hung with a pendant. She popped it open. A portrait of a young girl lay inside. She showed Soren, then put it back.

The woman pulled back the curtain, platter set with steaming, thinly sliced potatoes topped with cream of goat milk. She set them down at the table and urged them to take a seat.

"So," she said. "Why have the Order of the Golden Sword found themselves in my house?"

"Forgive us, good woman," Diana said. "We heard rumors of your—"

"My devilry and my heresy," she interrupted. "I assume?"

"Yes."

"I wouldn't think such trifles would concern the Order; great arbiters of truth that you are."

Soren grunted. "Normally, yes, if we were to investigate every frippery, pockmark, or wayward spouse under the influence of the Great Devil, we would find ourselves with no time to deal with serious matters."

"What are serious matters, then?"

"When half the village is convinced that you're hiding pointy ears under your veil," Diana said, "and a mouth lined with fangs the size of fingers. Yet, the other half seems to sing your praises. Those think you're the next coming of Ginevra herself."

"I make potions and poultices from time to time, sell them to womenfolk, mostly. One that'll settle your guts, one that'll do the opposite. Don't drink my tea if you value your bowels."

"Hm. I suppose you could answer a few of our questions, then?"

"And what if I said no?"

"I suspect you know what comes next."

"I do. What did you do to your arm, Sword?"

Diana wouldn't be deterred. "What's your name?"

"Lorena-Maria Ulgart."

"Lorena-Maria? Are you Republican?"

"Alanian, yes. On my mother's side. She came here to be with her love, my father, oh... sixty-two years ago. My memory is a bit fuzzy these days, but that's the right of it."

"Right. Married? Children?"

"None. Been alone my entire life, the way I like it."

"No children? Who will look after this place when you die?"

"No one, I suspect. Let the forest grow over it, I won't mind." *Acerbic, and tight-lipped, too.*

"Let me move on. Why did you think we were here for a 'Master'?"

The woman sighed. "Oh… I shouldn't have opened my mouth. You're not with the baron, are you?"

Diana shook her head. "Most certainly not. The Order answers only to Sigur himself."

"Right. The baron has himself rather a problem with a rash… in his nether regions. His wife won't touch him until he rids himself of it. Doctors tried and failed, so he came to me. I guess one of the folks here had spread the word that I had remedies for all sorts. That was an afternoon, let me tell you. The man was so nervous I thought he might shit himself on the chair. I inspected the man's horn, and between you and me, I think the surgeon'd tried leeches or something… it was angry, red, like a newborn." Soren shifted in his chair. "I gave him a paste of wolf's bane and ground willow bark to ease the swelling and itching. It's probably Night Pox, so there's no cure, but it'll go away in time. They came here… oh, two days past, to say it's not working. I say the only way that's like to happen is if he's not putting on every day, the lazy bastard. I've seen more than my share of it in the menfolk, so I know what I'm doing. Anyway, I been sworn to name him the Master to all his servants. I thought that's what you two were, 'fore I realised."

"I see. I gather we won't have this information confirmed?" Soren asked.

Lorena-Maria shrugged. "Likely not. Sorry."

"And where did you learn to make these medicaments?" Diana said. "I understand that the academies do not take women, one of the few doors that are closed to us."

"If you think there's only a few doors that are closed to us women, you're sadly mistaken, child." She paused. "My mother taught me, just like her mother before her."

Diana turned. Wild clucking came from the garden, raising the alarm. Something was out the front. She went to the window. A crowd of peasants had assembled outside the garden. They stood in silence, but their faces were frozen in anticipation. *Don't get any closer now. It's dangerous.* Diana turned back. She noticed the woman's eyes flash for an instant to the pendant on the shelf. She tensed up. It went silent, anxiety charging the air.

"Hm," Diana said, narrowing her eyebrows. "There's one thing that's bothering me. I think you're lying to us about not having children."

Lorena-Maria laughed. "What are you talking about? I don't have children."

Soren leaned forward. "There's something you're not telling us, isn't there?"

"I have no idea what you're talking about."

"I think you know where this is going. Either you answer our questions truthfully, or we'll be forced to use other measures."

"Ain't answered 'em nothing but truthfully."

Soren got to his feet without a word. He walked over to the hearth. Embers smoldered quietly. He chanted a prayer to Sigur, closing his eyes.

"*Lightfather,*" he said. "Fire given by your name, I purge you by the holy God. Bathe us now in the light of purification for the salvation of all faithful. Let every unclean spirit be commanded by Him who is to come to judge the living and the dead and the world by fire."

Diana saw Soren's hand flick almost imperceptibly towards the flame, tossing some sort of powder on it. The blaze erupted in yellow, filling the room with a slight metallic smell. Golden light bathed the room. It died down, returning to its regular orange color, but it burned stronger than it had before.

"Step forward, Healer. Prove your innocence in the pyre."

The woman gulped. "You can't be serious."

"Prove your innocence. No more than a hand's worth. If your skin blisters but does not catch fire, we will know your purity."

She sighed. Coming over, she said, "If I pass your test, will you leave?"

"Without hesitation."

Soren pulled up a chair. Lorena sat, waving her hand over the fire. Sorenius took hold of her wrist, pulling her into the flames. She yelped. The heat licked her skin. Her flesh turned red and angry. She groaned. Diana saw a flash of something in her eyes, but it disappeared as soon it arrived. The woman screamed. The peasants raised their voices in alarm. Lorena gasped in surprise, covering her mouth with her free hand.

Diana ripped her hand aside. Teeth, as long as fingers.

Soren leapt to his feet. The herbalist dove, grasping the side of the dining table. She flipped it with a grunt. Hot potatoes and cream sprayed into the air. The table crashed into the Swords, thrown with surprising strength. Diana groaned as she hit the floor.

A growling noise filled the air then a flash of dark red fur, the same color as the woman's hair. It tore past them, hurtling through the door. The peasants yelled in surprise. Sorenius helped Diana to her feet. They burst outside. *Twang-thunk.* The beast gasped, half-woman, half-demon falling to the floor.

The peasants cried fury and pelted her with stones as she died. Soren squeezed her shoulder for a job well done. The trap had been Diana's suggestion and only a last resort. She was just glad the peasants didn't trigger the trap themselves. Rigging up the twine had to happen under the cover of darkness – and Diana counted herself lucky that the woman's garden didn't look tended to, giving her plenty of dense bush to hide a crossbow in, and less of chance that she would accidentally trigger the trap prematurely.

The village folk looked satisfied that Lorena was dead and stopped throwing rocks. Diana played with her hair idly. It seemed that the peasants were all too ready to turn brutally against a woman who'd lived there for years, as a long-standing pillar of their community. But Diana understood. It *was* betrayal. She had lied for so long. The people of the village had a bright future ahead of them.

"Let's go," she said to Sorenius.

He nodded. "I trust these people can take care of a pyre by themselves. Her body is to be salted and burned, and her ashes are to be taken to the preceptory to be disposed of. Yes?"

The folk nodded.

INTERLUDE

BALTAS

B ALTAS KNEW THERE WEREN'T much promised to a man in this world. Even less for someone like him. He'd inherited his smithy from his father, like his father before him. But he knew someone would try to take what he'd built, eventually. His wife, his children. All of them would be taken, eventually. It was the way of the world.

When he heard screaming coming from behind the mill, it was no surprise. He ran around the corner. A scruffy man was dragging Toldas by his collar. They were in the middle of the barley patch. Caldas was kicking at the man's legs, trying to force him to let go.

Baltas sprinted over to them. He recognized the man as one of the strangers from the forest.

"Stop," he boomed, "What's going on 'ere?"

The man put Toldas down, and replied, "What's going on here is that I caught this bloody thief, red-handed. He stole a valuable trinket of mine."

Baltas stepped forward. "'ang on... Toldas, is this true?"

"But Da..." The boy looked down. "Yes."

"Alright. You still have the trinket?"

"Yes, Da. It's in my pocket." On saying this, the man started rifling through Toldas' pockets.

"Hey, stop that!" Toldas squealed.

The scruffy-looking man found the trinket and snatched it out of the boy's pocket. Baltas felt his anger rising. He would have to suppress it. His boys had not seen him Change, not yet. He would have to tell them about it, one day, since it seemed more than likely they would have the curse as well, like his father before him. But that day would not be today.

"Good. Now you've got yer bauble, be on yer way," Baltas spat, pointing to the forest.

"I don't think so, this boy needs to be taught a lesson," the stranger said, drawing a dagger that was tucked into his pants. He held it near the boy's wrist.

Baltas felt a lump in his throat.

"I'll remove a hand, and we'll consider it even."

"No, Da!" Toldas screamed.

Baltas' world slowed down. Anger and terror rose in his stomach as he shook. He would not have his son being hurt. Just because he knew someone would try to take everything, that didn't mean he had to be fine with it.

The pit opened beneath him. His mouth unhinged, opening wider to accommodate huge canines. His chest expanded. His arms ballooned. Brown fur grew from every pore, blanketing his body. The stranger dropped the boy and trembled in terror as a giant wolf, standing on its hind legs, picked him up by the head and carted him away.

T HE STRANGERS FLED, SCREAMING, as the wolfman tore through their camp. Baltas had finally pressed the issue. He would deal with them once and for all. How dare they harm his son, he might have thought, had primal rage had not consumed his mind. Baltas threw the screaming man he'd been holding. He hit a tree with a sickening crunch. The travelers ran, panicked. He caught up with them all, butchering them where they stood. Gods, he felt good.

B ALTAS FELT THE BOLT slide into his back. It had not gone far in—his fur-covered skin was exceedingly protective—but gods, did it hurt. All he tried to do was scare the poor raven-haired lady, so the two strange hunters would be quick to leave. He yelped in pain and took off into the bushes. Then his heart beat strangely. He slowed, feeling sluggish.

What's happening to me?

Baltas clutched his chest and coughed blood. Then the Changes reversed themselves. He got shorter. Fur pulled back in. His jaw cracked as it re-formed to its normal shape. He could no longer smell the manure from the farm five miles away. The wolf turned back into the man as everything sealed back up inside him. His legs gave out, and he fell to the ground.

The black-clad man and woman ran to him. The woman had a look of worry. He hoped he had not hurt her, but she seemed to be fine. He felt himself dying. He thought of his children and hoped they would be alright without their father. He thought of all the things he would miss. Their first beard hairs, their first loves. He had planned on apprenticing Toldas next year. The boy had natural creativity.

He hoped with all his heart that the boys would not have the curse.

"My children..." he muttered.

Baltas' lungs burned, and his heart ached in his chest. He groaned as the black-clad man pulled out the bolt and wiped the blood off. His blood. His vision went hazy.

The man and woman were talking, but he couldn't hear what they were saying. His chest trembled—it was getting harder and harder to breathe until finally he couldn't anymore. His vision went black as he breathed one last time. In that moment, he could have sworn there was a white wolf waiting for him in the darkness.

12

CALLED

TRIBUUM, 1043

*Demons organize in packs. Such hives of devilry and malice
must be rooted out and eliminated with extreme prejudice.*

— LORD NOTARIUS GIAN ADALLA

THE NEXT POST THEY went through, Soren received a letter from the
Notarii Inquisitorum, calling them back to the Citadel. Inquisitor
Rotersand wanted to congratulate them personally for their hunt of the
Kuhurt blacksmith and the noble defense of the preceptory at Avercarn.
Diana couldn't believe her ears. She didn't have the stomach for the pastries
the kind clerk's wife left them.

"That's what he's calling it?" Diana said when Soren finished reading the
letter and handed it to her.

Soren shrugged. Inside the emperor's post, a few quiet clerks milled
around, while the horses nickered softly outside by the hitch. These posts
were a hostler and letter service all in one. If you knew where someone
was heading or hoped their travels took them, you paid a rider to take your
letter to the nearest post. Diana imagined Swords were their main clientele,
having occasion to travel long distances and receive communications. But
knowing all that, never once did she find a letter from a young man from
Invereid named Tristain when she had occasion at all to receive one. That

darkened her mood already, so when the clerk behind the counter told them to move for the next patron, she took issue.

Diana looked behind her. "There's no one there."

"Make way for the next patron," he said. His voice thrummed with the authority that came with having a little scrap of power that he could lord over others.

She chuckled, shaking her head in bewilderment.

Soren continued. "Rotersand took over a few years ago, and he..."

"He, what?"

"Never mind. He has been ordained by the Grand Inquisitor, and it is not my place to question him. He just likes to name things in grand ways."

"I see. What's he like?"

"Rotersand? Tough. Demanding. But ultimately reasonable, as long as you get results."

"Got it. He did my confirmation."

"I remember. I was there."

"Right. Should we go, then?"

"We wouldn't want to keep him waiting," Soren said, carrying an edge of exasperation.

Swords liked to be kept in the field, Diana found. The bureaucracy and the staid procedures at the Citadel kept most people at arm's length. She was no exception.

"**G**OOD MORNING, INQUISITOR SORENIUS and Warden Diana," Lord Inquisitor Rotersand said. He wore a black velvet robe with gold trim. Selene wondered if the finery was overkill. She had only ever seen the Archduke wear such nice clothes.

They bowed their heads in greeting.

"Good to see you," he continued. His voice was deep and commanding. Her nerves crested like a wave. He waved to the two chairs in front of him. His office was fairly small, lined with bookshelves stuffed with papers and books, with titles ranging from *How to Hunt Wolfmen, vol. X* to *The Histories of the Modern Istryan Empire*, all ten volumes. His office overlooked the ocean. Diana appreciated the view. Hanging on the back wall was the sigil of the Order—a golden sword pointing to the sky on a black background. Light rays shone from its base, symbolizing the penetration of the night by the golden light of truth. Functional, really, as a description of their jobs.

They took their seats.

"I must congratulate you, Warden." Rotersand grinned.

Diana breathed a sigh of relief. The inquisitor was unnerving when he greeted her at her confirmation, though she decided to give him credit. Perhaps he was having a bad day.

"Thank you, Lord Inquisitor," she replied. She told of the events of the day, and felt the compliment was a little undeserved.

"But I can't take the credit," she finished. "Soren killed the wolfman."

"Yes, but you faced your first lycanthrope and survived," the Inquisitor said. "From what Soren told me in his report, you were very gallant under pressure."

"Gallant?" she said, blinking. "I almost fainted out of sheer terror!" She laughed.

The Inquisitor didn't smile. The room was silent, swelling with pressure. Diana flushed. She always did have a talent for jokes at the wrong time, she realized.

Finally, Inquisitor Rotersand spoke. "Modesty is a fine quality until it becomes cumbersome."

He stared at Diana. For a moment, she thought she deep, profound rage flashed in his eyes. Then he smiled.

"Then, of course, you killed your first in Avercarn. Using a poison trap. Well played."

"A crossbow trap, actually." She found his nerve tiresome.

He nodded and turned to Soren. "And what of you, Inquisitor," he asked. "What is your perspective of your apprentice?"

"She is progressing very well," Soren answered. "As you'll remember, I was six weeks out of my confirmation before I killed my first. She beat me by a week. So, I do say it's going well."

"Yes, I do remember," the Inquisitor replied. "The one at Vosfeld... If I remember correctly, it led you on a chase for a week, and it was back and forth. You chased it, it chased you..."

He sighed. "It still cracks me up, to this day."

Soren chuckled and waggled his eyebrows in agreement. Selene had no idea what was going on.

The inquisitor turned and faced the ocean. "My father once told me that fate is a woman's game. Our lives are like whores in heat. Sometimes you need to force the bitch down."

After a pause, he said, "I have news. You are to march for the South Hills, to a town called Esstadt."

Diana looked at Soren, who cleared his throat.

"Why there, Lord Inquisitor?"

"It would befit you not to question me, Inquisitor," he said. He turned back around. "We are marching there because I have received information that an enclave of lycanthropes hides there. You will go with a force to secure the town and detain those determined to be harboring the creatures there. Find the demons and kill them."

He lifted his head. "And get it done. Find the demons, not excuses."

"Very good, sir," Soren replied.

Diana nodded her understanding. She wasn't going to open her mouth again.

"WHAT IN SIGUR'S LANTERN was that about?" Diana said.

In the yard, Sigursday celebrations exacted their streaming vengeance on the eaves of the Citadel for another year. Colorful streamers, that was. Priests carrying censers chanted through the vestibule and smudged up the grounds. Little carved swords hung from candelabra, made from white wood, of course, while she could smell the cinnamon and raisin strudels baking in the ovens, the delicious smell wafting from the kitchens.

Soren flicked a throwing knife between his fingers. They armed themselves in the Citadel armory. She restocked her poisons and quarrels, dipping their tips in a dish of adder venom. Alongside and between her were others doing the same rearming. An inquisitor here with his pin, two arbiters there. A huge man in full plate that moved with the grace of a dancer. He had his helmet down, and there wasn't a single gap between any of the pieces.

She leaned close to Soren, careful not to raise her voice. Speaking ill of a superior could get her killed, or lashed, at the very least.

"It was like Veles, two faces in the same man, and with all the bluster of a storm!"

Soren held a hand up in deference. "Inquisitor Rotersand is an intense fellow, but he is fair and just."

Diana grumbled. She felt Rotersand was humorless and rude, even if he was 'fair and just'.

She thought on that flash of hatred in his eyes. She read the *Histories*, had heard the sensational stories about the Order, but her experience was that they were nonsense, or they were justified. Besides, she'd done awful things in her quest to make the world right. If skin had to be cut open along the way to get to the canker, well, that was just the right thing to do.

She rubbed her eyes, frustration coming to a head as she moaned in displeasure. Soren glanced at her but didn't react.

"You should consider yourself lucky," Soren offered. "Rotersand appears to have taken a shine to you."

"I wouldn't say that."

"Look around. All inquisitors and veterans." She glanced around. The convoy did seem to be made up of some of the most senior and cutthroat Swords Diana had seen.

Nials the Bitten stood nearby, smiling at her. She shuddered.

He had survived an attack by two lycanthropes—finishing them off with just a dagger. Nials had dusty brown hair, yellow eyes, and was mangled. Missing an ear, bitten off by one of those werewolves, if you believed the stories. But his appearance belied his strength. He had a survivor's build, having lived alone in the forests of Osbergia for years. He hunted werewolves with only knives in some cases, and his own wit.

Standing beside him was Lena Ulnstadt, an arbiter who once threaded a knife through the crook of a statue's arm, twenty yards away, and nailed a wolfman through the eye. She was a slender woman with a pointed chin. Tansy, she was known as. A daffodil was tucked above her ear, pinning her blonde hair back. She armed herself with a heavy-looking crossbow, giant drum under the stock, full of bolts. It looked impractical, and certainly Diana couldn't use it with only one arm. She was curious, though, and wondered if she'd get to see it in action.

Soren continued, "The Inquisitor clearly sees your potential."

"I'll admit, I do feel a bit outclassed," Diana said.

But why would the Inquisitor choose me to go on this mission, what possible use could I be?

13

THE ASSAULT

FERVUM, 1044

*Give a soldier a man to kill, and no other choice, and he'll keep
fighting till his own death.*

— DUCHESS ELSE ADOLAR

THE HORNED RAM BATTERED the gate as anxiety charged Tristain's lungs like a thousand knights' lances. Wood splintered. Strings
twanged and arrows whistled. Broadheads planted in the ram's rawhide
skin and wood frame, unable to hit the drivers beneath. Soon enough, the
archers gave up. Tristain shuffled his feet in the muddy dugout, thirty feet
from the gates, arming sword and heater shield in hand. His shield was a
spare, clumsily painted with Sir Vredevoort's colors—a red bear on a green
field.

It had been two weeks since he'd left the general's quarters and joined
Vredevoort's regiment, under a gruff sergeant named Dengeld. They were
all gruff. It came with the territory. When you knew only a few of your men
would survive a battle, it was hard to get attached. Vredevoort's regiment
had the highest casualty rate of any.

Tristain had laid low, not attracted attention. The graycloaks hadn't
shown themselves since that night they'd questioned him, but still he kept
his head down, keeping to his tent between drills and chores. Not getting

to know anyone. Eventually, the ram was completed, and the catapults measured for distance. The general declared it was time to take Rennes, and the night outside the alehouse became the last thing on Tristain's mind.

Two men down from him, someone dropped silently, an arrow through their chest. The gap was quickly filled. A whistle. An arrow landed in front of him. He blinked. Mismatched feathers—one from a raven, another from a goose. The shaft was nicked. He raised his shield, protecting his face. His open-faced pot-helmet would provide very little protection if they hit him in the face, despite the grimness of their make. Over the rim, he spotted the gate crashing open. A mighty cheer came up around him.

Vredevoort the Grim led the charge, all steel and plate. Enormous longsword in hand, he bellowed as he charged. Tristain clambered over the chest-high trench, arrows planting themselves all around him. Shields up. Swords and spears were ready. Boots thumped on the ground. Shouts all around. The drivers moved the wooden beast back, out of the path of the charging line. Tristain felt the world melt away. All that stood in front of him was their enemy, red and blue acorns. Their terrified faces above those surcoats.

Until the pitch started flying. Horrible screams rippled the air. Heat from the boiled tar hit him, nearly knocking him off his feet. Torches descended upon them. Fire roiled in waves through dozens of them. Tristain's skin sizzled. The pitch itself hadn't hit him, but it still burned. Alongside him, men turned into bright candles.

He pushed forward, nudging the stone down in his gut. He stabbed what he could. A boy dropped. He was younger than Tristain. The man next to him stabbed back. Tristain put his shield up, feeling the point glance off. He lashed out, slicing his foe's face through a gap in a helmet. Another took their place, bringing their axe down on Tristain's still-extended sword arm. He gasped. Someone leapt in, turning the blow aside with their shield. They brought their sword around and through, chopping and chopping, using their sword more like an axe.

"Feel the fucking terror in the air!" the man cried.

Cries and shrieks reinforced his battle cry. Another Badonnian fell as Tristain's sword opened his neck. Blood jetted out of the wound. An axe planted in his shield, jarring his arm. His attacker cried out. The axe was stuck. He cried out again as Tristain planted steel in his belly. His face contorted in pain as he coughed blood onto Tristain's face.

Tristain turned to face another, yelling in fury. A sickening crunch rang out as his opponent's helmet caved in from a hammer. At Tristain's rear, someone caught a spear in their gut. They were pressed in, and troops on both sides fell as the tide went back and forth.

He felt his cheek open, recoiling and grunted in anger, bringing his sword to bear. A shove, a grab for his shield. Tristain ripped the shield away, slashing wildly. There was no room for finesse. Stab, stab, stab. Stab until they stop moving. Deep inside, he wished he had a spear. But swords were weapons for knights—and knights in training. It was a matter of pride and tradition. Who was he to say no to tradition?

The battle went on for Gods knew how long. Exhaustion came for Tristain, until he couldn't lift his shield anymore. He felt the battle open behind him. He stumbled back. Breaths came shallow and quick. This wasn't his first battle, but it was his first with so many casualties on either side. Despite their year of isolation, starvation and disease, the Badonnians were still putting up a fierce fight.

A discordant horn blew from behind. He turned. Hundreds of knights in black plate streamed in from the north. He glimpsed a red flag with a black lion *rampant*. The arms were not familiar, though red and black meant they were Annaltian. Annaltia, their northern brethren. From what he knew, the Annaltians were in Annaltia. *Are they here to help us?*

The Annaltians formed a wedge. Tristain admired their discipline and their tactical genius. A wedge now would destroy what remained of the Badonnian line.

The knights charged into their rear. The Osbergian rear. Tristain gawped. Frantic shouts rang out as panic set in. Tristain's countrymen were taken by surprise. White hot pain shot up through Tristain's chest. He twisted his face as he turned back. A spear shaft stuck out from his breast. It planted deep in his sternum, nicking a rib.

His skin prickled with fury. *Oh, Gods.* The surrounding crush slowed. His stomach lurched. His vision narrowed. He thanked Ginevra the change was less painful this time.

LEON HEARD SHOUTING. HE came to the edge of the cage, kicking a rotten bit of cabbage out of the way. Panicked cries echoed as camp followers and injured men ran, those that could. A mighty roar sounded in the distance, but still loud enough to be heard. *Huh?* A flaming arrow whacked into the dirt nearby. *Fuck.* A knight in black plate galloped past. What was happening? There weren't no Annaltians here. *Shit.* He kicked over his slop bucket, sending foul smelling brown over the ground.

"*Hey!*" He smacked the bucket on the bars. It made a clanging noise. "Someone get me out!"

The fire from the arrow spread, igniting dry straw on the ground. Even though it had rained two weeks past, it had been dry since. The ground was waiting to go up—a few hours of wet that long ago wasn't enough to stop that. Leon banged furiously.

"*Someone get me the fuck out!*"

BLOOD HAZED AROUND TRISTAIN. The air was thick with violence. He raged, thrashed, destroyed. Friend and foe alike fell to his claws, teeth, strength. The battle thinned on both sides as the black beast felled them. Those who weren't killed ran.

The air vibrated with a sudden eruption. A head-sized boulder, thrown by great engine, brought down a tower above. The side crumbled, filling the air with a cloud of dust. He felt something strike the side of his head, and the world went black.

C AEN LIFTED A ROCK off a boy from the Twentieth. The poor lad had a mangled leg beneath, his tibia poking from flesh. The boy went stiff, falling silent. Caen looked down. Short, white feathers prodded from his chest. *Shit.* Caen threw his shield up.

A bolt chunked into the wood. He flinched as the narrow bolthead poked through. It was only a thin layer of dyed cloth covering a few planks, after all. The dust cloud resolved, and he'd lost sight of the beast. He thanked Sigur for that.

Now he had a new problem, in the form of twenty crossbowmen in black and red, fresh to the fight. He stepped back, hiding behind his shield. One bolt. Another. He cried out, a bolt stabbing into his arm. He jumped behind a fallen chunk of wall and breathed again, yanking the bolt out. Vredevoort in his steel came clambering into sight, bloody and limping. Dead of all colors surrounded him. He raised his sword.

Behind his helm, he bellowed, "*For Sigur—*"

A bolt cut him off, punching through his leg plate. He howled, push-ing onward regardless. Two more bolts. The Grim dropped to his knees, and the third one finished him. Caen looked up. Vultures circled above, patiently waiting for their meal. *Piss off. I'm not fucking dead yet.*

The wall cracked open again, hit with another boulder. Somehow, the siege engines were still going. Caen coughed, dust rippling over him. *Now, you idiot!* He ran for it, diving over the rubble.

The dust settled, and Caen found himself inside the walls of Rennes. *Now what?*

T RISTAIN'S HEAD POUNDED AS he awoke in the dust-covered street. His helmet was gone, and his armor in pieces. He rolled over and groaned. Slowly, it came back to him. He'd been knocked out when the tower fell. He crawled, getting to his feet. Rubble blocked the gate. With no other choice, he went the other way. *Maybe I can find a postern gate. Get out of here.*

"Monster!"

Tristain looked around. An Osbergian had his sword pointed at him, trembling. Tristain's heart sank. He'd seen him transform.

"Die, devil!" The soldier swung his blade.

Tristain leapt back. He patted his side. No weapon. *Shit.* He tripped, letting out a grunt as he landed.

"Sigur, give me strength," his attacker yelled as he raised his blade.

Tristain closed his eyes. This was it. You lived your life and tried to survive a fucking curse. Then some prick does you in because he thinks you're a monster.

He heard a cry and something warm spattered his face. He opened a single eye, unsure whether he would see his death barreling down on him. The soldier gasped, clutching at his chest. Steel flashed, and the man dropped.

Caen came into sight behind. "I think Leon would have my head if I let you die," he said, pulling Tristain to his feet.

"Caen? What in Ginevra's name are you doing here?"

"What does it look like, squire? Making us even. C'mon. We need to go."

Tristain dragged his heels.

Caen turned. "What are you doing?"

Tristain felt an overwhelming ache in his chest as his lip quivered. "Why? Why do you care? I'm a monster."

"Look, I'm no priest, and I'm not here to pass judgment. But right now, it's only a matter of time before the Renneans, Annaltians or, Gods forbid, fuckin' Sigur comes for us. We need to go."

"Go where?"

"The army's done for. Ginevra knows why, but the Annaltians are tearing us to shreds. Both Waters and the Grim're dead. I wouldn't 've believed it had I not seen it myself."

"Gods... The general?"

"Probably dining with Sigur already. Let's fucking go."

Tristain pushed down his fear and followed Caen. They clambered over the rubble, following a line of fleeing peasants out of the city.

"Down!" Caen dropped prone into the long weeds.

Tristain went down as well. A group of black armored horsemen rode through, carving their way through the peasants. A flash of blades, and their screams went silent. Tristain felt his breath hot against the weedy ground. He wondered how much blood would water these wildflowers. *They might even develop a taste for it.*

Caen lifted his head and moved it on a swivel. "Let's go."

The camp was soon within spitting distance. Fortunately, the Annaltians were so preoccupied with butchering the assault force that they left any deserters alone. *Imagine if Father could see me now, running like a coward.*

They rounded a building. Tristain's feet ached—it was then he realized that his transformation had torn his boots to shreds. He ran on bare feet, cut up by the gravel and dry ground. "I need to find some boots. Where in Sigur's name are we going?"

"I was hoping you might know," Caen yelled back.

I can't go home. Not to how things were. Father would hang me if he discovered I'd deserted.

Tristain came to a halt just as a squad of spearman in black passed.

"Hide," Tristain hissed. They hid behind a wall.

"*Attack!*" the head of the squad led a charge into the parade ground in front of them. Screams and shouts came over the wall.

Tristain breathed hard. He and the corporal looked at each other shamefully. Creeping along the wall, the battle grew louder. Hitting the ground from the around the corner, a servant fell all bloody. Tristain held his breath as a spear came down. The shaft twisted in his guts, and the servant stopped moving.

The clash grew quiet, and they crept along further. Rounding the corner, death unfolded before them. It was a massacre. The camp followers who remained were mostly servants armed with tools. The few men-at-arms that had remained behind—to guard the camp from a counterattack by the Badonnians—had been slain. The spearmen disappeared behind a barrack, marching back towards the parade ground.

Tristain swallowed hard, leaning down. Sheathing his sword, Caen came to his side, rifling through their pouches. Tristain blinked, watching Caen as he took two pieces of silver, placing them in his own belt pouch.

"You gonna' stand there staring, or you gonna' help," the corporal said. "We need coin if we're gonna eat. Gotta survive. Not like they need it, not anymore."

Tristain looked over the dead. Something felt wrong. "Are we to be cursed?"

"Sigur strike me if there's something wrong with it." Nothing happened. "See?"

Tristain sighed. Ten coins they found in total. Enough for a few tavern meals. *I need a weapon, too.* He found a sword that had a few nicks but was otherwise well-balanced and sharp, and a pair of worn boots, but they did the job and fit well.

"Good," Caen said. "Let's go."

They ran for the stables, hoping one or two horses would still be there. Even a pony would've been enough to get them to the nearest village. They'd be stuck in Badonnia, but anywhere was better than this field of death.

Tristain heard a shout in Annaltian. He looked behind. Smoke rose above a line of tents, toward the parade ground. *They're razing everything to the ground.* An arrow hit the ground to the side of them.

"Run!"

They bolted. Tristain turned. A black rider kicked up dust behind him, hot on their tails. The enormous destrier under the rider bared down on them. An alleyway appeared between two buildings. They ducked down it. Caen threw open an armory door and they headed inside. Chest and legs aching, Tristain leaned against the wall as Caen shut the door.

"Quiet," Caen hissed. They were silent, the sound of their breath the only noise. Then came the brief sound of hooves clattering on dirt. Tristain willed his breath quiet. He slid his sword from its scabbard, as Caen did. The door creaked open. Heavy clanks of plate foretold the rider's entrance.

"*Du kannst dich nicht verstecken,*" he said. The voice muffled stupidly under his helmet. *You cannot hide.*

Caen swung his weapon, catching the Annaltian off-guard. He caught the blade in his lobster-shell gauntlet. Smashed Caen in the face with the other. They wrestled and Tristain drove his sword through a gap at the back of his knee. Yelling, the knight fell forward in a crash of metal. He tried to pull himself up, seething beneath his helmet.

Tristain found the gap between his breastplate and arm-plate and drove the point in, cutting through the mail and jacket. The knight grunted, twitched, died. Blood leaked from beneath the breastplate.

Caen chuckled slightly, wiping red from his mouth. "Thanks. Eme's tits. Bastard should know better than to turn his back."

Tristain eyed the blood dripping through the floorboards. "That's a knight. I just killed an imperial knight."

"No shit."

"I'm a deserter, too. And a demon. How many men have I killed?"

"Maybe they'll tell you his name when they're hanging you for it."

"Hmph. Don't know about you, but I don't plan on sticking around for that."

"Me neither." Caen stuck his head out of the doorway. "Let's go."

Tristain spied the knight's blade, a longsword with a ring pommel. Set in the center of the gilt cross-guard was a polished sapphire. He eyed it enviously. He drew it from its scabbard. It was well balanced, perfectly weighted. *Stealing from the dead, now? You've pilfered a bit of silver. What's a sword?*

He stepped outside, ring-pommeled sword in hand, duty arming sword tucked into his belt. The knight's giant destrier waited where he'd left it. Shouts came from elsewhere, and he could hear sounds of battle within the camp. Someone was fighting back.

"Let's see..." He walked up to the beast. The horse whinnied, clearly expecting another master. Tristain brushed his hand. *It's not biting or bucking, so that's a good sign.*

"*Sie angreifen!*" someone bellowed. Tristain turned his head. The twenty spearmen in black came rushing at them.

"Get on!"

He climbed on the horse, taking the reins with one hand. He pulled Caen into the saddle. The beast whinnied in protest, but after some cajoling, took off.

They sped along, flitting between buildings. This was nothing like his other horse. This was a beast bred for war and he had to fight to keep it under control. Eventually, they neared the edge of the camp. Tristain heard fighting. He turned his head for a quick look.

Behind them, beside a barrack that was now an inferno, they saw a pale, red-bearded man in sackcloth fighting off a group of axe men. It was Sir Vorland. The two swore.

The copse outside camp and freedom beyond opened out to them. Only screams and fires lay behind them. The horse pulled, wanting to run, to be free of this place. No one was chasing them. They could ride away, and no one would follow them. *No. No more running.*

"We have to help him," Tristain said.

"What are you fucking waiting for," Caen replied. "Permission?"

Tristain dug his heels in, wheeling the destrier around. The horse kicked up dust as it took off.

The Annaltians were taken by surprise. The sapphire-set blade flashed as Tristain charged, yelling. The destrier knocked an axeman down. Tristain sliced a hand off. Another swing severed a neck. He slashed wildly. Caen jumped off, cutting away with his blade.

Leon blinked in surprise. He snatched an axe off the ground, jumping into the fray.

Fending his attackers off, Tristain felt the horse lift, rearing and kicking. He held on for dear life. *Shit.* An axe came down on his leg. He blocked it, spinning around and planting his sword through his foe's face. The last one fell as Leon cut him down.

Tristain caught his breath, his legs, arms, shoulders burning from exertion.

Leon panted, helping Caen to his feet. "Nice sword," he said. "Nice horse."

Tristain nodded, climbing down. Leon laughed, throwing his arms around him.

"Good to see you, lad."

Tristain groaned. The knight with melons for biceps squeezed the ever-loving life out of him.

Tristain stumbled as he released him. "And you, Sir. I'm sorry we didn't come for you sooner, and about the ale—"

"Ah, forget it. Sigur's blessings that we're all uninjured. Now... I'm done with this place."

They found their way to the stables. Only a sumpter and a shabby pony remained.

"Sir—" Tristain held the destrier's reins to his knight.

"No, squire. You've earned it."

Out they rode, smoke clouds blowing along their path to the Pass. Tristain looked back. Rennes was aflame. A stream of black dots rode through the camp. They cut men down where they stood. He swallowed. They were the few that remained, a long way from home. *Has the world gone insane?* He supposed it had. A myth lived inside him. A civil war. The Annaltians served no master but themselves—Rennes burned under their torch as well. Perhaps it was the same disease inside Tristain, turning these men into monsters.

"Tristain," Leon said, pulling him back. "Come. The leviathan awaits, and then home."

14

MEMORIES

LEVITUM, 1043

The South Hills are the wildest of the wilds. Kings, queens, and emperors have all tried to enforce their reign on the place, only to find that hillmen stubbornness far exceeds their patience.

— GERAINT FALLSTADT, EMPEROR'S HISTORIAN

WHEN SHE TRAVELED, DIANA liked to avoid small villages. Distrust and superstition imposed themselves on their visitors, and nasty folk usually congregated together. Especially in the South Hills. People would behead you for staring at them wrong—not that Diana couldn't handle herself, of course. The advice for people living out in the Hills was: don't.

A few pitiful fields clung together around the village like curdled milk and beyond that, in every direction, stretched forest. Wild country, well past the archduke's reach. The mountain range of the South Hills grew towards the horizon in pale granite and snow above the tree line.

The air stank something foul. A crooked palisade, like a mouth full of bad teeth, surrounded an animal-churned circle of dirt, ringed by a few houses. Several outbuildings flirted with a logging site nearby. A dog barked in the distance, and as they pulled closer, she heard the frantic scream of a woman. The crying of a child and swearing. Soren sent Nials ahead to investigate.

Diana pulled alongside Soren. "What do you think it is?" She shifted in her saddle, her arse having long gone numb from the day's ride, the day before, and the day before that.

"That screaming means only one thing in the Hills."

Diana grimaced. People inflicted themselves on each other in the South Hills, they said. Neighbors and friends; the worst enemies. That was why everyone lived so far away from each other.

The screaming stopped as Nials disappeared. Then dust blew over the set of buildings, and Nials galloped out of the village, followed by a group of riders in red and silver. Twenty of them, she counted. Diana recognized the arms as the Count of Esstadt's. The image of a fluttering banner stuck in her mind, that day on the lists, when Tristain fought bravely—

No. That's not you, not anymore. He's gone, dead in Badonnia. Face-down in the muck.

She clenched her jaw, cursing Sigur under her breath. If only she could've seen him once more before then, even just to say goodbye.

"Ho," the horseman at the front cried. All of them wore armor, mail and padded jackets, prickling with lances and boar spears. Atop their heads were open-faced bascinets, glinting faintly in the gray sky. They came to a stop thirty paces away.

"Who would you be?" the one at the front called.

"Inquisitor Sorenius of the Most Holy Order of the Golden Sword," he said. "And you're in our way."

"This man thinks he's a king, by the look of it," one of the ill-tempered interlocutors remarked.

"Well, Inquisitor arse-licker, you're in *our* path. We are the Count of Ineluss's men, the Count von Pfalzberg. And your men are interfering with a royal decree that permits us, as the reach of the count's arm, and the archduke's arm in turn, to levy taxes from the people. We were doing just that before you arrived."

"All the men are dead, Inquisitor," Nials said. "These bastards killed the husbands and took the wives."

Diana's hand tightened around the reins. When she relaxed, she noticed Soren's hands do the same. He didn't answer.

"They refused to pay, simple as that," the leader said. "In the Hills, you take what's offered. I would think it's none of your business, Holy Arseling. The Order is concerned with wolfmen, no? None here. So, remove your arses from our path or von Pfalzberg will hear of it."

"And what of the children?" Sorenius said.

"Three boys tied up. None else."

"Good. Kill these men."

Diana drew her crossbow, gladly.

The count's men reared their horses in shock, trying to arrange themselves. Diana fired a bolt, punching one between the eyes. She dropped the crossbow, let it hang by the loop off her belt, and in rapid succession she threw knives at the men, killing three more.

Before they could draw their swords, Tansy studded two with five bolts apiece, her machine crossbow making loud sucking noises, like the inflating of a bellows, but sharper. Nials leapt off the back of his horse and came down, sword first, on the leader's back. He screamed.

Manus, the big man in plate, drew his giant two-hander, and pushed his equally giant destrier on, swinging a blow that curled the air and made it sing. The blade moved through the air faster than seemed possible. Split one man in two and had half the head of another man who was unlucky enough to be nearby.

Soren's horse bucked as one stabbed it through the chest with his boar spear. Sullen roared in pain and went over on his side. Soren flipped off the saddle as the beast fell. Almost danced in the air, then came to land on his attacker's horse behind him. Had his head nearly sawn off in a ring of steel and screams. Close work.

Diana leaned forward in her saddle to push on, throwing knife after knife. More men dropped. Half-dead men laid in their own filth. Half of them fought on, eyes hanging out of their heads, mouths cut open. Chests, guts. Keep killing. That's all she needed to do.

She leapt off her horse, came down with her sidearm. The dagger. Something hard struck her in the side, deflected off her plates. She killed that one and went on. Her arm ached, sweat filled her eyes. She twisted a knife again, into a gullet this time. Found things. That's all she did. Pink things, and she stabbed until they stopped moving, stopped breathing.

Blood filled the gulch next to the road, a tribute to the God that looked over her. A tribute to Sigur, who gave her strength. Diana could save this land from monsters, and the Order had given her the power to do so. In His name.

She panted as the sun filled her eyes again, wet and shadowy. No, that made no sense. Sweat filled her eyes, blurred the sun. Her hand tightened around the dagger, and she wiped her face. They were all dead.

Except one. The last one wheeled his horse around and fled. He beat down the road, back the way he'd come. Tansy aimed a shot. He was nearly past the buildings, more than forty paces away, already. Diana breathed. The bolt would miss. They'd have to catch him—

Click-thwock-thwock. Two bolts punched through his horse's flank, and the creature reared, casting off the rider. Free of its burden, the beast raced off past the village, presumably to die somewhere. The rider crawled forward, clearly winded, groaning, grasping for air.

Nials cleaned his blade on a dead man's tabard. "What should we do with him?"

Soren nodded. "These men were lycans. You saw it yourself," he said. He walked up to the one who'd run, and Diana followed. She bared her teeth, seething. She wondered if this man had touched the women, too.

"What about the count?" Tansy said. Manus came up behind, hefted his greatsword over his shoulders. It dripped red.

"This one'll tell the count that one of his fellows was a demon, and us Swords came by to save them." Soren turned over the man with his foot.

He looked no older than twenty, and stunk of shit, had brown on the braies under his hose. He nodded his head rapidly. "Yeah, I'll tell him that."

"Sadly, we didn't arrive in time to save them all, and it was a great confusion. We had to cut down a few of them to save ourselves, since we were afraid the corruption had spread."

The count's man nodded. "Got it."

"Good. Go on, run. Go tell him."

Scrambling to his feet, Tansy and Nials cackled with laughter as the count's man ran, waddled, heavy in the rear from that brown.

"Alright, form up," Soren said. "Take the horses and the children."

They continued into the village. Diana remounted Eda and now moved through the buildings. A few of the women cried out as they tried to stop their boys from being taken.

"What will happen to them?" Diana asked Soren.

"They'll be taken to the Citadel, to train. Their mothers should be proud, with them given a chance to have a proper life without their fathers. They'll be compensated, which makes the medicine easier to swallow. Hey!" he called. He took a purse from his belt and gave it to a woman, and she nodded tearfully.

"It's strange," Diana said. "Why kill the men?"

"These kinds of men have no scruples. They're godless. They were taking their payment from the women right before we arrived."

"Nothing wrong with a bit of rough-and-tumble, now and then," Tansy added, giggling.

Diana turned. *Did she take a tumble and smack her head in the fight?* On their journey, Tansy and Nials had kept to themselves, along with that big Manus fellow. That had suited Diana just fine.

"It's the heriot, milord," one woman said. She was old and had an air of authority about her gray hairs. None of her clothes were torn, unlike the others.

They looked at her. "Heriot?" Diana asked.

"They'd been asking it from everyone from Norstraad to Lichheim. But we thought our simple village would escape their notice. It's a tax. They take it from the dead, like vultures."

Nials gave a flinty smile. "It only gets worse for you hillmen, doesn't it?"

Soren cleared his throat. "Let's move on. We'll send these boys ahead to the nearest church, where the priests there can send them on to the Citadel."

"The nearest church be Esstadt, milord."

15

KNIVES

LEVITUM, 1043

*If demonic influence spreads beyond the immediate vicinity
of the hive, to the town or the village at large,* exterminatus *is
required. This entails a cleansing of the entire area to return it
to Sigur's light.*

— LORD NOTARIUS GIAN ADALLA

KNIVES HAD AN HONESTY to them that people could never match. Heriots and death taxes and thieving, raping men-at-arms aside, a knife lets you know the truth of something. If it cut, you bled. If you held it wrong, bounced it off a rib as you shoved it in a chest, you jarred your hand. And it didn't matter if you only had one hand. Sort of the point, really. Cut, stab, parry, throw. That was about the length of things for Diana.

Which was far more than could be said for the people of Esstadt when Diana and the other Swords entered the town. They came out armed, staring at the strangers riding the muck-filled road to the center of the town. Out of lopsided hovels and from behind busted doors. Insects trilled a low hum in the full heat of aestiva, Solni suspended in the cloudless sky. But then it wasn't cloudless, as she looked down. Nipping at the horizon like dogs at its heels were black threats of a storm.

Diana's nose stung with the full punch of the town's stench as they passed a little road shrine, this one dedicated to Eme, protector of travelers. Flowers had been placed at the foot of the shrine. The sculptor had poured the goddess's curves into a tight kirtle, all the stranger for the modesty of the piece. Usually, Eme was depicted as naked. Nearly always. At least in Invereid, and Ostelar, and everywhere else. The distraction proved no remedy for the smell of the place, and certainly the bright flowers, laid there like on an old grave, covered nothing.

Houses emptied their contents like a drunk emptied a tankard into his mouth. Folk carried hatchets, scythes, knives, and sneering looks almost as deadly.

"Get out a' here!" a woman yelled. More yells followed.

A low giggle, like the noise from a hissing adder, came from Nials's mouth.

"Sigur brings the judgment," he said.

Tansy clicked her tongue. "Guilty, guilty, guilty."

Sorenius followed that with a quick, "Hold your tongues. I'll do the talking."

Ending abruptly, like a poor lover, the road came to a halt at the foot of what looked to be a rathaus. Well, what passed for a rathaus in the Hills, which was nothing more than a house that sat fat on the eye by being even more ramshackle and tacked-on than the rest.

An unshaven, flaxen-haired man pushed open the rathaus door with his foot and stepped out. He made some motion to the people around them, and Diana thought of that old expression: *the wolf hunts in packs*, and she knew this man posed the greatest danger out of all of them—werewolves aside. At his hip he carried a flanged mace, the symbol of his office. The sheriff, invested by the count's authority.

Soren pulled up his new horse, a brown gelding taken from the count's men, thirty paces from the man. The rathaus's courtyard—if it could be called that—was little more than a throwing of lime and dirt, baked by the heat and rutted with time. Like this bastard land and its bastard people. Half-starved dogs raced each other, barking and snarling, and skidded to a halt at the crowd's edge. Even the animals here hated them. Diana could easily kill one with her crossbow, and Tansy's engine-crossbow would make quick work of the rest of them. It might even be a mercy.

"Well met," Soren said. "I am Inquisitor Sorenius, vested with the authority of the almighty Lightfather, and the duty to pursue all His enemies. Announce yourself."

"I am Rutger of Esstadt," he said, making himself taller. He had a deep, resonant voice. "Known in these parts as the Giver." The Giver might've been a name to drape on a priest, or a gentle man of good breeding. This man was neither.

Skin the color of onions, he was flecked with the grays of middle age, graced with the broad, wide chest of a swordsman. His blond hair cared little for a razor, settling long around his shoulders. A red-specked beard jutted from his chin.

"I know what you are, Sword. The Order aren't welcome here."

More hillmen filed into the flanks. Diana put her hand on the stock of her crossbow.

"By the decree of His Holiness, Pontiff Benedictus, the sixth of his name, as named at the Council of Istrya—"

Someone threw a rock, and it struck Soren's horse, causing the beast to reel and whinny in pain. Diana lifted her crossbow and leveled it on the crowd, cheeks searing with anger.

"Easy, Warden," Nials said, in a voice that told her *we'll get our chance, soon enough.*

Soren caught his horse, pulled it back around. He ignored the attack. "The Council of Istrya in 445 gives us the power to seize and question any suspected to be involved with harboring demons."

"No demons here, friend. See, I know my laws too, and you don't need to be comin' here with them expensive low-country words. The council's decree says you haven't got four wheels on your cart if there's no demons here."

"We have leave to arbitrate the level of demonic influence, however."

"Isn't nothing demonic about the right people getting what they deserve."

"What they deserve?"

"Aye, we have had some attacks here. But they have got only thieves and rapers. I see no problem with that. They all deserve it."

"It's the gods intervenin'," a man said.

"Takin' out evil people." Someone else. "They're servants of the gods."

"These people have the right of it. Like I said, there isn't anything demonic going on here."

Diana's thoughts roiled, caught like a bird in a storm. "Are you justifying what they've done? Werewolves kill and maim without discrimination."

"Yeah," the sheriff said, like it was a forgone conclusion. "Discriminate to the right people. Isn't no one good in this village that's been ate."

Diana tightened her mouth. Tears stung her eyes. She pointed to her arm.

"A demon clawed my arm off. Are you saying I deserved it?"

"If you're askin', I'd say aye. You're Order. Nothing makes me smile more than hearing that you got done."

Diana blinked. She couldn't believe her ears. Anger punched through her chest. Never in her life had she felt such rage—like the heat of a blazing pyre. If they were talking about what was deserved, this bastard deserved a fucking bolt through his lungs. She thought about doing it herself.

Soren spoke. "If you have nothing to hide, you won't mind my questions."

For a moment, only the wind replied. Diana eyed the sheriff who watched Soren in turn. Only the three of them existed in the world.

"You know the old gods?" the sheriff said finally. His scarred hand fingered the mace at his belt. "I suppose you wouldn't. It's a hillman tale."

"We don't need to know your cunting tales," Tansy said.

"Tell us where the fucking werewolves are, before we slit your throat," Nials added.

"When Sigur and Eme and Ginevra, even Veles, were but babes in their cribs, or so the legends go, the Continent went by another name in another tongue. A tongue better suited for a wolf's mouth than a man's."

Tansy giggled. "This man's crazier than a whore with her tits cut off."

"I can see we're getting nowhere," Soren said. "If you won't comply, we'll be forced to take aggressive action."

The sheriff stiffened, closed his hand around the haft of his mace. "I've heard the Order put whole towns to the torch. It's time someone—"

A sharp, sucking noise. Diana jumped. A bolt plunged through the sheriff's throat. He gurgled. As he opened his mouth, blood vomited out. He dropped head first on the hard-packed ground with a crunch.

Tansy giggled, lowered her crossbow. "We weren't getting nowhere with him."

Numbed by shock, the folk took a moment to groan and sigh. Diana smiled at the dead man.

"Kill 'em!" someone screamed. All hell broke loose.

A blockheaded man roared and charged Diana with his hands, grabbing hold of her leg. She kicked out savagely at him, dashing his mouth in. He reeled back, gushing blood. Another man took his place armed with a hatchet. He charged in at the same time as a woman with a chopping knife. Diana jerked Eda on with a "Hya!" and wheeled around.

The sucking noise of Tansy's crossbow underscored the screaming and the anger. Folk of Esstadt dropped, set upon by quarrels. Some ran. But in the small courtyard, horses and crossbows were useful only to a point.

Diana turned too sharp. Eda lurched, and Diana lost her grip on the reins. The mare bucked, shrieking, and she fell out of the saddle.

The world tumbled. Faces screamed by as she landed hard on her arm.

"Get your fucking warden!" Nials yelled.

The air buzzed around Diana's head. She threw her head forward and the glint of something metal shot past. An axe head, right where her head would've been. She scrambled back, kicked herself onto her feet, and crashed into something hard. The back of her head flared with pain. Her eyes streamed with tears.

She honed her mind. These people meant to kill her—peasant folk or not. Hesitation for a moment meant death.

They're all demons, anyway. As surely as they held the curse themselves.

She pirouetted, drawing her dagger. It sunk to the hilt as it bit into a man's ear. He jabbered and turned limp, the iron fireplace poker falling from his hands. Her hand ached from her fall, and she lost her grip on the handle. She ducked a swing from a hatchet, jumped back from a falling shovel.

Her dagger kept her honest. She had no chance in this fight. Not in the thick of it.

A great scream of metal rang out. The man with the hatchet and his two fellows split in two. One was cleaved at the waist while the other was opened at the shoulder. Blood bathed her face, spat into her eyes. Behind them, the thundering plate and giant sword of Manus. He'd saved her.

She wiped her face, then something hard bit into her side. She reeled and turned. A scythe, point curving out. She danced out of reach as the nasty looking fucker who got her came around for another blow. Fingers found their marks in her jacket. She tossed a knife and lodged it in his eye. He howled, hands scraping around. He dropped the scythe. She ran up and snatched it from the floor. In the same motion, she drove it up beneath his chin, hooking the point through his mouth. Like a fish.

She pulled him forward and off his feet. He slammed into the dirt. She ended it with a swift kick to the knife still stuck in his eye and he dropped dead.

She checked her side. The scythe cut through the cloth of her jacket, the wadding, but not the plate beneath. She sighed in relief. As she stood there, she trembled for the heat in her blood. She could barely breathe.

Townsfolk were slain left and right. Men, women, children. It did not matter. They all met their ends. A townsman crashed into a clay pot, trying to escape Nials's blade. Water went everywhere as the pot broke into dozens of pieces. The man slipped in the mud as he tried to crawl away. Nials kicked the man in the head, flipped him onto his back. He grinned wildly as he plunged his sword into the man's stomach. Manus's blade danced through flesh and bone as easily as cutting butter with a hot knife. People fell apart, in stinking pieces. A woman cried as her baby laid limp and gray in her arms, the fletching of a bolt sticking from its side. The woman soon fell after, catching a bolt to the neck.

All the chaos appeared to move in slow motion. She found her dagger in the mess, planted the sole of her boot against the jaw of the man she'd lodged it in. For safekeeping. She fixed her hand around the handle and yanked. His head shifted as it came with difficulty. It loosened with a popping, sucking noise, and she pulled it out.

A man raced across Diana's path. She stabbed him through the chest. He cried out—eyes wide in terror.

She looked down at her hand. It quivered pink and bloody.

A roar shook her from her reverie. A blur of dark shapes and four werewolves scrambled, fighting back against Nials and Tansy. They were cut off. Manus raced after them, quick, but not quick enough. The two Swords would die.

Three men closed in around her. Impossible to tell if they meant harm to her, she just stabbed and kicked. One dropped, clutching at his chest, gasping for air. Threw out a knife, ripped her hand against the jacket, came away with nothing. Blood in her eyes. She swung the dagger and caught a man's arm, hard enough he dropped his hatchet. He fell. The last one pulled her forward by the neck, other hand around her knife arm. Her eyes hurt with the pressure. She twisted out of the grip on her hand. When she freed herself, her blade came down like hard rain on his neck, forcing his other hand off.

Something made a huge crashing sound. Shrieking as heat poured over them.

"Diana!" Soren yelled, gripping her by the shoulders. He dragged her away from the massacre, behind a house. People fled down the wide streets, screaming. She still heard cries from behind the building.

"What are you *doing*?"

Her mind hadn't caught up yet. Eme's tits, she'd really fucked up. Fire roiled over the courtyard. A werewolf shrieked, burning like a pyre, slapped his back trying to put himself out. The stench of burning flesh and hair made her sick. She watered the dry-packed dirt with the contents of her stomach.

As she lifted her head, she said, "What *is* that?"

"Liquid fire," Soren answered. A man rushed him, and he turned, making quick work of the man's throat with a single thrust of his estoc. Compared to her, his movements were graceful and effortless, even in this chaos. "Come! We need to find a more defensible position." He stuck his head around the wall.

"This is the place," she said. Esstadt was a hive of cursed beings and their sympathizers.

"What?"

He looked back, his comely face like a beautiful white rose smattered in blood. A knife as sharp as anything, and honest. His look made her breath stop.

I could never love anything, not after I left Tristain to die. And I won't get obsessed, like a little girl at a pretty smile from a stableboy. But she cared deeply for him, the man that cared enough to pull her from certain death, time and time again. She realized the Order had given her more than she ever imagined.

"The rathaus," she said, moving alongside him. "See there?"

The fighting blazed in the center of the courtyard, but beyond that, a gulch broke before the rathaus, while the building itself overlooked the entire square.

"You're right," he said. "It's defensible. We just need to break through."

"Do you have more of that liquid fire?"

He yanked a ceramic gourd from his belt. The last one. "One more. We'll make it count."

"You'd think these hillmen would give it up after seeing their neighbors killed."

"You would think."

"Ready?"

He nodded. They raced out of their hiding spot towards the rathaus. The hillmen had given up, in fact, only a few stubborn bastards still fighting in the courtyard, clashing with Tansy and Nials.

But the werewolves fought on. Three of them surrounded Manus—he swept his blade in wild arcs to keep them at bay.

One snapped its wolfen head around and snarled. It doubled over on all fours, charging them.

Diana ran with Soren. He threw the gourd. It hit the ground with a crunch. Fire roiled upwards, casting an arc toward the leaping werewolf. Flames licked its belly but didn't catch it. Diana dived out of the way as the beast landed with a skid along the ground. Claws caught a fist of her hair, yanking it out. Pain scraped across her scalp. She growled.

Soren yelled, "On high!"

He stood ten paces away. The werewolf skittered along the dry ground, between them, hair between its fingers. *On high!* Anger boiled her belly. She ran for the werewolf, dodged a quick slash of claws.

Eight paces.

She kicked her legs forward. Sliding beneath the beast. She lashed out with her dagger, two fast blows. The demon yelped in surprise. It did nothing, but the effort was for the shock more than anything else.

Four paces.

She rolled, heard the whoosh of a claw behind her. She landed on her feet and kept running. Soren waited for her with his palms braced against his knees.

Two paces.

She sheathed her dagger and unhooked her crossbow.

Now!

She jumped and planted both her feet against his hands. He tossed her. The world spun across her sight. She dropped her hand. The werewolf looked up. Black eyes, wide. She could have said... terrified.

She soared over. Took aim. The beast swiped a claw up, skimmed the stock. It wasn't enough. She depressed the trigger, smiled. As the demon opened its mouth to roar, the bolt slipped straight into it.

She landed hard on her side and rolled, her hand forced open. The crossbow went clattering violently nearby. She looked up, pain shooting through her neck where she'd struck the ground.

The werewolf stumbled, making a horrible choking noise. Then it raced off, bounding over them. Diana flinched. When it landed, it landed hard. Crashing to its knees, it pulled desperately at its throat. Claws tore into flesh. Scrabbling horribly and wincing in pain, its movements dulled. Then it crashed forward into the dirt, dead. A mercy.

Something to keep the creatures honest. It wasn't a knife, but a weapon that did short work—poison. Adder venom.

Out of the corner of her eye, something moved. A man. She drew her dagger and pushed up against his throat.

It was Nials. He breathed and laughed once the shock wore off.

"It's well, warden. Danger's over."

She looked around. Manus had pared the two werewolves open like apples, and they gushed stinking, black blood all over the dirt. He walked up and planted the end of his blade in the dirt, and came to a knee, leaning on the sword. Dark blood pooled between one of his plates, where it had been bent open, like opening a metal box to reach the goodies inside.

Tansy came over as well. Blood painted her face, and she smiled, only her yellowing teeth visible from beneath the crimson canvas. Like she'd bathed in it. Diana wouldn't have been surprised if she had.

Silence fell on them like dogs on a meaty bone. Diana lowered her arm. "What now?"

"We found and eliminated the werewolves," Soren said.

"What about the rest? They defended them."

"Yes... I'll send a letter to the Lord Inquisitor."

"A letter? This town needs to be given to the fire."

"You're getting ahead of yourself, Warden. Only Grand Inquisitor Vetterand and the emperor can sanction *exterminatus*."

She remembered a mention of it in her training. *Exterminatus*. The High Istryan word for extermination—complete removal of a hive of demons. Diana thought she saw scared, childlike eyes from behind shuttered windows. Maybe it was something said in anger—only those guilty deserved to be punished.

"Leave the children, if you can."

"Everyone is killed, Warden. That's the definition of it."

She nodded. The idea that *everyone* was killed made her balk at the brutality of it, and it made her conflicted. They'd protected, harbored, lived with the demons, and lied, tried to kill her and the others.

"It's unlikely it'll happen, anyway. It hasn't happened for twenty years. The emperor won't sanction them anymore."

"Congratulations, warden," Nials said. "You'll make an arbiter yet."

The high attack. Diana nodded. He leaned in close, giving her more of his hangdog, mangled look than she ever wanted. His breath stunk worse than the viscera that coated the ground. She grimaced.

"I've heard it before, this lycan worship. Think they can do no wrong, and they only kill those that deserve it. Horseshit, really. I never deserved this, either." He pointed to his face. "But you don't listen. And if they don't shut their mouths, you shove a blade in it."

There was nothing else to say. "Indeed."

16

THE FOOTFALLS

FERVUM, 1044

There're secrets in this world. Leviathan Pass and the Giants'
Footfalls are among two of them, hidden in plain sight. They
speak of a land that was once very different to our own.

— GERAINT FALLSTADT, EMPEROR'S HISTORIAN

TRISTAIN, LEON, AND CAEN ran their horses ragged. They rode far
as they could manage, through the night and another day. It seemed
like they'd outridden any pursuers. Night gripped them and Tristain's head
spun. He slowed. The world flipped until the sky became the ground and
his mouth filled with dirt. His head throbbed and he realized he hadn't
eaten for nearly two days.

The destrier snorted, grumpy at the constant riding. He found a tasty
shoot of ryegrass and was content. He was soon joined by the sumpter and
the pony. Tristain was helped to his feet. A fire was made, and Leon sat him
down. Tristain felt cold and beyond hungry. The fire helped.

"I don't think I ever thanked you, lad," Leon said. Tristain blinked lazily,
his vision blurry. He made a vague sound of agreement. The corporal
handed him a heel of bread. He didn't have a bag or a pouch. Tristain didn't
want to know where it came from.

"Here, *Althann*," the knight said. "Eat."

Slowly, things became normal again, as he ate. He didn't feel so faint. "What was that, Sir?"

"Don't think I forgot how you two saved my life," Leon replied. "Charging in like that was reckless, but still..."

"Don't forget it when you're back in the halls of good grace," Caen said.

Leon chuckled. "I don't see that happening anytime soon. The general will have almost certainly made my disgrace known; written a letter to the emperor to have my investiture rescinded. And even if she hasn't, people talk. Nothing sets tongues wagging like a disgraced knight."

They went quiet. Tristain took another bite of bread and broke the silence. "What will you do?"

"I'm not sure yet. I suppose I'll leave it to the gods for now. What about you, lad? What will you do?"

"I... I don't know. I don't even know what to make of it all. I'm a monster... some evil writhes inside, waiting to get out."

"Well," Caen said. "Do you *feel* evil?"

"I feel cold, despite the fire," Tristain said, hugging himself. Caen chuckled. "But no. I feel uncertain. Not quite like myself, but not evil either. My stomach turns at the thought of what I've done."

Leon leaned forward; his eyes cast in bright orange from the fire. "You remember what happened?"

"Not quite. I remember... I think I died. I felt impossibly cold, then a bonfire beneath me. The pain was... I can't describe. One part, I remember distinctly." Tristain held up his hand. "Claws came shooting out from beneath my fingernails. It felt like I was having them removed with pliers."

Caen shivered. Leon remained as stoic as ever.

"But after... it was like my whole body was filled with spirit, both in strength and feeling. I felt... better than anything. I killed those Badonnians, and I enjoyed it. At the time at least."

Caen laughed. "Those bastards deserved everything they got. I would've loved to 've seen their faces. I bet they didn't expect that."

"Neither did I. I suppose the priests would say I'm cursed."

"Let the priests and their incense-addled heads theorize what in the gods' name it means. We're alive because of you."

Tristain looked down at his feet. There was a lingering sense of shame about it, stirring deep inside.

"Lad," Leon said. "I can't say I know much about this, but I do know sometimes you can be a gloomy prick. You could've killed us too, and you didn't." He took the flask from his belt, giving it a swig.

"I guess that's true. There must be something inside, something holding me back."

"Let's get some rest," Leon said, wiping his mouth. "On the morrow we'll be nearer to the pass."

"How are we getting through? Isn't it full of... well, full of ours?"

"Yep. That's why you're not Tristain, son of Sebastian, or Caen son of... whoever the hell you're son of. Not Leon Vorland the Strong and his retinue anymore. I'm a farmer, and you're my two sons."

"Fuckin' blessed Ginevra," Caen said. "I've always wanted to know my father."

Tristain snorted with laughter.

"Yeah, and I'll spank you like your father should have," Leon replied. "Smart mouth."

"I expect we'll have to leave the destrier behind, too," Tristain said.

"You'd be right," the disgraced knight replied. "That warhorse'll give us away for miles. Even the pony might be a bit much."

Caen grumbled. "Right, so you get the only horse."

In the morning, they sent the destrier and the pony on. Perhaps they would live out their lives in the wild, or maybe they would fall prey to starving hunters or village folk. It was hard to say. Tristain thought of Onyx and Nikkel, and his letter for Selene. He wondered if Nikkel had made it Invereid already, although he only had a week or so on them.

By the time the sun was highest, they came upon a group of peasants driving an oxcart—two-wheeled and high-sided. *Farmers, by the look of them.* It was risky business considering the war raging around them, but determination on their faces made it clear they wouldn't be stopped. Some of the folk noticed their approach.

"Have a care," Leon said. "They might take us for outlaws."

Caen shot him a discourteous look. "We ain't?"

Leon stepped forward. He spoke in Badonnian, *"Buojour, sono vri?"* The ploy seemed to work as the headman turned his head and smiled at their approach. He said something back, and Leon conversed with him. They shared a laugh, and Leon turned his head to the other two and nodded.

"They're going to the pass," he whispered. "And they'll let us tag along. It's safer in numbers."

"Helps if they 'ave food," Caen replied. "Aye?"

Leon nodded.

T RISTAIN'S MUSCLES ACHED AS he tried to push the wagon through two peaty grooves, known as a road to the locals of the Footfalls. The Giant's Footfalls was a sparsely vegetated place, and sparsely developed at the best of times, and these were not the best of times. During the war it had been burned, and the trees that dotted the place were blackened. Soft peat under the oxcart's wheels had jammed it in place. Ash from fires. Weeds choked the fields around.

The Footfalls were sparse of most things, most of all people, which had bidden well for their travel to the Pass. Strange craterous formations made the land pockmarked. They looked like footprints of giants, hence the name. Eagles circled above, howling cries echoing across the barren place.

To the north were the wall of mountains that was the South Hills—south for an Osbergian—and the Avallano Mountains further south of that.

They gave up as the headman said something in Badonnian. Leon answered, and Tristain wished his tutor taught him the language before he left to join the war. Either way, Tristain soon realized what was happening as they broke off and started preparing a fire. Leon ushered him and Caen on.

"Let's get some firewood," he whispered in Osbergian. He kept his voice low, taking a swig of his flask. "Make ourselves useful."

Tristain nodded and followed.

Caen was close behind. "I thought I was gonna' shit my pants," he said as they moved out of earshot.

"That face you were pulling, Corporal, made me think you were pretty close," Tristain replied. "Let's just hope we make it to the Pass before too long. I can't keep answering their questions with a nod. They'll think I'm mute or something."

Caen nudged his elbow. "Let 'em think you've been mule-kicked in the head. Wouldn't be too far off."

Tristain blew his lips. "Shut up."

"Stop your yammering," Leon grumbled, belching. "Find some fuckin' firewood before I strangle you both."

Tristain scratched his head as he looked for good branches. He wondered what had brought on the knight's bad temper of late.

The headman, thankful for their bundles, offered them all a swig of a wineskin. Tristain took a sip. It was deeply acidic, like strongwine, but worse, and foamed around his lips. He coughed. They laughed.

"Soured milk," the headman said in Osbergian, laughing. Tristain wiped his mouth, flicking his eyes to Leon. Then his eyes went to the longsword hidden under the sumpter's pack. "It's okay. We tell from first day. Clothes—" he said, gesturing to their rags "—not ours."

Tristain glanced around. The headman was right. All the villagers wore similar clothing, cuffed woolen tunics in blues, and very few hoods. They wore box-shaped wool hats instead. The three Osbergians wore what an average Osbergian soldier would under their armor; knee-length woolen tunics in brown and yellow.

The headman held his hand out. Tristain took it. "Roupert. You are?"

"Tristain."

He turned to Leon. "And we know you, *Chevalier*. You are fearsome to kill the King's brother and all his men in such a way."

Caen coughed. "*King's brother!*"

"*Wi*. We call you the Flame. Is okay. The King's brother was a cruel man." He spat on the ground. "He under the mountain now."

Leon crossed his arms. "The Ox's Balls?"

The headman nodded. "You are hero."

Tristain and Caen looked at each other incredulously. Caen laughed. "*Hero—*" Leon flashed Caen a stern look. The corporal shut his mouth.

"You know... we're probably going the wrong way, Sir," Tristain said, smile flicking across his face. "You might be in good stead with the Badonnians."

Leon snorted. "Might be."

"Oh no," Roupert said. "King Pineton want your head. He loved his brother."

"So much for that," Caen said, taking another swig of the fermented milk. He inspected the skin. "It's horrible and tastes like cow sweat, but I can't stop drinking it."

"Is too bad. We have lots back home."

Tristain sat by the fire, warming his fingers. It was colder in the Footfalls, close to the ranges. "Was it the war? Why did you run?"

Roupert sat as well, joined by the others. Tristain caught the eye of a young, brown-yellow haired man and smiled. The young man smiled back.

His big hazel eyes held a glint of mischievousness to them. He was all chiseled jaw and high cheekbones.

There were eight in total—five, discounting the head man, his wife, and the blond man. One man wore a fraying straw hat, who looked like he was a few teeth short of a full set, with a pockmarked, sun-damaged face. Accompanying him was a woman who was either his wife or his sister, or perhaps both, as they had the same features, and seemed very close. The fourth was a stocky, weather-beaten man, who could've been a fisherman or sailor, down to the blue woolen cap and pierced ear. A small boy with a matching red cap, travelled with him.

Roupert glanced at his wife, an older woman with greying hair. "This is my wife and son, Marie, and Luka." Luka was the young man with blond hair. "We flee the war, yes, but we try to start a new life. We hear the empire will take anyone who work hard. Life is bad here. The King is cruel, like his brother. Anybody who say a bad word against him ends up..." He drew a line across his neck, grimacing. He looked at his wife again. "Marie father, he end up like this. The war was just the push to make the journey. The King's brother was his *chasseur*, his devil. Anyone refuse to pay tax, he is there. Anyone refuse to swear fealty, he there. And..." He made a squeaking noise as he drew a line across his neck again. "We owe a great debt, *Chevalier*."

"You owe me nothing," Leon replied. The head man's wife nodded, a small tear gathering at the corner of her eye.

"Thank you," Roupert replied. "Still, anything we can offer, is yours."

"How about a fire and conversation?"

Roupert nodded. They were eight in all, and the three deserters made eleven. He told them of how each of the refugees had been picked up along the way. They'd have to be on the road before long, lest they make a tantalizing target for criminals or slavers. But Tristain would protect them, if it came to it, and he was sure Leon and Caen would, too.

"So, what was it you wanted to be? A father and his sons?" the one with the blue cap said, laughing. He spoke better Osbergian than the others, and definitely wasn't Badonnian by his accent. "Bold claim, that. A damn sore sight if I've seen one. How does a ginger make a strawhead, *and* a blackhead? Your wife rainbow-haired?"

"Sounds like a mummer's jest," Caen replied, laughing.

The blue hat laughed. "I suppose it does. Well, Ginevra be praised. For the Flame'll get us to the Pass, and then."

"And then, what?" Leon replied, running his hand through his beard.

"I've a debt to settle. You've no doubt heard of the *Arabella*? The fastest ship in the south? No? Anyway, that bastard of a captain Chesterfield marooned us in Ammercy. This is Bean, and I'm Lorrin. We've been trudging through marsh, avoiding both the Badonnians and the Osbergians, on our way back to calmer waters, if you'll excuse my expression."

"Bean is your son?" Tristain asked.

"Nah. He's a stray that hung around long enough for Chesterfield to take him on. Eventually he just became part of the crew." The boy looked at the sailor but didn't say anything. "'e don't speak. We don't know his real name but he loves beans, so we called him Bean."

"You talk enough, we eat," Roupert's wife said, and no sooner than she had did Tristain find a steaming bowl in his lap. As he chowed down, the sailor started singing a ditty about a woman pregnant with a horse, and her husband's consternation at the birth. Tristain caught Luka's eye again and smiled.

Luni was high in the sky when Tristain laid back on the straw that was his bed under the stars. A gentle breeze blew over his face. It was peaceful. He could almost forget the horrible events that had led him here. A shadow moved across the sky. It was just an eagle making its way home, he imagined. He drifted off to sleep as he imagined he was the eagle, soaring his golden wings over the grey steppes.

TRISTAIN SAW LEON AND Caen lag behind as they crossed a ridge. He looked over the landscape. At first, it wasn't clear what they were looking at. But eventually he spotted bleached bones and tattered cloth. A field of dead men. They'd been left behind for the crows and the wolves. Already picked clean, they'd been there for months. With so many dead, he wondered how anyone would've survived. He wondered what it was all for, in the end.

Leon was taking a swig from his flask as Tristain walked up. Remembering that they'd both fought in the pitched battle, he kept quiet. The knight sniffed. "I knew we'd pass by here eventually," he said, dejection in his voice. "Doesn't make the wound any less nasty."

Tristain looked at the knight. "Was this...?"

"Yes," he replied. A few moments passed. "I never buried him. Did you know that? I saw him fall, but when I went back, I couldn't find his body."

"What would you say to him if he was here?" Caen asked.

Leon sniffed again. "I'd ask for forgiveness, and for dragging him into this stupid war." He let out a great sigh. "A cursed man I am, to outlive my child."

Tristain thought on Caen's daughter.

Caen patted Leon's shoulder. "The gods have their ways."

They let the silence drag out for long breaths until he said, "I think it's best if Erken didn't see me like this. I'll admit, I've not been the best knight I could've been. I apologize."

Tristain opened his mouth to say something smart, but there was a time and place for jokes, and it wasn't now.

"Anyway," Leon went on. "We should get back to the caravan before they leave us behind." Tristain looked back as they left. He caught the silver of Leon's flask by the edge of the ridge.

A yell came from up the road. They ran, coming around an outcropping. The caravan was being waylaid by thugs. Roupert's wife screamed. Tristain bolted. He breathed hard, his legs carrying him as fast as they could. He drew his sword as the thugs were within spitting distance. They pinched at the wagon, tossing through the contents. The head man and his wife tried to stop them. The others watched on.

"*Bastards, get!*" he cried. They looked over. One of them yelled in Badonnian, throwing himself on the ground.

"Please! Don't hurt us! We're only hungry!" They were Badonnian but spoke Osbergian reasonably well. Tristain wondered if he was the only person on the Continent who only spoke one language.

"Get back," he warned, waving his sword. They quickly backed off. Tristain felt a hand on his shoulder.

"*Goddess,*" Leon said. "What's happened here?"

"Please," the bandit said with ragged breath. "We just want some food." He stepped closer.

"Get back! I'll gut you where you stand," Tristain said, feeling his skin prickle with anger. He wasn't sure why, but his fury needed to free itself from his body. He advanced. Leon gripped his shoulder hard.

"Tristain," he said firmly. "*Sal'brath.* Look at them. Not a weapon among them."

Between quick breaths, Tristain glanced over them. They were half-starved, rags hanging off them, and Leon was right. They had nothing that could even be considered a weapon. But Tristain remembered what his sword instructor, Master Loren, told him.

He found himself yelling. "Fists, knees, elbows... what are those if not weapons? They're hoping we'll let our guards down and get us when our backs are turned."

"Please," the bandit pleaded again. "We've nothing left."

Caen went to speak. "Just give 'em a scrap—"

"We're not bloody priests, Caen," Tristain snapped. "This isn't a charity."

"Can I offer a solution," Leon said. "Enough food and ale for a day and be on your way."

"Thank you, sir."

Roupert nodded as he handed the men a skin of ale and three heels of bread.

"*Mercee.* Been much kinder than the other imperials we've seen."

Leon's ears pricked up. "Imperials... Osbergians?"

"*Non*, not white but black like night. They burn from the north. They burn it all."

"They burned us, too," Caen said offhandedly. "Why *are* the Annaltians here?"

"To take advantage, would be my guess," Leon replied.

Annaltia's disruption of their war in Badonnia likely stemmed from some feud between the Archduke and his brother, Prince Reynard.

"Of course..." Tristain felt the lull and started to calm. The prickling under his skin went away.

Caen crossed his arms. "Want to enlighten us?"

"What are brothers if not envious? Gods know I was." He was envious of his brother's looks, his age, the admiration of his father. Until Bann died, slaughtered by brigands on the road. Perhaps that was the reason for his outburst.

"Prince Reynard," Leon said. Reynard ruled in Annaltia. "I don't know much about him. But if the princes are going to war..."

"All the more reason to get through the Pass," Caen said.

"What of these ones?" Tristain said, sheathing his sword, but keeping it close.

The starving peasants looked on with haggard, tired eyes. They were probably simple village folk, their lives destroyed by the war.

"Let them be," Leon replied. The others seemed to agree that was best. "No sense in slaughterin' men down on their luck."

The sailor Lorrin offered a small bit of hope. "Maybe the Annaltians'll give up soon enough—after all, if it's as you say, they'll be at war with Osbergia, and everyone'll forget all about Badonnia. Who knows, maybe they'll need folk to rebuild."

"Thank you, sir," the leader said. "Gods be with you all. Gods bless your journey."

They parted; the bandits going east, Tristain and the others west.

17

THE ARBITER

LETUM, 1043

*Lower Market is one of those places where you can find every-
thing. Bodies—warm and cold—drink, coin, dice and cards,
luxuries of all kinds. Including and especially death.*

— CAPTAIN PARSSON OF THE OSTELAR WATCH

"ARBITER DIANA," THE CLERK shouted over the noise. "Arbiter!"

Diana got to her feet. Her black cloak dropped down by her
sides as she stood up, cramped, the uncomfortable seat making her legs lag
a little behind. Numb from sitting so long. Cold wind washed over her
as someone pushed through the door, a gray drizzle falling on the frosty
streets outside. Set into the walls, hearths burned feebly trying to heat the
foyer.

The Ostelar Watch garrison crowded with folk of every color. A
night-skinned Saburrian woman sobbed as she pressed her hands around
her little girl's while the poor girl tried to free herself. Two men with the
color of oil shoved each other while a third man tried to pry them apart.

The place was about as crowded as a flock of vultures at a carcass.

She tilted the silver badge on her chest, the mark of arbiter, and stepped
forward.

"Ah, the captain will see you now. Come with me."

She followed the woman up the stairs and onto a landing. The clerk stopped, looked around. Throngs of witnesses, suspects, and timewasters all approached the front desk, competing for the clerks and men-at-arms attentions. She waved to a clerk standing among the teeming mass. He looked up and waved back.

The woman's cheeks colored. The flush of blood of budding romance. If Diana cut that skin, red would run everywhere.

She remembered feeling something similar for Soren. Had it really been six months since Esstadt? She smiled crooked, like all the pieces didn't quite fit together. *The last time you say goodbye to someone never quite feels like long enough.* He'd been sent on another hunt not long after their return from Esstadt, while she'd been advanced to arbiter—no longer his apprentice.

The clerk led her down a narrow, carpeted hallway. Gruff watchmen passed them, giving Diana looks. She ignored them. Warm air pushed over her cheeks, and she untensed. The offices here looked to be as luxurious as it got in the Watch.

At the end of the hall, the clerk gestured to the door. From the inside, she knew the door faced outwards onto the street. Perhaps the captain even had a balcony. Diana went in.

"Good, the Order finally sends me a Sword," the captain said, sarcasm dripping from his words. "Captain Tollsen." A Salzheimer name. He was a tall, middle-aged man with a broad chest and waspish waist. A huge scar ran from his brow to his chin, but both eyes appeared to still be in working order, if a little walleyed.

"Have a seat. What's wrong with you? Sit, please."

Diana started. She pulled the chair out and sat.

"Arbiter, aye? And they think they can barge right into an ongoing investigation? We're stumped, please help us, dear Order of the Golden Sword. More like Golden-fucking-privy. I've got enough problems with these refugees from Badonnia without you adding to my mess. But if it's really true, I'd rather send one of you to your death than one of my men."

Diana stared and laughed. If she had expected something, he proved to be the opposite, like finding out a gentle, placid-looking dog was actually a vicious biter. A slightly walleyed one.

"Are you quite finished?" she snapped, eyes flashing with fury. "Sit down."

The captain gawped and made a choked-off noise. He sat.

"Now, Lord Inquisitor Rotersand has appointed me as arbiter because that is what I do, I arbitrate the level of demonic influence and seek to right the balance of the world. If the Watch could handle it by themselves, why haven't you? The Gutter is wreaking havoc on the slums, and you want to compare cock lengths? Please... I'll let you men handle that, but I'm here to do my fucking job."

"Alright," he replied. "The Gutter's last victim, as with the rest of them, as you're probably aware, are blonde women from the slums. Whores, most of 'em. I wouldn't normally care—we have vengeful clients all over the city—but these... you've never seen a body in such a state. I almost don't want to describe them, for your constitution."

She leaned back in the chair; eyebrows raised. "Try me."

"Well... they're usually missing one part, or several. Like... they've been feasted on by wolves. But these women couldn't have been sitting there more than two days before they're found, and there ain't any wolves in Ostelar."

"Dogs?"

"Could've been. But I've seen people ate by dogs." He shook his head, turned slightly green. "There's rarely anything left. This one's been feasting on particular parts and leaving the rest."

She nodded. "Where do you keep them?"

"Keep them? We ain't a witch or any of the Godsdamned churches. Certainly not the fucking embalmers. Go talk to them if you're wanting cold bodies to keep you company. Me, I'll take them warm."

Warm? Her skin crawled. She shook her head, putting a hand up to her temples.

"Alright. Which embalmers took them?"

"I don't know. It's a different one each time. They all stank, like they usually do. Ask around."

"There's nothing else? Truly? That's as far as your great investigation has proceeded?"

"Yes, now get out of my office."

She stormed out of the chair and out the door.

D IANA PACED ALONG THE Lower Market promenade, the main strip where stalls sat in the shadow of the Osterlin Hill. Hawkers avoided her gaze, noticing her black cloak and badge. Smoke from cookfires stunk the place up, and though the rain had now stopped, fog settled on the city. Wet ground squelched beneath her boots, wet air settled on her skin, in her hair. Everything was wet. *Fucking bruma months.* She returned to Ostelar just in time for the worst season of the year. At least in Invereid, Solni peeked out every now and then, as though it missed the little faces it looked upon. Not in the north of Osbergia.

She began to think on contrasts. The wet and cold north of the province to the warm south and warmer months on the road with Soren. Her advancement came as soon as they returned to Ostelar.

A day like today had visited the jut of land that was the Citadel, fog turning everything gray. Gray like dust. Gray like the common demon pelt. Gray like the sheen of a blade in dull sunlight.

For all the accolades, the ceremony was remarkably short. Nothing like her confirmation. Advancement meant receiving the pin and being called arbiter from then on.

Then Soren had left for somewhere in Annaltia, and she hadn't seen him now for months, a shred of loss stopping her breath short.

"Vallonian pirates pillage Republic towns," a herald announced just ahead, tearing Diana out of her memory. "Rumors of werewolves in Badonnia, and news from Annalt: is the prince really marching to war?"

Diana walked over to him.

"Oh, no-no-no," he said, scrambling off the upturned box he announced from. "I did what you Swords asked me to. I always make sure to say a word or two on werewolves. I mean, you just heard me, right? Please don't hurt me."

She softened her expression. She could do nice when the occasion called for it. Now and then, reluctantly. Once, she could've been called kind. But like a butcher, time had cut her old life out, tossed it into the maw of a devouring beast, and left her only the gristle.

"I'm not here for that," she said. "You spend time in the Lower Market, don't you?"

"Ain't no law against it."

She pointed to the garrison. "Would you have seen embalmers coming out of that building, carrying a body, perhaps?"

He looked at her sidelong. "Maybe. How badly you want to know?"

"Anything you can—" She frowned. "Oh, right."

She pulled out a few coins—three gold archdukes, his face stamped on the front. Very original choice for a name, those coins. The prick was probably vain enough to imagine a world where his name was spoken in conjunction with gold, and he got it.

"More."

Her frown deepened. "Five."

"Seven."

"Fine."

She handed him the coins and they flew into a pocket she hadn't seen and would likely never see again.

"Two days back. They went off to the outskirts, with a dead girl on a cart. Blonde girl."

"What did they look like, do you know?"

"Didn't catch much of their faces. They kind of blend in."

"That's the point."

"Oh, yes. Don't they fucking know it, living on the edges of society and all that."

"Anything about this cart? Any markings?"

"Uh... how—"

She flicked him another Duke. He snatched it out of the air.

"It had like uh, a cross?" He held up his hands, drawing the sign of an *X*. "With a ring around it."

The symbol she'd seen before, though in a different context. *These embalmers worship Veles?*

"The outskirts, then?"

The herald nodded. "If there's nothing else..."

She walked in the direction of the outskirts, pulling her cloak tighter around her shoulders.

D IANA HEADED TO THE outskirts, far from the shadow of Osterlin Hill, and even further from the gaze of the archduke. A pack of stray dogs marked the occasion, barking and running across her path. She reached for her knife reflexively, then relaxed as they passed. She kept her wits about her as she crossed onto an unnamed avenue, the main thor-

oughfare. The sign for the street had been scratched, burned, and shot at
with crossbows so many times, it was unreadable.

Carting baskets across the pockmarked road, washwomen sung a bawdy
song.

"I walked the Alba long
Found a sleeping girl
How could it go wrong?
Made my heart swirl
All of a sudden
Didn't hear Alba for long
Ripped off her button..."

And on the song went, though Diana approached now. They looked up.
Their kirtles were worn, heavily patched, but repaired with care.

"What's this then? Silver sword?" the first one said.

"Sword," the other one said.

"Aye, it's a sword."

"Not the pin, you mummer. *She's* a Sword. One of them Sigur fanatics."

"Right. Well, what do you want? We're a bit busy here."

"Where are the embalmers?" Diana said. "I'm looking for those that have
a cross within a circle on their carts."

They looked at each other and laughed. "Wel's Chosen."

Wel? "That's the symbol for Veles. Is Wel another name for him?"

"Aye. That's what the embalmers call him, anyway."

"Alright. Where can I find them?"

They rattled off a complex set of instructions that, in Diana's mind, were
intended to lead in her circles.

"Well met, then, and thank you, goodwomen." She extended several
coins their direction, and like the herald, they disappeared them into pockets never to be seen again.

But she followed the instructions, and found the *X*-sign on a cart, sitting
in front of a brick building. It was square set on an immaculately clean,

wooden cart that had been polished and sanded. She raised her brows in admiration. Covering up the filth of dead bodies must've been hard work.

She walked into the building. The smell hit her nose immediately.

Cadaverine. The smell of rotting bodies and chemicals—she'd smelled it enough in the Gray Citadel. She peered around a corner. A man stood there, gloves up to his wrists, apron over his chest. He was peeling back the chest flesh of an old woman, naked and pallid on the table. A man with a crossbow pushed in from the side.

"Excuse me, are you—"

"No Golden Swords here," the guard said.

"I'm willing to pay," Diana said.

"Hold, Prouso," the man said, not taking his eyes off his work. "You'd better explain what you're doing here before you find yourself on this table." There was a pop as the man levered open the woman's ribcage.

"I'm looking for the embalmer. Arbiter Diana."

"You've found him. I'm Van Vinland. Mind telling me what you're doing here, Arbiter Diana?"

Vinland turned, his eyeglasses glinting in the dull, greasy light that was coming through the dull, greasy windows. "Oh-oh, yes. You're far more interesting than your voice would suggest. It's my singular pleasure. One of my chosen told me of you, told me of the beautiful trans-humeral amputee."

He put his tools down and walked closer to her. Her left shoulder started to hurt at the base. She wiggled it reflexively, bound under her custom-made jacket's straps.

"You know..." he said, reaching gingerly for her left shoulder. She flinched. He put his hands up in deference.

"My apologies, I couldn't resist. You know, I work with the dead every day. It's not so often that I find someone who bridges that gap, the gap between life and death."

She sighed. Was every man in this city a fucking cretin?

"I'm looking for the Gutter's victims," she said. "Pretty, blonde, from the slums. Bedwomen. You would've picked them up at the Lower Market garrison."

He looked past her, his eyes unfocused. Then he looked back.

"Ah, yes, I remember. Yes, the captain wanted us to burn the bodies."

"Burn them?"

"Yes, a strange request. We embalmers never burn bodies. We preserve them so when the Gods return again, our corporeal forms look as they once did. We do it for those who don't have their own rites, or don't have anyone to do it for them."

"I heard it was because you make people look pretty at funerals, which, according to the funeral parlor owners, helps with the grieving process. Helps that you get an extra kickback, off the side."

"Yes, that does help. Each of us must find a way to survive in this world. But yes, we have the bodies interred below. No one came to claim them, of course, and they were in such a grisly state that it was difficult to make them look nice. I'd be looking for a reasonable sum before I handed them over."

"Can I see them?"

"No, I'm afraid not. Bodies have been going missing from our rooms. No one other than embalmers are allowed down there. Unless you would deign to... let me see your arm?"

Diana screwed up her face. "Fuck off, worm. I should gut you where you stand."

"Then, my answer is no," Vinland said, shrugging.

She huffed. She strode from the building, fuming.

S HE WAITED ON THE roof opposite the brick building. Solni dropped behind the horizon, leaving night to coat the outskirts in darkness like a painter that was too generous with his brush. Tallow must've been hard to come by, since not a person burned a candle in their homes. Not from her vantage, anyway.

All of the embalmers had left to their homes, or so it seemed.

She dropped down onto the street, rolling silently. She waited, making sure she couldn't see any movement inside, then stepped in.

The cadaverine smell punched her nose. She peered around the corner ahead, but it was hard to see without a candle, and what little light fell through the windows from Luni filtered through layers of grime. The dead old woman laid on the table, her chest popped open. Flies didn't seem to be an issue.

She found the candle she had seen at Vinland's side when he was cutting at the body. She took the tinderbox from her belt and lit the wick, filling the room with warm orange light.

Proceeding further into the building, she held the candle ahead of her. The room opened to a hallway with doors along each side. She took the nearest one. It was a supply closet, stinking of those chemicals. She quickly closed the door.

Each door appeared to be empty rooms, until she reached the last one on the right. It led her out to another hallway, roofed with glass, Luni hanging there half in light, half in shadow. Her face like a smiling bone. The hallway moved off into the dark distance, while other doors flanked the hallway all the way down.

He said below. Below is where I'll find the bodies.

It took a while, and each room was a grimmer sight than the last, bodies in various states of decomposition, all exsanguinated, ready to be pumped with that awful pink embalming fluid, if she understood the process herself. The whole place was excessively clean. Not a single bloodstain or stray dirt mark in the entire place.

At last, she found the stairwell down to the basement. When she reached the bottom, the smell came like rounding a small rise, only to find a new, harder rise before you. She gagged. As she looked up, she saw a candle on a table. She came over to light it and saw a gray, pallid foot at the end of the table. Push out of the darkness.

She shivered not from the cold.

She lowered her candle and lit the one on the table.

She found more, lighting them as she went. The room expanded in size as the candles were lit. It was a vast, underground morgue, filled with bodies upon bodies, all on tables in various states of decay. All grey and naked. One cadaver was in the process of having its gold teeth removed, while another had its organs preserved in jars of the pink fluid. Sutures pieced its body back together. There were so many bodies, it would have been hopeless trying to find the right ones. Or it would have been, had they not had tags on their toes.

Setia Lobissen, forty. Natural causes. 202

She went to the next one.

Almaty, no family name. Thirty-two. Death by strangulation. 431

She looked in pity at the pallid woman's forlorn face, the red markings around her throat. The women from the slums weren't strangled, so she moved on.

Name and age unknown. Death by evisceration and hemorrhage. 639

All the tags had a number on them. Couldn't have been the date they died, there wasn't enough numbers, and they all jumped around. Must've been the asking price, their cost for delivering the bodies back to their loved ones to be displayed as an open casket.

Six-hundred and thirty-nine Dukes. That is a reasonable sum. No one will ever claim her. And evisceration? This must be one of them.

Diana looked over the body. The woman was young, no older than Diana herself. Her skin was soft, and still had some color. The corpse was no longer than a few days dead. Diana brought her face right up to the woman, prodding with her gloved right hand. The woman's eyes were glassy, brown. Her hair was blonde, and she was likely a very beautiful woman in life. But missing teeth, and broken nails showed her lot. She had a deviated septum as well, upon closer look. Likely a powder addiction of some sort. There was a faint scar on her chin, as well.

The sum of her life had been reduced to a cold table in a butchery, tagged for its worth.

Diana looked further. An x-shape gashed across her chest, sewn up. She had sutures, dry and pocked, bloodless, done by the embalmer that worked on her, probably. She looked closer. There was another cut, made across the stomach, just below the liver. It was sewn shut, but the cut looked swollen, bruising around the incision. It was done while she was still alive. An incision. Precise, as though it were done with a knife wielded by a practiced hand.

You poor woman. But this doesn't look like a claw, and I've never met a werewolf that strikes with this kind of precision.

A chinking sound came from the door. Diana spun and caught a shadow in the doorway. She drew a knife and tossed it. The dark figure cried out in pain, rounded the corner and out of sight.

"You, stop!"

Luni cast gloomy half-light on them in the hallway. The figure raced up the stairs. It left a blood trail. A clinking noise followed each step. Mail. It reached the top, but she was nearly on it.

She flicked a knife. A man's voice cried out as her quarry fell to the ground.

She walked up to him, drawing her dagger. The man rolled over. The walleyed captain of the watch. His nose was broken, pouring with blood. Diana kneeled by his side, deftly stealing his sword from his scabbard. She threw it away.

"Fuck you," he squeezed out through wheezy breaths. "Cunting Order bitch."

"Mind telling me what you're doing in an embalmers' body room, in the middle of the night?" She dug her thumb into the wound. She found that pain often loosened the tightest tongues.

"Don't! Just... ah, fuck, my leg!"

"Don't be a child. Now, answer my question."

"I was... look, it's probably going to sound strange, but I was paying my respects to my wife."

She dug her thumb in again.

"Ahh! Fuck, stop! Alright! I was looking for those women. The women the Gutter killed. I needed them gone."

"Vinland told me. You wanted them burned. Why not burn them yourself?"

"You think I've got a fucking pyre laying around? I'm just going to put up a bonfire, burn some fucking women in a stack, in the middle of Lower Market? Fuck... no. I thought the embalmers would do that when no one paid, and then I found out they wouldn't, so I came here to finish the job."

"Why?"

"Why what?"

"Why burn them?"

"Dispose of them. I told you. You hard of hearing?"

She screwed her face up in frustration. "Why dispose of them?"

"Oh! I can't."

"You can't?"

"You must be hard of hearing."

Diana groaned, getting to her feet. Planting her dagger in the man's spine looked like a decent option. She could pin the murders on him.

She made a frustrated noise. There was more to it than that. "You fucking walleye. So, you were going to burn the bodies, and you can't tell me why. I'm guessing you're not doing this of your own accord—someone is telling you what to do, right?"

He staunched his nose with his hand. "Yesh, that's the gist of it."

"You know what the Order does to people who won't answer questions, right?"

"Yesh."

"And you're willing to go through that for what, a bit of coin?"

"A lot of coin."

"And the noble who's paying you to do this, he won't seek retribution when he finds out you blabbed to the Order?"

"No, Bugold won't find out... he—oh, fuck. Forget I said that."

"Bugold, eh?"

The man groaned. "Fuck. He's going to kill me."

"And you think I won't, walleye? I might just kill you now for how fucking maddening you've been."

"Ah, I guess I've got nothing to lose, now. But you got to promise me you'll look out for my wife."

"Your wife? All right, we'll send her to a preceptory, make a vestal out of her."

"What? No, I mean *look out for*," he said, making a cutting motion across his throat. "She's a fucking bitch who took off with my money."

Diana blinked. "Fine."

"So, Bugold pays me to keep it hush. Not sure why, but he's definitely not the Gutter."

"How do you know that?"

"The old prick's probably eighty, or near that. I don't see a hunched old patrician gutting these women, don't know about you."

"Where can I find him?"

"Aloysius Bugold. His house in the Noble Quarter, on uh... Riemark-strasse."

She got up.

"Wait! You got to help me! I'm injured!"

She didn't turn, not even when the captain cursed her, her children, and her children's children.

18

NOBLE QUARTER

LETUM, 1043

The villains of the Outskirts take their lead from the villains of the Noble Quarter.

— LORICH, EX-CAPTAIN OF THE OSTELAR WATCH

THE YOUNG SELENE WANDERED down the main hall of the Oncier-ran Estate, finding her way to the kitchen. She had been woken up by a scream, or so she thought. She figured it was a nightmare. Unable to get back to sleep, she decided on a midnight snack. Sausage, or some braided braid and milk, perhaps. The vast, paneled hallways looked ominous at night as always, soft orange glow of her candle illuminating unknown horrors in the shadows.

They're just shadows, Selene. Her heart thundered in her ears.

Bright moonlight drifted in through the leaded glass of the windows of the kitchen, casting a slightly green hue on the floor. The moon goddess sat full in the sky; indeed, if it wasn't a full moon, it was certainly close.

It pained her to make the decision, so she took all three: the sausage, the bread, the milk. She put the jug in the crook of her elbow, the bread in her teeth, and the sausage in her hand. As she left the larder, she heard a crunching noise. She looked around. The hatch to the buttery was open—she had not noticed before. Fleshy, wet sounds and heaving grunts filled her ears when she came to the top of the stairs.

It's probably just a fox. Got into the buttery somehow. Someone must've left the hatch open. She took the candle with her.

Selene took a step down. The stairs creaked and the grunting stopped. Her candle flickered, barely penetrating the gloom. She became painfully aware of her loud breath.

A huge wolf's face appeared at the bottom, lips pulled back in a snarl.

A wolf!

She screamed, dropping the candle. She ran. Legs tumbling down the hallway, the food flew out of her arms, splaying across the carpet. The jug smashed, sending milk and ceramic scattering. She heard the tumbling of heavy paws on the boards—it was behind her.

"You blooded bitch," it roared. "You let me die!"

She screamed for help. No one heard her. She dared not look back. The front door was open. How had she not noticed before? The wolf got in through there. Selene bolted through it, then ran towards the stables. The grass squelched under her feet, her nightdress trailed in the mud. She panted as she reached the stables, the horses whinnying at the disturbance. She looked behind, taking shelter in the stable. A great black wolf stretched on its hind legs—long human-like arms hanging below its waist, muscled chest more like a man's. It was something between.

No, it's a werewolf! Her eyes widened in panic. *Eme, Ginevra, help me!*

"You let me die," it yowled. Its mouth called out a voice as familiar as breathing. *Tristain?*

The creature looked like it was sniffing around, trying to find something. Selene put her hand over her mouth and shrank against the wall. It paused, sniffing the air. Then it withered in size, turning into a human, naked as the day he was born.

Tristain. The same fluffy black hair, the same jaw. A little older, perhaps. She gasped, then started shaking, and woke.

D IANA WOKE WITH A start. That horrible dream played out for
her again. She sat up and rubbed her shoulder, the tense, knotted
muscles that enclosed the stump, what remained of her left arm. The bed
above the Riemarkstrasse Park was uncomfortable, but she'd slept in far
worse. She rubbed her eyes.

Justice. That's why you're here. Tristain made his choice. But that dream
felt as real as the fog that settled on the windows, touching its shroud to
everything.

Too many fires to put out. She took out her dagger and eyed the point. It
grounded her—kept her honest. The same purpose. A knife honed for one
task, and one task only. Same as her.

She yawned, stretching as she stood. The Noble Quarter had its share
of hostelries for merchants, pricier than those in Lower Market, but the
pockets of the Order ran deep, and when the proprietor had seen the badge
of her rank poking from the breast of her jacket, he'd given her a good deal.

When she'd eaten, the day stretched out before her. *I'd better find Bugold.*

She walked down the street. Unlike Lower Market, the Noble Quarter
was not so much filled with life, but with austere, proper-looking men
and women. Minor nobles: sons and daughters of dukes and counts. Rich
burghers.

A few scornful looks were thrown her way as several women came her direction, dressed in lavish, tight-boned dresses that accentuated their breasts
and hips. Gift-wrapped. She found herself admiring the fabric of some of
them. They were plush, thick velvet. Perfect for the bruma months, and
on the edge of fashion, but also tastefully put-together. In another life, she

might've been one of these women. Part of her missed that lifestyle—traveling to Invereid to try on the latest Tanerian or Alanian styles.

The knife of the Order whittled her away, leaving her strong, all hard edges. A better woman, she told herself. But she'd also been known to lie.

"I'll wager she doesn't know what a comb is," one of them muttered. The others sniggered. Diana scowled, flashing her teeth. The women scarpered off.

"Alexei," a voice ahead of her shouted. "Don't make me come up there!"

A gorgeous, blonde woman stood on the porch of a manor, shouting. Diana walked over.

"What's this?" she said.

"Oh, just my good for no—" She turned, noticing the pin. "Oh, nothing, good inquisitor! I was..."

"Arbiter. And you were loudly requesting the presence of someone named Alexei?"

The woman looked shameful. "Yes."

The door opened and a handsome man with dusty blond hair walked down the front stairs as though the world belonged to him. Diana recognized him.

"Sorry to disturb you, mistress," he said. "This is my wife, Margot."

It was the handsome man from the garrison the day before. His blue eyes held not-quite-wholesome intentions. She ignored this, noticing a cut on his chin. It looked fresh, starting to scab. She hadn't seen it yesterday.

"What's the cut from, master?"

"Oh, this?" he said, laughing slightly. "I'm terribly clumsy, as Margot will tell you."

She laughed, nodding.

Diana saw no reason to believe him, since he was clearly lying, but this was a distraction she couldn't afford. She needed to rule out demonic influence. Helping these women against whoever intended them harm.

That was why I joined the Order in the first place, right?

"Tell me, where might I find the Bugold household?"

"Oh," the woman said. "Why that's down the street. But may I be of assistance? My name is only Margot Ginevra Bugold."

"And your father is Aloysius Bugold?"

"Yes, he is. Can I ask, what do you want with him?"

She was sharp. Diana hadn't said anything about wanting to talk to him.

"I have some questions for him."

"Ah, splendid. Might we go there together?" Alexei said. "We were just heading there ourselves."

"Fine."

T HE BUGOLD HOUSE WAS the largest on the street. A ninth-century, three-story mansion, set back from the street by a large garden populated with topiaries and privet hedging. In the center of the garden, naked, curvy Eme poured water into the fountain beneath. The water sparkled with Solni's light, catching Diana's eye as the three of them walked into the garden. The fog of the morning had faded. Holding each other in the crook of their arms, the couple walked ahead.

"My great-grandfather built this place with his own hands, Arbiter," Margot said. "Not his *own* hands, of course, but he drew the designs. Well, no, he didn't *draw* them, but he did tell the designer what he wanted."

"It's lovely," she said. She cared little for propriety and wealth these days, but she could understand the mechanics of the conversation well enough. Ply a few compliments, give a little, hold your true intentions behind your back like a dagger, until you stab them in the eye.

"And where are you from, Arbiter?" Alexei asked.

"Invereid."

"Ah! I thought I noticed the hint of an accent. See, I'm quite good at noticing things, much like you, I suppose."

Margot wrapped her hand around the ring pull, thudding it twice against the great white-oak doors. A few moments later, a footman in wild colors, purple and red slashed doublet, opened the door. A halberd rested on his shoulder. The telltale sign of a breastplate and pauldrons pushed out from under the doublet.

Merovian Guard? The guard was stoic, unblinking as they passed under his gaze.

The Bugolds are royal?

"Margot, my sweetling." A portly, elderly man with at least sixty brumas under his belt reached forward to hug the woman. "And Alexei, my boy. How are you both? And who's this? A Golden Sword, come to visit?"

He passed a look to the guard.

Diana smiled quickly. "Lord Bugold, I am Arbiter Diana, appointed by His Holy Lord Inquisitor Elias Rotersand, noble champion of the Order of the Golden Sword."

"Pleasure to meet you, Arbiter," he replied, bowing as far as his aging back would allow. "Call me Aloysius if it pleases you. I have only agreeable views of the Order. Demons would have us by our necks if we let them run wild. Would you like a refreshment? I can have the butler bring you something."

"No, thank you. If it suits you, I would like to ask you some questions, in private."

"Of course!" He waved at his daughter and son-in-law. "Margot, Alexei, please take a seat in the parlor. I'm sure the arbiter and I won't be long."

They both nodded, heading off to the west end of the foyer. Alexei flashed her a smile as they walked into the room, closing the door.

"Follow me, Mistress Arbiter," Bugold said. They headed to the opposite end of the foyer, into an oak-paneled office lined with bookshelves. A lovely, silver-embellished bureau sat in the corner, its lid securely over the desk.

His guard followed them inside, taking up a position in front of the door. Diana took note of the gaps in the man's armor.

"Please, have a seat," he said, indicating with his chin a high-backed chair opposite a large oak desk. The window in front of her overlooked a small courtyard that held a smaller copy of the fountain at the front, stark with the greenery having shed their leaves for the cold bruma months.

Diana considered the chair. From that position, with her back to the door, she'd have to push the chair back and move around the table to get at Aloysius. The chair was heavy and the floor carpeted. This would give the Merovian time, and they were known for their alacrity.

Diana sank into the chair. Aloysius groaned as he did the same.

"Now, please, ask your questions."

"Lord Bugold, know that I seek the answers that I do because I do what arbiters and the Order have always done: get at the truth. To take offence to a question I might ask is to take offence at Sigur Himself. Do you understand?"

The man gave her a wary look. "That is quite the disclaimer. You must be waiting to ask me something terrible."

"Shall I proceed?"

Bugold nodded and brushed off his fine-point hose. "Ask."

"Where were you two days ago, on the twentieth of Letum?"

"Let's see. I'm old, so my memory plays tricks on me. If I remember correctly, I was here, receiving a visit from the playwright, Senechartis. My butler can confirm this for you. He keeps meticulous records of the comings and goings at the house."

"Why would a playwright be visiting the Bugold household?"

"I wish to keep it a secret, but I am organizing a play for my daughter. It is about her love of flowers and romance."

Diana leaned back in the chair. Behind she could sense the Merovian's gaze. He could drop his halberd on her head without much effort. She'd have to throw the chair back, but from this low position that would be quite the trick. If she kicked off the desk, first, she could send it leaning backwards, and she could roll out of the way of any blow. The desk looked fixed to the ground—easy enough.

"That's nice of you."

"Indeed, I thought so. Anything else? I'm waiting for the question that will shock." He reached out and took a dried fig from a bowl on the desk and offered her some. She shook her head.

"What is your relationship to the captain of the Ostelar Watch?"

"What relationship?"

"Captain Tollsen. Walleyed. A Salzheimer, though his accent is barely perceptible."

"These details mean nothing to me. I do not know who you are talking about."

"He would beg to differ. He says that you've told him to dispose of some bodies."

Aloysius sighed. "I see. He's taken it upon himself to ask for a higher rate. You see, the man is upset that I have him on a retainer, and yet it is not high enough for his vices. I do know that he is lying to you, to blackmail me into losing my standing, unless he received a raise."

After a pause, Diana eyed him with a cold expression. "Lying to a Sword of the Order is a grave crime. The bull of Istrya, *Salvus Benedictorum*, named by Benedictus gives me the power to arrest you to determine the truth."

Aloysius's eyes drifted for a moment to the Merovian, then back to Diana.

"You've been taken in, I'm afraid, Arbiter. The man is desperate. I lied about my involvement with him because it is, quite frankly, embarrassing."

Bugold nodded. The guard stepped closer, the sound of his heavy plate thumping. Diana felt the hairs on her neck stand.

"Mistress, you are aware of the Merovian Guard, yes?"

"I am aware."

"The emperor is my second cousin. He holds me in high regard and receives me often when I visit in Istrya. So, if you're quite finished, I would like to you leave."

They went silent. His hands trembled though his face remained calm. *Could he hold a knife anymore?*

"Why would you be covering for the Gutter's crimes?"

The old man licked his dry lips. Diana felt the tense silence stretch out. "Make it quick."

Diana kicked the desk and threw back the chair. It slammed quite short into the guard's hips. She rolled out of the chair just as the halberd went down. It gouged a huge hole out of the chair, where her head would've been. He kicked it aside. She spun, pushing her dagger under the man's helmet.

He shoved her away and smashed her in the face with a closed gauntlet. White pain dashed across her eyes, blood filled her mouth. She'd bit her tongue, she was sure. Something tightened around her throat, and her dagger hand stuck fast. He held it. She tried to wriggle out, but there was no wriggling. Her breath choked, eyes watered. Through blurry eyes she kicked at the man's chest. The Merovian was strong, and though he stumbled back, she'd lost all of her power. She stamped her foot. The blade at the retractable opening of her boot's sole shot out. She flicked her foot upwards, slamming it home. The man groaned as blood gushed from his neck. The hand at her neck went slack and he dropped, thumped in a heap of armor and flamboyant clothes.

She rubbed her throat, gasping for air.

Aloysius stood dumb, mouth apart. Then he cried, "Guards!"

She jumped over the table and threw her arm around his neck. He let out a squeal. A pig without qualms. As easily as though he'd killed those women himself. "Who is it? Who killed them?"

Three more guards burst into the room, stopping short of the desk. They gave her fierce looks, brandishing the points of their halberds towards her.

She glanced behind. Diamond-shaped iron bars enclosed across the window. She could never break through there. It was fight her way out or take a hostage. She didn't fancy her chances with three Merovians.

"You have no idea what you've just done, do you?" Bugold squeaked. "The emperor will tan your fucking hide, and all you godsdamned Swords."

"If the emperor wants to come down from Istrya, let him. Tell me who the Gutter is, and I'll let you live." She pushed the blade tighter against his throat and kicked his knee, so he fell.

He groaned. "It's Alexei! Alright!"

He'd come to the door to see them. The guardsmen looked at each other but kept their weapons trained on Diana. Alexei gave a flinty smile. He had something in his hand. A flash of steel, and one of the Merovians dropped his halberd and clutched at his neck. Blood soaked into the colorful jacket, adding another layer of dye, nothing too garish by comparison. He stumbled and fell to one knee.

The others turned, shock dulling their movements. Alexei punched out again with a short blade. A dagger, suited for close work. The Merovians barely had time to bring around their halberds before they died, too, in a clatter of steel and blood.

Alexei walked forward, wiping the dagger on the tail of his doublet. A brocade doublet that wouldn't look out of place at a banquet in the White Palace.

"Alexei, what... what are you doing?"

"It's about time someone dealt with you, old man."

Diana guessed. "You're hoping to make a deal, aren't you?"

Alexei burst out laughing. "You're incredible." He grinned, eyes touching every bit of her. "Just incredible. I suppose there's a reason you're an arbiter and not a washwoman. Tell me, who are you? I know Swords take the names of Martyrs on their confirmation."

Diana stared, kept her dagger pressed to Bugold's neck.

"You clearly come from good breeding."

"Alexei, what is the meaning of this?" Aloysius snapped.

He chuckled. "Father, I'm certain you know my cousin, the prince?"

Aloysius suffered under Diana's grip. "Reynard? What does he have to do with this?"

Prince Reynard of Annaltia?

She shook her head. Politics—to be avoided. She thought she had turned her back on that life, but like a rock crashing downhill, it struck everything in its path. The guards were just another set of heads to be pulverized on the way down.

"Be quiet," she yelled. "I don't care. You're a murderer, Alexei." *So am I, but we're different. I kill to protect the innocent, he kills for the thrill of it.* But she enjoyed killing, too—*no, we're different.* "These women were innocent."

"Where's my daughter?" Aloysius barked.

"I was sorry to tear open her precious neck, but things are developing. See, in a few months, there won't be an Osbergia."

"You killed her?" Bugold sighed. He seemed to have forgotten the dagger at his throat. Diana saw no need to hold it there as he stepped away and threw his hands on the desk and sobbed. She dropped her arm by her side.

"Margot!" He cried. "You monster!"

"Enough!" Diana roared. "Come with me, demon."

"Demon? I'm no wolf." Alexei blinked. "I'm just a killer, like you."

Diana ground her teeth. *Bastard.* She sheathed her dagger and threw a knife. Alexei's smile faded as he clutched at his chest, around his heart. She never missed her mark. Not anymore. Not the meek little girl, playing at swords with Tristain. Not the crying girl hiding in closets. Monsters died at her hand. She was a Sword of the Lightfather and brought His justice.

Never suffer a demon to live.

This man was a demon as easily as one that took a wolf's visage.

"You covered up his crimes."

Bugold looked up from his sobs. "What? Don't kill me—"

She inserted the blade of her dagger between his skull and his vertebrae. A quick death. More than he deserved. She lowered him to the ground, closing his eyes.

Silence aired its ugly bits. The room stank of coppery blood, and she tasted it on her tongue.

She found the butler and the staff and killed them too. No witness to this monstrosity could survive. She got kindling and wood from the back shed and when she was done, flames licked the ceiling. A pyre wrought at the manor, a purifying blaze. Their crimes could never be undone, but she could fucking get close.

There was beauty in the pyre, and as she departed, Eme's statue poured sparkling fresh water.

"I T'S NOTHING WE CAN'T smooth over," Rotersand said. "You demonstrated good judgment by leaving no witnesses." He grinned. "I never thought that young warden who barely survived her first *Velitore* would grow into such a blossoming killer."

Diana kept her head forward, didn't engage. He liked to bait her, she noticed. His scarred face turned a rictus grin.

"Well, I must say, this is a first."

"A first?"

"The first time I've appointed an inquisitor in my tenure."

Diana gaped her mouth. "Inquisitor?"

He nodded and opened a case that had been sitting in front of him. Inside was a gold sword pin. He stepped around his desk and up to her. The hairs on her neck stood on end. Repulsive man, though they all had their scars. Diana forced herself to face him. She would no longer be cowed by anyone.

She kept her chin high as he put his hand inside her jacket, finding the pin. He lingered his hand there for a moment. Paused. His scars twisted into a smile.

"I'm proud of you." His voice was gruff but his tone genuine.

She blinked in surprise. "Thank you."

Her chest flooded with pride. All her life, recognition had been scant and pride even scanter—she'd almost forgotten what it had felt like. Like a warm aestiva day with wildflowers in bloom. Life, choices, and circumstance cut her away like a practiced sculptor, leaving a sharp, violent, determined woman. Not a better woman, but one who faced the hard things and came out victorious, annihilating anyone who crossed her path.

He stepped back. "You are now Inquisitor Diana. May all demons fall before your dagger and your bow."

She bowed her head. "Thank you, Your Eminence."

"You are welcome."

"I THINK SHE HUMPED him," Tansy said, wiping her mouth between slurps of soup. The dining hall at the Citadel emptied towards Vespers, but Tansy, Nials, Diana, and big Manus lingered.

"I didn't touch that scarred fuck." Diana worked the handle of her dagger between her fingers, point resting on the table. "You watch your mouth. I'm your superior, now."

Lena gave a flinty smile. "Got it, Inquisitor." She said it in a sing-songy way.

Manus sat there silently as always. She noticed he never ate and didn't have a bowl in front of him even now. He still wore his helmet. His breath threaded through the holes in the cheek, a punctuation to the silence.

"So, Inquisitor," Nials said after a few moments. "Did he pull out his worm? What's it like? Mangled, like him? Or did you just bend over his desk and let him have his way?"

She pushed to her feet, scraping the bench on the stone. Nials jumped up on the table and folded himself over his knees.

"I wonder who's quicker?" He tapped his face with both hands. "I'm ugly, but I've two hands."

Diana's stomach boiled, but in the interests of exhaustion of the day settling across her brow, she sat back down. "Once more, and I'll hang your guts over the cathedral altar."

Nials climbed off the table and sat as well. "It took ten years for Sorenius to get inquisitor. I mean, it begs the question, surely."

She sat in uncomfortable silence with them, Manus's breath underscoring.

Tansy slurped some more. "Beggin's what she did, on her knees—"

Diana grabbed a fistful of Tansy's hair and slammed her face into the bowl. It broke, shattering into slivers of ceramic. Blood poured from her teeth and her cheeks, cut up. With a grin, Diana slammed her down a few more times, then dragged her off the bench by her hair, the woman screeching, twisting, trying to break free.

"Say it again," Diana roared. "Tell me you think I humped him. Go on!"

"You earnt it!" Tansy squeaked in pain and swallowed. "You earnt it, I'm sorry!"

Diana let go.

Nials had been looking over his shoulder at the violence. He laughed as Tansy wiped her face of tears and blood, and Diana thought even Manus cracked a smile.

19

OUTRIDERS

FERVUM, 1044

The chrysalis event refers to the subject reaching terminus and returning as a fully realized demon. It is described as a moment of complete peace, until the spirit is yanked back into the body, whereupon a feeling of fire consumes the flesh and an agonizing transformation takes place (the colorful words of one such subject).

— LORD NOTARIUS GIAN ADALLA

EIGHT OUTRIDERS SILHOUETTED AGAINST the grey sky on a ridge to the north as the wagon rumbled along the rocky road. The ox grumbled as the headman brought him to a stop.

"Who are they?" Luka the farmer's son said.

"No sudden movements," Leon replied, resting his hands on the weapons at his belt. Tristain turned his knuckles white as he squeezed his hand around his own weapon. They waited there, unmoving on the ridgeline. *It's them. The hunters. Those graycloaks told them about me.*

Tense moments passed. Eventually, they moved off, disappearing.

"Must've thought we were someone else," Caen muttered to himself. Tristain didn't relax. He knew they'd be back.

"*Bon*. Let's go," the headman said, sending a lash across the ox's back.

"Stay on your guard," Leon whispered as the ox started moving again. "That won't be the last time we make eye nor ear of those."

Lorrin sang a song and they fell into good spirits. At last, the keep came into sight, and the pass beyond that. The leviathan itself stood looming in the distance, so enormous as to be seen from miles away. So enormous and distant, in fact, it was half obscured by mist and fog. A snow-capped peak in the shape of a dragon, it was said to be the bones of an ancient dragon that lived before the time of the gods, and depending on the legend, made the world. Tristain thought it was just a weirdly shaped mountaintop.

Eventually, they crested a rise, and the keep drew into sight all at once. Banners of the Archduke flew over the walls—a gold bear on red field—as well as banners of the empire; split black-and-red field with gold lion. Pennants in different colors dotted the towers, representing each army that had taken the keep. A man every ten feet on the walls, armed with crossbow, oiled mail, and steel helm. The keep itself was a hundred feet wide, spanning the narrow gap between two slopes. There was no other way across the mountains, at least not one that Tristain knew of. This made the keep a good strategic position to have on hand. But for them? They weren't in the army anymore—deserters. For them, it was another obstacle to get past, preferably with their necks intact.

The gate stood open and the ox lumbered into the bailey, hard-packed ground beneath its hooves. The dray creaked and swayed as it shambled in, its axles about ready to snap. It was a small wonder it had made it this far, and yet it still had further—the whole ten-mile-long Pass still laid before them, and wherever they were off to after that.

So long as the deserters kept their faces downcast, and their hoods high, they would avoid scrutiny. They would pass as father and sons, and last they checked, seeking refuge in the empire wasn't forbidden. Of course, as a last resort, they carried swords and axes under their cloaks.

The guards didn't immediately intercept them. At first, they circled the wagon, observing their quarry. Tristain sent a glance over the captain. He had a patch of three silver trees on a black and green field. Invereid's own, but he wasn't immediately familiar. He carried spear and shield, sword at his hip. He looked like he knew how to use them.

"What business have you in Osbergia?" the captain spoke at last.

"Refuge, sir," Roupert answered. "We are only simple folk."

"And the wagon?"

"All we have left, sir."

The captain walked around, giving the wagon another look. Tristain felt his cheeks flush as the man lingered on his face.

"You travel in odd company, Badonnian," he said, not taking his eyes off Tristain. "These two look feral—what, there wasn't a single razor amongst any of you? Even a simple knife and some water... though you've not been the strangest to have come through, I suppose. No matter." He clicked his tongue. "Yes. There's gonna be paperwork, of course. You'll have to wait until it's been returned from the capital."

"The *capital?*" Caen choked out. "That'll take weeks!"

"Months but needs must. Where're you from, Osbergian?"

"Uh, the Spear, sir. Came to Badonnia to see my cousins, got mixed up in the war."

"Right. Well, there's that small matter—we have to notarize your entry into the empire. Wouldn't want any deserters slipping through the cracks."

"Of course not."

"Naturally... it could be rushed. For a fee."

Caen smiled, expecting the bald-faced suggestion of a bribe. "We have coin."

"Aye... ten a head... three for the women. Seventy-eight silvers," he answered without hesitation. "Aye, two for the lad."

Caen grumbled. "That seems steep." It was steep. Ten silver would buy a week's worth of ale. Forty silver was the price of a well-made sword. No chance a few farmers would have that much between them.

"*Wi*, we have not that much," the headman added.

The captain clicked his tongue. He was about to open his mouth when a white-haired, broad-shouldered woman in plate walked out of the barracks at the other end.

"Hold, Captain," Gida said in her strong northern accent. Tristain laughed. Caen chuckled. Leon folded his arms, seemingly indifferent.

"Ah, here's the commandant," the captain said, leaning on his spear. "She'll sort this business out."

"Lieutenant?" Tristain couldn't believe it. He pulled his hood down.

A smile flicked across her face. "It's commandant, now." She gripped him by the shoulders and laughed. "I'm glad you're not dead, Squire. And who's that? Is that the corporal?"

"Come 'ere, you big bitch!" Caen threw his arms around her. She laughed, gripping him tightly. The captain and the others seemed positively thrown. She turned to Leon.

Leon kept his distance. The memory of his time in prison, his impending date with a noose was still fresh. They stared at each other tensely. Finally, he said, "You're not dead either, aye?"

She laughed, and so did he. They embraced. As they broke apart, she said, "Gods know they tried! It's good that I should run into you three, actually. Who do you travel with?"

"The enemy," Caen said with a smirk. "Good people, it turns out."

"If only we knew," Gida replied. "Before we burned their fields to ash."

The captain made a gesture. "These ones, Commandant, they ain't pay yet."

"Let them go, Captain. Any who aid a Knight of the Empire prove themselves worthy."

"Very well, sir."

The refugees thanked them profusely. In good spirits, the headman threw his whip over the ox. They yelled goodbye, and Tristain wished them luck. The wagon creaked as it rolled over the uneven ground. *They're gonna need it.* He caught Luka's eye. He wondered if he would ever see the man again and felt a pang of *something*... it wasn't quite regret, but perhaps the feeling a man might have in choosing between two meals and wondering what the other meal was like.

"Commandant," the captain said, gesturing to Caen. "This one said he was visiting cousins in Badonnia. Who are they, really?"

"This is Leon Vorland the Strong, Knight of Ineluss," she replied. "These two are his retinue. The coal-hair is the son of the Count of Invereid, Tristain Oncierran, squire to the noble knight. The straw-hair is Corporal Caen, formerly of the Spear."

"Well met," the captain said, bowing. "I am Vidan Geldchen, of the Geldchens of Ostelar."

"Burghers?" Leon said, scratching at his ever-growing beard. It was touching his chest, now. Vidan nodded. "Heh. Count on a merchant to earn his gold. What's a merchant's son doing at the edge of the world?"

Vidan smirked. He was dark-haired, with complex eyes—brown, with a hint of gold and green. *To match his name, I suppose.* He had thick dark eyebrows and a shadow of stubble on his shaved chin. "Yes, Sir. It's complicated, and a story I won't tell, excepting over an ale that's been bought for me."

Caen laughed. "I think the man needs an ale!"

"Yes," Gida said. "That's a good idea. After duties."

"Yes, Commandant," Caen replied, saluting.

"Back to your duties, Captain," Gida said, slight annoyance passing over her face.

Vidan saluted and disappeared.

"So... Commandant," Caen remarked. "That's quite a step."

"Right," Gida said. "We should talk."

She took them to her office at the top floor of the barracks. It was roomy and had comfy furnishings. Her window overlooked the pass but was facing the wrong way to spot the leviathan. Tristain wondered what the leviathan looked like up close. Probably just a bunch of big rocks stacked on top of each other, and like nothing at all. The effect was given by observing it from the right distance and perspective. There was something to that, though. Why would it happen to be at just the right angle and distance to look like a dragon? And from both the Osbergian and Badonnian sides? No, that was nonsense. He put it out of his mind.

Gida smiled, genuinely beaming as she sat at her desk. "Gods, it's good to see you. I thought you three were dead, for certain."

"No such luck," Leon replied. "Now, what happened?"

"With what, sir?"

"You said it was good that you should run into us."

She smirked. "You've always been sharp, sir. I have a request of you three. There would be silver in it, of course."

Tristain cleared his throat. "How much?"

"More'n you've seen in some time, by the look of you." She grinned. "No matter, we have warm baths, and servants that'll clean you up in no time."

Tristain glanced down and silently conceded the point. "What's the job?"

"Vyahtkenese horses."

"Warhorses?" Horses of Vyahtken were native to the eponymous wild lands far to the east. They were stronger, livelier than other breeds, and absolutely fearless. They were perfect for battle, and highly prized for that reason.

"We need a guard," Gida replied. "Someone to transport them to Avercarn."

Caen's uncertainty was clear from his tone. "Why us? You've a whole keep of men, by the look of it."

"There's simply no one else for the job, Corporal." She was cagey, holding something back.

"They weren't legally obtained, were they?" Leon asked. Gida declined to answer. After a few moments, he said, "What do you need a guard for? We hold the pass from both ends."

"I suppose you've not heard, being on the road."

"Heard what?"

"The roads are dangerous, and war is coming. Th—" She stopped herself.

Leon leaned forward in his chair. "What is it, Gida?"

"There's talk the empire is unravelling. Annaltia has attacked Osbergia. Nothing like this has ever happened. The archduke is scrambling. In fact, I should probably mention that every knight has been called to arms."

Leon sighed. "Brother against brother. This bloody Prince Reynard. What is the meaning of it? Surely, it's not just bald-faced greed."

"I cannot say. But he holds our trade routes to the capital hostage." Gida was right. Annaltia was directly north of Osbergia—and all routes to the capital, Istrya, ran through the province. Trade, taxes—both would be disrupted.

"A lot of people are going to be angry," Tristain said.

"They already are," Gida replied. "We've been spared the worst of it, out here... but there's already shortages, and the archduke has proposed a new levy to fund the coming war."

Leon swore. "For Ginevra's sake."

Caen threw himself upright. "Any news of the Spear?"

"Nothing, as yet."

Caen sighed, leaning back, deep in thought.

"So, you see, we need all the men we can spare, here. The Badonnians can't be allowed to just march back into these halls, especially not when we fought so hard to take them. Rennes is the least of our concerns, now, but we can at least hold onto what we gained."

"Then let us stay," Tristain said, looking to Leon. The knight sent him a glance. "We can help."

"I understand you want to help, but—"

"You said you need every man you can get."

"True, but... this is, arguably, more important. If we can use these horses to resupply our army, it might mean the difference between victory or defeat."

"It surprises me to hear an Annaltian say that."

"My loyalty is to the empire, squire. Not to a single man. I would see the prince in chains for what he's done."

"Forgive me, Gida, I didn't mean anything by it."

"No harm done." She whistled and some servants bundled in with towels and razors. She rose from her chair, carried herself with strength, a stiff spine. Her eyes held harshness, but there was sadness in them, too. Something happened to her, Tristain was sure.

A servant boy led them to a squat building opposite the barracks, filled with steam from natural hot baths, where a bath and a shave were in order.

A T DAWN, THE MEN loaded grain, wine, sacks of flour, and what else they could spare into wagons. The smiths straightened horseshoes, fifty down, and fifty more to go. The head smith's voice was a lash, spurring them to work as fast as they could. The farriers worked themselves furious and red-faced, shoeing the Vyahtkenese by the dozen, their hammers ringing out in the cold mountainous air.

By mid-morning, Captain Vidan rustled the dozen or so grooms into the muster, who led the hundred or so horses. The beasts were black as pitch, a sea of smooth midnight coats. They stormed, stomping at the ground, kicking up dust, butting up against each other, gnashing their teeth in shows of dominance—to be expected from lively horses bred for war.

Tristain wondered how in Sigur's name they were going to make it through the pass without losing a few to falls or fights. Blessedly, that wasn't his problem. The grooms had that joyless task. Tristain's only job was to protect the convoy on their way to Avercarn.

Tristain secured the chinstrap of the bascinet around his shaved chin. The servant boy handed him a spear and shield, decorated with the Osbergian bear. On his belt sat the sapphire longsword in its scabbard. He reveled in the familiar smell of leather, the weight and feel of oiled steel. The armorer had fitted him with padded jacket, mail, and breastplate with spaulders, and the bascinet, of course. Over the breastplate and past his thighs he wore a tabard of Osbergian red, with a sigil of a white eagle stitched to the breast, thanks to one of the men's wives. It was cinched in with a dark leather belt. Nothing fancy, but it offered more protection than a sackcloth shirt. He wondered if it would last, or he would simply tear it at the seams within a week. The memories of that horrible night still haunted his dreams, even if he knew what happened was right.

"Apologies, Sir Strong," the armorer said, bowing his head. "A' know it's no harness an' plate, but I simply had nothing better for you." Leon had much the same as Tristain, the best the keep's armorer could spare.

"No matter," Leon replied. "A good shield turns blows aside just as well as plate."

The armorer chuckled. "Too right." The armorer was in his late fifties, in his twilight years. The wisps of hair on his head were white as snow. He'd come to see them off, as did Gida and a group of soldiers. His upper back was rounded slightly. He had a solid frame, and hard, callused hands. The man had commented on Tristain's blade when he'd visited the armory.

"That's a stately blade," the man had said. "Fit for a prince."

"I suppose so," Tristain had replied. "The Annaltian I took it from didn't seem like a prince, though."

"Princes and traitors seem close company these days. Maybe it's only right that the blade ended up in your hands."

"Why do you say that?"

"I'm near the end of my life, son, but I've still enough wit to tell a good man from the rest."

Tristain had been stung. He'd felt like a coward, a craven. Deserting his country, his duties, bringing shame to his family name. Failing Mother, failing Selene. He expected nothing more than the end of a rope, and yet as he threw his leg into the saddle of his own Vyahtken, he felt like a knight marching off for empire and glory.

"We'll have to get that ale some other time," the knight said to the captain. "A shame we won't hear the story of the merchant far from home."

"Aye," the captain replied.

The commandant whistled, calling a groom. Tristain turned. Gida was as striking and beautiful as ever in the haunting white light of the pass, but at the same time, cold and distant.

"No such luck, Captain," she said. "You're going with them. A letter arrived in the night, from Lord Galeaz. You're to deliver the horses to a village ten miles south of Avercarn, Passtadt."

The name slapped Tristain's ears. *The steward? What's he to do with this?*

"Very well, Commandant." He had a slight smile play across his lips, perhaps looking forward to the chance to get away from this frosty place. Tristain knew that he was.

They said farewell to their old friend Gida with a few tears and headed through the gates west. The frozen ground beat under the weight of hundreds of hooves, the thundering sound filling Tristain's ears. He wondered if this many horses would bring the weight of the mountain down on them. *Don't be ridiculous, Tristain. Thousands marched through the pass on the way to Badonnia. You were with them.*

The pass stretched out before them as the sun reached its zenith. They were headed toward home at last. He wondered if he would see Selene before war called again—and what he would say to her. *Gods, I hope you'll forgive me.*

T RISTAIN TOOK IN A sharp breath. The Dragon's Alley opened before them. The sky-piercing apex of the leviathan was drenched in shafts of light, impaling the snow atop in a bristling, moving line. Then it happened all at once—the clouds above broke like foes before the might of the mountain. The dragon's mouth stood open, drenched in sunlight, ready to swallow the world. Mist grabbed pathetically at the sides of the towering beast, settling for draping its foothills, and the valley below, in a veil of smoky white.

"That's even better than last time," Leon said. The captain, Vidan, whistled his agreement.

They assembled at the edge of a plateau. Below them in the valley, thick grass and virgin forests of conifer and cypress broke only at the bank of a narrow stream that came from higher up the mountain. Glacial flows, now melted, turned rocks in the cold bruma months, creating enormous heaps of stones at the foot of the mountain. Gazing ahead, a winding path left the forest behind, passing over talus and grey rock, and up, switching back until finally squeezing through a gap between the mountains, the way out the other side.

The sight was aweing, filling Tristain with an almost sacred quiet, despite the hundreds of hoofbeats. Maybe he'd grown used to them now.

"You know why it's better?" Caen said. "'cause we're going home."

The pass broadened on the other side of the valley, leading through a ravine. Some of the horses grew spooked, but the grooms led them on. Eventually, the pass led into a thick wood, where dry branches fell over the trail. The horses grew wary of the unsteady ground, and so they stopped, and the grooms had to clear the path. It was like this. The Pass was only ten miles long, but they moved at a glacial speed, making sure none of the horses didn't get separated from the group.

"Can't they just beat on 'em until they move?" Caen wondered out loud.

"You try and beat on a hundred destriers, corporal. They'll beat on you, most likely," Leon replied.

Before long, the path was cleared, and the pass opened again. Eventually, the keep on the other side drew into sight, the back of its walls much less guarded than its front would've been. The sentries waved their hands in greeting as the sun started to set. *All things considered, not a bad day's work.*

Tristain sat with his knight and the others as the smell of chargrilled lamb filled the air. The commandant of the western keep, a hefty soldier known as Gerold Milkwine, for his ability to drink wine like it was milk, welcomed them with open arms. He offered them all the meat they could eat, and more than enough ale and wine to wash it down. Tristain suggested the best cuts should go to the grooms.

"They worked harder than the rest of us," he said, unbuckling his armor. They cheered him half-heartedly—not ungrateful, but exhausted. The Vyahtkens had been corralled in a hastily constructed pen, now resting for the night. "How they managed to do it without losing a single one, only Sigur knows."

The commandant passed it along, and the cooks brought the grooms the king's cuts: the shank, the legs, the shoulder. Caen sung a ditty as servants brought the ale out.

"There once was a Countess from Delph,
Whose breasts sat as high as a shelf,
So only the tall, could see them at all,
And the Count had to take care of himself."

The men laughed, cheering with their tankards, beer sloshing onto the dirt. Milkwine joined in, telling his own ditty.

Tristain noticed Leon hadn't taken one. "No ale, Sir?"

Leon smiled but didn't respond. Tristain saw his eyes turn glassy, orange reflection off the fire. *What's going on with him?*

"Oi, here," Caen said, thrusting a second ale into Vidan's waiting hand. "It may not be bought, but you've an ale. Tell us: what's a merchant's son doing out here?"

Vidan took a sip. The froth sat on his upper lip as he spoke. "Our family's cousins of the rich Geldchens, you see. Same grandfather, but my father didn't inherit his father's talent for business, or anything really. My father was a gambler. Unlike my grandfather, he had some deluded idea in his head that money could be made through luck or chance. He would go down to the port every Lunsday and put money on cockfighting. You can guess how that went. When I came of age, my father had already lost the house, and was in a large amount of debt to some important people."

As the night grew on, the grooms faded away, going to bed. Milkwine belched and said goodnight, and Caen and Leon went to bed as well. Tristain couldn't sleep—his thoughts fixed on Selene—so it was just Vidan and himself left by the fire.

"So, where do you go from here?" Vidan swirled the wine in his cup and sipped.

The fire popped a shower of sparks, its last breath before the darkness of the night would descend on them. Tristain shivered. "Once we get to Avercarn, it's back home to Invereid."

Vidan's dark, serious eyes passed over him. "Are you cold?"

"A little."

The captain gave the ground next to him a little pat. "You could come here, and we could keep each other warm."

Tristain blushed. The idea of being so close to another man was intriguing, and he'd wanted to do the same to Luka on that night in the Giant's Footfalls, but his parents had been there. "I'll get more wood."

"Oh, come on. I don't bite." He laughed. "Unless you want me to."

Swallowing, Tristain got up and walked over. He crouched, and Vidan made room next to him. The ground was cold, but Vidan's body radiated warmth. Tristain soon stopped shivering.

"What's waiting for you in Invereid?"

"My mother and sister... well, she's not quite a sister, but she's close enough. She's my father's ward."

"Your father's ward?" Vidan's breath was warm and boozy on Tristain's neck.

"Yes."

"You don't talk much, do you?"

Tristain turned. He didn't like this line of questioning. Hurt and guilt ripped through him like the claws of the beast that lived inside him. "I've been trying to get them away from my father for years. He's a brutal man. He hurt me and my brother. When my brother died, and I left for the war, he hurt Mother and Selene." Tears wet his cheeks. "It's the greatest failure of my life that I didn't take them with me, and I didn't find a place for them."

Vidan rubbed his chest, his fingers brushing against mail. The feeling wasn't unpleasant, and Tristain felt a stirring in his groin. "You're still young. Your greatest failures lie ahead of you, I think."

"That's comforting."

He chuckled. "There's nothing we can do to control others. Your father is a bastard, it's true, but there's only so much we can control in this world. You say your mother and sister were stuck... but that's not up to you. They could've run, at any time."

"You're not one to temper your words, are you?"

"I don't see the point. We've only got one life in this world, until the gods take us again to fight in their eternal wars."

Tristain turned and kissed the man. "You're right. I might die at any time—life is short." *It's even shorter for a man with a demon inside, with hunters after him.* Thoughts of Selene shoved into the back of his mind, and Vidan let out a surprised grunt. Then he pressed in deeper, matching Tristain's enthusiasm. Hands made their way down to the loops and belts of their hoses and Tristain took Vidan's manhood in his palm and Vidan did the same to Tristain. Tristain broke the kiss and moved to the captain's chin, neck, Adam's apple. Vidan let out a soft groan that sent a shooting thrill up Tristain's spine.

"Silence, you'll wake someone."

"Let them be woken."

T HEY WERE ON THE road again. It was a hard task, and slow going, while two horses broke from the corral and were lost in the forests surrounding the road. One was found dead, half-eaten by wolves by the time they'd found it. It took two days just to get within sight of the emperor's road, where they moved like clotted blood. Another two days from there to Avercarn. He and Vidan hadn't spoken since that night, and Tristain put their tryst down to something like an experiment—a meal tried and found curious. He only cared for Selene. It was nothing like that with Vidan, and he didn't know if it would ever be. The next day passed without losing a horse or the road, and the marches of the Avallano Mountains moved to thick wood.

He awoke that morning, on the third day after the Pass, after dreaming of Selene. She had grown into a lovely woman, now, but deep sadness nestled in her eyes, like Gida's. Then great clawed hands reached from behind and tore her into pieces. He breathed in sharp as he woke, squinting in the early morning sun. Fog still settled in the air. He was cold, without a lick of clothing on him.

What in Sigur's name...?

The air smelled strongly of copper. He looked around. A black Vyahtken lay next to him. He got up and realized blood covered him. For a moment he thought it was Vidan's and his stomach turned until he looked at the dead creature. Its belly was cut open. Intestines lay strewn across the ground. *Gods... I did this...* Tristain's hands shook as he tasted blood around his mouth.

20

HUNTED

LEVITUM, 1044

*What troubles the soul the greatest is that demons live among
us, living their entire lives without enkindling their natural
inclinations, as the chrysalis event never comes to pass. They
may live full lives and die in their beds having never known
they were cursed.*

— LORD NOTARIUS GIAN ADALLA

TRISTAIN STOLE BACK INTO the camp, bare arse in the morning sun.
They camped on a bald hill, forest and mountains behind them.
Yellow fields of broom-like wheat bloomed ahead of them. The air smelled
crisp, while the porridge stodging over the fire warmed Tristain's cool skin.
Caen and a few of the grooms laughed their heads off.

"Breakfast," Caen yelled, "When the naked prince is ready!"

Vidan offered him a spare set of clothes. "I won't judge," he said. "Everyone's got their own interests."

Tristain turned beet red as he stuck his foot in the pant leg.

"*In*—It's not an interest! I lost my clothes when I was bathing in the
river!" Vidan murmured his agreement, walking off to check the fire. "I
did, I swear!" He blew greasy hair out of his face in frustration.

When Tristain was dressed, he went to join them by the fire. Leon intercepted him.

"Are you okay, lad?" he asked.

Tristain scratched his cheek. "Not really. Can we talk more... privately?"

Leon nodded. They walked down the hill, passing behind a tree. "What is it, son?"

"Well... I went to sleep last night in the camp and woke up out in the forest. I've never walked in my sleep, so imagine my surprise when I find a fucking half-eaten horse at my feet."

Leon wiped a hand over his face, blowing his lips. "You're saying..." Tristain nodded shamefully. Leon took his arms in his hands. It was comforting. "It's high time we learn to control this, no?"

"*Control?* How?"

"Well... how does it normally happen?"

"The first time it happened, it was when I nearly died. But now it happens whenever I get angry, or sad, or—"

"Overwhelmed with emotion?"

"Yeah."

"I imagine it's like any other skill—it needs practice to master. Take your clothes off. Don't be shy, we've both been in the army, son."

"What are you..." Caen said, walking up. He was picking grains out of his teeth. He grunted in surprise, seeing the naked squire in front of him. "I'll leave you two to it, shall I?"

"Tristain slew a horse. I'm training him to control his emotions."

"Sig— *A horse?* Did he look at you funny? Don't mind their long faces."

"Corporal."

"Oh, that. What happened?"

"It makes me sick. I ate its liver and heart, by the looks of it."

Caen leaned on the tree. "So? What brought it on?"

"I can't say. I don't remember having a dream or nightmare, anything that might make me angry or upset."

"I guess we'll have to kill you, then. What? That's what brings it on, right?"

"You better be joking." Leon glowered.

"All right!"

"That's not a bad idea, though," Tristain said. "I can't believe I'm suggesting this, but... what if you attacked me?"

"Eh?"

"Hit me."

Caen wound his fist back. He sunk it hard into Tristain's stomach.

"*Ogh!*"

"Anything?"

"Harder."

Another uppercut.

"Harder!"

A jab to the chin.

"Wait! What if I lose control?"

"Don't worry about it!"

Caen pummeled Tristain, again and again. Leon kept him upright, so he didn't fall over. White pain washed over him. He clenched his jaw, pushing through it.

It was like a floodgate opened in his mind. Leon and Caen jumped backwards. Tristain felt a rush as he transformed. He loomed over the two men. He groaned, feeling the urge to thrash and destroy, but he calmed himself. *I'm in control!*

Leon bellowed a cheer. "Ginevra be fuckin' praised!"

Caen glared, his face turning slightly pale. "Holy Gods! Fuck, up close..."

"Terrifying. That'll put hair on your balls."

"What d'ya think? Looks like a dog's face, right?"

"Bear. Or maybe a wolf?"

"Aye... I could see that. Would explain the teeth. Can you talk?"

Tristain tried to speak, but his mouth and tongue were unfamiliar with the process.

"Yiiidddiot." It sounded a little like a cross between a moo and a yowl.

The knight and the corporal howled with laughter.

Tristain's chest heaved, sniffing the air. Something wasn't right. He glanced around. His ears pricked up. Something rustled in the distance. A whooshing noise drew closer and closer. He dodged, feeling the slight brush of metal past his fur. The bolt thudded harmlessly into a tree.

Caen and Leon spun, drawing their swords. "What the hell was that?"

They're hunters, he wanted to yell, but it sounded more like a distended growl. The two men turned. Confused. *Fuck!*

Tristain ran. The two men cried out after him. Tearing through brush and forest, he tried to get a better look and head the hunters off. But if they were who he thought they were... well, he wasn't sure what he could do. But now he was in control, so maybe he could finally deal with them once and for all.

High in the branches of an elm, Tristain sniffed the air. Two of the hunters were heading this way. They smelled like sweat. Both of them had eaten soaked beans and barley meal for breakfast. The way they barely disturbed the ground as they walked suggested they were light on their feet. They moved like predators, back against back. There wasn't a way to get the drop on them.

The smell of lavender and roses drifted into his nose. Fresh herbs and Tanerian reds. The smell of silver maples blooming in vernia. *What the hell? It couldn't be...* He shook his head, focusing on the task at hand.

He roared. Leaves shook. Birds scattered. The hunters came running.

Racing through the tops of the trees, he led the hunters away, howling every so often to draw them further away from Leon and Caen. He used thick arms and bendy branches to vault his way across the forest. He understood the movement implicitly, somehow, like his expanded hearing—he knew where and how the hunters came after him; which leaves they stepped over; which branches they snapped. The only time they became obscured was when they stopped moving, and Tristain had to rely on his less sensitive, but still improved, sense of smell.

He dropped onto a leaf bed. The hunters were lost; it seemed. They moved in circles, running into each other like headless chickens. He smiled, baring his teeth. *Now, to get back to camp.*

Click. A mechanism thundered to life. A clattering of metal and pulleys. His world spun upside down. Thick chains bit into his leg. Tristain howled. He swung there, helpless.

Shitshitshitshit—

The hunters came running. Tristain reached up, trying to work the chains free. He couldn't get any purchase. The chains were thick. He tried to wrench the links apart, but they were too strong, and he was too exhausted from running. He wondered briefly how far he had run—miles, and yet the hunters seemed to be around every corner.

They drew closer. *Fuckfuckfuck*— The chain loop caught around his ankle. He tried to wriggle his foot loose, but he couldn't get the angle. Then he had a stupid idea. He reached up and snapped his ankle in two. He groaned, blinking back stars that circled at the edge of his vision. Slipping free of the chain, he twisted in the air and landed on his side with a thump. He looked down. His foot dangled at a weird angle.

Using his arms to propel him along the ground, he ran on three legs. Even with a broken ankle, he still moved faster than running on two human legs. He made it back to the edge of the forest, the hill ahead. He looked around in a panic, hoping that Caen and Leon hadn't followed him or the hunters. But no, there they were, standing at the edge of the forest.

How do I transform back? Hm... he focused on his breathing. In. Out. In. Out. Slow. The urge to thrash and destroy was a distant memory. Slowly, he felt his chest relax, and his breath grow steady. He thought of his sister, and their childhood. A picture of Selene formed in his mind, of them giggling as they tricked Bann—making him think their father wanted him at the stables, when he was really in his office. The look on his face as he marched back up to the house, of which Tristain and Selene had a prime view of from Tristain's window. Other moments, too, flashed in his mind.

Remember when you lost a horse's bit? Father was so furious. I took the blame, remember? You didn't see it, but he gave me a flogging. You owe me one.

He recalled the song his mother used to sing as she brushed his hair.

"Oh, sweet child,

Oh, sweet child of Juniper.

Blessed that rests on her knee,

Never have I seen such a likeness,

But in the child before me."

Tristain studied his body. His arms had shrunk back to their normal size; his sense of smell returned to its usual mundane state. Black fur sheathed itself under his skin. It was a strange feeling. The Change was taking less of a toll on his body and mind now, he noted, as he did not collapse from exhaustion this time.

Pain bit into his calf. Caen and Leon looked up as the squire cried out at the edge of the forest. They raced over.

"Shit," Leon said, cradling Tristain's underarm on his shoulder. He had a shirt for him to put on. "C'mon lad. We'll get that foot fixed up."

"Hell of a thing," Tristain said, chuckling.

"Oye, what happened?" Caen asked, helping with the other side.

"They're miles deep in the forest still. I led them on a wild chase. But then they caught me in a snare. I had to break my ankle to escape."

"Gods be good."

When they reached the camp, the horses were already being corralled, and were ready to go. Clearly, the grooms hadn't noticed one missing. The captain nodded as they returned. The sky darkened as a drop of water fell on Tristain's cheek.

"**S**HUT THAT SIGUR-CURSED DOOR!" someone yelled. Their cloaks spilled with a deluge as freezing wind battered the inside of the taphouse. The captain closed the door behind them as he strode over to the barkeep, putting four fingers up, and joined the other three as they thumped down at a table.

"The ale's good here," Vidan said. "Have a drink. It's on me. Pay's in my chest upstairs. Give me a minute, though. I'll have to take a cut of the missing Vyahtken out of it."

Caen raised his hand to ask how much that'd be, but the merchant's son was already up the stairs and out of sight.

Tristain wiped long wet hair out of his face. Water dripped from his sodden beard onto the table. He laughed inside. Seventeen years and not a whisker, and now it was practically impossible to get rid of it. It paled next to Leon's, of course.

Tristain glanced around. Two dancers twirled by the minstrel in the corner, dressed in vests traditionally with bells, tilting their hips in time to the music. They were muscular, more muscular than Tristain would imagine a dancer to be, with bulging shoulders and firm necks.

At a table next to them sat a merchant in fine clothes, speaking in strongly accented Osbergian. He was probably from the republics, the same as that bastard steward. Which one, though, Tristain was never sure. Alania, probably. The man across from the merchant had his lean, powerful arms crossed and seemed deeply uninterested. His long, dark hair streaked with white was tied back in a ponytail, while the scars on his face spoke to an interesting and dangerous life. Not wanting to linger on the tough, Tristain moved his gaze along.

Next was a farmer and his wife; their small child was in a swaddling basket alongside. The wife had a tansy flower tucked behind her ear, blonde hair framing a youthful face. She looked the part of a young mother, but something about her seemed uncertain, like she was expecting something to happen at any moment. In fact, both of them looked like they were waiting for something. Their food lay untouched before them.

Along from them stood the barkeep, who was wiping the same spot on the bar, compulsively, like he was trying to clean a year-old stain. Over by the door looming like an enormous shadow, was a man. A gigantic man, dressed in an oversized black cloak. The fabric blanketed him, darkness obscuring his face under his hood. Tristain glanced down. A steel sabaton poked out from beneath. He was a knight, like Leon. Others sat around, drinking alone. He hadn't expected the alehouse to be busy. *The ale must be good*, he thought. *So why is everyone cross?*

The minstrel plucked a cheery tune, and the brawny dancers twirled again, though the patrons' faces remained unsettled. The barmaid came up to them with their tankards. Tristain thanked her with a smile. She was young, younger than himself. She would've been the innkeeper's daughter, most likely, though they looked nothing alike.

"Hey, lass," Leon said. The woman gave him a curt nod. "Any news of the war?"

Caen added, "Must've been hard to see all the young men leave."

"Oh, been fine," she replied. As she spoke, her accent seemed strange for a southerner, speaking more with the refined tones of the capital. "There's no war here. Sigur protects this house." *Sigur? Sigur doesn't give a toss about travelers and alehouses. That's Eme's job.*

"Thanks, lass," Leon said. The barmaid walked off and joined the barkeep. She lingered her eyes on Tristain before someone else called for her.

Tristain took a sip of his ale. It was light and fruity, slightly sweet. It slid down easily. Soon enough, they needed another round.

"Where's that Sigur-cursed idiot?" Caen yelled, drawing a few eyes. "He better not 've gotten lost on the way to our money."

"Ah," Leon said. "He's probably hoping we'll get bored and piss off so he doesn't have to pay us. You know those burghers. They could sit on a pile of money and still have their hands outstretched, looking for more."

Caen laughed. "That one'll go to his grave with his hands outstretched, I'm sure."

Tristain got up after a few more rounds. He needed a piss. The giant man in the corner got to his feet as well. Tristain froze. Gods, he was tall. The top of his hood grazed the ceiling. He was wide, too. His dark grey blanket, because that's what it was, gave him the appearance of a mobile wall.

It was only at that moment that he noticed the minstrel had stopped playing. Tristain sat back down. He leaned forward. "Something doesn't feel right."

Caen turned his head. "What?"

"Have you seen that giant by the door?"

Caen glanced backwards. "Hmph. He's big."

Leon rested his hand on his sword-hilt. "I see what you mean. Have you seen the state of those dancers? I've seen lither woodcutters."

"I've not heard that woman's baby cry once since we arrived," Tristain added. He gestured with his eyes. "And what about that merchant? Annaltian clothes, but Tanerian accent? If he's Republican, I'm the emperor."

"I think we need to go."

Leon nodded. They stood. Chairs scraped on the ground. The farmer and his wife stood. The merchant and his bodyguard. The dancers and the minstrel all came closer, moving to surround them. All of them stared daggers.

Caen drew his sword. "What are you lookin' at, ugly?" He directed his words to the farmer. As he drew closer, Tristain noticed he had nearly half his face missing. Mangled, like a dog had attacked him. Tristain pulled his longsword. Leon drew his sword and axe.

Laughter came from above the stairs. The treads creaked as a woman in a black cloak descended upon them. Tristain felt the blood drain from his face. Like a jab to the nose from a powerful fist, the scent of lavender punched his nostrils, almost knocked him off his feet.

"Selene...?"

"You always were a little dull, cursed beast," she said. It was her, but she was different. Her raven hair came in waves, vibrant and lustrous, but her green eyes, once bright and curious, now stared at him coldly, completing a cruel sneer. A small scar on her chin rounded out the look, as if she'd dodged a knife or a sword a fraction too slowly. The way she carried herself was new as well. No longer the meek child. She pulled her shoulders back, commanding the room. And the biggest thing... it took Tristain a second, but he realised. He wanted to throw his arms around her, offer her comfort, but... *Holy gods! What happened to her arm?*

"It took half an hour for you and your friends to see through our mummery. And I am Diana, a vessel of the holy martyr, and an inquisitor of the Sigurblessed Holy Order of the Golden Sword, and you'll address me as such, demon."

Tristain's jaw went slack. "Dem— What are you talking about? I'm your brother!" *She's the one hunting us. Gods, what happened to her?* Martyr and inquisitor... she was in the Order now, a Golden Sword.

Caen laughed. Leon scratched his neck with the sharp end of his axe.

"I knew that captain was a bastard liar," Caen muttered.

"Had us fooled," Leon remarked.

"That'd be Karl." She laughed, a bitter laugh that was completely foreign to Tristain.

"What do you want from us?"

"I'd want your heads on spikes if it was up to me," she replied, as calm as if she were giving directions. "But it isn't. So, will you come quietly?"

Tristain felt sick. "Heads on spikes... Gods, what happened to you?"

"I have been blessed, demon. I am a sword of the Lightfather, shield of the innocent."

Silence fell as he pondered the question. *Would he come quietly?* Tristain snorted, twisting his hands over the hilt of his sword.

"Sorry, Selene. I won't go with you. Step back. I don't want to hurt you."

She smiled. She *wanted* him to say that. "Oh, don't worry. You won't." A crossbow *twanged*. The bolt bit into Tristain's shoulder. A flare of pain shot up his arm to his neck. He grit his teeth, ignoring the pain. He dropped to one hand, bursting forward with his sword. Selene moved aside easily. Tristain stumbled on his hurt foot. His vision blurred. The woman he'd grown up with, the woman he'd once thought he'd marry, grinned, wicked and cunning, as he collapsed to the ground. Tristain's body wracked with fire, prickling with needles.

The giant marched over. Caen swung his sword, cutting through the enormous cloak. The blade glanced harmlessly off the plate underneath. The huge man grasped Caen's face, lifting him easily. He brought the corporal up, then drove his head into the floor. The wood cracked. His eyes were glassy as his body went limp. Blood pooled from his head. Tristain could only watch in agony, helpless... unable to move or change.

Leon clashed with the merchant and his bodyguard, crying out in fury, until he took a sword in the chest. He collapsed to the floor, coughing dark red blood onto the wood.

"Take them," the inquisitor said, her face stretched out in a wicked grin.

VOLUME THREE

Pages from a leather-bound journal:

I was framed! Unbelievable. Albrecht will regret this. I've had to flee from the city, but I will return one day, to seek my rightful place as Lord Silberwald at the Archduke's side.

I was attacked on the road. I cannot see out of one eye, and my face hurts something terrible. I have lost my voice. Ditchborn bandits took a shine to the chain around my neck—I suppose it's only right. It was a gift from the Archduke, and I didn't deserve it. When I fought them off, one of them transformed into a monstrous creature.

Some Sigurian priest saved me. Gods. He's given me some drug to help with the pain, and slathered my face in a poultice, but my hands tremble as I write this. It's tiresome.

I woke up in a dingy stone temple near Etzen. He tells me that given a month or two, I'll be getting around again.

Some visitors came to the temple today. They were armed to the teeth, but stopped for no more than a chat and a waterskin. Golden Swords, even though they wore black. One of them eyeballed me. I'm sure he didn't know what to make of a highborn down on his luck as I am.

Getting around gets easier every day. I regained my voice, though it is still scratchy. I'm holding a sword again. Praise all the Gods I haven't forgotten how to fence. Only having one eye has affected my depth perception, but it isn't anything I cannot get used to. Maybe soon I can return to Ostelar, reclaim my rightful place. Though they'd probably run in horror from my horrible face. I was beautiful once. What a cruel joke the Gods have played.

The black-clads returned today. One of them came up to me as I was practicing. We sparred, and he complimented my technique, as I knew he would. He asked how I acquired my disfigured face. I told him of the beast that attacked me. He suggested I should join the Order. Apparently, they hunt the creatures. I was going to say no until I asked a few questions. It's incredible. They're rudderless. Unfocused. They only fight for tradition's sake. They have no idea what potential they have. The laws of men don't apply to them. They could do incredible things, and answer to no one. I was wrong. I won't return to Ostelar. No, the Order will suit my ambitions, just nicely.

21

TO THE CITADEL

SANGUINUM, 1044

*Three drops of morel berry sap, also known as atropine, causes
disorientation and paralysis of the demon within minutes. Five
drops, death within seconds. Keep this at the forefront of your
mind if you wish to contain the demon rather than kill.*

— LORD INQUISITOR ELIAS ROTERSAND

FOLK PASSED DIANA AND the other Swords on the road north, young,
old, little children, babes at their mother's teats. The south offered
refuge, safety from the coming war. The north only offered death. Some
drove wagons, or carts as they did, their families walking alongside them.
Most came on foot, their goods on their backs. All wore hard looks. The
men and the women carried weapons. Axes, scythes, sickles. Some gave
lingering looks over Diana's cart. The allure of the covered wagon might've
been too much to deny if it were just Diana on her own. The inquisitor had
silver at her belt. Even that might've been tempting enough, but the three
other Swords deterred them from getting any closer. The armored giant,
Manus, likely kept them away with his sheer size alone. He was practically
a walking mountain, seven feet tall, at least.

They stopped by a brook. Diana led Eda to the water for a drink. She
brushed her fingers through the horse's chestnut mane, drawing it out,

watching the hair fall, strand by strand. She reflected on the capture. *Did I go overboard? Eight seemed a little excessive for just three of them...* The four others had moved on—wardens sent back to their duties at the local preceptory. *It felt necessary, but I wonder if I was overcompensating. How many hunts have I been on? Twenty-five, thirty? Why is it that one mention of family and I'm hesitating like a damn novitiate?*

"Brother, huh?" Tansy said. Diana turned. Her affinity for silent movement was enviable. She danced a bolt between her fingers, leaning against a tree.

"What?"

"You heard me."

"Yes, the beast is my brother. So what?"

"No need to get defensive." She snatched the bolt from the air and walked up. Right into Diana's face. She had blonde hair, with viperous blue eyes, and the practiced, purposeful step of a professional. She was shorter than Diana and looked up. "I don't want to let any attachments impede what needs to be done."

"Hm. They won't. And Arbiter... you step out of line again, and you know what happens."

The woman smiled. "Evening, Inquisitor."

Diana breathed and released her jaw. *I'll have to watch her...* Lena had confronted her again without regard for seniority. That meant trouble.

They continued along the road. Diana kept her gaze on the cart. Muscles in her neck clenched involuntarily. She took a deep breath, trying to calm herself and adjusted in the saddle. Eda shook her head, whinnied. Diana felt the creature pull at the bridle. She wanted to go faster. Diana obliged.

"I'm riding ahead," she declared as she cantered past. She gave a few flicks with the reins, turning the pace into a gallop. "Hyah!"

The horse pulled ahead, further, further, along the road, over a bumpy path, on damp grass, splashing over silver puddles, under leafy birches. A scared fox flashed its fluffy, bright orange tail as it disappeared into a bush.

Wren, magpies, all sorts screamed into the air. Eda threw her neck forward as her strong back muscles worked between Diana's thighs.

They went further, further, until the wagon was long out of sight. Then Diana slowed, moving to a trot, then a walk. She sighed, looking around. She had a job to do. After all, she had the duty of protecting the cart. She could do that from here. Protecting them until they delivered the cargo to the citadel. *Protecting them from what?* The Lord Inquisitor wanted the Black Beast and The Strong alive. He clarified that if they were harmed, it would mean all of their heads. *Why?* That was a dangerous question. She buried it in the back of her mind.

The road was empty. The train of refugees had reduced to a trickle. Tristain was a monster, a horrible beast. The bodies outside the alehouse in Badonnia made that clear. *Galeaz reported a field of severed heads and body parts... he wasn't wrong. It was a massacre. It resembled how those children the tax collector killed looked, but on a larger scale... he's much more dangerous than Father ever was. He wouldn't be alive if I had anything to do with it. We may have shared a home, but it was luck he didn't claw my eyes out when he cried for Mother.* She squeezed the reins. Her face screwed up. Angry tears rolled down her cheek. *Now he's just a few hundred paces away, more than capable of killing again.* She could only hope that the sleeping drug held its sway.

She stopped, wiping her face. *But he is like Father: Cursed. Is it his family? Maybe it's what Sigur wants. His family was cursed, and I'm the only one who can save them.*

A strong wind blew through the trees, leaves whipping up into the air. Eda shuffled, got nervous. *Storm's coming... We'll need to make camp soon. I'll find the firewood and light the fire. Lena will hunt our dinner. Manus will lift the swingle-tree from the sumpter and undo the traces. Soren'll set up the tents, hitching the poles and setting the lines. I'll sleep with Lena. It wouldn't be proper for the men to share our tent.*

And then... then we'll have to deal with them.

TRISTAIN DREAMED HE LAID with his face pressed against timber, the deck of a ship in a nameless ocean bobbing up and down in the waves. His body ached. He went to speak, but nothing came. He glanced behind. The sea rippled with green forest and grey rock. His mother stood in the center, staring back at him, holding her eyes in her hands. Her sockets were dark pits, but he could feel them boring deep into his soul. She turned her back on him. He ran through the trees, crying out all the while for her, again and again, until she disappeared.

Stabbing pain in his shoulder thrust him awake. The world was blurry, bloody. Every roll of the wagon's wheel was pain, his head pounding. He concentrated, trying to change, but he couldn't. There wasn't anything he could do—he was as helpless as a drowning man begging for air. Things went black as the motion of the cart and drowsiness took him again.

He dreamed he was in camp again, delusional as he was. Propped up like a deserter on the rack, bent low by a whip. The crowd egged him on. Caen and Nikkel, Leon the Strong, Andrea and Maria from Badewald, Lombas the Small, Herrad and Caspar... all dead, all hollow. The noble knight had a hole in his chest, sucking air. Andrea had her head split in two. Caen had his tongue cut out. They howled for him to help them. Unending... their howls wracked his skull until he cried out for them to stop.

A white wolf appeared and ate them all, devouring the world until it was nothing but a void. Tristain fell, tumbling down and down, to the deepest pit below it all. Everything was black. *This is Hell.* He knew it in his heart. It wasn't a pit of fire, or death, or demons. *Black... unending black, for eternity. Cold nothingness.*

His breath was icy in front of him. A chill passed over his body. His blood felt icy in his veins. The pulsing of his freezing heart in his chest, beating faster and faster and harder and harder until it ruptured, tearing and gnashing with wild teeth through his skin. He screamed for it to stop. He screamed for his mother.

"*Squire!*" a voice from the bowels of the earth said. Tristain groaned, fluttering his eyes. The wagon came into focus. It was Leon. *You're alive!* He went to scream but found he couldn't talk. His mouth was gagged and refused to cooperate, anyway. The walls spun as he sat upright. His head felt like it was made of lead.

"Squire!" The knight's muffled voice. A foot shoved his shoulder. "Oi! *Sal'brath!*"

"Sigur, be quiet," a woman yelled from outside the wagon.

Tristain tried to move his arms. They wouldn't cooperate, either. He looked down, his head unsteady, unable to support its own weight. Thick ropes wrapped around his wrists and ankles. Leon was bound in the same way.

The wagon slowed, then stopped. Heavy clanking feet came to the back. The flap opened. The giant man in plate, towering and immense, stared at him, then reached over and scooped him up. He carried him with ease, as if Tristain weighed as much as a feather. The giant propped him up against a tree, orange light coming from a crackling fire. Tristain's head slumped. The giant laid down Leon next to him like a sack of potatoes.

A green-eyed, raven-haired, vicious woman sat across from him on a log. She leaned over, staring at him. She'd tied her hair back in a tight knot, while a dagger and crossbow sat at her tooled-leather belt. A black boiled leather jerkin over her top, and black trousers under a black cloak. She wore a gold brooch of a flaming sword at the fold of her cloak. One arm was missing, a metal plate over the shoulder. It did nothing to tame the savagery in the look she was giving him.

A strong wind chilled him to his bones. She said nothing. She simply stared.

"So," a blonde woman with a yellow flower tucked in her hair said, squatting next to him. It was the farmer's wife from the alehouse. She wore a similar set to Selene, though without the brooch of a flaming sword. *No, she's not the farmer's wife. That was a fiction. This woman is a Sword. She hunts my kind.* Tristain narrowed his brows as she eyed him up and down vigorously. She had freckles and pale skin, and a taut scar down her cheek in the shape of a crescent.

"He's a pretty one," she said. "But skinny. Hardly a beast. Shame. I like my men with a bit of meat on them."

"This one's for His Revered, Arbiter," the silver-haired, broad-shouldered, handsome one said, walking up from the horses. "If we gave him to you, Tansy, he's apt to end up like the last one."

"I'd like to get him to the Citadel in one piece," Selene said.

Tansy stuck her chin out. "His Revered like young, pretty boys?"

"I don't concern myself with the Lord Inquisitor's predilections, and neither should you. Enough. Let's just eat."

The big one wasn't a giant, after all. In Tristain's much less deluded mind, he was just an enormous man. Though he was taller than any man he'd ever seen. He cooked three skinned rabbits over the fire as the sun went down and a strong wind whipped up. He turned them with care, roasting them until they were golden on all sides. He wore his plate and helmet even now, beside the fire.

Tristain glanced at his shoulder. A bloody bandage had been wrapped around it, and the bolt was gone. They had stripped him of his mail and sword. He looked around. The hilt of it stuck out from under one horse's saddle. Clearly, one of them had thought it was worth something. Perhaps they would sell it.

"Do we give them some?" Tansy said, munching on her rabbit. She nodded to Tristain.

"Give him a nibble. Enough to keep him going," Selene replied.

What happened to her?

The woman did as she was told, taking Tristain's gag off first.

"How could you, Selene?" Tristain's voice came hoarse and strained. The inquisitors looked at each other and laughed.

"Just take the food and shut your mouth," Selene said.

Tansy chuckled and shoved the roasted haunch into his face.

Tristain took a bite.

"There, was that so hard?"

"Gods curse you."

Tansy's eyes flashed with excitement. She smashed him across the face with the back of her gloved hand. He cried out and blood dripped into his mouth.

She laughed. "You demons... it's always the same thing. All bark, no bite. Some morel berry, and you're as weak as babes at their mother's tit." She tapped him on the nose with the half-eaten rabbit leg. "Any more of that, and we might just forget to feed you." She yanked the gag back into place.

Leon watched what happened. He was silent and ate without complaint. *I'm sure he figures they'll let him go, eventually. They'll have to. He's a knight of the empire, a hero, even disenfranchised as he is. If the archduke or the emperor were to find out they have captured him...*

Tansy sat next to the fire, picking up her lute as the others ate. She plucked gently, singing as the fire popped and the dark overtook them. She sang, like they sat at a minstrel show. *"Brigida and Dietrich, they slew the heretic..."* Her voice glided over the melody. The silver-hair joined in. Selene just leaned back on her log. Her expression was... content? It was hard to tell, but she certainly hadn't been broken up about killing someone—or an underling killing someone on her orders. Who was this monster who sat before him?

She's gone. The girl you knew, the girl you relied upon, could count upon, could understand you... loved you... she's gone. The Order has taken her. They've taken her humanity.

Tristain saw Caen singing along with them. He blinked, and the corporal was gone.

D IANA ROSE WITH THE dawn. Journey on the road these days necessitated her rising—bandits might mistake them for refugees—and she huddled close in her cloak at the dead fire. She poked at it with a stick, hoping to find some embers to start another fire and warm her bones, but the day stretched long ahead, and they'd warm up on the road.

The sky was a limp gray, threatening rain in the afternoon. The two prisoners sat back-to-back, sleeping, making soft babbling noises. Diana put the whetstone on her thigh and began to sharpen her dagger. Soren woke with the rasping sound, though the others slept.

Except Manus. She could never be sure if he slept—even in sleep, he kept the helmet on. In either case, he laid flat on the ground, arms spread wide, crushing grass under his bulk.

Soren joined her beside the ashes. He didn't say anything, and she didn't either.

"Brother," he said after a while.

"Adoptive brother."

"What will you do if he tries to escape?"

"Kill him, of course."

He nodded at that. After a pause, she said, "I don't feel anything for him. I can perform my duties." She couldn't tell who she was trying to convince more, him or herself.

"As long as you're in top fighting shape. We can't afford distractions."

"I didn't kill him when I was a girl. I should have. I would've rectified that mistake in that tavern, but Rotersand wants him alive. It's not my place to question it, of course, but I'm left to wonder."

"Good." Soren slapped her leg. Any feelings they held for each other were long gone. The feelings of a meek little girl. A lot had changed in a year, while life and circumstance kept her honed. Fit for purpose. She needed to remember that.

They set out again, nicking the Black Beast—that was his name, not Tristain—with the poison, and he went as limp as a worm. The emperor's road picked up more refugees, all going against them. A group of men and mules pulling drays covered with canvas lumbered along just ahead.

Soren rode alongside her, while Manus drove the cart.

She spurred Eda on and yelled, "Yah!" She waved her arm. "Off the road! Make way! Order business!"

The men scattered, pulling their mules off the road. A dray rolled, bumped, hit a rock, and toppled over. Cloth pulled back to reveal weapons—spears, swords, shields, armor. Cries from the men went up.

"Get this off the road! Now!"

They hesitated, expecting her to care about the arms.

"This isn't Sword business. I don't care if you're deserters or Annaltians or Veles-cursed brigands. Get this off the road!"

Dispersing, they gathered up the blades and armor and started to move them. But it was slow work, since the dray had to be righted, and it had snapped one of its traces.

Soren rode up. "What happened?"

"One of the drays hit a rock and toppled. This'll take the better part of the day to clear. Should we double-back and see if there's a way around?"

"You itch to be at the Citadel?"

"I itch to be free of our fucking charge." She slapped the air with her hand, in the direction of their prisoners. "How much morel sap do we have? How long will that last?"

"Long enough." Soren narrowed his eyes.

"I'll go back and see if there's a way around."

"Now?"

"I've never known you to be cautious, Soren. When you took me from Invereid to the Citadel we stopped for nothing."

"He's your brother."

"I could leave you behind, find the path on my own."

Soren winced at that. "You are the inquisitor-in-charge on this mission."

"I know."

"What's got into you?"

Tansy shouted, "What's the fucking hold up!" Nials sniggered by her side.

"They're like children," Diana mused. "I do better alone. When you were gone, I found a depth of faith and strength I never knew existed. And now you're back, on mission, and I can't stop being distracted."

"Is the problem me or your brother?"

"Stop talking about my fucking brother! He's not my brother, he's a demon!"

"When was the last time you saw him?"

Her throat tightened. *The—*

"Tournament. The August Griffin Tournament, in Invereid. Father hosted it every year, until Bann died." The words spilled from her mouth. "No, I turned my back on that past. You said it yourself. We forget our past as soon as we set foot in the training hall."

He leaned in. "I lied. You can never forget your past. It's like forgetting how to breathe. Tell me."

She looked back. "Will our companions overhear us?"

"We're scouting ahead," Soren shouted back to them, preempting Diana.

Tansy made a face like a spoilt child that had just been relieved of its toy. "Fine! Don't hump for too long!"

22

THE TOURNAMENT

Three Years Ago

WHEN THE ARCHDUKE'S SON arrived at the Oncierran estate, the field already swam in bright colors. Selene pressed her thumb down to still her fingers. She could do nothing for the heart thrumming in her chest. Fighters had arrived ahead of the archduke's firstborn, the guest of honor, and the entire household was to meet him at the front of the house. He would one day be emperor, after all.

It had rained in the small hours of the morning, and the deluge passed before the dawn, leaving a bright sheen on everything. The smell of wood sap and blossoming flowers. She could almost ignore the bruise on her thigh, given to her by Father. It only hurt a little when she walked, now. Otherwise, it just felt numb.

She dug her nail into her thumb, stopping just shy of breaking the skin. Tristain turned his head and smiled. She smiled back.

He looked like a lord, today. Not that he didn't all the time, but today, he stood out. Green silk danced up his narrow waist, meeting his broad shoulders in a tantalizing *V*. Brocade cut across the front, in a panel in the center, buttoned by pearls carved into the shape of acorns. Their family emblem. Well, the Oncierran emblem. Selene's family wasn't important enough to have an emblem, but they were important enough to repair a ward to a count—a daughter, no more—so there she was.

Father and Mother stood side-by-side at the head of the assembled household. All the servants stood behind Selene and the other children,

Bann, and Tristain. The firstborn, Bann, penciled things into a soft-leather journal. He wore an iteration of Tristain's outfit—both were iterations of Father's, really—but his straight-up-and-down body did nothing for the eye. Where Tristain held a sword, Bann held a quill. He was off to the archduke's court, as second secretary to the revenue service. But not before one last chance for Father to show him off.

The deal was struck that when the archduke's son repaired to Ostelar, Bann would go with him.

Good. I'll be glad to be rid of that snake. Something about the boy, and now the man, always creeped her out. Gave her goosepimples across her neck, made her shiver.

Mother wore her perfume of lavender and crushed roses, which washed over Selene now as the gentle breeze changed direction. She looked at her, a smile shared between them that gave Selene strength.

The archduke's entourage rode up the rise, shining in steel and bright fabrics, brighter banners. They'd see the count's strong walls, dressed in silver acorns on green fields. Loops and wooden hoardings hung from the stonework, ready for defenders to make any attackers' life hell.

Father said it was about presenting a unified front against the archduke, after all. "Rudolf," he'd said, "and by extension, his father, must see his vassals are strong. We will, of course, be his one day."

To this end, Father had every guard dressed in bearded helms and armed with spears and lined the rise with them like roadside flowers. Flowers to go unwatered, but the threat that blood could spill would give Rudolf and his entourage a lesson that the Count of Invereid stood strong. As an ally, for now.

Riding on strong Vyahtken horse, they issued from the gate over hard-beaten ground, pluming dust behind them. Father smoothed his doublet, adjusted his wide-brimmed felt hat. Tristain followed suit while Bann watched with interest, tapping his chin with his quill. Mother smiled her gentlest smile, her own suit of armor, and Selene straightened her shoulders and prepared her best coquettish look.

If Father saw her charming the archduke's son, maybe he'd ease the beatings. She dug her nail into her thumb, forced her smile.

From the side of Rudolf's entourage, the herald approached on a delicate-looking palfrey, raising a silver baton.

His voice struck their ears like a thunderclap. "His Highness, Rudolf, son of Albrecht, Duke of Taneria, and Prince of the Lion Throne."

He wore as many shining curves of plate as he carried names, his face obscured by his lion-faced helmet, as though he rushed to do a quintain before the tournament had even started. Rudolf lifted his lance to salute the count and turned about, gave his horse gold-plated spurs. He threw the beast towards the lists, back the way he came. Hooves clapped the ground as he returned down the slope. His entourage followed, kicking up dust. Father turned the color of beets.

Trumpets sounded. The guest of honor had arrived.

S ELENE WAS ALLOWED WHERE she liked before supper, and so she went down to the field to watch the fighters prepare. Squires in bright livery and little pageboys rushed around cleaning bits of armor, fixing saddles, washing clothing. If she were to count all the streaking bodies on the list field, it would be like counting the heads of wheat in a windy field.

Bann sought to inflict his presence on Selene, intercepting her at the top of the hill. His ever-present quill was tucked behind his ear. Usually there was never much said between them—he had his plans, and Selene was never in them. They involved his betters; he was always striving to be noticed.

A boy and now a man obsessed with pleasing Father. It was pathetic, really.

"What do you want, Bann?"

"Can a brother not see his sister for one of the last days he might ever see her?"

Selene smirked. "What do you want?"

"What?" He folded his arms. "I have to want something?"

"You haven't called me sister in all the years I've been Father's ward. Not once. I can only assume you want something."

He smiled, calling images to mind of a rotting carcass. Selene shivered.

"Yes, I suppose so. Perhaps I'll have you join me in Ostelar once I'm established. You seem perceptive enough. But you should've let that dog die."

Color washed from the sky and her breathing came sharp as she recalled that day, a week prior. She dug her nail into her hand again. Her bruise flared to life, a stinging whip across her thigh.

"That'll be the death of you. You care too much, it's dreadful."

Selene snorted. "I care too much? I rather think not caring enough is the problem."

The dog had come in from the rain, wet and limping. It wasn't theirs—it was a stray, from the village, maybe, or it belonged to one of the serfs. Either way, Selene had taken pity on it, and hidden it in the stables. Father didn't want the mangy runt—his words—stinking up his estate, and they'd have to care for it anyhow.

He brained the animal with a cleaver. In front of her. A quick death suited it better, he said, and he wanted to teach her a lesson. After, he gave Selene a thrashing with his belt. She could still taste the fear and blood on her tongue.

"What should I have done? Left it to die?"

"Yes. There's no sense in helping a creature that can't help itself."

"That may be good for you, Bann," she said, drawing out the last syllable. His name, wrung tightly in disgust. "But I refuse to live like that."

"Then I can't help you, either. Don't come to Ostelar. You'd die there. Goodbye, sister."

He shouldered her as he walked off, the back of his head fixed, shoulders fixed, immovable. Black hair the color of midnight, the color of death.

She scoffed. "*Should've left it to die,*" she whispered. If chance or circumstance ever had it that she could leave him to die, she would.

S HE SAT ON THE lee side of the hill. A field stretched out like a lazy lover to the stream and forest on the other side, long grass flattened by the arrivals over the last week. In the center of the camp, there was what looked to be the nailed-together sides of a barn that the builder forgot to put the roof on, with a set of stairs built up around the sides. The lists. Where men would battle for their honor, though there were a couple women too. A duchess, Ilse Adolar, among them.

Father would never let me fight. Courage fled her and fear needled her when she imagined it. He'd beaten her for as little as play-fighting with Tristain in the garden. That didn't mean she didn't practice in secret, of course.

Men from Annaltia, wearing surcoats of the black bear on red field, argued with men from Invereid, silver maples on green field. Their words garbled on the wind, and she heard boots behind her.

"Warriors can't resist a good joust, no matter where they're from. Especially when the fighting hasn't started in earnest."

She looked up. A thick-shouldered man in a plain doublet exploded with muscle and red hair. Alongside him, a boy no older than Tristain, with the same eruption of thin red hair on his head, and not too different in size either. The man's son.

She went to stand when he waved a jovial hand. His hillman accent danced along the syllables. "Sit, sit. Don't stand on my account, lass. Do you mind if we join you?"

"Of course."

"You're Oncierran's lass, ain't you? His ward? I'm Leon, and this is my son, Erken."

The boy waved, curled up over his knees. Leon did the same, his hose tugged down over his thighs, leaving the top of his arse slapped with the wind. Selene covered her mouth and tried not to laugh.

"Pleasure to meet you. I'm Selene."

Leon leaned in. "This ain't a real fight. Those men wouldn't be so eager if this was a tournament of old."

"When they fought to the death?"

"Aye. This is just peacocks havin' a go, trying to make each other look small."

"Are you fighting?"

"Aye, lass. Are you?"

She laughed. "No, of course not."

Solni dipped his toes below a cloud, shooting bright shafts of light through gray motes drifting across the horizon like logs floating lazily down a river. Out beyond the field to the north, the forest broke to wheat farms licking the air with their yields—Father's tenants. He owned the land from here to the horizon, and one day it would be Bann's. She bit her lip. How old would a man have to be before he couldn't hold a belt, anymore?

How many years would she have to live under his roof? She needed to find a husband, someone who would take her away. Maybe that could be these hillmen—she'd live in the South Hills if it meant getting away from Father.

She turned to Leon. "Where is your wife, lord?"

"No lord, aye. Just a lowly knight."

She drew back her eyelids. "Ginevra's chalice! You're Leon the Strong, aren't you?" She jumped to her feet and bowed, which was awkward on the side of the hill. "It's an honor."

He laughed. "Aye, lass, that's what they call me."

"I'm sorry."

"Aye, it's not your fault. The name stuck. I mean, it's fitting."

"No, I mean, I didn't recognize you. Are you fighting?"

"Aye. Tell my son he's being ridiculous by not trying his hand."

"I won't take the chance of fighting against you, Father," Erken said. He had a soft, innocent voice. It wasn't only the words, but the way he'd said them, that spoke to his generosity.

"The men will think you're a coward."

"I don't care."

The longer they talked, the more she realized she wouldn't gain much from this conversation. Erken was only a knight's son, and one from the South Hills at that. It was no Annalt or Ostelar. She hated that Father forced a brutal calculus—when she wasn't moving ahead in the world, she was falling behind. With a belt or a smack waiting for her if she fell too far.

"Excuse me," she said, interrupting them. "I just realized I have duties to attend to. Enjoy the feast." She smiled, and they looked a little dumbstruck by her sudden departure.

Erken said, in a small voice, "Until then."

She walked up the hill, holding her skirts so she didn't trip. The castle's curtain wall dripped with banners like it sweated heraldry. Bolt holes stared back like eyes between the banners.

A team of servants carted three whole goats, the goats dead and hung by their legs from wooden poles. Ahead, a pair of oxen drove ahead at the goad, the servant driving them was a wizened old man who had a stooped neck. His voice slapped their ears as he pushed them up the hill to their ultimate fate.

A hundred people had to be fed, after all. Selene didn't quite know how they'd fit them all in the estate's great hall, but Mother would certainly try. She had a talent for that sort of thing, and she made sure no one went hungry.

Mother waited at the top of the hill, in fact. She waved the train of servants inside and smiled as Selene approached.

"Father's not here," Mother said, sounding thrilled with that. "He's gone to talk with the archduke's son for a spell."

Selene's chest flared with excitement. "What about?"

"He wants Rudolf to sit next to you at the feast."

She couldn't hide her surprise. "*Father*—of course. Does he want me to marry him?"

"Effortlessly practical you are, my daughter. Not there!" she yelled, waving to the line of servants. "Behind the arches!"

The team of oxen were corrected with the goad, making snorting noises. The servant cursed Sigur for their difficulty.

Mother tucked a lock of hair behind Selene's ear and looked on her kindly. "If that is what you want."

"Of course, Mother."

"I'm only asking."

"Yes. If it'll get me away from him." Mother knew about the bruises, what Father did to Selene. He started with Mother, after all.

Mother took Selene's hands in her own. "I only want a better life for you than I had."

Selene frowned. Bann's words infected her, although maybe she was already like him more than she realized.

"You're acting like you'll never see me again. If I marry the archduke's son, he'll become archduke, one day. Albrecht wastes from gout, they say, so I doubt I'll have to wait long to sit the White Throne. Then I can have Father imprisoned and take you as far away from him as possible. Maybe you can even live in the White Palace, with me."

"That would be nice."

"If Father thinks it's his idea, all the better."

"Alright. Have the servants draw a bath and get you dressed for the feast."

S ELENE DRIFTED IN THE beaten copper tub, pruning her fingers. By the water clock on the wall, supper floated somewhere soon, leaving her with time to soak now. Time to strategize. What did the archduke like? Pretty women, she'd heard. The daughters of minor nobles, people without titles but rich blood. Daughters whose fathers weren't important enough to sue for marriage. Were the rumors true? Did Rudolf have a string of illegitimate children across Osbergia?

Selene liked children. And Father was important enough to sue for marriage. *So, get him in a tryst, then? A hump before the tournament?* Perhaps. Guilt steamed over her as easily as the hot water. Tristain was never promised to her, but they'd always imagined it to be so. Holding hands, kissing in the stables. They'd showed their bits to each other, out of curiosity. Selene's hand drifted underwater, thinking of it now.

Rudolf meant nothing to her, and Tristain did. That handsome nose, the boy she'd known growing into a strong young man. A man with calloused hands from sword training, pushing himself into jousting and tournament fighting like a man with the spirit of a lion. That was apt.

The movement of her arm swirled the water. She laid back, making soft noises.

All she'd have to do was imagine Rudolf as Tristain, really. And the real one would forgive her, eventually. She'd get them all free of Father. Practically speaking, it didn't matter how bad Rudolf was. No one could be worse than Father.

The thought of Father soured her enjoyment and so she sighed heavily and climbed out of the water.

"Come," she called, and the servant came with fresh linens and a cloth to dry her, wrapping the cloth around her waifish frame. Even at fifteen, she still had yet to mature in her hips and breasts. She wondered if she ever would. Not like her servant.

The woman was a local farmer's girl, a little older than Selene, though shorter than her, with a wine-colored mark on her pointed face. Her short, blonde hair wisped around her ears, and a woad-dyed kirtle framed a generous chest. Joanna was her name.

The splotchy bruise on Selene's leg went unmentioned.

"What do you think of our guest of honor?" Selene asked.

"The archduke's son, mistress? He's a Prince of the Lion Throne."

"I know his titles. I mean what do you think of him?"

"I've not seen him, mistress, only that leal armor of his. It's handsome enough, but you can't hump a man in plate. The bed would break underneath you."

They laughed, their noises echoing off the oak-paneled walls. Selene shushed her, failing at her effort of shushing herself, knowing that at any moment Mother—or worse, Father—could burst in at any moment checking on her before supper.

Selene dug her nail into her thumb as the water dripped off her and Joanna gathered up a bodice and dress, stiff with many layers and smoothed with starch. If Joanna placed it on the ground, it probably would stand on its own. Little white embroidered flowers trailed over the skirts, moving into larger ones towards the top of the bodice.

"Mother chose that dress?"

"His lordship, mistress."

"I'm to look like a garden."

They laughed. Joanna passed behind Selene, who let the towel drop. Selene pulled on the linens, but not before wondering if the girl stared, though the thought did nothing for her below her waist. It took Joanna a few moments to gather up the dress and lift it over Selene's head. When she found the sleeves with her arms, and the head hole, Selene worked up the courage to ask.

"Have you humped anyone?"

"I have, mistress."

She dug into her thumb again. "What's it like?"

"Most men are useless, so it ain't much fun. Think their cocks are a gift from Sigur Himself, and care naught for the lady."

"Most men? How many men have you shared a bed with?"

She laughed. "A few, mistress," she said, drawing out the words as though teasing her. Somehow, Selene didn't think she was telling the whole truth.

"Well, what does it feel like when it's good?" She imagined it being good with Tristain. Somehow, it felt right. She wondered if Rudolf was the same, though the rumors about him muddied the waters some.

"Like..." She spoke into Selene's ear as she fastened the ribbons at the back, pulling the dress across Selene's chest. "Feeling good, over your whole body. Like that tingly feeling you get after holding your breath for a long time, but all over, and ten times better."

Selene shivered without meaning to. "How do you know a man's good?"

"If he's kind, and gentle, and giving, there's a better than good chance he'll be a good hump. Do you think Master Tristain is a good hump?"

Selene jumped forward and turned, still tethered to Joanna by the ribbons. "No! I mean... maybe." Her cheeks flared as bright as the candles burning in the stands around the room.

Joanna laughed. "I won't say nothing, mistress." She placed her thumb, index, and middle finger against her mouth and made the motion of turning a key. "A locked box."

Selene turned back and let the girl continue. "Yes... I think he'd be a good lover." Gentle, generous, always giving.

A knock came at the door. "Father wants you at the feast, Sel." Tristain's voice.

Selene and Joanna nearly bowled over with surprise. Then they giggled, and there was no chance of stopping.

T HE GREAT HALL OOZED with music and mirthful speech. Elaborate pastries on buffets filled the air with earthy, fragrant smells. The herald announced Selene, and she entered demurely, though her feet danced under her skirts like horses biting at the bit to run free.

Father sat between an Annaltian knight with a bushy mustache that fell into his mouth and a squat but rotund woman, likely the knight's wife. Mother and Tristain sat side-by-side, at the other end of the long U-shaped table, while Bann entertained—a strong word—a plump, red-haired woman with a hook nose who looked half-asleep. There was a priest here, too, all eyebrows, from a Sigur's church nearby. Radimir, she thought his name was, though she rarely went to Gebet.

All the fighters' servants and the pages would stay in the camp, and food would be taken to them after supper in the great hall. She wondered if the company there might be better, but then she remembered her mission. To charm the archduke's son. Rudolf. She'd better remember that, and not to call him Albrechtson.

Or maybe he'd prefer *Prince of the Lion Throne*, on her knees?

"Have you a proper horse, Arnaud!" A great, wide knight wearing several pastries shot up from the table and made a joust. "Or is it a mule, again?" People laughed.

A Badonnian knight vaulted over the table, sending cups and plates flying, and brandished his beltknife as a weapon. Two guards rushed forward to intercept him. The knight screamed his frustration against the shafts of the guards' halberds, then marched from the room, blaring past Selene, nearly bowling her over. Father clapped the good sport.

In the distraction, she hadn't noticed a man come alongside and loop his arm into the crook of hers. She stepped back, but he stepped with her, looked down on her. He was tall and not disagreeable in his long face and blond hair, trimmed brown beard.

"Allow me to walk you to your seat, my lady," he said, voice like a deep song to her ears. Like the voice of a mountain.

"And you are?"

"Do you find the music at these events to always be boring? Always better to turn a quintain than a canso, I always say," he said loudly, following the jest with a bout of laughter that others mimicked.

The rapidity of the change in subject snagged her and so she only laughed in response. He extended his hand as they stepped up onto the dais, helping her climb despite her stiffened skirts. Who was this man that joked about song structures and knew the whimsy of women's dress?

Whoever he was, he was dressed well, and looked to be drawing more than a few eyes from the room. Father even cracked a smile.

He bowed and kissed her hand when they made it to the center of the great table, to the seat of honor. *Of course.* She kicked herself for not realizing.

"Prince Rudolf Osterlin, at your service, my lady."

She couldn't deny she got a tingle across her nape. "Pleasure, Your Highness."

Green eyes like polished emeralds fell upon her. She also couldn't deny their agreeableness. They sat as the servants drew their chairs out for them. Wine came to them as well, from carafes of silver, whose tops were pulled into lion's mouths.

The servants came around with silver basins of water to rinse the face and hands—one to each, which she was glad for. Many of the men, in rinsing their faces, pressed an index finger to their nostril and blew the other one hard, swapping hands to do the other side. Grossness hit the water.

But not Rudolf. He splashed his face modestly and dabbed it dry with the offered towel.

She smiled at that.

The herald announced a few more stragglers and the viols and the pipes began again, bubbling under the conversation.

"The count sat us together. Do you have a problem with that? I can move." Rudolf's accent glided over the syllables—a city accent to her rural one. Invereid, that city on the river, seemed like a hovel by comparison.

Moving would be an embarrassment to Father—the guest of honor moving from the center of the feast? And besides, she needed to keep his company close.

"Of course not. Have I offended you, my lord?"

"Not at all. I do not concern myself with the whims of fathers, so I thought I should inquire as to whether my company is agreeable from the person it concerns."

She blushed, despite herself. This man had already proven himself by leaps and bounds ahead of Father. Why was she worried again?

Two seats down from her, the Annaltian that had antagonized the Badonnian laughed and stuffed his face with a hunk of goat's leg.

"I'm surprised he didn't hop out of here," he said to the table. "Badonnians sound enough like frogs, I thought he might," he roared, face turning red as he laughed louder than anyone at his own joke.

Selene didn't laugh, and neither did the archduke's son.

"Oh, come on. The princeling here have a soft spot for Badonnians? That's sadder than an embalmer that gags at the sight of a dead body!"

Rudolf leaned forward, his eyes flashed with mirth. "That's a good joust, Dietrich. If you hold a lance half as well as you hold a joke, you might stand a chance at the top three tomorrow."

People laughed. Dietrich laughed louder, clearly misunderstanding the wordplay.

"Demon's Disgrace," the herald announced.

More servants came around with meat-filled pastries. As they broke apart, soaring over the tables like birds, it gave way to 'oohs' and 'ahhs', as the main dish revealed itself. Kitchen women hefted the spectacle on a giant wooden platter.

A wolf, roasted and sewn back together, skin and all, with a dagger planted through its sad, dead head. Demon's Disgrace.

The priest rose and bowed to Father, who returned the gesture with the charge of his cup.

"Sigur be praised," he said, and the entire room followed his lead.

The dagger was pulled back to show that it wasn't entirely stuck through at all, only planted into the top of the skull which revealed a garlicky stew pungent with rosemary and white bits that were almost certainly the beast's brains.

"DO YOU KNOW MUCH about my title?"

They enjoyed the second course—beef medallions set on roasted leeks. The viols and the pipes changed in lockstep with the conversation that had now become more drunken and rowdier. Selene's eyes buzzed with the good wine the servants poured as freely as though she put her mouth to the cask.

"Prince?"

"Duke. Of Taneria." He plopped a finger of bread soaked in the beef sauce in his mouth and chased it down with a giant gulp of his cup. "It's a relic of my great-grandfather's day, when Taneria was part of the empire. He handed it to my grandfather, and my father through him. Though

Taneria's not part of the empire anymore, not practically speaking, anyway, it's only ceremonial. My father passed it to me when I came of age."

"The firstborn of the firstborn."

"What's that?"

"Your father is the firstborn of the emperor, your grandfather. It's poetic, in a way."

"I suppose it is."

"Would you ever press your claim? Pull Taneria back into the empire?"

"That's a dangerous question."

"That's not an answer."

She laughed, cheeks warming. Rudolf grinned in return. He returned to the leeks and talked between mouthfuls.

"You know, I composed a song for the first woman that caught my fancy. See, all the women in Ostelar are painfully boring, though Father would like me to marry some man with a purse bigger than the White Palace. Sorry, I meant a woman with a father with a purse bigger than the White Palace."

Selene giggled. "Is that so?" She tested the waters. "Would you perform it for me?"

"I suppose I might. And what would you give me in exchange?"

"A kiss."

People around them gasped. She felt a tap on her shoulder. It was Tristain, his eyes boring into her like drills. Guilt colored her cheeks.

She mouthed a 'sorry'. "Yes?"

He bowed to Rudolf, who laughed. "Excuse the interruption, my lord."

"Yes, go on, then. What is it?"

"May I speak to my sister alone?"

"Yes, fine." He turned back to his cup, snatching another medallion up with a fork.

Selene got up, holding her balance on the edge of the table. *I don't think I can walk very far.* She held onto Tristain's arm.

They went to a carpeted side hall, paintings of Tristain's forefathers on the walls. A great-grandfather leered down at them, following them with his eyes, it seemed.

"What is it, Trist?"

He grimaced. "I'm sorry, Sel."

"For what?"

"You know Rudolf's reputation?"

She folded her arms, then fell forward a bit and caught herself on a console. "Yes." She sighed and made sure Father was still in the great hall. He was—reminiscing loudly with a cluster of knightly looking men.

"It's too good of an opportunity to ignore. If I marry him, we can be free of Father. I can tell Rudolf what he's done to us, and he'll have him imprisoned."

"That's a big 'if'. I have another plan."

"Oh?"

"Get a knight to take me on as squire." Both plans were flimsy, they knew that. "If I prove myself tomorrow, if I win, even—and you know how hard I've been training—there's not a knight here that wouldn't take me on. If that happens, it's just the beginning. If I get knighted myself, I'll be able to bring you into my household, along with Mother. Get you both away from Father."

"That sounds even flimsier than my plan." Selene planted a kiss on his cheek. "Let's see if Rudolf will be swayed. I love you, Tristain, but it's time to grow up."

Tristain's lip creased. He looked to be holding back tears. "Tomorrow. I'll prove myself. You'll see."

She clasped her hands around his own. "Alright. We should return to the hall, lest Father get suspicious."

T HE FOLLOWING MORNING, SELENE dragged herself out of bed, head pounding. Joanna attended her, giving her a village tonic of more wine, which actually seemed to help once she could stomach the thought of it.

The lists rocked with noise and nervous chatter, while around the camp, the tents stuffed with bodies—servants and pageboys and squires all dressing and arming their knights. The herald called the first match: a joust between a Vallonian knight and a Badonnian, one of the less interesting matches.

Each knight drew lots, and Tristain was one of the last to fight. Selene came to his tent to wish him luck, with Joanna, who attended her skirts to make sure she didn't trip over them in the mud. The stink of horses and oiled steel drifted over the camp as thick as a cloud. When she walked into the tent, a page who wore a hillman tunic—red and yellow, lined with fox fur—was doing up his buckles. The page had been loaned by Leon the Strong, who had no need, since his son wasn't fighting.

The sound of a great crash, something punching through hard steel. Roars went up from the lists. Someone had been unseated.

Tristain's breastplate was barrel-shaped, ending at his waist. Forged from a single piece of steel, thicker in the middle than the sides, the design was twofold: to deflect blows, and for fashion, intended to cut a masculine figure on the battlefield. By creating the effect of a huge chest and small waist, it was the height of style for men. Riveted to the bottom of his breastplate were the faulds—articulated pieces of steel that protected the abdomen and groin that slid past each other if he needed to bend over. Besagews hung over his armpits.

Under his breastplate he wore a mail shirt, made of interlocking steel rings meant to prevent a cut from getting through. Under that he wore a jacket padded with many layers of linen, meant to stop a thrust. In a first blood-style tournament, as this one was, stopping the blade as much as possible was important above anything else. On his legs he wore plates attached to a girdle underneath. Under the plates themselves was a set of wool chausses, which sat atop breathable white braies. His lower legs and feet were guarded by a pair of pointed sabatons—articulated steel shoes that strapped right on top of his boots. Someone would have to peel him open, like a metal casket, to get inside.

"How do you wear that godscursed thing? How does every knight not just topple over?"

Tristain and the boy laughed. He was about to answer when the page answered for him.

"The weight is distributed by the harness. It goes over the shoulders and around the waist, so it uses the whole body for support."

"Huh. Good luck today, Tristain. Please be careful."

Sounds of shouting and arguing came from outside.

"Are you daft?"

A man's voice drifted in. Tristain stepped out of the tent, grabbing his longsword. Selene followed. Though she suspected he would not need it, tourneys were a bout of violence and honor, and the lines between friendly contest and a bloody one blurred easily.

"You blithering idiot!" the man shouted. Rounding a corner, she saw Rudolf dressing down a servant, and she could only look on with pity. The servant had dropped a decanter in the mud. Rudolf's fierce eyes cowed the servant, and he apologized profusely.

It wouldn't be the first spoiled son of a lord—he was a Prince of the Lion Throne, after all. Not many men could claim higher potential for spoiling than that. And besides, all he had to do was treat *her* nice. She walked up to him, hoping to calm his nerves and ingratiate herself further.

She touched his vambrace, a fluted, silvery plate that clasped over his forearm.

"Don't let it get to you, my lord," she whispered. "All these men see your outburst and know that anger is an uncontrollable beast for you. They could use that against you."

He nodded. "You're right. You're very wise, Selene."

She smiled. Her plan was working.

He stepped closer. "Though a wiser woman might have realized I saw you leaving your brother's tent, after talking with him in private last night. See, I notice things too. You seem very close and I wonder where I fit in that tally."

She laughed, passing off their interaction as a misunderstanding. "You worry too much, my lord. My brother and I are close, it's true, but it can only be expected from two children who came up together from a very young age."

He snorted, then gave an appreciative shrug. "I suppose so." He bowed with a flourish—quite a feat in full kit, apart from the helmet. "I wrote a poem for you, my lady," he announced. "When I win, I'll perform it for you."

Selene couldn't deny the flutter in her stomach, as though a thousand butterflies swarmed inside.

She squeezed his arm over the plate. A useless effort at physical touch, but the thought was appreciated by Rudolf, who smiled.

"Then win, my lord."

TRISTAIN HAD TWO WINS, and one draw, where he'd drawn blood at the same time as his opponent. A Vallonian was his next bout—Domingo Miguel Santa Clara de Alves, wore a leather coat-of-plates over mail and jacket, and they drew lots of foot battle, not the joust. The coat's shoulders were greatly stuffed, with alternating stripes of green and gold, the colors of Vallonia. Invereid was far from Vallonia, so Selene had only ever seen a handful of them and did not think much of them. She recalled they were known for their beautiful women and their sailing prowess.

Bodes well for a battle on land, then.

On his head he had the most extravagant plume of peacock feathers, crowning behind his pot helm, much like a peacock's tail. Tristain wore a stuffed maple tree strapped to the top of his helmet. Mother had made it for him.

"Hear me," De Alves announced in heavily accented Osbergian. "I will win this day for the grace of my princess!"

Some in the crowd clapped. Tristain slapped his visor down.

De Alves circled him. He had his sword pointed directly at Tristain, crossguard behind the buckler in his other hand. Tristain followed the circle. He shifted his left leg back, moving into another guard, bringing his sword to his left hip, point towards his opponent's throat. De Alves would have to sidestep the point to avoid a nasty thrust.

De Alves burst forward with surprising speed. Selene felt her heart in her throat. Tristain's sword was deflected with the buckler, and De Alves got the point of his sword on Tristain's upper arm. It got under the pauldron. Selene gasped.

The crowd whooped, expecting blood to be drawn. The fight was stopped. Selene saw Father curl his lips in disappointment. When the marshal checked Tristain, a shake of the head provoked boos from the crowd. Selene took a deep breath and willed her nerves to quiet.

Tristain moved to a high guard, his sword above his head. He shifted onto his left foot, and advanced forward with his right. De Alves brought his shield up, anticipating a strike. Tristain pivoted on his right foot, sidestepping, then advancing forward again. The maneuver took less than a second. Moving behind De Alves, he brought his sword down. The edge walloped the Vallonian's back, lurching him forward. He spun, striking Tristain's arm, the blade bouncing uselessly off his rerebrace. Tristain turned at the same time, slicing across De Alves' unarmored heel. The Vallonian fell to the ground, letting out a shocked grunt.

The crowd cheered. Selene sat forward. The marshal checked De Alves' foot, which was indeed pouring with blood. Tristain's arm was raised to declare him the victor, then the crowd gasped. Blood spattered the ground in big drops.

Selene breathed in sharp. The sight gutted her, as easily as Tristain's blade had cut through the Vallonian's leg.

But he'd been fine. The draw didn't disqualify him, though De Alves could no longer stand, removing him from the tournament.

Leon the Strong had lost gracefully, after wrenching the helmet off his opponent—the Badonnian that had been antagonized at supper—snapping the strap. In the moment, Leon had earned a cut from a burred edge of the Badonnian's helmet tearing through the leather of his glove. The Annaltians had lost to the Osbergians, nearly igniting a brawl outside the lists, but the guards came.

That left the final two: Tristain and Rudolf, with drawn lots of a joust to decide the winner.

It might've been poetic, something out of a song, if it didn't wrench at her lungs to think of either of them falling. *It's only a first blood tournament, Selene. Killing's been outlawed for years.* Though accidents had been known to happen. Like the Vallonian might, Tristain could end up with a life-changing injury.

It was rumored Rudolf, as the archduke's heir, had been granted a grand allotment to make the best armor in the land. Steel from Annalt, leather from the stoutest cows in all of Osbergia, and the finest armorsmiths on the Continent came to Ostelar, at the archduke's behest, to forge the best armor ever beheld. Then Rudolf had polished the absolute crud out of it, making anything beauteous or elegant about it disappear.

Like a preening cock in the field, he rode his giant destrier into the lists, throwing his hands in the air, asking for the audience's cheers. They gave them to him. Selene clapped, doubt plaguing her mind. The Osbergian bear reared on his helmet, swiping a paw to Tristain as he entered from the other side.

Tristain entered on his more slender but still sizable Onyx, who pulled against the reins as though impatient. Leon's page handed him a lance, and he slapped down his visor. Rudolf did the same, waving his lance for more cheers. The crowd obliged.

The field opened for them. Forty paces. Enough to build up speed. Enough to crash horribly. Selene held her breath, and shuffled to the edge of her seat, digging a nail into her thumb.

"Hoooooo!" the crowd roared.

The horn sounded.

Tristain and Rudolf spurred their horses at the same time. Dust kicked up behind them—the field had already been turned to dust—and they charged. They seemed to be heading right for each other, no barrier to stop them. It was simply a matter of pride.

The crowd swelled around Selene, pressure building in her head. Pain. Pain like a lance in the leg or in the eye or in the neck.

Rudolf lowered his lance. Tristain immediately after.

Rudolf went low, glancing off Tristain's leg. The end wobbled but didn't shatter. Tristain's missed. The stands went "Hooooaaa!" in response.

Selene breathed. *Win, Tristain!*

The fighters wheeled their horses around and made for each other at a sprint.

Tristain leaned forward a little, it looked like. The lance crashed into his side in an explosion of wood. Selene screamed and jumped to her feet. He recoiled, dropping his own lance and he fell from the saddle in a clatter of steel. His horse, Onyx, kept going for a handful of paces.

She raced down, pressed herself up to the fence that separated the list field from the stands. She couldn't see anything. There was no blood leaking from Tristain's armor. Leon's pageboy ran up to him as the marshals called a stop to the contest.

Rudolf threw back his visor and spurred his horse over to Selene. He took a flower that he'd tucked into his belt and offered it to her. She looked up at him, chewing her lip, worry for Tristain battling a bloody war over her appreciation for Rudolf's sweetness and generosity.

"Continue the fight," the marshals yelled.

Selene almost yelped in surprise. Tristain was pulled to his feet, dazed but standing. He lifted his visor and gave Selene a flinty smile.

"The master from Invereid's saddle has broken, and no second horse is allowed in the contest, as per the laws of the land. The remainder of the contest must be fought on foot!"

The crowd 'oooh'ed and 'aah'ed.

Rudolf kicked his horse over to the middle of the field and dismounted, leaving a groom to lead it out of the lists.

"As the one remaining on the horse, the prince gets to decide the weapons."

"Longsword, of course," he answered without hesitation. "What would an Osbergian be without a stiff blade in his hands!"

"A soft one!" someone yelled from the stands to laughter.

"Indeed."

Tristain took his blade from the sheath and threw it down. Rudolf did the same. They wouldn't need to sheathe their swords until the contest was done.

The horn blew again and they threw blows at each other. Tristain pivoted, trying the same trick he tried on the Vallonian, but Rudolf was too quick. Light on his feet, lighter than he should've been considering the bulk of his armor.

But it was as Leon's pageboy said—the weight was distributed, and where better to find that than in the finest set of armor in all of Osbergia, possibly even the empire. The difference was plain enough comparing the two of them. Tristain moved at speed, but Rudolf was always quicker. Outmatched and outclassed.

Selene edged around the fence to get a better view.

Rudolf put Tristain on the defensive, forcing him to deflect a series of savage strikes. Any time Tristain launched an attack of his own, Rudolf deflected the blow and countered immediately. Tristain would have to rely on feints and surprise to get the upper hand.

Tristain shifted his hands closer together. They circled each other. Rudolf charged, stabbing. It was something he had tried before, and Tristain was prepared. He punched his gauntlet out, repelling Rudolf and knocking him off balance. Rudolf grunted, then regained his form by stepping laterally. Selene expected a strike at any moment. Sure enough, the prince's blade moved low for a leg shot. Tristain burst forward and snatched his own blade halfway with a gauntleted hand. He put himself between Rudolf's sword and his body.

The duke's son grunted in astonishment. Tristain hooked his blade under Rudolf's helmet and shoved him over in a crash of steel. The crowd jeered. Selene covered her mouth, suppressing a chuckle. Rudolf rolled out of the way, anticipating a strike. Tristain allowed him to get to his feet. He would never strike an unguarded man.

The throw had achieved its intended purpose though, proving that Tristain could get around Rudolf's guard. He needed to do that again, but this time drawing blood. He needed to aim for a vulnerable spot. Though where the vulnerable bits were, Selene wasn't sure. There wasn't a single gap in that thick plate, as far as she could tell.

Rudolf grunted as he stood on shaking feet, louder this time, infuriated from the humiliation.

"I'll kill you, you bastard," he yelled, his voice stupidly muffled by his helmet. The veneer of gentleness had worn away like the elegance he'd so easily scrubbed from his armor.

Rudolf charged, trying the halfsword trick that Tristain used. The point of his longsword like a short spear punched into Tristain's breastplate with a crunch of metal. Selene gasped.

It pushed Tristain onto his back foot but didn't get through. The point came around again, *crunch, crunch.* Tristain tried to deflect each one, but Rudolf was too quick. He sidestepped and raised his own sword-spear but got his arm tangled around Rudolf's scalloped pauldron. The straps on Tristain's rerebrace popped open.

The stands lit up with a "Hooooaaa!"

Selene slapped the fence and shouted, trying to get the marshals' attention. Surely there was some rule against fighting with a bit of armor flopping around!

In the tangle, they brawled for control. Metal chewed and crashed, fusing together. Rudolf's bear slapped off somewhere into the dirt. Selene held her breath as he tripped, landing with a din of steel. Tristain followed, his sword plunging forward. Right for Rudolf's neck.

Fuck, he's going to kill—

"HOOOAAA!"

Tristain slid off at the last second, sword glancing off, shoulder punching into Rudolf's helm.

"HOOOAAA!"

Anxiety frazzled every nerve in her body. She plunged her thumbnail into her finger, trying to ground herself. She couldn't call an end to it—not only did she not have the power, only Father did—but it would insult both their honors and mar Father's reputation.

The men would fight until one of them drew blood, or worse.

Rudolf made a coughing sound and rolled over onto his stomach. Still on top, Tristain drew his stabbing dagger, eager to find a gap. Rudolf pressed upwards and tossed Tristain off and got to his feet.

The crowd roared. It was a huge feat of strength. Tristain rolled. Selene dug her nail deeper.

Rudolf stepped forward, raised his sword. He coughed, blood exploding from the breaths of his helmet, leaking out.

"Stop!"

"Quiet," Rudolf hissed at the marshal, swinging his sword at the man as he ran in to stop the fight. He stomped on Tristain's breastplate, keeping him fixed to the ground.

"I am a fucking prince! I will not lose!"

Father did nothing.

He flipped the sword over, point down. He raised it, lifting the point over Tristain's unarmored upper arm, the rerebrace loose and flopping around. Father still did nothing. He would watch while his son was killed.

Selene had already squeezed through the fence and pushed onto the field. *Don't, don't, don't*, her mind screamed, and she charged forward, crashing into Rudolf's back.

The stands vibrated with a raucous "BOOOO!"

Rudolf stumbled forward, shoving her out of the way with a plated hand. "Sigur take you, wench!"

Selene hit the ground on her tailbone, hard. "Get up!" she cried, biting back tears.

Tristain tried to roll, unable to sit up from his back. Rudolf kicked him down again.

"GET UP!"

Rudolf raised the sword.

Selene got up behind him, drew the dagger hanging from his belt. A dagger from Alania with a round handle—curious she would notice such details in the panic.

She fished out a gap under his helmet with the tip. He froze.

"Enough," she screamed.

"STOP THE FIGHT!"

Father's roar of a voice. It seemed impossible she should've heard it so clearly, but it was as though he spoke right into her ear. Her knees were suddenly weak. She held a dagger to a prince's throat!

"STOP THIS FARCE!"

Father burst out of the stands and raged down to the fence, pushing himself through.

Selene dropped the dagger and felt lightheaded. Shame slapped her cheeks. *What have I done?*

The ground fell away from under her feet until all she was left with was the tiny shard of her choice, shredding all hope with its alacrity and its clarity. She'd ended both of their plans with a single movement. Tristain would never get a knight, now, and Rudolf would never marry a murderess—even an attempted one.

She stumbled standing, and her eyes glazed over. The world tumbled around her head, and she was on her back, then in the dark, as though the sun had suddenly been snuffed out.

23

SEA OF BLACK AND RED

SANGUINUM, 1044

*The three little princes; Albrecht, Reynard, and Harald, grew
up stealing from each other's playpen. They continue this game
into their adulthood, taking what they rightfully see as theirs,
without care for the lives that are destroyed.*

— WORDS SAID BY A COURTIER IN THE LION PALACE

"YOU ATTACKED THE ARCHDUKE'S son?" Soren gaped his mouth.

She laughed. He looked like he'd just had his tongue caught in
a trap, opening and closing his mouth like a fish.

They sat on a log as their horses ate grass nearby, hitched to a tree. The
sounds of the marshy forest around them cricked and thrummed—frogs
and crickets and all manner of life. The air carried the powerful scent of
rot and fecundity, of trees and swampy muck, forcing the stench down her
nose and throat so she could taste it.

Death hadn't visited this part of Osbergia. Yet.

"I thought nothing shocked you anymore."

"So did I."

She laughed harder.

"What happened?"

"The embarrassment of being taken unaware by a girl was too much to bear for him. He swore everyone to forget if Father punished me. You'd better believe he did."

He laughed now. "I get it. Then, Tristain meant a lot to you. And now?"

Relief washed over her as she realized the truth.

"No. I know now I was a stupid girl with a stupid infatuation." A part of her knew she was convincing herself as much as him.

He smiled and patted her shoulder. "Good. On to Ostelar, then."

A SEA OF BLACK and red surrounded the city. They arrived in the afternoon, orange light falling on the gathered army, tens of thousands strong. The estuary around Ostelar was a bustle of soldiers and knights, camp servants and followers, all wearing the Annaltian colors. They were laying siege to the city. *No smoke... they haven't assaulted it yet.* They were surrounding it. In preparation, and they'd been there long enough to set up earthworks and a palisade around the camp.

She wondered how it would go—what would the Swords do if the Annaltians invaded the city? The Order, as an arm of the church, was apolitical, uninterested in choosing sides between the conflicts of men. In theory. Many examples of usurper pontiffs and inquisitor assassins in history stood out in practice.

A cadre of riders cantered past them, scouts on the emperor's road. The captain eyed them as they rode past, the four Golden Swords with their wagon in tow. Diana wondered if they would turn around, demanding to see what was inside. They could easily believe it was supplies or vittles for the people, and it would be entirely reasonable for them to seize the cart. Though it was entirely within their rights as Swords to refuse, it would be much easier to avoid the scrutiny of whoever led this host of thousands.

The hooves of their horses and the rattle of the wagon's wheels echoed over a freshly hewn bridge. *There wasn't a river here before...* She gasped. From the surface of the water poked roofs, structures, poles. They'd flooded the Outskirts. A mile north, a huge, curved dam of stone buttressed against the Tibor, diverting it down constructed trenches, emptying the river out to sea a mile further east than it would normally have been. It also had the side effect of submerging the low-lying Outskirts in three feet of water.

It wasn't clear what happened to the people who lived there, but they weren't here now.

The earthworks were incredible. Normally, Ostelar sat at the confluence of two rivers: the Alba and the Tibor. This made it incredibly hard to siege, as only a narrow strip of land permitted entrance from the north. Normally.

Somehow, the prince had changed the very landscape in order to bring all of his thousands to bear.

Swift hooves clattered behind and over the bridge after them. *Here we go...*

"Halt!" shouted the riders' captain.

They stopped and turned. The riders approached swiftly. There were twelve of them. The riders were going too fast to see before, but they were very well-dressed, too well-dressed to be scouts. They prickled with lances, while one of them carried a black lion standard. Diana saw Manus lift one of his giant hands off the wagon's traces, placing it on the hilt of the greatsword sitting next to him in the driver's box. It had a cloak over it, but the shape and size of it was undeniable.

"Who are you, and from where do you ride?" The captain spoke with a strong northern accent, and in Osbergian for the sake of the group, though Diana understood and spoke Annaltian just as well. Not that different, though some verbs differed slightly.

"Who comes?" Soren calmly straightened himself in the saddle.

"I, Prince Reynard the Second of Annaltia, have."

Soren bowed his head. "Your Serene Highness. We are servants of the Most Holy Order of the Golden Sword. I am Inquisitor Sorenius, and this is Inquisitor Diana, Arbiter Lena Ulnstadt, and Arbiter Manus Ironhand. We come from Avercarn, important cargo for the Lord Inquisitor in tow."

Nials had been called to Istrya at the last Imperial post, which, in flagrant opposition to sense, still worked.

The prince returned the bow with a slight bend in his neck, representing their unequal footing.

"Well met. Lord Inquisitor, hm."

Diana looked the prince over. He wore a fine, embroidered burgundy jacket over a breastplate, undone at the front, tabs fluttering in the wind. He had a lance in his right hand and a decorated sword in a scabbard at his side. A handsome man, like most of the Imperial family, with hair cropped close to his head, bright blue eyes, and high cheekbones. His helmet was hooked to his saddle, a bascinet with klappvisor, like the rest of his retinue.

"Can you verify this information?"

"We wear the badges of our office, Your Serene Highness *Raginardus*," Inquisitor Diana said in Annaltian, turning on the charm by using his High Istryan name. "We are simply what you see before you."

Soren gave her an amused glance.

A clever grin spread across the prince's face. "Yes... you are, indeed, Mistress Inquisitor. Fortunate I should make your acquaintance. Please, dine with me. The caprices of camp upkeep can wait."

The Swords fell in line with the retinue, moving at a gentle pace. Reynard moved alongside Diana.

The prince kept his eyes trained on her, only correcting the courser between his legs when it drifted out of line.

"Whence do you hail, Mistress Diana?"

She kept her eyes forward. "Invereid, Your Serene Highness."

"Please, call me Reynard." She nodded. The prince chuckled. "That iciness could freeze smoke, Inquisitor. Come, tell me... where was it you said you were riding from? Avercarn? I have but a small confession to make... you take those, don't you? A confession for Sigur's ears, or as close as it gets." He laughed. Diana couldn't help but smile. "I don't know my brother's province very well. Where is Avercarn?"

"The south, Serene Highness," one of his advisors said. "Near the border with the Alanians."

"Thank you, Anselm. And how long did that take? A month? You must be terribly exhausted, Mistress."

Soren snorted. If the prince heard, he didn't react.

"I'm fine. Thank you, Your Highness," she said.

"No, you must rest. I can hear it in your voice. Stay for the night, at the least. Enjoy a fine meal, a hot bath. I'll have the servants prepare one for each of you at once. Though the big one might need a horse trough and a scaffold."

"Excuse us, Serene Highness, but we are carrying important cargo that must be delivered expeditiously. If you'll but let us pass."

"That's no way to talk to your soon-to-be liege lord. Please, join me in my tent. At least long enough for a drink."

Diana sighed inwardly. She was itching to get rid of that damn wagon, and what was inside. But she would humor the prince. "Very well."

They passed through the palisade gate: the perimeter of the siege camp. The camp was a set of rings, the eastern side of which sat in the depression that was the former riverbed. At the fringes stood the tents for the men-at-arms, and the camp followers. Campwives scattered throughout, cleaning pots, washing linens, sweeping built-up ashes from campfires, and delivering stew and strongale by the cask to the men. Inside fenced yards, soldiers drilled with spear and pike formations. Further inside sat the cavalry's tents, the knights, and their lieutenants. Beyond that were sets of trenches alternated with rows of spiked poles facing towards the walls, deterring any sallies of defenders from the city.

"This siege ought not to last," the prince said. "My brother's walls will come crashing down soon enough."

She saw what he was talking about and let out an involuntary sigh. Three giant trebuchets—each over a hundred feet tall—were being erected in the center of the ring, a few hundred yards away. On the road, they'd passed teams of woodsmen felling trees by the dozen, and now she knew what he was using all that lumber for. Carpenters and craftsmen clustered like bees around a queen, lifting, hammering, tying, and nailing pieces into place. They were nearly finished.

Between the trebuchets braced a few bombards, giant tubes of bronze, on giant wooden frames. She'd heard they were a new Vallonian invention, used on their ships and by the vicious corsairs around the Bright Sea and the Cape of the Knife, but had never seen one. Their power at destroying fortifications was considered unmatched, though they were next to useless in an open field.

"Your Serene Highness must have dazzling engineers," she said.

"Thank you. You are *very* agreeable, Inquisitor. From which house do you hail?"

"You wouldn't know them. They are a minor house."

They arrived at the prince's tent; a marquee large enough to house a company. In the center, in front of them, stood a parquetted oak table, flanked by high-backed oak chairs set with rosewood inlay in the shape of a lion roaring. Both the table and chairs had carved feet in the shape of lion paws. The tent was empty apart from the dining set, other than an armor and weapon rack. Diana supposed it would've been for assembling, when all the knights and generals met for battle preparations. The two inquisitors filed inside after the prince, while Manus and Lena were told to wait by the wagon. The prince noted their absence, but Soren told him they should keep watch over the wagon.

"What are you hauling in there, prisoners?" the prince asked as they sat. Soren didn't answer.

"I get it, important cargo. Besides, that's not the reason I called you here."

Diana leaned over the table. She cringed a little inside. She was ignoring decorum on purpose, but her training throughout her youth had given her hard-to-break habits, and that all came rushing back in this lauded company. "And what is the reason, Your Serene Highness?"

"I *am* fond of the Order." He leaned forward as well, letting the moment draw out. Diana wondered if she was too obvious, that he could misconstrue her behavior as disrespectful.

"It's important work that you do. I believe very much so. In fact, that's why I allowed you into my camp, allowed you to see my fortifications, to see where I store my supplies, to tally how many soldiers I have, to examine my siege-works, and it is why I will let you travel onto the gates when we're done here."

A servant approached with a tray of drinks, placing a goblet of wine for each of them on the table. Reynard picked up his cup and gave it a slow swirl.

"I truly believe it. That's why the Order in Annaltia has flourished under my patronage, and it would disappoint me very much if the Order in Osbergia did not."

"I'm not sure what you mean."

"My patronage, of course." He took a sip of the wine. Diana's and Soren's wine stood untouched.

"I believe we can end this war, you and me. My profligate brother must answer for his crimes, but I have no wish to throw the lives of his people away. You, you could be heroes, lauded for your efforts in preventing bloodshed, and praised as loyal servants of the Emperor."

"Prince Reynard," Soren said.

"Please! Why don't you have a drink? You—" He slapped his head softly. "Of course! My apologies, I'll rectify this at once. Anselm! Two apple juices, please!"

"Yes, Serene Highness."

Soren looked back at the prince. "Prince Reynard. The Order does not answer to the emperor. Canon law is clear."

The prince smiled. Gods, it was a cunning smile. Diana got a little frustrated with that perfect smile and perfect teeth.

"Inquisitor, please. Don't take me for a fool. I know well canon law—that the Order is loyal only to Sigur himself, and I have no problem with that. I do not wish to interfere with that. But, as the largest patron of the Order in Annaltia, I am deeply familiar with its inner workings, and its reliance on donations of both men and money from its lords and its princes. Not to mention the land that you lease for your citadels and your preceptories. It is but a simple request. I ask that you to deliver a message to your leader—the Lord Inquisitor Rotersand. Ask him to throw open the gates on the fifth day of the next week, and he shall have all the men and money he could ever want."

The servants brought out apple juice. Still, she didn't drink. Who knew if it was poisoned?

"And if he doesn't?" she asked.

"Well, then... nothing. Nothing immediate, of course. But after a few years, a crack might appear in the walls of your great fortress. Nothing major, nothing that cannot be delayed. Then another appears, and it's larger, possibly structural. But there're no funds to be found to fix it. You might find that you must choose between fixing a wall and purchasing an alchemical reagent to fight the demons, and we both know which you would choose. On and on it goes until you find that your great fortress has fallen out from under you and buried you within it. Who knows, it might even fall into the bay. Wouldn't that be something?"

Diana's face grew hot. She glanced at Soren. He nodded. *We have little choice.*

"I think we understand," she said.

"Good." The prince clicked his fingers. "Anselm, have whatever the inquisitors need brought to them. If you require fresh horses or waterskins, please take them. Whatever you need." The prince stood, and the others followed.

"Thank you, Serene Highness."

He walked them to the opening of the pavilion. He talked directly to Diana now. "It is truly a shame you can't stay the night. I loved the stories my inquisitors in Annaltia would tell me. I can only imagine yours are just as entertaining. What a night we could've had."

"A shame indeed, Serene Highness, but we must be going."

"Very well." He bowed deeply, deeper than he should have. "Sigur be with you."

"Farewell." Diana matched the bow and came to her horse. She threw her leg into Eda's saddle and up and over, and they began the final length of their long journey to the citadel.

Her chest released as they walked over the trenches, over the makeshift drawbridge the prince had lowered for them. She glanced back. He was smiling at her. She looked away. *Thank the Gods I didn't become a courtier.* She screwed up her face. *I might've married a man like him. I almost did.*

"What's wrong with him, Inquisitor?" Tansy asked. "He's a bit too pretty for my liking, but he looks like your type."

"I'll remind you, Arbiter," Soren said. "Our codes forbid physical intimacy."

"Who said anything about intimacy? I meant fucking."

"Who approaches!" a voice boomed from the top of the wall. A row of guardsmen pointed their crossbows at them, tense-jawed, ready to fire upon them at any moment.

"Inquisitors of the Order," Diana yelled back. "Returning to the Citadel!" There was no answer for a while. Then the gates opened, chains rattling as the mechanism pulled the great metal-reinforced doors wide enough for three wagons astride.

On the deserted, cobbled stone road, the Strand Osterlin, stood a man in a black cape. He had it wrapped around his throat, passed over his shoulder. Black hair slicked back with oil, his vulture-like eyes examined them. It was Galeaz, Lady Adolar's former steward. Their agent.

"Come," he said. "The Lord Inquisitor waits."

24

REUNION

SANGUINUM, 1044

Family reunions are often a messy business. Old grievances rear
their heads like unwanted, stiff cocks.

— COUNT ANDREAS OF VERANIA

T HE COVE SMELLED LIKE mucky sand and seaweed. Waiting in a
damp, smelly place after such a long journey was the last thing
Diana wanted. Tansy wore a face of disgust. *That makes two of us, Tansy.*
Crates lined the walls of the smooth, black hollow, stacked high on the
rough-hewn wharf. Sunlight outside the cove reflected off the waves in the
Bay of Empires, sloshing up against the stone.

Out in the water, the tri-masted carrack *Iustitia* anchored, its impres-
sive black sails rolled up and away. A twenty-man tender was rowing to
the wooden jetty that extended out from the wharf. On it was the Lord
Inquisitor, dressed in a raiment of white and gold. The captain threw the
rope, catching it around a pole, and pulled them in.

Rotersand and his retinue stepped off the boat. The jetty creaked under
their weight.

"Inquisitors," he said in his smooth voice. "Well met."

They bowed.

"How was Istrya, Revered One?" Sorenius said.

"Always a pleasure. We have much to learn from our cousins in the north. My delivery?"

"Yes, my lord. The beast waits for you in the prison. It's been given the venom as you requested. The other one waits in the western tower."

Rotersand turned to Diana. He smiled, or at least the closest approximation of a smile he could manage. "Very good. I'm thrilled to hear that. I'm retiring to my quarters. Inquisitor Diana, please see me as soon as possible."

She nodded. "Yes, Your Eminence."

The Lord Inquisitor departed and Diana waited a few moments before following. She passed under the solid steel portcullis that would seal the prison in the case of escape, and climbed up the levels, up to the top of the Citadel. Beyond that, a spiral staircase took her from the cove through storerooms, the prison, the training halls, overseers' offices, and finally to the top of the eastern tower, where the Lord Inquisitor's office was.

Her legs burned. She looked through a window as she reached the top. The sun was bright over the bay. A gentle breeze washed over her face. It was peaceful. She could almost forget about the army that surrounded the city and her adoptive brother, who lay drugged up and caged so many feet below.

"Good morning, Diana," Rotersand said as he entered. Diana thought of home as she walked in, though the room stunk of the ocean, and was the furthest thing from home. She forced the thought from her mind. He'd changed into a white velvet robe with gold trim. The finery was a little overkill. She had only ever seen the Archduke's son wear such nice clothes. She bowed her head in greeting.

"Have a seat."

Diana forced her nerves down. He waved to the chair in front of his desk. His office was circular, like the tower, lined with bookshelves stuffed with papers and books. Hanging on the back wall was the standard of the Order of the Golden Sword—a golden sword pointing to the sky on a black background. In truth, it was quite phallic.

She took her seat. His desk was in a bit of a state, papers and files scattered all over. Clearly, the man didn't have time to clean up since she'd seen him last. An unassuming leatherbound journal that stood out, though. There were no marks on the book to identify it and he had cleared papers to make space, as though he took particular care.

"I must congratulate you, Inquisitor," Rotersand said. Diana breathed a little sigh of relief. After all this time, after all she'd been through, the knife that she'd been honed to, she still hated seeing him. He made her blood run cold.

"Thank you, Your Eminence," she replied. She told of the events, how she'd captured the Black Beast, and Leon. She told of their return to the city, and Prince Reynard's offer.

"Yes, Sorenius told me of your meeting," he replied. "Very interesting. I should reflect on this."

She blinked. "You're considering it?"

"And why shouldn't I? If it can avoid needless bloodshed."

"Because the Order's impartial, beholden to canon law. That gives us our immunity to act as we please, but if we interfere with the laws of men, we'll be dragged down with the rest of them. We rise above the muck of politics and war and pledge ourselves to a higher calling."

The Lord Inquisitor smirked. "Yes, we do. Now, this knight, Vorland. Is he cooperative? Do you detect evil within him?"

"No, my lord. No trace of the beast within him. I checked with the archivist. No traces of it in his heritage, either. There were many moons between Avercarn and Ostelar, and I did not drug him with the morel. If he was going to transform, escape, he surely would've done so before now."

"Did you cut him?"

"Cut? No."

He tsked. "If a demon has sufficient control over his abilities, he may suppress his transformations. An adequate emotional stimulus, such as the removal of a finger or an ear, something vestigial so as not to cause premature death, should provoke the metamorphic response. No matter. If you believe he has no trace of the Great Devil, I believe it. Should you talk to him, turn him to our side, he could be a valuable ally. He is highly respected among the people for his legend and commands a sizable force in the Hills under his white eagle banner."

"Did Galeaz not try to destroy his reputation, to sow discord in the ranks?"

The Lord Inquisitor's eyes darkened. "Who told you that?"

"A rumor, Your Eminence. I should know better to ignore such trifles."

He sighed. "Yes, he did. A mistake. I did not know Reynard was marching into Badonnia not as an ally, but as an opportunist. Thankfully, Galeaz failed."

"Reynard is a snake," she offered. The Lord Inquisitor nodded. "Should we trust him?"

"I saw the great siege engines from the deck of my ship as we were pulling into the harbor. The walls *will* fall within a fortnight. I've seen these bombards in action, and the great trebuchets will outrange any counterattack the archduke might muster. There are rumors the archduke has already fled Ostelar for Vallonia. And if the prince's threat is genuine, we could find ourselves without a patron, and we would wish our heads decorated the palisades like those in the White Palace."

"Is it that serious?"

Rotersand rubbed his temples. "I cannot say. Talk to this knight. He may know something we can use. If not, he could be a bargaining chip. Convince him to join our side. Who knows, if we can get him close enough to the prince, perhaps he can solve the problem."

Is he suggesting... "Yes, my lord." It was a sound plan. Bring an end to the siege by killing Reynard. *The assassination of a Prince of the Lion Throne.* It had happened before, in history. Inquisitor Behler the Blackguard, who killed Emperor Fortis in 339. The church and the throne had a long, troubled history.

"Good. We've made him comfortable. I have a feeling he'll come around. Now, please send for the jailor. I wish to pay someone a visit."

TRISTAIN WOKE, BLOOD STINGING his eyes. The dark room he sat in was blurry. His throat felt numb and his tongue swelled in his mouth. He coughed.

"Ah, you're awake," a voice said. A rag wiped his eyes and the dark stone walls of the small room came into focus. A broad-shouldered man in a white and gold robe stood before him. His eyes were familiar, like he'd seen them before in some half-dream. The man was wiping his bloody hands with a rag.

"Tristain Florian Oncierran, second son of the Count of Invereid," the stranger pontificated. "First a son, then a squire... now an abomination. Or was it the freak all along?"

The man came closer. He seemed to appraise his work. Tristain tried to move and found he could not. His arms and legs were numb. Strength completely fled from them. This differed from the other drug. His torpor seemed deeper, and there were no chains or ropes on him. There was no need.

"You'll find yourself unable to move, and much to my benefit, my black beast: unable to synthesize."

Tristain tried, but when he concentrated, the wall in his mind was still there. He went to speak, but his lips seemed unfamiliar with the action. He twisted his lolling mouth to form the word: *how*? It sounded more like, *oooh*, but the Inquisitor understood his meaning.

"The Gods were truly sadistic," he said. "Handing us this corrupt world they created and all the horrific things within it. Have you heard of the sand adder? A nasty creature, from the northern dunes of Saburria." The slick-haired inquisitor held a glass syringe in front of him—white liquid glistening off the tip. "Dreadful, isn't it? Can't move a muscle? Can't blink or even swallow? Don't worry, it's not fatal to lycanthropes, at least not at the dose I have given you. Although... that does not mean you won't be uncomfortable. Following paralysis are spasms and hallucinations. Uncontrollable feelings of terror. Grinding of the teeth. It will be so bad you may even break a few. You may think... it must wear off at some point. At some point, it will release you from your torment." He let out a rattling laugh. "Indeed. But I inject you again and the process begins anew. It will only stop when I say." The Inquisitor grabbed Tristain's jaw, wrenching him forward.

"And only when I say."

Tristain's fury bubbled underneath, under a layer of helplessness.

"Poor boy. I can see it in your eyes. You want to kill me."

He went to move but found he could not. His body was unresponsive. Painful tingling spread through his legs and feet. The tingling spread through his body and up through his body to his jaw. His eyes glazed over, and his teeth started gnashing together. Something in his periphery darted by. He looked over.

Only black mold and dark stone. Another shadow moved in the periphery. The stranger's throat rattled when he breathed. It was nearly imperceptible normally, but to Tristain's ears, it sounded like a thousand thundering hooves. He thought his head might burst from the pressure, and he whimpered inside. The experience was wholly disconcerting. Ribbons of white light danced down by his nose and up towards his brow.

The ground shook and bubbled up before him, as if it had turned liquid. The black stone floor rose like liquid foaming in a cup and popped right in front of his face. His jaw hurt from the grinding. Shivers ran up through his body, shivers that he could not control. Hours passed like this, hours of Tristain's mind straddling the edge of insanity. The stranger watched him the whole time. Finally, the ringing in his ears subsided. He wiggled a finger, cautiously. It moved, and Tristain rejoiced internally. Strength was coming back.

"I see you're recovering," he said, looking down on Tristain.

"Fuck *yooo*," Tristain mumbled, tongue still taking up far too much room in his mouth.

The stranger's countenance shifted.

"I should kill you for what you've done," he spat. "What you've done to our family."

"*Ouurrr fami-lee?*"

The stranger's face twisted into a grin. It called to mind white maggots wriggling in a carcass. Roaches squeezing through gaps under doors. Fat horseflies infesting an abscess.

"Do you not recognize your own brother?"

The floor fell out from under him. His jaw went slack. "*Noooo... mmmmyy bbbb—*"

"Died? Bann Oncierran did." He turned his head and peeled back a flap of skin—the skin wasn't real, somehow. It was a mask. Beneath the scarred skin, pink, smooth skin revealed itself. His brother showed his face underneath, then the mask descended again. "I am Lord Inquisitor Rotersand, now. You're surprised? I suppose you would be. I took care to cover my tracks."

"*Whyyy?*"

"Because I have plans, brother. Plans that cannot be interfered with. Plans for our family."

Tristain started trembling. "No..." The stranger took the syringe and stuck it into Tristain's neck. "*You whore-sooo...*" Then he went as still as a corpse.

25

DECEIT

SANGUINUM, 1044

*It is well known that Istryan conquered a people that lived on
the Continent before his arrival. Yet we know nothing about
them—any detail or elaboration on Istryan's enemies has been
completely expunged from history.*

— GERAINT FALLSTADT, EMPEROR'S HISTORIAN

DIANA STRODE INTO THE room with purpose. The knight sat unchained by the window on his bed. It was a narrow bed, with a hair-thin mattress, but the room was well-supplied, with fresh apples on the table, and a trunk by the wall full of fresh clothes. A gentle, salt-laden breeze blew into the room.

"Making yourself comfortable?" she asked, pushing the door shut.

Leon turned to face her. "Selene, right? I remember you."

She smiled. "Diana. Inquisitor—"

"You can keep your titles. I'll have my freedom if you're offering."

"Very droll. I won't mince words. Consorting with a demon is a serious crime in the eyes of Sigur. You will be tried in the eyes of the Lightfather, according to His laws."

He scratched his chin through thick red beard, making a rasping noise. "Hm. Tell me, can you see the army from here? Humor me."

She glanced outside the window. The army were still there, static, fixed, gathering around the walls like a sea of tar.

"They're still there."

"I think I've seen fewer Annaltians in Annaltia. What do you think is going to happen when those walls come crashing down?"

She walked to the table and sat. "They won't harm us. We won't fight on either side, so they'll have no reason to."

"Could be. D'you really think the prince will believe that?"

"He has no reason not to. Besides, I didn't come here to give my opinion on politics."

"No. You came here to talk me into joining your cause, didn't you?"

Diana smiled. "You're smarter than you look."

"What other reason would you have for keeping me alive?"

"A fair hearing. You will have the chance to defend yourself."

Leon crossed his arms, waving a hand to punctuate his point. "And Caen? Did he get the chance to defend himself?"

"That was a mistake. We believed him to be a demon."

"It's hard to tell, isn't it? They, we... we all look the same, we all bleed the same..."

"Don't be ridiculous. They're uncontrollable beasts. Left to their own devices, they would kill us all."

"Aye, and your brother? What happened to that brave girl that charged into the path of sharp swords and attacked the archduke's son?"

"He was never my brother, and you're talking of the actions of a stupid girl."

"I'm sure he's thinking the same thing. Not my sister, not anymore. You know, he never stopped talking about you. He used to say he would bring you a gift. Pearls or something."

He leaned back on the bed. "I imagine he's going to be burned at the stake, or whatever you bastards do."

"Yes, I suppose so."

"And you're just fine with that... all fine and dandy. Thanks Tristain, for all the childhood memories."

"You speak as if our childhood were honey and roses. His father was a demon, too. He killed his mother and gave me this." Her voice turned thready, as though on the verge of tears. As she pointed it out, her arm tightened with phantom pain, as though a blade plunged into the webbed skin between her imaginary fingers, where they once might have been. She promised herself she wouldn't cry. She wouldn't give this hillman bastard the satisfaction. "My biggest regret is that I didn't let Rudolf kill him."

"Aye, but can't you see? That's what they do. The Order. They prey on the meek, the dregs. People that have been left behind by war, or death. They turn you. They make you believe that what you're doin' is right, and good, when really, you're just doin' everyone else's biddin'. You never had a moment of hesitation? Never had a moment where you've really asked yourself, *is this right?*"

Diana sighed. *I don't think he's going to be convinced.*

"Y'know the name Palerme?"

"No. I suppose you're going to tell me."

"Aye, lass, an' you'll listen. Palerme's on the border of Alania and Osbergia, in the mountains. Yonder, it was a trading post. But then the traders started havin' children, started t'settle down—buildin' shacks, then houses, and it grew into a vibrant little community. The people even pooled their money and had a watchtower built that their sons and grandsons turned into a keep. Palerme became *the* border crossin', but the former Duca of Alania, Alessandro, took notice. The Duca thought they were cutting into his profits too much when people could just come to the border for their Alanian wine, their Varangian marble, or their Tanerian silks. In those days, trading by merchant ship was uncommon. But you know what they say—never come between an Alanian and their coin. So, what did he do? What else? He paid off the Order to invent a fallacy that they were harboring demons, and the Order did what they do best, declarin' a cleansing. No defense. No fair hearing. Extermination was the cure for a disease that never existed.

"But here's the thing. The people of Palerme were tough. They fought back. Lots of 'em died. The rest retreated to their keep deep in the forest and waited the Order out. They'd stockpiled for the winter, and there were only a dozen left, so they had enough for years. Or they would have, had the Order not thrown their dead over the walls. We threw them over in such quantity... faster than they could bury them. The people inside got sick. Very sick. The last merchant threw open the gates in desperation, begging for the Order to spare his life, treat his young son for the corpse sickness... and they cut his throat. Just like that. We burned the son at the stake."

Diana rolled an apple between her slender fingers. "You expect me to believe that?"

Leon shrugged. "I don't expect you to believe it, lass, but it happened. I was there."

"Horseshit."

"It's true. Speak to Velstadt."

"Velstadt? Lord Inquisitor Velstadt? He's dead. Elias Rotersand is the Lord Inquisitor now."

"Rotersand, huh... Well, go look at the archives. It's all in there. Some of them in gray robes kept records of it. I saw it, they made notes in those huge ledgers of theirs. It's going back, uh, twenty years now. 1023 it was."

She tapped her fingers. "No, I don't think I'll do that." The man seemed convinced of his own lies. The bell rang for noon. They would serve luncheon in the west wing, if she remembered correctly. "Excuse me," she said, unlocking the door and leaving. Leon didn't say a word. She sighed, locking the door again. *I really don't think he's going to be convinced.*

L EON'S WORDS WEIGHED HEAVY on Diana's mind, even a week
later. She practiced alone in the training hall, shooting her crossbow
at targets idly. Memories like decanted wine came pouring back. Leona,
Salim, Ebberich, Ruprecht... the moments spent together in this place.
Half of them were dead, the others, she wasn't sure. They could've been,
too. Of course, she'd done things she'd regretted. Leona was dead because
of her, all because the girl just wanted a friend. Diana had killed that.

She killed Salim because the Order told her to. The rector threatened
her life. *No... that was me. I could've refused. I might've been punished, but
I wouldn't have been killed, no. Soren would've stopped that before it could
happen.*

Other names flashed in her mind. *Lorena-Maria. Baltas.* She remembered every name, every demon she'd killed. Some were outright murderers, but others... others were less certain. *I wonder... I wonder if we left
the herbalist alone, would she have just lived her life in peace?* She nocked
another bolt, mechanical in her movements. She squeezed the trigger, not
caring if it hit the target or not. *It can't be true... the Order helps people,
they saved me... well, Soren and that priest did. Soren found me, saved my
life. One of many times.* She paled, realization washing over her. Everything
they had taught her, the self-realization she felt... it was all him. She let the
crossbow fall by her side.

Palerme... if that was true, there'd be records of it, surely... The Order
recorded everything. The archives were a trove of information, but they
were tightly controlled. The archivist had eyes everywhere, his assistants.
No records could leave the halls. Only inquisitors or higher ranks even had
access. She would have to be careful. Leon's words weighed heavy on her
mind.

T HE ARCHIVES BUILDING SAT atop the immense Osterlin Hill, opposite the White Palace. Diana shivered, pressing her arm closer to
her jacket as she ascended the stairs. The Inner Ring's stone architecture
and vast thoroughfares funneled wind, making it chilly most of the time,
even in summer. Their height at the top of the hill did not help matters,
funneling the wind even further.

Diana turned. From here, she could take in the entire palace. The curving
form of its arches and buttresses gave the structure a sound foundation,
while the tops of its towers extended into fine parapets, where even fin-
er gold-and-red pennants flew from their tops. White birds circled the
sky-piercing structures. A bronze statue, greened by time, of Istryan the
Conqueror stood imposing above the central doorway. The man was a
visage of strength—one hand gripping the haft of a winged spear, the other
by his side. A huge brazier burned in front, evoking comparisons to Sigur
and his golden lantern.

Diana walked into the archives. They paled compared to the palace,
though it was nice enough. Beyond the columned front was an open-air
courtyard of colorful tiles in the center of the building, built in the sixth
century. Sets of assistants and notaries in their gray robes stood in quiet
conversation about the latest gossip or the latest discovery. She asked for
directions, and they pointed her to a stairwell off the left side. Down she
went, following signs to the records section. Through a candlelit hallway,
she came upon a large, dimly lit room filled with row after row of book-
cases. In front of her sat a man at a desk, his head bent over a piece of
parchment. She was about to speak when she saw his hands as he wrote.
They were pinkish and misshapen. They seemed to shake whenever he
took them off the page. The left side of his face was heavily scarred and
seemed to melt into his neck. She cleared her throat. The man looked up.
He laughed and put his quill down.

"Selene, is that you?"

Diana narrowed her eyes, trying to place him.

"It's me, Ruprecht!"

"*Ruprecht?*" This was the man confirmed before her, and she had heard nothing from him for years. "Gods, it's been..."

"Years! Sigur, time has been kind to you. You're as beautiful as ever. Meanwhile, I'm... anyway, what are you doing here?" He spoke fine for someone with half a face hanging off.

She smiled. It was exciting to see him again, even if it was like this. "I... I didn't know you were an archivist."

"Assistant. They transferred me here after... well, after this." He pointed to his face. "A case of hot pitch exploded in my face. My fault, really. I was setting a trap and overbalanced."

"Gods... I'm sorry."

"No harm. I wasn't cut out to be a Sword. I prefer my books, anyway. But you—Inquisitor! When did that happen?"

She laughed, feeling giddier than a month-old pup. "Ah, not that long ago, really. A few months."

"Well, it suits you. From the day you landed that knife flick on the second try, I knew you were heading places."

"Thank you."

"How about this siege, eh? They say the archduke's in talks with the prince. We can only hope brotherly love wins the day, eh? Well, you didn't come here to let me talk your ear off about politics. What are you after?"

"I suppose I don't know. Do you know of a place called Palerme?"

"Palerme... no, never heard of it."

"It's on the border with Alania. What about... operation records, from 1023.

"1023... there was an operation down that way, but I can't recall if it specified where exactly. It's over there, third row in. Operation Heregeld, I think it was called."

She found the book, a thin wafer of calfskin, bound with twine. *Operation Heregeld...* She found a seat in the reading area. The room was quiet.

She and Ruprecht were the only ones in the room. Though that didn't mean there weren't eyes watching from the walls.

She flicked open the first page. *Hmm... Operation successful... locals grateful... ten inquisitors, twenty prosecutors, thirty arbiters, forty wardens... an auxiliary of mercenaries, under a Leon Vorland—sum-total one-fifty, led by His Eminence Lord Inquisitor Velstadt.* Diana hesitated. The knight had been right. He was there. This was a major operation. There were over a hundred Swords. *And I thought I was being absurd by having eight of us... Surely something this big would've caused a stir. There's also no mention of the number of kills or captures of demons.* Whoever notarized it left no mention of the demonic presence.

She turned the page and snorted. Someone had taken to it with a quill, scoring deep lines of black ink across the surface. To cover their tracks—the depths of their guilt as black as the ink itself. She could barely read any of it. Only fragments remained, and nothing useful. The next page was like this as well, and the next. On the last page was a table of financials. She checked if there was a payment from the duca or an Alanian, but there wasn't. The seal of Lord Inquisitor Velstadt sat at the bottom of the page, along with his signature.

She sighed. *Useless. There's nothing here.* She heard footsteps. She turned, hand shooting to her dagger.

"You'd do me a favor by killing me," Ruprecht said. "But I thought you might want to see these first."

Diana relaxed. He carefully placed a pile of assorted tomes, books, and ephemera on the table.

"Everything I could find that talks about a place called Palerme in the year 1023. Census reports, business transactions, deed transfers, law proceedings, you name it. Now, you want to tell me why you're so interested in this place? And why you were all but ready to cut my throat for sneaking up on you?"

She rubbed the side of her face. "It's... it's nothing."

"You're a terrible liar, Selene." He sat at the table. "You don't have to tell me, but you're going to need help if you're going to get through all this before sundown."

"It's Diana, now," she whispered.

He grabbed the first book off the pile and started flicking through. "Hm?"

"Never mind."

She flicked through them. None of them had anything useful. *Legal proceedings of a M. Talbert and D.F. Chamfer regarding steel tariffs... Financial records of Palermean Holdings, blah-blah...* Surely, if the whole town had been wiped off the map, there'd be some trace of it. Everything looked right. All the legal records wanted to talk about were trading and inheritance disputes, while all the financial records itemized in excruciating detail the income and outgoings of twenty different trading companies in the area. Two hours later, and she was getting nowhere fast.

She tried the next book—*Census Records of Osbergia, 1023.* It wasn't a large book, but it was comprehensive. She rolled her thumb over the thin pages. Ostelar had twenty of them alone. *Come on... O... O... P... Paarville... Paen... Palberg... Pale... Palerme, finally.* She glanced down the page. *Records count three men married of chief means, eighty men married of moderate means, four men married of low means. Twenty men unmarried of chief means, six men unmarried of moderate means... twenty heads of cattle, blah-blah... here. What's this? Records could not be confirmed in the following census?*

She looked up. "Ruprecht, is there a 1024 here?"

"For the census? They do it every five years. I'll go get 1028." He winced, favoring his right side as he left the room. She frowned in pity. *It must pain him so... it looks like it was his hands and the whole right side of his body. I knew those traps were dangerous—I've used them. To think, one moment of inattention and that could've been me.*

Gods, it was silent in here. She could've heard a pin drop. Her heart was in her throat. The still, underground air seemed to want to choke her for even stepping foot in this place. Eventually, after an ungodly amount of time, Ruprecht returned. She breathed a sigh of relief.

"Here," he said. "What is it?"

She took the book he offered, flicking to the P's. "Here... but... there's nothing. Paarville. Palberg. Pale. Passtadt. Perm. No Palerme."

"That can't be right."

"Here, look... the page is missing."

He looked at the pages, flicking back and forth. He flipped it over, inspecting the spine. "It's aged, but it's fine. No pages missing."

"What does that mean?"

"They skipped it. Either the census wasn't done, which is possible, or... or the town no longer existed."

"*No longer existed*—what in the four hells?" It was *exterminatus*, but there was no demonic presence whatsoever. They'd buried a town wholesale for payment, like common mercenaries. No wonder the emperor didn't sanction them anymore.

"Selene, what is this?"

"Ruprecht... I think I've found something I shouldn't have. I don't think I can tell you, though. It would put your life in danger."

"Please be careful. I would hate to think *I've* put *your* life in danger."

She sighed. "Thank you, Ruprecht."

"Anytime. If you need anything else, you know where to find me. Good luck, Selene."

She embraced him, and he let out a small gasp. Then he returned the embrace, and they parted without saying any more.

She walked back to the Citadel. The night-time streets were a blur around her. She didn't even notice the nearing auctumnitas celebrations of Eme; bawdy girls and innkeepers in the street alike bellowing for patrons, fragrant lavender and rosemary being burned in every window in every street, and the men and women alike ignoring usual modesty and going around in nothing but their boots. No, she didn't notice the excessive drinking and celebrating going on around her, as the city wanted to break free of the bondage that the siege brought upon them, and she especially didn't notice the great flaming ball of hay and pitch soaring through the air and dashing into the side of the White Palace.

26

THE ATTACK

SANGUINUM, 1044

Assaults of cities during sieges contain the worst of humanity. A man whom, having waited for months without success, now has the opportunity to finally deal with the enemy who humiliated them from the walls, runs amok and does things he would normally never do.

— DUKE ESTRAD, COUNT PALATINE

THE CITY STREETS WERE in a panic. People screamed, running to get to nowhere. There was no escape. The hill burned, as well as the port. Another ball of fire soared over her head, crashing into houses a few hundred yards away. The flash was incredible. The heat of the explosion nearly knocked her off her feet. She threw her hand up, covering her face. Crowds gathered in the street, trying to see what the commotion was. Children wailed, unable to grasp what was happening. Women clutched at their husbands, begging them to run, but there was nowhere they could go. They'd have to run to the sea, like rats diving from a sinking ship. They could only watch their city go up in flames.

Thunder across a cloudless sky rocked the ground, the air clapping with distant explosions. Bombards, striking the walls with boulder-sized stones.

It wouldn't be long before the walls fell. A few hours—dawn, if they were lucky.

Diana raced up the hill to the Citadel, her legs burning. She burst into the cavernous cathedral. A procession was happening, burning censers filling the air with sweet smoke. No one seemed to realize what was happening outside. It was no surprise. The walls of the citadel were thick stone, muffled the blasts from the siege engines. She bolted down the hall and up the stairs. She had to find Leon. The sky lit up again through a window. Screams and smoke drifted into the stairwell.

She threw open the door.

Leon snorted, waking from his sleep. "I'm up!"

"Knight, you see what's happening out there?"

"What—Ah... 'tis time, then. What are you doin' here?"

"Palerme, it's real. It was a coverup. They wiped a town off the map for money, and everyone forgot about it. We have to do something."

"Of course, it's bloody real, girl! Now, calm down. We're not in any danger here, at least not at the moment. What's your plan?"

"I... I'm not sure."

"Well, what do you want to do? I won't lie. I'm hopin' whatever you say gets me out of 'ere, lass."

What do I want to do? "This isn't right. This isn't what the Order should be. All those children, all those innocents."

He turned to face her, coming to the edge of the bed. "Althann. That's what us Hillmen call 'em. The demons. Althann are friendly spirits, ambivalent to humanity. If you left him alone, he'd leave you alone. There are even stories of him helpin' humans out if they got lost in the mountains, like givin' 'em healin', sup, and water."

"Like the herbalist."

"Who?"

"Doesn't matter. But wait, you said you were in the Order?"

"I didn't say that. They hired mercenaries. Paid us enough to keep our mouths shut. Don't look at me like that, lass. I wasn't always Sir Leon the Strong. I'm opening my mouth now."

"So, these Althann... Hillmen were here before the Empire, weren't they?"

"Yeah. We got absorbed as Istryan and his armies pushed east."

"It's known that Sigur came with Istryan. If the hillmen have stories of the demons that predate Sigur... maybe that's what they originally were. Friendly creatures, who were forced to adapt to a changing world. Their descendants are what we see as demons, forced to live in a world that was never meant for them. And they made up the curse to justify hunting them. Althann, huh..."

"Might be. Might be nonsense. But I *know* Tristain. He's like a son to me. He killed no one that didn't deserve it."

She slumped in a chair. "What do we do? He's locked up down below, and I don't have the keys—" *But Sorenius would.* "I know what to do."

S ELENE BIT HER LIP as she opened Soren's door. His room was austere, just as hers was. A nightstand sat next to a boiled leather jacket mounted on an armor stand. Two sets of white robes were draped over hooks on the wall. A narrow bed sat in the opposite corner. She glanced at the nightstand again. On first pass, she hadn't noticed them, but there they were, a set of iron keys on a thick ring.

He sat there, on the bed, shirtless, sharpening a dagger by a tallow candle. Her eyes lit up. Gods, he was handsome. His shoulders and chest rippled with taut muscle. Powerful arms curved enticingly. Silvery hair filled out his chest and stomach, framed by two rosy nipples.

He looked up. "Inquisitor? What are you doing here? Have you seen what's happening out there?"

Selene shut the door behind her. Her mind swam with possibilities. Wonderful possibilities. This could be the last time she would ever see Soren again. She wanted the key, and she wanted him. She wanted him more.

She strode up to him. He placed the dagger and sharpening stone on his nightstand. "What are you—" She grasped the side of his face, and pushed in with her lips, and straddled him with her legs. A jolt shot up her spine.

He pushed apart. "Diana, we shouldn't do this."

She let go, and undid her nightshirt, and her hair knot. The lacing slipped effortlessly, sliding down over her shoulders, breasts, belly, past her waist until it settled around her hips. She tousled her hair. Her raven curls cascaded in flowing black. Her green eyes twinkled in the candlelight. His mouth gaped slightly.

She smiled, enjoying his gaze passing over her. "Haven't you ever broken the rules?"

He regained his wits. "Not in a long time."

"Allow me, then." She leaned in, her locks brushing across their faces and grasped him tight. He gave in, pushing deeper into her, tongues wet, breath heavy and hot. He tasted like salt and honey, and her mind buzzed with excitement. He grabbed her with both hands. If it was a jolt before, this was a storm. It felt incredible. *Soren and I had so many months together... why weren't we doing this the whole time?*

She moaned as she ground herself against the swelling in his trousers. His rough hands danced across her neck, shoulders, back, arse. She felt her wetness slipping onto his hard belly. His engorged cock begged to be freed. She obliged, undoing his trousers, and lowering herself onto him. Her body wracked with pleasure. She rocked her hips and pushed him back onto the bed. She brought her head down and took his nipple in her mouth. He let out a moan. It stirred something deep inside her, and she bit down, drawing blood. He made a sharp, lowing noise, but he never stopped. His hips moved in time with hers, and neither of them cared they were no longer quiet. She felt his body jerk beneath him, and the same feeling swelled within her. They writhed and spasmed and quivered together and fell exhausted onto the bed.

They were silent as they filled the room with their hot breath. Selene turned to him. He looked back at her. His grey eyes like the ashes of a long-dead pyre begged her to ask. Begged her to ask him to come with her. The belfry rang midnight, tolling across the black cape and out to sea. She sighed. *I can't ask. I can't do that to him. The less he knows, the better.*

"What is it?" he asked.

"Nothing. I should get back." She wiped herself off with his covers and got up from the bed. *I should get back. It's nearly time.*

"Is something wrong?"

"You've never asked before, so I don't know why you're asking now," she said as she threw her nightshirt back over her head, deftly palming the keys.

"Is this about—that was a long time ago. I apologized, didn't I? And it's never happened since."

"It's not that. Really, I'm fine. Look, I should get back before anyone sees I'm out after curfew."

"Stay here, then. I have a spare robe. You can leave in the morning."

"No... Please. I have to go."

"Diana." She turned her head. He waited for her to say something. She didn't. They stared at each other. She forced herself to leave. The door latched as she walked into the hallway.

Right... now to get Leon.

She avoided anyone in the hallways, and her room was as she left it. Her armor was on the rack, waiting for her. She threw it on, clasping the jacket closed, laced her trousers, and pulled her gloves on. She dropped her dagger into her belt frog and hooked her crossbow across her back. Three adder vials in her belt pouch, along with a dozen bolts and the iron keys, and she was ready to go. Ready as she could ever be. Her hand hesitated as she reached for the door pull. *Come on, Selene. Do this. He's counting on you...*

She pulled open the door slowly. No one was outside. The halls were empty. They were all still in the cathedral. *Good.* She crept along the narrow hallways, avoiding the major thoroughfares and sacristies. She knew the way, had trod these halls for more than two years, and this last week refreshed her memory of the place. *Ten more paces, then a right. Fifteen paces, there's the candelabra with the one broken arm. Twenty paces, then down the stairs.*

27

BREAK

SANGUINUM, 1044

*The psyche is an interesting thing. With the right application
of force and substance, you can make a man do anything you
want, or leave him in a hell of his own making, forever.*

— LORD INQUISITOR ELIAS ROTERSAND

LEON HEARD A SOFT knock on the door. His eyes shot awake. He was just resting them. He wasn't sleeping, really. The lock mechanism clicked. The door opened slowly. Leon crept behind the door, chamber pot in hand. A dark figure strode into the room.

"Leon," she whispered.

"Oh, it's you," he said. Selene looked unimpressed. He expected her to be frightened that she was standing behind him, but no. She had nerves of steel. *Good. We're going to need them.*

She held out a set of black robes for him. "Put this on. You're overly all too big and recognizable. Keep your head down, and pretend like you're not four feet wide, and they might not know who you are."

"Alright," he replied, throwing the robe over his head and his hood up. "I'm not sure how I'll pretend to do that, but I'll try."

S ELENE WALKED SLOWLY ALONG the tiled floor, keeping her head down, nodding briefly to the clerics passing them in the hallways. Leon was in lockstep, head down as well. For a knight famed for his honor and known for his bluntness, he was well-accustomed to subterfuge.

They walked down the spiral stairs as if they were inquisitor and novitiate. She took a candle from a candelabra on the wall. Down here, it would just look like they were a mentor and apprentice situation, perhaps a little later than usual, and Diana the Inquisitor was just taking the novitiate for a tour of the prison. *During an assault on the city... who am I fooling?*

She heard shuffling from a cell. One of the prisoners must've been awake. Hushed tones and whispers alighted her steps to the door, and she lifted her candle, lighting up the room through a small grate at the top of the door. Selene peered inside. A little girl snuggled with her mother, both trying to negotiate the chains shackled around their wrists. The girl looked at Selene and huddled closer to her mother. They were both shivering. The mother looked at Selene with a sense of sad weariness. Selene felt a twinge of guilt. She thought back to herself as a little girl—the one who felt scared and alone. She felt for the girl in the cage, but what could she do? Tristain wouldn't rescue himself. She left them alone and moved on.

They rounded the corner. The silence buzzed in her ears, and she smelled the stink of the bay below. The hairs on the back of her neck stood on end. Turgid with a hollow, reverberating quiet, something slinked out of the darkness. Sharp cheekbones, lips that could charm the pants off a queen, and skin as pale as the brightest white silk resolved from the shadow.

"Inquisitor," Soren said, his arms crossed. He was in his own armor now, estoc sitting at his belt. "What are you doing here?"

"You followed me?" she asked.

"You weren't yourself. What was I to think?"

"And you know me?"

"Of course, I do. I know you better than anyone else."

She placed her hand on Leon's back as the knight tensed up. "Why do you suppose?"

"Please don't tell me... You're going to rescue your ward's son, aren't you? I knew it. You almost convinced me, but as soon as family comes back into the picture..."

"Hang on, just ... hold a minute." *If I can convince him...* "It's not just about my family, Soren. I can't do this anymore."

"So, you turn your back on us? After all we've done for you?"

"*We?* What about you? What do *you* want? Come with me. They *deserve* to be free. The Order just wants to exterminate them, the demons. See, I don't believe that's what they are. I may have once, but not anymore. They're victims. Victims of a thousand-year-curse that is passed down, generation to generation. A curse that turns the rest of the world against them, for nothing other than their difference. They've done nothing to deserve what they get—"

"*Done nothing?* What of all the families and good folk that've had their lives utterly destroyed by the creatures? What of the innocent, Inquisitor? You saw it yourself!"

"They... can't control themselves. The Order makes it worse, as it is. We hunt them, force them to hide their abilities, rather than seeking help. The world hates them, but we could be different, show the world that there's a different way, a better way. We could *protect* them. There is no chance that they would harm anyone if we offered them a place to change in a controlled way. We know more than anyone else about them, and we can use that knowledge for good."

"What about someone like the tax collector from Annaltia? He escaped his bonds and slaughtered *everyone* in that village. Even the children. You don't remember that? He nearly killed you, too!"

"Of course, I remember that. But it's no worse than what we've done. We destroyed Esstadt, put *exterminatus* on them!" Leon turned his head and snorted. He was from the South Hills. "Have you seen what's in the archives? We burned whole towns to the ground for the sake of a few potentially harmless beasts. What about Lorena-Maria, the herbalist? What about the blacksmith? They were just living their lives until we came along, and we destroyed them. The Order is rotten. The way we do things, it's not right. We need to change it for the better."

"I see you've been reading that *Truth*, gross falsehood. No, Selene, now come, I know you. You don't mean this."

"It's rotten to the top, Soren. You know, Leon, Rotersand just wants to use him to assassinate Prince Reynard." Leon turned his head. He hadn't known that. "I can't... *pretend*... like what we're doing here is good and right. Not anymore."

He clenched his jaw. "No."

"I... please, Soren. Please, you have to."

"No, Inquisitor. I'm sorry." He drew his blade slowly. "I can't let you do this. Surrender, and I won't harm you."

A tear slid down her cheek. "I know you won't." She closed her fist around the dagger's hilt and unsheathed it. Leon backed up. The dagger felt heavy in her palm. "I'm sorry, too."

They came to blows. Lunging, thrusting, parrying. Selene did a half-turn, lashing out with a kick. He caught her leg, and she quickly did a spin to get out of his grip. He brought his thin blade around for a low blow. It skewered her calf. She yelled.

"Stop, Inquisitor," Sorenius begged. "Surrender, and we can forget this ever happened!"

"No," she spat through ground teeth.

"You won't win. I taught you everything you know." He withdrew his blade. Blood spurted onto the stone, black. She cried out. "You'll throw it all away for someone you barely know anymore. You've spoken of your ward's son *how many times* in the years I've known you? No. Your place is here. Now, I'm going to the belfry to sound the alarm. They should know there's someone trying to escape here." He eyed Leon pointedly. "You should go back to your room and pretend like none of this ever happened."

No. She would not let that happen. He passed her. She lunged.

Sorenius clutched at the blade in his heart. His eyes went wide. His voice was weak. "What..." She let go of the blade as his legs gave out from under him.

She kneeled next to him, head hung low. She started to cry. Soren swallowed hard, then coughed blood. He grasped her hand weakly. Then his face relaxed, and he died.

Leon rested his hand on her shoulder. "I'm sorry, lass."

She sniffed, letting the silence draw out. The air hung heavy with sadness. Minutes later, she spoke, "Me too... I... I loved him."

"We all lose those we love. It's part of life." He released her and stepped past and down the hallway, peeking around the corner. "Lass, I'm sorry, but we have to go. Grieve later, but please—"

Selene got to her feet. She wiped her face, sighing. "Yeah." *Tristain waits for us...* They couldn't linger here. She looked at the silver-streaked man with the gray eyes for one last time.

"**S**ET HIM DOWN HERE," she said, the red-bearded man nodding as he gently placed the Tristain's gaunt frame onto a long crate. The storeroom down the hall from the cells would do for now, but they needed to move soon. She tended to him, uncapping her waterskin and putting it to his mouth. Tristain's eyes were glassy, unfocused. He was muttering nonsense.

"Sigur! What is wrong with him?" Leon was watching a line of drool that had worked its way out of Tristain's slack mouth.

"How long has he been like this?" she wondered. "It looks like he hasn't eaten in... Ginevra knows how long." She glanced over his skeletal form, bones poking from scarred flesh, covered in a layer of grime. His thick beard was home to all manner of dirt and things she did not want to put a name to.

She stepped back, watching Leon try to feed her poor brother. Tristain muttered something, and Leon put the piece of apple in his face again. He flinched.

"I'll shove it down your fucking throat, Squire!"

Tristain remained unresponsive.

She looked back at her guardians' son, her childhood love, and her lip quivered. She had a flashback to the last time she'd seen him. Tristain was the magnificent knight in his armor, the great tournament, the battle of two lords: a song for the minstrels. That man now sat before him, propped up not by his own strength, but by another's. Dark, greasy, matted hair, and sunken eyes. There was nothing behind them, they were just bloodshot, lifeless. Her hands trembled, then her breath quickened. She stumbled backward and landed softly on a box. Leon glanced at her and said something, but she did not hear him. A cascade of thoughts assaulted her.

How long has he been like this...?

Her breathing became quick, and her hands cold and damp.

Who did this to him...?

The color drained from her face.

The Order did this to him... They're not the only ones... All those people... What I've done in the Order's name?

She lost her bearings, and the room spun.

All those terrible things I've done... the people I've killed. Mother, I've become as horrible as the demons I tried to stop. And worse: I liked it.

She tried to control her breathing, cradling her head in her hand. Desperate tears spilled onto the ground. A vicious thread between the thoughts ripped her to pieces. The thread did not have a name, but sobs wracked her body as it ran her through. An inordinate amount of time went by. The desperation broke to a thought—the Order preyed on people like her. Broken people, people lost to grief, to injury, and they knew just how to pluck the right threads until the seams came apart, and they were remade into killers. It wasn't an excuse. Just a reason.

"Lass!" Leon cried, finally reaching through. She jerked with recognition, fuzzy eyes darting towards him. "Where are we going?"

"There's... there's a ship." The *Iustitia*. The Lord Inquisitor's ship. It was the only way out. "Out in the bay. We can take a boat from the cove."

"Well, are you coming?"

It took all of her will to force words out of her mouth, but she finally said, "Yes."

28

LIFE AND DEATH

SANGUINUM, 1044

*Present a man with no other options, and he is capable of
impossible levels of effort.*

— GRAND INQUISITOR ULRICH VETTERAND

THE STEEL GATE WAS down, shut tight. Thick steel barred their
escape to the cove. The inviting sound of gently lapping water sat
tantalizingly out of reach.

"*Raaaaggh!*" Leon booted the gate in frustration. "*Sal'brath!*" He yelled
louder than he should have, really. He limped, juggling Tristain as he
hopped around on one foot.

"It's no use," Selene said. "This is made to keep demons—Althann—from escaping."

"There's gotta be some way!" He put Tristain on the ground. "Come
on, lass, give me a hand!" He lowered himself, gripping tight, his thick
back muscles flaring as he tried to budge the gate. It didn't move a hair.
He yelled, giving up.

"Shit... what do we do, now?"

There must've been something. *A novitiate's body cut to pieces... a soft
splash...* "The arena!" She grimaced. "You might not like it, knight. We
might have to crawl through some awful things. After they train novitiates,

they test them in a Trial, a test against an Althann. They dump the dead ones from a chute."

"Oh, *sal'brath!* And you really thought the Order was good? Sorry, lass, I'll leave it. Ah, shit... If it gets us out of 'ere, I'll crawl through Sigur's arsehole."

"That's... vivid. But reassuring. Let's go. We'll have to go back the way we came."

"Lead the way."

"Arms tired yet?"

Leon laughed. "I'm used to carrying his weight."

They walked back through the dark halls of the prison, moonlight contrasting starkly on the basalt. The air was tense. Selene imagined coming around the corner to a full complement of arbiters and having her body filled with crossbow bolts. She soothed herself, tugging on her hair.

"*Wait!*"

She turned her head, stopping dead. Leon bumped into her. "You hear that?" Leon shrugged. The silence stretched.

Someone poked their head up from behind the barred viewing window. It was a shabby-bearded man in sackcloth, naked from the waist down. Clearly, the guards hadn't thought it important to give him pants. "Oy! You're not Order, are you? We saw you pass before, the stark-raving one with you-"

"Who the hell are you?"

"Frischeid, son of Frischeid. Call me Frix."

"But what are you doing in there?"

"Oh... they thought I was a demon, didn't they? I mean, I am. But I did nothing wrong. My business partner, *that bastard*, told on me. Was given a fat reward, I'm told."

Behind them, another person stuck their head up. It was the young mother from before. "You heard the screams, milady? What's going on out there?"

Selene swallowed. *Shit... these people are going to die. If it's not the Prince's men, it'll be the Order... or maybe they'll forget about them, and they'll all starve...* "What's your name?"

Leon tugged her along. "Lass, we have to go—"

"It's Meszel, milady."

"Meszel, Frix... I'm going to get you out of here."

They breathed a sigh of relief, thanking her profusely as she pulled the set of iron keys out of her belt pouch. *Now, which one is it...*

"Nope, I think it's that one—No, try that one—Ah, turn it the other... Okay, not that one," Frix said.

Leon put Tristain down, leaning him gently against the wall. Selene glanced at him. He was still unconscious. A line of drool ran onto his sackcloth shirt. *Come on, Tristain... you have to wake up eventually...*

"*Ahah!*" Frix yelled.

"Who's there!" someone called harshly, out of sight. They were near. Selene swore under her breath.

"Shit, shit, shit," Leon swore louder.

"Here! Take the keys!" Selene threw the keys past the bars into Frix's cell. They would have to free themselves. "Let's go!"

Leon scooped Tristain up and ran. They ran through dark halls, past cells, over hard stone, up stairs and down stairs. Finally, they reached the tunnel that led to the pit. Selene swallowed as they entered the sandy, dimly lit killing ground. Blood still stained the sand. The circle smelled of terror, and piss. A bleached finger-bone stuck up from the tan-colored earth.

The giant iron door roared to life above their heads. Selene looked up. It was quickly coming down on them. They dove forward. Leon landed hard on the sand, trying to stop himself from crushing Tristain's frail body.

"What in the four fucking hells?"

The sound of clanking plate filled the smooth-stone circle. A giant stepped out of the darkness. Above, the brazier roared to life, scattering light across the room. The light reflected down onto the sand, giving the giant a reddish-orange hue. In hulking plate, he glared. Manus Ironhand.

"Gods, I'd forgotten how big that bastard was," Leon said. Behind the metal giant, the iron door slammed shut. The soft sound of a lock being turned. Selene looked up as a rasping voice spoke.

"Hello, Selene."

"Lord Inquisitor," she said.

The man grinned wider than seemed possible, stretching his face to absurd proportions. He let out a chuckle, and his voice dropped its harshness. No, it was his authentic voice. It more than resembled her guardian father's in passing. "My father's ward."

Tempered by the realization that it should've been obvious in hindsight, she smiled. "Bann."

"I see you've finally realized, after all this time. I must admit, I thought my act was very good." He yanked at his face, pulling skin. Scars revealed themselves under the false skin. He rolled the skin up in a bundle, like dried glue, and tossed them into the arena. The wad hit the sand with a gentle *plop*. "You enjoy my work? Brother was always entirely too much of *himself*, wasn't he? The boy always needed to be taken down a peg. I'm only sad we were too far distant by age, that I could not have more time with him, to work on him, to mold him. Ah well, needs must."

"*You* did this to him?"

"You're lucky he's still alive. Sorenius told me what happened with Father. He gave you that freakish stump, didn't he? Where is your lovesick puppy, anyway?"

"Dead. I killed him." She spotted someone coming up the stairs next to Bann, taking up position, crossbow pointed towards them. Someone with blonde hair, and a tansy flower tucked above her ear. *Lena.*

"You... Selene! That's cold. I thought you loved him."

"I wouldn't expect you to understand, Bann."

"Yes... well, this is getting tiresome. It's about time you dropped these heroics and kill the knight, already. He's lived well past his usefulness."

Leon glanced at Selene.

She raised an eyebrow at Bann. "Why would I do that?"

"Because if you don't, I'll kill Tristain, and then I'll take my pleasure in taking each of your fingernails, one by one. Oh, I suppose I'll have to settle for toenails as well. Five is entirely not enough. And *then* I'll kill you."

"You're insane."

"*Insane? Insane? Father is the insane one! He did all of this! He turned us against each other! The great hypocrite!* Blabbing on about family, and honor, and respectability... while he murdered and ate his own wife, the Godsdamned *monster!*"

"No, *you* did this. The Order... was it just a means to an end? What end?"

He chuckled. "Yes, I suppose it was... but what end? Power, of course. Control."

"Power is never for power's sake," Leon mentioned quietly. Selene nodded.

"But I digress. Regardless, this is the ultimatum I present. Kill the knight, and I'll let you return to your duties in the Order. I'll let you live and forget the disrespect you showed me."

She looked at Leon. The man still held Tristain in his arms. The knight wiggled his jaw, cricking his neck. He nodded.

She unhooked her crossbow and shot at Bann.

The shot was quick. Bann was quicker. All the spryness of his youth was now undisguised. He threw himself out of the way. Tansy let out a shocked cry. Selene swore.

"*How dare you!*" he screamed. "*Kill them!*"

Manus stalked up to them, his giant two-handed sword at his side. His dead eyes seem to light up behind his faceplate. He raised the greatsword, ready to strike. Leon placed Tristain in the sand gently, drawing the axe at his belt and the shield from under his robe. "Let's go, you big *sal'brath* bastard!"

Selene bolted for the gate behind Manus. It was the only way up to Bann. The sand pounded under her feet. Ironhand swung a wide arc. Selene barely ducked underneath it. Gods, the sword was enormous. The brute swung it far too fast to be human. *What the hell is he?* Suddenly, the sword was bearing down on her again. She jumped out of the way. She scanned his armor, looking for a weak spot. There wasn't much. A small gap under the helmet, maybe. She had to try something.

LEON BELLOWED IN FRUSTRATION. Manus kept them both at bay with wide sweeps. The ground felt warm under his boots. He kicked up, sending an arc of sand into the air. The giant stumbled. Leon jumped, driving his axe forward. The axe slammed against the plate, glancing off harmlessly. Leon pushed his advantage, driving his heel into the brute's knee. Manus didn't budge. *Fuck.* The greatsword came behind Manus's head for a cleaving blow. Leon held his shield high. He swallowed. The moment moved in slow motion. *No, it's going to go right through it!*

Leon changed his footing at the last moment. The shield turned aside the cleave, used its own momentum. The sword kicked up sand as it planted. Leon's arm felt stiff, sore, but he smiled. The brute had overbalanced. The back of his neck stood exposed. Leon brought his axe down. Flesh split. Blood gushed from the wound.

The giant didn't seem to notice. Suddenly, Leon's vision spun. A sharp pain hurtled through his chest. He thumped into the sand.

Leon coughed and spat. He lost his bearings for a moment. His vision swam. He narrowed his eyes, focusing on Manus. Bright red blood gushed down the giant's breastplate. *He should be dead... but sal'brath, I just tickled him.*

He went to get to his feet. A bolt glanced off the sand near Tristain's head. Leon looked up.

Tansy was laughing. "You've left your pup to fend for himself, red-beard! There's scorpions in the sand!" Leon grunted in surprise. He threw himself over Tristain, shield ahead. A bolt planted itself in the shield. Another one. Another. The woman's laughter became manic. She pinned Leon down.

Selene cried out. She flew past his eye, crashing into the sand. She spat up blood. Leon clenched his jaw. *Fuck... some help... some help would be nice... we're gonna die... a man-wolf would be nice right about now...*

"Squire, wake the fuck up!"

T HE PRESS OF DARK trees loomed over Tristain. The air hung heavy with mist. His feet pounded against the slippery dirt. He could feel something approaching. His breath came hard and fast. He wasn't sure where he ran, and where he came from, but he knew he had to run. As fast as he could.

A familiar scream rang in his ears. He spurred himself on. His heart felt like it might burst from his chest.

"Selene!" He waited for her reply. Nothing. He threw himself over an uneven embankment, sliding in the mud. He burst through a bush and caught his breath. A little girl with dark hair sat before him, cradling her knees, and crying.

"Selene," Tristain said, giving her his hand. "Let's go."

They ran. Tristain looked behind. Something large moved between the trees. His eyes went wide. "Faster!"

Their breathing grew panicked. Tristain tripped on a rock. He groaned, face bleeding. A giant wolf pounced on Selene. She screamed. Tristain pulled himself to his feet.

He charged. "*Get away from her!*" The beast slapped him aside with a powerful throw of its shoulder. It loomed over Selene. It licked its chops. She cried.

It spoke with Bann's voice, "*I'm going to kill you, you horrible little urchin, and I'm going to enjoy it.*"

Tristain went pale. The wolf took her by the collar and ran off. "*Selene!*"

She screamed. Tristain was too far away. *No! You're not taking her away! Not now, not ever!*

He felt the familiar pit in his stomach. A burning began in his chest. Fire rippled through his lungs, his nerves, his muscles. The pain was welcome. He knew what came after. Sigur came to him in that moment. He remembered himself thinking about what he might've done to deserve his damned fate, Sigur's curse. This was no curse—this was *strength*. He was *might*, given flesh. Power surged throughout his body. Fur glided from his skin. Snout grew from jaw, nose and face re-formed. Teeth grew finger-sized, sharp as a wolf's. His hot breath curled in the forest. The air seemed to tremble as he rose to his full height. He took a deep breath, filling his lungs with night air. It was the freshest air he'd ever smelled. A bellowing roar rattled the trees and shook the ground.

He blinked. He was no longer in the forest. Hysterical laughter filled his ears. Sharp grunting. He felt the sand under his feet. The surrounding walls were high, but he could see the top, and no longer would fear affect him. He sniffed. The blonde woman started shrieking. With his sharp hearing, he heard a derisive grunt behind her.

The steel-covered giant turned from his fight with Selene. Tristain leaped and crashed into him. Smashing through the gate, he sheared the iron gate off its hinges.

Tristain ripped his helmet off. Bright, luminescent eyes widened as Tristain tore his throat out.

T HE GATE HUNG OFF its hinges. Selene darted in behind. She flew up the stairs, turning a pirouette as a bolt skimmed her arm hairs. Tansy screamed in surprise.

"*Wait, Dia—*" The blade under her chin cut her off. The venomous woman finally died.

Bann backed up. "Selene, you know me... kill me if you have to. Everything I did, I did for our family."

She cried out, howling in pain. Her dagger pierced his chest again and again. He fell. She saw herself from above, taking his life, wound by wound. When it was over, her hand felt stiff, and Bann's blood covered her jacket.

"No!" It was Leon.

Selene turned. She ran to the stairs and froze. She slumped on the wall. Her eyes glazed over.

Tristain was impaled. The giant two-hander had run him through when he'd charged at Manus. Tristain drew his lips back, snarling in pain. A deluge of dark blood ran down the steel, saturating the stone. He looked at Selene, his jaw going slack. He stumbled and collapsed. Leon rushed to him.

"*Pleeeaaase!*" he cried. His voice was ragged. "*Not again!*"

Selene fell beside them. Tristain's body shrank and his fur receded. His face turned back to the glowing child she remembered. She shrieked, pleading for his apology.

He couldn't have heard it. He was already gone.

29

THE ARABELLA

SANGUINUM, 1044

A SOFT KNOCK FROM behind the heavy iron door broke the desolate silence. Selene wiped her face and picked up her dagger. She hoped desperately they weren't Order. She didn't think she had it in her to fight anymore.

"Let us in," Frix's voice came. "Someone help!"

Selene gasped. She raced up the stairs, and the mechanism thundered to life. A loud clinking of chains and pulleys, and the door raised slowly. Threadbare and unkempt, they threw themselves under the door, flooding in. Forty, fifty of them. Selene smiled through the pain she was feeling. At least they were still alive. Leon shut the gate when the last one came through.

"Milady," Frix said, his pale legs in full view. "'Tis good to see—" He cut himself off, looking around. "What happened?"

She didn't answer. People were getting restless, wondering out loud if this was another dead end.

"Let us help you, milady," Meszel said, her daughter at her side. "Is there anything we can do?"

She turned to Leon. "Come with me," she said.

People gasped, looking at the carnage in the stairwell. The body chute was off to the left, and that was where they headed.

"Down here," she said. Her lip quivered as she tried to organize her thoughts. Leon held her shoulder. His touch was calming. "It'll take you to the sea. Be careful, though. I don't know what it's like in there."

"What is this?" someone asked. "A corpse chute?"

Selene didn't answer. Frix shrugged. He spoke to the crowd. "Milady, if this is our only way, we'll take it. Better than burning at the stake, or getting slaughtered by Gods know what, right?" They all murmured in agreement. "Let's go, then. I'll do the honors." He crawled into the chute. "It's dark!" He cried out. "But it's metal, and smooth-*woah!*—" He landed with a soft splash. "*It's fine! Bit cold! Oh, don't mind the bodies!*" came his voice.

The prisoners murmured with uncertainty. "It's our only chance," Meszel said to her daughter. "Come, Gretel." They followed Frix into the chute, screaming as they fell. *Splash*. They were fine.

They formed a line, following one after the other. It was easy after that. Finally, the last one made it through, and Selene was next.

"I'm taking him with me," she said to Leon. She looked over Tristain's body. The greatsword was still planted deep within him. Her lip quivered again. "I can't do it on my own."

Leon nodded. "Of course, lass." He grabbed the sword's quillons, pulling while Selene put her weight on Tristain, closing his eyes quickly. She glanced at his soft neck, his bearded face. His body was still warm. He looked like he could be sleeping. She blinked back tears, trying to focus on the task at hand.

The sword pulled free. Leon stumbled back. "Gods, how did that fucker carry this, let alone swing it... it's gotta weigh thirty pounds..." He let it fall to the stone with a clatter.

They put Tristain in the chute.

"And your other brother?" Leon asked.

She clenched her jaw. "He made his choices. He can rot in this horrible place for all I care."

Leon nodded. "He won't need this anymore, will he?" He had cut Bann's purse from his belt. It looked heavy.

Selene shook her head. "No, he won't."

She pushed Tristain forward as she crawled into the dark tube. Forward, forward, forward, until it fell out of sight. She swallowed, taking a deep breath. There was enough room to maneuver. She threw herself, feet first. It was a sheer fall. She shrieked, not knowing how far she would plummet. But then, soft orange light came from beneath.

Water engulfed her. The fall was only twenty, thirty feet. She swam to the surface. The prisoners swam to a nearby ledge, helping each other up. She looked up. Orange light filled the black sky. The air smelled of ash and salt.

Selene pulled Tristain's body along with her as she kicked her legs. The sea was calm enough to swim with only her legs. Eventually, she made it to the ledge. Frix was there, helping everyone up.

"Take him," she said. "Take him first."

Frix called for help, pulling Tristain out of the water while Selene pushed. They groaned with the effort. Once he was on solid ground, Frix helped Selene out. Leon wasn't far behind.

"What now?" Frix asked as Selene wrung her raven locks of seawater. The others shuffled, not sure what to do. Meszel kneeled down, shushing her daughter, wiping her face. The girl was crying.

"There," Selene said, pointing to a shadow on the horizon. "We can escape on the ship."

"How do we get out there?" Leon asked, Tristain cradled in his arms. "I ain't swimmin' that far. Not with him on my back."

The prisoners murmured with hesitation.

"Around there," Selene said, pointing to a curve in the cliff. "There's a cove. Should be a boat there."

They followed the curve of the cliff, rounding the corner. Water sloshed around their feet as the wind picked up waves. Selene shivered. She wasn't the only one.

The cove stood ahead of them, bathed in light. Men in short sleeves and shabby trousers were loading crates into moored boats. A man in a red coat and peaked wool hat was barking orders. They did not look like Golden Swords.

"That crate! No, Sev, leave that one! Too heavy! Yeah, we can always use more rope!" He turned his head, squinting into the darkness. "Oye! Blades!"

His men drew their swords, axes, and knives, dropping whatever they were holding.

"Who's there?" he cried.

Selene drew her dagger and stepped out of the darkness.

She lifted it into the air. "I'm unarmed," she said, stepping onto the stone wharf. She threw her dagger aside. "We're looking for a way onto that ship."

The leader looked at his men. They all laughed. "Good thing, mistress. You've found it."

"I'm Selene. Are you the crew?"

"*Her* crew. The *Arabella*, or the *Iustitia*, as that pompous fuck calls her."

"What are you doing here?"

The leader waved for his men to sheath their blades. "Gods honest, men, keep loading! I swear, they'd trip over their damn noses if I wasn't there to tell 'em where to step. Mistress." He bowed. "Captain Bennington Stuart Albrich Chesterfield, formerly of Marberg, now of the high seas. The city burns, and the Order with it. We're taking what we can from this place and leaving." He rested a hand on his sword hilt. "I trust there's no issue?"

"Gods, no. Come, everyone. It's safe." She waved to the group behind her. They filed into the cove. She glanced behind the captain and breathed a sigh of relief. The steel portcullis was still down, so it was likely no one else would stumble upon them.

"Selene. Just Selene," she said, shaking his hand firmly.

"Well, Just Selene, we're—"

"*Leon!*" someone cried. Selene turned her head. A man with a silver earring clapped him on the shoulders. "It's Lorrin!"

"Sailor," he greeted.

Lorrin looked down. "Oh... is that... Shit. I'm sorry."

"Me, too."

"I'll see you on the ship," Lorrin said, and went back to loading crates.

"Let's go, men," the captain cried. "Mistress, we can offer you passage, but... are you this many? I'm afraid we'll have to ask for some compensation."

She gave him Bann's coin pouch. He flipped the heavy bag over, inspecting a single coin. "Yep, that's enough. Too much, in fact. Here." He handed it back. It weighed about half as much.

"Into the boat," she cried. The boats could hold twenty of them, with all the other sailors and crates. They would have to make at least two trips. It got heated.

"I'm not fucking staying here," one prisoner yelled. He had graying hair and a thick-set body, with the musculature of a blacksmith. "I've spent a year in this place. No fucking way am I spending one more second!"

A man shoved him. "Back off! Let the women on first!"

"Bullshit!"

"Aye!" Leon bellowed, getting between them. "We're in no danger 'ere! This ain't right! Fighting amongst ourselves gets us nothing!"

Frix chimed in. "Lackwits! Can't you see the Order 're laughin' at us? We have to stick together!"

"What about a lottery?"

"How the fuck we do that, Heinrich?"

"It's just an idea, Gregor!"

"First on, first off!"

"Oy!"

Gregor the blacksmith threw a punch. It missed his target, smashing Leon in the face. He reeled but kept his footing.

"That's Leon the Strong, you idiots," Frix yelled.

Selene strode up to him, worrying. She reached out, checking his cheek. "I'm alright, lass," he said. "I've taken harder drinks. How do you know me, Frix?"

"I saw you at the Red Dragon Tourney... oh, ten years ago? *Phwoar,* you were incredible. Unseated Gustav Vredevoort three times, he did. See, lackwits, that's who you're messing with. He'll drop you faster than a sack of potatoes."

Gregor turned red, giving him a stiff bow. "Sorry, Sir. I'm ashamed."

"That's alright, lad. Now, we'll have to draw lots or something."

"No, I volunteer," the blacksmith replied. "I'll take the second round." The man he was arguing with, Heinrich, volunteered as well. Then ten others did, then another ten.

"Right, well, anyone who didn't volunteer on the boats," Selene said.

The captain took up the helm, barking for the rowers to pull. "*Pull,*" he yelled rhythmically. "*Pull! Pull! Pull!*"

T HE *ARABELLA*'S DECK WAS a flurry of activity when the second wave of boats arrived, and soon everyone was on board. The reddish-orange sky grew brighter, and the smog was getting thicker. Selene coughed, leaning on the railing.

"*Haul anchor! All hands away,*" the captain yelled, and the black sails loosened. The wind inflated them, and the ship moved out to sea. Selene looked around. As the ship reached its cruise speed, the deck mellowed out. She walked up to Leon. He stared off into the distance, still holding Tristain in his arms.

"I've decided," she said.

The knight looked up.

"We're going to Palerme."

Leon nodded. "We'd better bury him."

She bit her lip. "Yeah."

They had Tristain wrapped in a shroud, and a bag of sand tied around his ankles. His face was left uncovered. Selene knelt next to him. She placed her hand on his chest and closed her eyes. She apologized with all her heart. But she knew. She knew she would have to beg for his forgiveness for the rest of her life. *I'm so sorry...* A tear fell, soaking into the canvas. Her heart hurt. It seethed in her chest.

As they lowered his body into the water, the deck was silent. The knot was slipped, and Tristain sank. The sea swallowed him whole.

Selene had to look away. She found her solace in up. She watched as the sails distended in the gentle breeze coming off the coast. The backdrop of the burning city behind them grew distant. Topsails floated like clouds in the night sky. The very top sail, the skysail, appeared to touch the heavens themselves, free from human hands. The water was so still and the breeze so steady that the sails looked like sculpted marble hanging there, pulling the ship through the water. It was breathtaking. She stood there a while, taking it all in.

Her lip quivered. She couldn't resist her grief any longer. It came unbidden. She leaned on the railing, unable to move. Her soul poured onto the timber. Like a piece of wood already burned and turned to ash finally crumbling at the slightest touch, Selene broke. She gasped as pieces of herself scattered to the seabreeze, sobs wracking her body as she cried about everyone she had lost, and a small voice inside her wondered if anything would be left.

EPILOGUE I

OTTILLE

"Come, mama!" Sanna cried. "It's just over the ridge!"

"Sanna, wait! Don't race ahead," Ottille cried out after her. The frost was coming and it was easy to get lost in the mountains. The smell of a coming rime filled the air. Ottille's feet were cold. Snow was soaking through her boots. "Come back!" She groaned. The girl disappeared from sight.

She walked over the ridge and sighed in relief as the forest opened to a wall of gray stone, the parapets of a castle behind. They had arrived. "Come, Ma," Ottille cried.

The old woman grunted, clambering slowly up the stone. "The spirit of youth," she croaked. "Impatient, no matter the age!"

Ottille helped her mother over a rock and onto the ridge. "A welcome sight, Gram."

"Indeed. I was afraid we might get lost, and I'd have to eat you to survive!"

Ottille laughed. "Now, where's that girl gone... ah, there!"

Sanna had raced ahead and talked with a man in a thick brown cloak. He had a bright red beard, and his shaved head reflected the pale sun. Ottille and her mother walked gingerly down the ridge, which hadn't proved a problem for the young girl, but Gram's brittle bones and stiff joints had her lingering.

"...and who do we have here?" The wide man in the brown cloak said, his beard building up a little frost.

The girl spoke, "This is my ma, Ottille, and my gram."

"They have lost my name to time, boy," the old woman replied.

Ottille rolled her eyes. "Her name is Lucia. We're from Invereid."

The man bellowed with laughter. "You'll have to meet our leader, then. She's from Invereid, herself." He bowed his head slightly. "Sir Leon Vorland."

"*Leon Strong!*" The girl cried. "Wow! I saw you fight every time you came to Invereid! Well... I peeked through the fence, but I still saw you!"

"Well, ain't I glad to have such a dedicated admirer? C'mon, warm yourselves in the keep. This ain't the time to be outdoors. Winter's almost on us."

They followed him up the hill and beyond the stone wall, into the bailey. The circular keep was seventy feet tall, capped with merlons, and flanked by a smaller tower to the right. The stink of horses drifted over from a squat building next to the smaller tower. To their left, a heavy-set man was tanning deer skin, the tanning solution making Ottille's nose itch. Next to the gate, a blacksmith was hammering away, making pickaxe heads. His apprentice was peaning the shafts, jamming the heads into place. The heat of the furnace made Ottille hunger for a place to warm her feet.

They passed through the wicket door of the keep, the person-sized door at the foot of the wagon-sized main doors. The knight closed the door behind them. The hearths blazed. Feeling heat wash over her, Ottille breathed a sigh of relief.

"Thank the Gods," she said.

"Thank Althann," came a woman's voice. Ottille hadn't seen her sitting on a chaise by the fire. "For that is what you are." She got up slowly, with one hand. The knight rushed over. She waved him off. Ottille snorted. This woman was superior to the knight, that was clear. He answered to her, but why?

"Welcome to Palerme," the woman said, walking over.

Sanna cried, "*Baby!*" and ran up to the woman, throwing her hands on the woman's plump middle.

"I'm sorry, milady, she loves babies," Ottille apologized. She eyed the woman. Under a loose red samite and wool dress, her belly was round and full. Her young cheeks were rosy from the heat of the fire, and long, beautiful black locks hung down past her generous chest in waves. A grey silk cape covered her shoulders, hiding her left arm. Clearly, she was of means.

No, she wasn't hiding her arm. The woman only had one arm. Ottille's heart poured out for her.

"Tis a welcome blessing, milady," Lucia said. "Expecting in winter, a bountiful harvest in spring."

The woman chuckled light-heartedly. Ottille breathed a smaller sigh of relief.

"It's quite alright," she said. "Hello, little one. What's your name?"

The girl grinned. "Sanna. What's your name?"

"Selene. I'm very pleased to meet you."

"Selene is our lady," Leon said, lifting his head in respect. "Our lord."

"I don't appreciate that word," she replied. "But yes, I manage the keep and its surroundings, as well as the day-to-day running of the place."

The old woman's countenance shifted slightly. "What was it you said before, milady? Althann?"

"Althann, from the old Hillmen tales. In truth, we don't know if he was a god, or who he was exactly. But he was a friendly spirit, we know that, and if you've found your way here, that means you are too."

"Hah! Brilliant!"

"Come, sit, warm yourselves."

Ottille sat by the fire. "Sit here, Sanna." The girl ran over, sitting by her mother and Ottille ran her hands through her yellow straw-like hair. "Sir Vorland said you were from Invereid, mistress?"

Smiling briefly, Selene replied, "Yes, once. I consider Palerme my home now. So, why did you come here? Other than the obvious, of course."

Ottille stroked the back of her daughter's head. "My husband, Dietmar, was hanged by a mob out for blood. Even our old friends. They knew we were them demons, and we lived in peace our whole lives, minding our own business, but that didn't stop them."

"I'm sorry, truly."

"Tis a shame. People are angry, ever since the capital burned. I know how they feel, but that doesn't make it right."

"Kings and emperors have failed us for centuries, for millennia. It's time we took our destiny into our own hands."

The wicket door swung open with a clatter, sending a cool breeze inside. A man in a woolen coat and fur-lined cap strode into the room, shutting the door behind him. "Frix," Selene said.

The man bowed deeply, dropping his hood. He was clean-shaven, with dusty brown hair, and had a broad, freckled nose. "Mistress Selene, we've found the iron."

Leon clapped his hands, letting out a bellowing laugh.

"Excellent news," Selene joined in the celebration. "I knew there would be some in these hills. Gregor'll be happy he won't have to buy iron from the Duca anymore."

The mood in the room shifted. A candle blew out without a breeze. Ottille turned her head and found the old woman's hand on Selene's belly. Tense seconds drew out as Ottille paled at her mother's lack of tact.

Lucia grinned, gaptoothed, wrinkled, and genuine. She spoke with the self-assured nature of a long life. "It's a boy. I feel it in my heart. He's destined for great things. May Ginevra keep him hale and healthy."

Ottille went to speak, "Mother—"

"Oh, he's certainly hale," Selene cut her off with a radiant smile on her face. "He keeps me up at night with his incessant kicking." She winked at Senna.

The girl looked at her mother with anticipation.

Ottille sighed. "Go on."

The little girl ran up, throwing her hands on Selene's belly. She squealed, balling her hands up in excitement. "*Ahhh!* I can feel it! He's kicking!"

Everyone laughed.

"If it's a boy, as the wise woman says," Frix asked. "What will you name him?"

"I think... Tristain would be nice."

EPILOGUE II

GERAINT

A SOLUTION WILL ALWAYS *come when you least expect it, Geraint, that's what your father always said*, he thought. His hunchbacked jailor had yet to come back. Geraint wished he wouldn't. He liked to poke and prod too much. And he inflicted his sour cheese breath on Geraint every time he got close. That was almost worse than the knife.

But your father also said mountains were formed when the gods passed kidney stones, so what does he know.

Geraint felt the tug of his chains, the metal biting into his wrists. He was intimately familiar with being bound. The women in Saburria, across the ocean, liked to use chains. At least the ones he had been with.

But not like this. This isn't nearly as fun.

Geraint had been in his damp, dark cell for three days now. He had not been fed, which he considered to be the height of rudeness, and subsisted only on the moisture dripping from the ceiling. The sound of crashing waves came through the tiny window over the last few days, meaning he was near the sea. The stone of his cell was dark and smooth. Basalt, he figured. When he was taken, he'd travelled bound and with a bag over his head, but only for six days or so, by his reckoning. At a pace of roughly ten knots on an honestly, quite bumpy boat. They'd also turned at one point, passing a cape of some sort. He could only be in one place. Vallon, the capital of Vallonia.

They couldn't pull the wool over his eyes. There was nothing hidden in this world to the old codger. He'd met horse-worshippers, Vyahtkens, and men from the north beyond Salzheim who spoke exclusively in clicks. Matriarchal societies who revered old men for their wisdom and their virility, since their culture warred constantly and none of the men survived past thirty. They were stunningly good company and had some bloody great jokes about getting old.

Alas, he was stuck in a four foot by four-foot cell, with nothing but a dullard for conversation. He had been asked repeatedly to tell the jailor what he wanted in Vallonia, and Geraint said all he wanted was to study the archives. This only prompted more stabbing, but Geraint did not know more than a sheep herder knows of fish. Which was to say, nothing.

"Vallonia closed," he snapped, the extent of his Osbergian. Geraint insisted he spoke Vallonian, in Vallonian, but the jailer simply didn't believe him.

"I demand to speak with the King, invoking the right of a scholar to the scholarly pursuit of genealogy and consanguinity," he had said. The jailor stared at him, the lackwit not quite certain of half the words he had said. "Family trees, and uh... cousin fucking." He imagined the jailor was intimately familiar with the latter.

"Vallonia closed." He poked him with his knife again.

He had come to Vallonia as the culmination of two decades of work. Tracing the history of a person on the Continent, with the many and varied ways of keeping records—if the local municipality kept records at all—often left him reaching for sanity and the wine cup. Not only had he traced the histories of all the noble families and some of the merchant families in the empire and the republics, but he'd also cross-referenced that with mentions of fouled blood or cursed offspring.

What he'd found had led him to Vallonia. He already had an idea of what he would find but getting out was the first step.

His jailor returned. Geraint heard the shuffle of oafish footsteps and a jangle as the idiot fiddled with the lock. Then a clink as the lock mechanism moved into place. The door creaked open. The one-eyed hunchback jailor stepped inside.

He spoke in quickfire Vallonian, announcing, "The prisoner is here, sir-ehm, Gran Maestro, sir."

An olive-skinned, tall, and regal-looking man in a set of chain and plate stepped across the threshold, thumping and ringing. A sword set with rubies hung from his waist, and he wore his hair close-cropped under a hat so wide he had to fold it up to get it through the door. Feathers stuck from it like some poor goose was out there, somewhere, missing a patch on its arse.

"Thank you, Malchos," he said, with a deep, baritone voice that commanded authority. Or at least it would have, had Geraint not been half-deaf.

"It's Palchos, Gran Maestro, sir."

"Yes, Balchos. That'll be all."

"Yessir." The jailor shimmied past the Gran Maestro's enormous hat and shuffled to the door, creaking it shut as he closed it behind him. The Gran Maestro was straight-faced as he stared at Geraint.

"You mind?" Geraint asked, voice croaky. "I've got a killer itch on my toe, could you scratch it for me? I would, but"—he jangled his chains—"I'm a bit tied up."

The man smiled, and said, "That's funny. Who would've known writers were so droll?"

"I am only what you see before you," Geraint said.

The Gran Maestro stepped closer to him, eyeing the man.

"You know, I read your book once," he said. "If only you'd managed to insert some wit into that ponderous tome, I wouldn't have fallen asleep halfway through."

Geraint cleared his throat. The length of the book was a bit of a sore spot for him. He'd planned on breaking it up into several collections of volumes—ninety-two in all. But because of how the press worked, it was easier—and cheaper—to print them all in one continuous session, which took over a month, incidentally, and led to some pre-sales falling through.

"Are you going to actually torture me, or just prod me with your words?"

"Yes, well, it was interesting enough when we heard of a man in the archives that wasn't supposed to be there. Even more interesting that this man was a northerner, too."

"Everything's north of Vallonia. You're going to have to be more specific."

"Imperials," he snapped. "Always trying to shove their fingers into places they don't belong. You know what we do to spies?"

"I can imagine, but Vallonia's like an old whore. She can take a few fingers."

The Gran Maestro leaned forward, his breath at least not worse than the jailor's. Like onion soup, and spiced sausage of some sort. Geraint had lost his hearing for the most part, getting old, but his sense of smell never diminished.

The Gran Maestro made a stretching motion with his fists, pulling them apart, making creaking noises with his mouth. "Your arms and legs will be tied to horses and their rears will be slapped and set off in opposite directions."

"I've always wanted to be a bit taller," he mused. The threat didn't scare him. "Might've had more luck with women had I been."

A vein threatened to burst on the grandmaster's forehead. Thick fingers closed around Geraint's cheeks, forcing his lips open.

"Do you have any idea who I am?"

Geraint smiled—quite a feat in his current predicament. His voice chewed through the gap of his lips. "Gran Maestro of the Red Blade, but you're not Hamedas. No, that must make you Mara Al Hammad dos Las Amida, also known as The Bear. I thought you'd be taller in person. How is your wife, Sofia?"

The Bear stepped back. "Taller... *donkey*—" He broke off with a series of swears, stringing them together like the finest jeweler. Choosing the right cut, the right stone, to fashion a set of curses fit for a king. A king of obscenities. The Gran Maestro continued to swear as he yanked the door open, folded his hat up, and stepped through.

Well... People often had the strangest reactions to knowledge. It gave him as much power as a sword and wielded in the right hands—his—it allowed him to cut just as deep. It had been a balm for him, as well, and saved his life on more than a few occasions.

Loud chatter filtered through the door, the individual words lost. Then a shout, followed by a crashing noise. *Someone's having fun out there.* Something huge smacked against the door, a thump of a skull, then another.

Crashing open, the door gave way to a big man and an even bigger guard, who had blood on his knuckles. The big man wore a shining brocade vest and had a giant grin on his face, one that held ill portent.

Or often did, for both of them.

A solution will always come when you least expect it, Geraint.

Shit, was Father right?

"Vargo," Geraint said. "You well-timed bastard."

Vargo laughed, his generous gut barely hidden by the tails of his doublet, wobbling with each laugh.

"You've put on weight."

"And you're barely there, you skinny old man." He brandished a key. "Let's go."

The Gran Maestro crawled into the room, blood pouring from his nose. "You've made an enemy for life! The Order of the Red Sword will never forgive—"

The guard raised his fist. The bleeding man snapped his mouth shut and whimpered.

"I will make sure the king hears of you holding such an esteemed scholar in chains," Vargo said, unlocking the chains.

The lock clinked and Geraint's wrists suddenly came free, flaring in pain as feeling rushed back. Geraint rubbed them. They itched, red and scabby where the metal had bitten.

"Some would say he's a national hero. I wouldn't, but some certainly would."

Vargo knew some of what it took to be a national hero. The king's ex-commander of all his armies, and reclaimer of all the lands south of the Cartenusia mountains. He'd taken the lands back from the Saburrians after they'd conquered them centuries ago. War hero to the Vallonians. Baby killer and woman raper if you asked the Saburrians. Both had a grain of truth, as with all stories.

A good friend to know if you found yourself in a Vallonian jail.

Geraint riposted like a good swordsman. "If they had a few fingers meddling around with their brains."

Vargo threw his arms around Geraint. The crushing embrace bent his bones. "Vargo, you're killing me—" The release came and made him stumble forward.

The Vallonian gave a flaccid grin. "You're not going to be happy."

"What's happened now?"

"King Cartenas freed you on the condition that you leave the country."

"Shit." Geraint interlocked his fingers behind his head and breathed a heavy sigh.

The Bear laughed, nasally from his bloody nose. "You northerner bastard, that's better than what you deserve."

"You're still on the floor, friend."

Vargo grabbed Geraint's arm, causing a wince. He either didn't know his strength—entirely probable—or he was trying to impress Geraint of something. They had a long history, but this was the first time Geraint had been afraid of his friend in a long time, since his eyes flashed with ill intent.

He whispered in Osbergian without missing a beat. "I'll escort you out myself, personally. I want to make sure you don't get lost on the way."

Geraint smiled, suddenly hit with a wave of relief. "Oh, you're going to escort me." He threw a pleading hand up. "Can't say I'm not disappointed."

"Yes, disappointing, indeed."

They went out of the prison to a carriage, where four huge Vyahtken horses were harnessed and waiting, a pure tragedy for the near-wild breed. Geraint had no love for the creatures, but he could sympathize with the feeling of being chained up.

The guard shoved Geraint into the cab while Vargo followed, stepping up the treads. Vargo sat across from him, half in shadow as the sun passed overhead, the sounds of Vallon deadened by the quiet that came of the customary snooze at midday. Only the demonic or the busy kept working during Highest, risking exposure. Already Geraint started to sweat in the festering heat. He wondered which category his friend belonged to.

The cab rocked from side-to-side as the guard took up the driver's seat.

"Times are tough for the king's favorite, then, my old friend?"

Vargo had his eyes shooting around the windows of the cab, and now looked at Geraint. "What was that?"

"You'd think you'd be able to afford a separate guard and driver."

"Oh, don't worry, Geraint. I show you exactly how much I want to show you, and no more. And I'll never tell you if times are tough, my old friend."

Vargo knew precisely how much knowledge to portion out to a historian with fingers in every court, knuckles in every countess—and some counts—from Vallonia to the frigid northern Sanarikki.

"Fair," Geraint said. That didn't stop him pulling the sign of the up-side-down cross at him.

Vargo laughed, then switched to Vallonian again. "Drive, Maria."

A whip cracked and the carriage lurched as the Vyahtkens took off, flying across the road at speed.

"Your driver's name is Maria?"

"Family name. What kind of name is Geraint, anyway?"

"I don't fucking know. Ask my father on that one."

"I can't. Your father's dead."

Geraint tapped his head. "He never shuts up in here."

"You should get that looked at."

They laughed.

The carriage was nearly out of Vallon. Geraint couldn't help but think that Vargo had strategically chosen the time of their flight, knowing that the streets would be nearly empty, and no one would notice a stray carriage, even if there was the king's favorite inside.

"You sly dog," he said. "You chose the time and day to come rescue me particularly when you knew it was going to be a hot day in Vallon. Which god did you promise your soul to, to know that one?"

"The goddess of a stinking hot Sanguinum. It's not rained in two weeks."

"Oh."

"I'm a busy man, Geraint. And I'm doing you a favor, by the way. I could've let you rot in the Red Sword's oubliette. I hear it's got nails fixed to the bottom."

"Thankfully I never found out. They just had me in that room you found me in."

"What were you doing in the archives, anyway?"

"Research."

"Are you still working on that stupid bloody theory?" Vargo shook his head. "It's too bad I didn't know you during the Reconquering. I could've thrown you head-first at the Saburrians, you're that fucking hard-headed."

Geraint squeezed Vargo's knee. "I'm a hair's breadth away from proving it! The last piece of it was in the archives. I just needed to prove a link between the Gevaudan and the Tenebrosi."

"The king won't take kindly to you proving a link between a monster and his family."

Geraint looked down, his voice carrying a thread of defeat. "I was hoping he wouldn't notice, to be honest."

Vargo leaned forward, glancing out the window again. The city passed by, only a set of enormous gates in the distance now, each stone of the wall as wide as an oak. A row of equally giant cairns marched down the hill in front of them. The cab rolled over a rock and swayed.

A frown deepened Vargo's face, sullied his cheeks. "You should've told your old friend you were in Vallonia."

"Why? We haven't spoken in ten years. I didn't think you wanted anything to do with an old man who can't even bend over to wash his feet in a river."

"Hard-headed bastard. I got married, you know that? I sent you an invitation."

Geraint nodded. "Seventh wife?"

"Sixth."

He smiled. "What's her name?"

"Ariella. She's Varangian. Doesn't speak a lick of Vallonian, but her father owns the largest marble mine in Varangia."

The Varangians had two talents, in his experience: marble-cutting, and comely, dark-haired daughters. "Branching out, are we?"

"One must have their interests."

They laughed and Geraint slapped his friend's shoulder with a bony hand. It was spotted, bluish. No matter how hard he tried, he couldn't put on a mite of weight, and his neck stooped forward from years of being hunched over books and scrolls with tiny text in dark archives. No wife stood in his future, nor did his work permit one anyway. He was fine with that. Ladies-in-waiting looking to curry favor with the lady they were waiting for often took him on. They smelled sweet and he liked their laughter when he told them his stories. Thrilled for his friend, though, he grinned.

"It's a shame I won't meet Ariella."

"The hells you won't. Where do you think we're headed?"

L IKE MANY VILLAS OF the Vallonian gentry, Vargo's estate crept up the lazy shore of Lake Marianasta, a stratum of painted brick and gray slate roof. Outbuildings clung to the villa like flies, while the air stunk of heat, hugging Geraint's sackcloth to his skin. A semicircle of servants awaited their arrival.

Geraint looked twice. A woman waited too, beneath yards of fabric. Bright reds and yellows swelled around her hips, her powdered breasts wrapped like a market parcel in swirls of ribbons and brocade, pushed up like a shelf by her bodice. Piled high on her head was a massively tall wig of white hair—a trend set by the queen.

"Ariella, I take it?"

Vargo just smirked, sneakily, at his old friend. As if to say, *you've seen nothing yet.*

The guard pulled the carriage to a halt and the horses snorted, eager for more, though they'd covered nearly fifty miles in about a quarter of the afternoon. People would just be rising now, and it was clear the servants thought little of their master demanding they wait in the heat.

Ariella took it in stride, though. *Brave woman.* Her brown skin shone with bespoke beads of sweat, almost designed to draw the eye. Geraint stepped out of the carriage first. Vargo's sixth wife bowed, teasing more of herself. To describe the effect it had on his loins would be to describe seeing a sunrise for the first time after spending a year in a cave. He nearly burst with excitement.

He spoke low to his friend. "I see why you married her."

"That's nothing. You should see what she looks like with her legs behind her head."

Geraint stumbled forward, his knees suddenly weak. Ariella made a concerned noise in response. "Master Geraint," she said. "You poor thing. We must get you inside, out of this heat." Even her voice twinkled like a shining constellation, a sailor's guide in the wild sea.

He straightened, taking a big breath. "Has Vargo spoken of me?"

"I cannot get him to close his mouth when the topic of conversation arrives at you, and that happens all too often!" She laughed generously.

The laugh of a pretty woman. His heart was set on fire, and he felt insanely jealous of his friend. He leaned forward to take her offered hand and kissed the back of it. "It is a pleasure to finally put those unflattering comments I'm sure he's made to rest, then. Geraint Fallstadt, at your service, milady."

"He speaks very good Vallonian," she said. "Perhaps he is as well-read as you describe." She smiled teasingly.

"Very good!" Geraint laughed. *Where does a creature like this come from?* In all his long years, and there were many of them, he'd never had the singular pleasure of meeting a woman like this. He thought—no, knew—Ariella could spar with the best of the Imperial court, the finest courtiers, and win.

"Do you play any instruments?" he tested. "We should like some music if we're to have luncheon."

"Of course. I've been known to finger a harp or two."

He laughed hard, tickled by her sharp humor.

"Saturos wept," Vargo said, waving them in. "How are you, wife? Let's go inside before we expire from heat."

Geraint looked at his friend, remembering that the Vallonian word for Sigur—Saturos—had dripped down like honey from the Istryan Empire, shifting in the process, and that got his mind racing again. He recalled his purpose here, having been swept up in all the perfume and fabric and brown flesh. Before they could go inside, he caught his friend at the door. Ariella and the servants went ahead.

"I can't be here, Vargo. I have my charge."

"Stay here, you hardheaded fool. After we eat, I'll take you to my archives. I think you should find everything you need there."

Geraint flattened his mouth. "Yo—your archives? Are you saying I could've come here all along?"

"It's not a fact I try to make public knowledge, Geraint."

"This makes me very happy, then."

"I thought it might. Come, we'll have the servants scrape the stink off you."

AFTER A PLEASANT LUNCH of melted cheese toast and fresh grapes and pomegranates from the garden, Vargo took him to the archive wing. An entire wing for scrolls and books looked exactly how you would imagine, stacked to the tops with enough animal skin and leather to make the king's armory blush.

Geraint wore a collared vest borrowed from Vargo's son, who no longer lived with them, having married into a duchess's family in the south of Vallonia. Vargo's ample stomach meant all his clothes hung loose on Geraint, while his ample name gave his sons the pick of any women from here to the Cartenusians.

"What was it you were famous for again?" Vargo asked him as they walked into the gallery.

Geraint had gaped his mouth. "The Proussians. I gave them their name, proved their tribes came from an offshoot of Istryan's brother."

"That discovery will pale in comparison to what you're about to do."

Geraint looked at his friend with disbelieving eyes. "I thought you considered my work to be foolish?"

Vargo smiled. "I do, but if you succeed, there's no doubt this'll overshadow everything that came before."

They embraced. "Which god do I owe for such a dear friend?"

They broke apart but clasped each other by the shoulders. "No god, just Vargo."

Laughter. Geraint's mind jumped from point to point, a reckoning with the immense task that still laid before him.

This would be the culmination of two decades of work. Describing the ancestry of every noble family in the entire Continent, and tracing back that abruptly, immediately after Istryan's arrival, werewolves arose in noble lines. Not before. He forwent the Sigurites' description of them as demons—they were far more like some pitiful manifestation of man's bestial nature. But at the same time, they weren't. They were creatures unto themselves. He'd met more than a few and knew that within the noble lines—though shunned—the creatures were still cared for and loved.

He culled the documents he didn't need. He barely noticed Vargo leave. Ariella came to visit with a spiced iced tea at one point, placing the perspiring glass on a desk out of the way of his culling. She said something and he answered it idly. Once he was in the mood, nothing could get between him and a solution. It was how he'd discovered the Proussians' roots.

Tenebros son of Cartenas, born under the sign of the Wolf—

Cartenas son of Loura, born under the sign of the Sword—

He flipped back. *Loura son of Cartenas, born under the sign of the Amphora—*

Cartenas son of Loura, born under the sign of the Chalice—

On and on, more Cartenas's, Loura's, and Tenebros's, like a bad minstrel song on repeat.

Cartenas, black issue—

Black issue. He'd heard that term before. He flipped through his mind, sorted the kill from the surrounding trees like the sharpest hunter. It was a term the priests used when describing a son that was stillborn. His thoughts spiked like it drove a spear through his skull. Tenebros son of Cartenas came before, ten generations back. But the records ended there.

"Older, older, I need older!" he called out at one point, and Vargo pointed him to a small cabinet.

The first scroll nearly crumbled to the touch. "A bit of tallow to keep them soft wouldn't go astray, Vargo."

"If I need an archivist, you'll be the first letter I send."

Geraint didn't deign to glare at his friend, the biting silence was enough to convey his hatred.

These scrolls were written in some cramped hand, in an ancient kind of Vallonian that resembled High Istryan, but not quite. A corrupted form, or perhaps an older form. Something closer to what Istryan might have spoken himself. Of course, Geraint could still read it.

Loura, black issue. Tenebros, black issue. Estomo, black issue. He read down the list. This would've been nine hundred years ago, when Vallonia was settled.

Estomo. He'd never seen the name Estomo before. Clues arranged before him like a golden way, but off the path led to a bottomless pit. He had to stay focused.

He lifted his head. Aches stretched their nasty hands across his back like a giant stretching his tendons until they threatened to snap.

Why were there so many miscarriages and stillbirths around the settling of Vallonia? Unless they weren't?

He reamed through more of the cabinet. *Estomo, Estomo...*

"Just make yourself at home, Geraint," Vargo called, a strong hint of sarcasm under his words, like a sour note of a fine wine.

"That bitterness doesn't suit you, Vargo. My work is more important than a bit of mess."

He'd returned from a horse ride with Ariella, who'd gone to get dressed for supper. *Gods... I'll be working on this all night.* It wouldn't be the first time.

Estomo par Tieloras was the fifth son of Istryan, the founder of the empire. Geraint stared at the page. *All of his children were black issue.* He couldn't believe his eyes. Tieloras was the Ancient Vallonian name for Tielor, the continent where Istryan was said to have come from. But if Estomo's children died in childbirth, who passed on the line?

The lycans. Who else would it have been? That meant the Vallonian kings all descend from werewolves, who lived in Vallonia and the western half of the Continent long before Istryan ever arrived. The monsters in the stories were invented whole cloth to justify their elimination and subjugation.

Geraint's guts churned. He knew he had done it. Naming the Proussians had given him a thrill, but this was higher than that. This meant everything. The culmination of two decades of work.

They were the original inhabitants of the Continent, and Istryan and his followers demonized them, to conquer them. It was a Sigur-sized hole in the world. No wonder the werewolves were wild, uncontained beasts. They had no choice but to fight their erasure, and their biggest sin was that they failed. Untethered from history, going back more than a thousand years, perhaps even further. Geraint knew the stories though. Where did the Great Devil come into that? Or was it just allegory, to further demonize the lycans?

He put the scroll down.

"Do you know what this means?"

"What?"

"That werewolves were the first inhabitants of the Continent *before* man!"

"Sigur," Vargo swore, without any passion. A statement of disbelief.

"Sigur, exactly! It directly contradicts—"

Geraint's chest erupted in a shower of blood, and his breath died in his lungs. Curiously, he didn't feel any pain, only a numb weakness as life left his body. He looked down. The nasty tip of a sword looked up at him.

Vargo jumped back in shock, his words numbed. "Ariella, why?" The voice muffled as though he stood at the bottom of a well.

"Speak up," Geraint meant to say, but it didn't leave his mouth. The words were killed in his chest, just as he was.

The tip of the blade slid back and Geraint—either no longer supported or the sudden movement making his body move in unison—flopped forward and smacked his head on the cabinet. Blood pooled under him.

Vargo shrieked as his vile wife named Ariella lashed her sword like a tongue across his face. The Vallonian dropped to the ground, eyes gone dark.

It's what your father told you, Geraint. A solution will always come when you least expect it. Just not a solution for you.

Life left his body as the woman started gathering up the papers, and he ebbed out of consciousness.

LIST OF CHARACTERS

- Tristain – second son of Count Sebastian of Invereid, squire to Leon Vorland

- Selene – fifth daughter of the Baron of Greifswald, ward of Count Sebastian

- Leon Vorland – knight of the realm, known as Leon the Strong

- Caen – corporal

- Sorenius – inquisitor of the Order of the Golden Sword

- Palia – rector of the Order

- Elias Rotersand – lord inquisitor of the Order in Osbergia

- Ebberich, Ruprecht, Leona, Salim, & Raul – Order novitiates

- Lena, Nials, Manus – Order arbiters

- Gida – lieutenant

- Andrea, Maria, Herrad, Caspar, & Lombas the Small – Leon's men

- Bann – first son of Count Sebastian of Invereid, missing, presumed dead

- Erken – Leon's son, died in the Battle of the Giant's Footfalls

- Vredevoort – knight of the realm, known as Vredevoort the Grim, commander of Count Andreas's regiment

- Andreas Pagehald – Count of Verania

- Reynard – Duke of Annaltia, third son of Emperor Franz II

- Ilse Adolar – Duchess of Osbergia, general of the Osbergian army

- Albrecht – Archduke of Osbergia, first son of Emperor Franz II

- Lorrin & Bean – marooned sailors

- Chesterfield – captain of the *Arabella*

- Roupert, Marie, & Luka – Badonnian refugees

- Captain Tollsen – Captain of the Ostelar Watch

- Van Vinland – head of Wel's Chosen, an embalmer

ACKNOWLEDGMENTS

IF THE FEAST MADE your mouth water, credit goes to Max Miller from Tasting History on YouTube and the very well-written *Food in Medieval Times* by Melitta Weiss Adamson. Alex West, whose steadfast guidance in all things arms and armor inspired Tristain and Leon's relationship. Credit goes to him and the Barony of St. Florian of the SCA at large for research and inspiration. For the tournament and the swordfights throughout the book, as well as the day-to-day life, thanks go to Jason from ModernHistoryTV, who knows more about the medieval period than any one person has a right to.

I want to thank Matty Parkin and Bjorn Burgher, for playing the DnD game this novel spawned out of. Thanks go to Megan Campbell, for being a reader and wellspring of encouragement. To all my other readers, as well. My ARC readers as well—thank you for doing what you do out of love and for taking a chance on an unproven author. Shannon, for being my foremost alpha and beta reader, and for her support. This novel wouldn't exist without her time, care, and love.

Lastly, if you like this book, please leave a review on Amazon or Goodreads! It really helps an author out, and lets me keep doing something that I love, which is delivering good stories to you!

About Author

NC Koussis was born in Perth in 1993 to Greek and Gamilaroi ancestry. He has moved all around Australia, settling in Newcastle for the moment, where he lives with his wife, son, and staffy dog, Nala. He's been writing fantasy books since he was a little boy, after falling in love with Lord of the Rings, Realm of the Elderlings, and Deltora Quest. He decided to publish a book in 2019, and it only took him three years. The Pyres of Vengeance is his upcoming novel. He considers himself an enthusiastic amateur of medieval history, historical battles and tactics, and food. When he's not writing, he's making sourdough bread and working on a PhD in neuroscience.

For more, check out art of characters from this book, and a high-resolution version of the map at https://nikitaskoussis.com.

Keep reading for the prologue of the sequel, *The Pyres of Vengeance*.

The Pyres of Vengeance

Prologue

R ICHTER SHOVED A BLADE into his gullet. Right as he did, the sheriff knocked on the door. *These southerners,* he thought as blood poured from his throat like the finest Tanerian red. *No sense for punctuality.*

Life ebbed from his left arm first. Peculiar how that always happened. He slapped it across the table, testing it. Felt like pins poked it, poked the ends, then nothing. Blood continued to splash across the wood and filled the air with a powerful stink.

As the knocking came again, more frantic this time, he slumped his head, unable to support his own weight anymore. He slid out of the chair and made a flopping noise as he hit the floorboards. A nail poked up at him like a rude gesture.

His vision faded to brown, then gray, then he looked at on himself, and warmth came, peaceful and quiet. He couldn't hear the knocking anymore, only a vast emptiness. Familiar but wanting.

It only reminded him of his failure.

Fire seared his skin and boiled his belly as he was pulled back inside his body. Fur erupted from every pore and claws as sharp as a lion's pushed their way out of his nail beds, tearing skin to make way. His head shifted, bones cracking and locking into place. His chest doubled in size and his feet broke. Bones had to break, had to restructure, to mend into something made for a predator.

He sighed. *Why do I ever think the next time will work?*

He considered whether he could kill the god that had cursed him. It seemed unlikely. Relaxing his muscles and his mind, he let the transformation take hold again and threw his clothes on.

When the sheriff knocked on the door for the fifth time, Richter opened it as a man.

"Yes?"

"Your pardon, master," he said. A stray lock of light hair untucked from his stained coif. At his belt, a flanged mace marked his station. "The lord said you were staying here. There's a family here what need your curing."

"I don't know about cure, but I'll certainly see if I can help."

"It's said you're a healer." He tried to stick his head over Richter's shoulder, likely noticing the pool of blood drying fast into the wood.

Richter moved into his path and smiled. "That it is."

The sheriff stepped away and a man in a dirty smock and felted hat approached. He took off his hat and pressed it between his hands nervously.

"Well met, master. I'm Reginald, though the folk 'round here call me Sod. I'm out at the lord's farm a few miles west of here. I'm a freedman, but I work for my liege lord."

Richter raised an eyebrow. "Sod?"

"It's what my mother called me. 'Bloody Sod.' It stuck."

You poor man.

Sod looked down, his cheeks flushing red. "Well... it pains me to ask, you know. But Sigur bless us, my wife's been havin' strange things happen of late."

"Of what nature? Menses?"

"Nay, master."

Richter smiled. "Please, be at ease, friend. I'm Richter, Richter Absault. My father was a Badonnian. Don't hold it against me."

Sod laughed. Richter gestured to the tavern across from his abode, over the main street of passing carts carving tracks through the mud. Feet, human and cloven, had churned the path into muck, frothy at the edges. Richter put his pattens on—wooden overshoes that set you above the muck—and with the farmer he went to the alehouse. The sheriff bid farewell.

When they sat at an uneven table, served warm ale that tasted like old shoes, and Richter cleared his throat, the farmer continued.

"My wife, you see... she's pregnant. But she's been having night spells, like she's been 'exed. Like a witch has got her."

"A witch, you say. What sort of night spells?"

"I'll find her in the garden, or down by the river bed in the morn. She'll be covered head-to-toe in muck, like she'd been crawling in it."

The peasant looked around, satisfied himself that no one was listening, and leaned in closer. Richter's eyes flashed with anger. He didn't like the invasion of his personal space, but then he remembered his teachings, passages that would get you through a hard day's work. *The Lightfather places His grace on every child who speaks His name.*

He took a breath and placed his hand on the knife at his belt for comfort.

"One time, I found blood on her skirts, too."

Richter pushed down his excitement. He had to remain stoic, impassive. Concerned, even.

"Is that so? This is grave news, then. Menses or no, this sounds like it requires urgent attention. Where is your wife, now?"

"At home, master."

"I see." Richter leaned out of his chair and called for the bill to be settled. "A few miles' ride isn't so bad in this country. If we were near Ostelar, I might be worried to come across Annaltians on the road looking for trouble." *Not that I can't handle a few Annaltians, but this hayseed doesn't need to know that.*

This was Forberg, a little town outside of Triburg. He'd made it his home of late, though his mission required him to move rapidly and very far, often. Traveling healers plied their trade along the roads south of Ostelar after the capture of that city, and it served him as the perfect cover.

"We can take my horse."

"Of course, master. I'd be happy to pay you for your time. I've been saving up in case a man like you ran across my path."

"Oh, what happy luck. Sigur has ordained our meeting, then."

"Indeed, he has, master."

T HE FARMER'S HOUSE STOOD on an embankment, elevated up from the flood pan on stilts. This part of the countryside flooded notoriously, as he was told by every cowpoke and hayseed the moment he stepped foot here. Richter steered his horse to the front of the house and swung his leg over, helping the farmer down with a gloved hand.

He smelled the blood before he smelled the stink of cow shit. Someone had been killed here, not two nights ago. The farmer was lying, or not telling the whole truth in any case, out of some protective notion. Only someone with Richter's nose would know, anyway. So, the farmer had thought to cure the curse.

When the Lightfather has delivered these tools unto your hands, you must seize them.

"My wife should be inside," Sod said, and led him up the set of stairs to the front door.

Inside, a woman whistled a tune that some of the Osbergians around here sung. A tune about a donkey having its way with a woman. He preferred the version where the woman's organs were so bruised, she died from bleeding on the inside.

The farmer's house consisted of a single, sad room, nested with moss-stuffed bedding around a fire, soot staining the ceiling. The farmer's wife tinkered at a small cot and seemed surprised to see them.

Her eyes passed Richter over, lingered on the knife at his belt. Around her eyes, he could see flecks of sleep, where she'd clearly had disturbance in the night. Wrinkles settled beyond that, couching the rest of her face in age and worry. But she was pregnant, and that was easily seen. Her belly pouched considerably over her thighs, ripe.

Richter pushed down his excitement. It pressed against his leg, hard against his hose. He remembered the training, what the instructors had beat into him. *What the Lightfather giveth, the Lightfather taketh away.*

"Woman, this is Master Richter Absault," the farmer said. "He's a healer, wot I said I was going out to do today."

"Well met, master."

Richter leaned on the wall. "Well met, goodwoman. I've heard you've been having some night-spells? Your concerned husband thinks you've been hexed by a witch."

She shook her head and laughed. "Sorry, I think my husband has pulled a nasty trick on you, master."

A frown. "What do you mean?" He kept his voice level despite the hate starting to build behind his eyes.

She fixed her eyes on his chest. Could she see the pin that he kept tucked inside his tunic? Surely not. Even if she was what he thought she was, he hid the thing well enough that a cursory glance wouldn't reveal much. Nothing about him was standard issue for his line of work.

And if she was what he thought she was, that made her very interesting indeed. He'd never seen a pregnant one, before.

Blessings come in all forms and sizes, and come at the most unexpected times, for He is good.

An unexpected blessing indeed. When he woke up this morning, he pissed into the remnants of the fire under the stove, relieved himself, then he'd taken the rest of the slop given to him by the good tavernkeeper's daughter into his belly, and shoved a knife in his throat.

He didn't really think it would work, but on the off chance... *For He is good*.

The woman placed a crown of daisies that she'd been sewing together at the head of the cot.

"My husband has these flights of fancy at times." She smiled. "But it's why I married him."

"Come, woman, enough jesting now. Tell him what you've been doing. The blood on your skirts that time."

"You told him..." She paused and let her hand slip by her side. "You told him about that?" He saw movement in her eyes.

In that moment, he also moved. The knife at his belt was no common belt knife, used for cutting cooked flesh at the table, or to spread butter on the stale trencher. It went zipping through the air and planted in the woman's throat.

She screamed. The farmer gaped his mouth and yelled. It was the last thing he did. Richter shoved a clawed fist through his lungs, punching through the ribs. Sod's throat made a hissing noise.

Richter wrenched his hand free, tearing more flesh open and Sod dropped. He might still be alive, but Richter wasn't taking any such chance with the wife.

As she sauntered, dazed, around the room, pissing blood on the floor, she saw him. She screamed as she lashed out at him with a knife. He turned to the side and punched a claw right into the woman's eye. The claw sunk to the knuckle. He scraped around as she gibbered in excruciating pain. It wasn't just the killing he enjoyed. It was the pain, too.

Something the Lightfather had cursed him with had also blessed him. *For He blesses and curses in equal measure*. Richter had made it his own blessing and seized the tools that He had given him. Using the control he trained himself in, and the Grand Inquisitor's beatings, he could manipulate the transformation at will. One part of him could be human, another part monster.

He chuckled. "Or am I *all* monster?"

She widened her one working eye. He lowered her to the ground and brought huge, club-like fists down on her head, again and again. When he finished, she was unrecognizable as human. Then he took hold of her head, or what was left of it, and twisted. Snapping rang out as tendons and bones twisted. He pulled, planting his foot against her shoulder.

Her head came free. He stared at it longingly and thought to relieve himself of the stiffness pressing uncomfortably against his leg, but then he remembered the other problem.

He looked down. The woman's belly sunk a little laying down, dead as she was, but it was still quite pronounced from the cursed offspring still inside. The babe would probably die without its mother to sustain it, but he couldn't take the chance.

He shoved his claws inside her belly again and again. Tearing the small, unborn babe to ribbons.

Mincemeat.

After it was done, and he'd taken care of the stiffness in his hose, he went outside. The horse waited there, the beast's stupid eyes staring limp back at him. As though it had not a single fucking clue what went on inside. What evil he'd dealt for a righteous cause.

Lightfather, I have brought war and spared no quarter. Let me be free of this curse.

Sigur did not answer him. He never answered. Still, he hunted the wolf-men, the cursed demons, in the hope that one day he'd be free, and he could die.

Have I not done enough?

He shook off his shoulders. He'd need to bathe in the river to get rid of the blood, but it was already getting chilly.

"A little fire would help," he said for Sigur's ears only.

When he rode away, the flames rose high and licked the evening air. He felt good. One more demon dead on the Continent. He would not rest until they were all gone, then finally himself.

Preorder *The Pyres of Vengeance* today.